LEAVE
a
MARK

LEAVE
a
MARK

GARY
MACKNIGHT

Raven Scott Publications: For any questions about usage,
please contact: ravenscottpub@gmail.com

To my daughter, Cassidy Rain,
who shows me all the wonders this world has to offer every day,

and

to my son, Connor Orion,
whose years of wisdom never cease to amaze me.
I love our conversations.

You have each left a mark on my heart
which I will carry with me long after I have left this world.
Hopefully the mark I made on you has been one of love.

And to my parents, Jack & Carole,
who have left their mark, not only on me and my brothers and sister,
but with everyone they have ever met.

I will tell you a story...

Leave a Mark
It started with a dream …

I know it's cliché to start a novel with the protagonist waking up from a dream, but in this case, that's exactly what made me write this book. I literally woke up one morning and told my daughter about a dream I just had about a man who was foretold of his death and needed to travel somewhere to find his past. She told me to write it down, and that it would make for an interesting book. Just then, I woke from that dream … I had a dream within a dream, and it was so vivid, I was disorientated all morning, wondering if what I was experiencing was yet another dream, that at any moment would I wake up again. At work, my friend Laura, noticing me in a state of bewilderment, asked me what was wrong. I retold the dream to her, and she also told me I should write it down, because it would make for an interesting story. That day, I wrote the beginning and end of the story, and with Laura's encouragement, I wrote chapter after chapter as the story began telling itself to me. For the next three months, I was typing till four or sometimes five o'clock in the morning, just to keep up with the characters' nagging voices, all screaming to me to tell their story.

As I wrote this book, I realized it wasn't so much about one man trying to reconnect with his past as it was about all people struggling to leave their mark in this world. And hence the title was born. *Leave a Mark!*

This story is very dear to my heart, and filled with so many of my personal experiences. I hope you enjoy reading it as much as I enjoyed writing it.

*"Immortality is to live your life doing good things,
and leaving your mark behind."*

— Brandon Lee

"Love as powerful as your mother's for you leaves its own mark."

— J. K. Rowling

*"Every once in a while your world stands still ...
There are certain friendships that are so important
they leave a mark on you long after the person is gone."*

— Art Buchwald

Prologue

The Horn of Africa

Modern-Day Ethiopia

Circa 8,000 BCE

In the silence of a dirt floor hut, an arthritic hand reaches forward. Ebony fingers, once strong, now weathered by time and toil, struggle to retrieve a small piece of wood. All fingers answer the call except one, the smallest appendage, stricken with pain, unresponsive; it remains closed, fixed tightly to the bright, pink flesh of the palm. In the other hand, fingers clutch a sharp tool and begin to scratch a word into the surface. One word, a single word, a word they have heard all their life. It is their word. The word a father cursed them with when they came into the world.

AETErNUM

"Find a mark. Leave a mark. It is time."
A quiet voice whispers in the darkness,
calling forth an ancient memory.

Place: New York City
Year: Present Day

In an Upper East Side apartment, Jonathan Taylor,

a 58-year-old architect, scrambles to his feet, lost and confused; he moves around the apartment he has called home for more than 20 years as though he's never seen it before.

"Cassandra! We have to go!" His loud, booming voice breaks the silence as he stumbles about his study. Cassandra appears in the doorway. It's quite unusual for his 25-year-old cat-like daughter to be up so early. Wiping the sleep from her eyes, she witnesses a most unusual sight: her father ransacking the otherwise well-kept room, tossing papers and books around as he frantically moves from bookcase to bookcase.

"Dad, what's going on?"

The morning sun is just breaking through the blinds, but already the city is alive and active. Steam escapes from steel plates lying on the black asphalt as the early morning taxis cut through the rising mist, racing toward Penn Station.

"Cazz, where are my books? The photo albums? From Africa—"

"Dad, you don't have to be at work for another two hours, and I don't have class today, so I'm going back to bed," she says, retreating down the hall.

"I'm not going to work today," he shouts as she enters her bedroom. "Or any other day for that matter." He speaks softer, hoping she doesn't hear him, but not softly enough for her young ears.

"What do you mean you're not—"

"Remember? Remember when I was in Italy with your mother, remember, I kept telling her I felt like I'd been there before? Do you remember me telling you that? I wonder if she would remember?"

"I think I remember," Cassandra says, scratching her head. Her long hair, the color of milk chocolate toffee, disheveled as a squirrel's nest, attests to how she is thinking. "What do you mean you're not going to work today?"

"Do you think she'll remember if I call her?"

CALL MOM? The mere suggestion stops her cold like a stinging slap across the face, dislodging any remnant of slumber.

"I think it was Florence? And, then, again in Scotland! Oh, and then, when we took that trip to Australia last year. Do you remember, I felt it there too," her father rambles.

"I don't think calling Mom is a good idea. She's still not speaking to you."

Jonathan shakes his head, dumbstruck. *Christ, it's been 10 years since the divorce.*

But before Cassandra can say another word, her father's thoughts race to another topic.

"I have to call my lawyer and then make arrangements with the bank. I have to call them, too. No, I'll go down there. Where are my keys?"

"Uh, Dad, I'll be right back." Cassandra slips down the hall, unnoticed by her father. She picks up her cell phone, and with frantic fingers calls her brother.

On the other end, a sleepy, disorientated voice answers the phone. "Cazz?"

"Trevor! Oh, thank God you're up!"

"Cazz, do you know what time it is?" His voice borders on delirium and anger.

"It's early. I know—" Cassandra begins, only to be cut off abruptly.

"EARLY? It's not EARLY in Arizona! It's the middle of the FUCKING night! And NO, I wasn't up. You woke me. I have to be up in three hours. Oh God, this better be good." Now fully awake, his confusion fades and only annoyance prevails.

"Trev, listen! It's Dad, something is wrong," she pleads into the phone. "He's acting weird."

"Weird how? Weird like he had a stroke, or weird like he's walking around the city with no clothes on?"

"He's talking about leaving! And not like when he left Mom. He's talking about leaving the city!"

"The city?" Trevor asks, now completely bewildered.

"Yes! And," she pauses, listening to the ruckus her father is making in the other room, "Trevor, he said he's not going into work!"

This captures Trevor's full attention. As far back as he can remember, his father never missed a day of work. He built his architectural firm by himself, acquiring one company after another until his company was the leader in the architectural world. "Put him on the phone."

"Dad?! It's Trevor. He wants to talk to you," she says, bustling back down the hallway and handing her father the phone.

"TREVOR! Oh, I'm so glad you called," unaware it was Cassandra who initiated the call.

"Hey, Daaaaaaad?" Trevor proceeds with caution, as slowly as a springtime bather entering a mountain stream. "So what's going on?"

"I'm going on a trip. Well, more like a journey, a trek. Sort of a voyage of, um, discovery, and I want you to come. You and your sister. You *have* to come."

"Dad, I have work. I can't just pick up and go. Wait, where are you going? What are you talking about? Dad, what is going on?" The questions tumble from his mouth as fast as his brain can think of them.

"I need to leave—"

"Leave? Leave for where?"

"I have someplace I need to be—"

"Like where?"

Jonathan fumbles for the right words, cautious not to scare Trevor, or worse, trigger something that would prevent him from coming along. "All I know is, I want you and your sister with me. To make sense of everything."

"Make sense of what?"

"Son, I need you to come with me."

The commanding tone reminds Trevor of the times as a child when his father taught him a valuable life lesson. It wasn't a demanding voice, but a powerful 'now, listen to me' voice that made Trevor stop and contemplate the events that were about to unfold.

There was a long pause, and before Trevor could say anything else, Jonathan's voice grew suddenly calm. "Trevor," he whispered. "I'm dying."

PLACE: NEW YORK CITY
YEAR: PRESENT DAY. LATER THAT DAY

"What do you mean, you're DYING?!" a shrill voice screams out of the phone's receiver. Sixty-seven floors above the streets of Manhattan, pigeons nesting on the window sill outside Jonathan's office take flight.

"Hannah, please try to calm down." Jonathan invokes the tranquil voice of a police negotiator attempting to coax a jumper off a ledge. Cradling the phone's receiver between his shoulder and chin, he looks past the glass wall dividing him and his secretary. With eyes fixated on her devilish grin, his outstretched hands emulate a strangulation gesture.

"Don't tell me to calm down. You can't tell my son that you're dying and think I'm going to be calm about it!"

Our son, he wanted to say out loud, but if it hadn't sunk in after 20 years of marriage, uttering the words now that they were divorced would just be inviting another argument. That was just one of her many annoying idiosyncrasies that drove him crazy. "I thought you would be elated to hear I was dying." He chuckled to himself as he rested the phone down on the desk before walking over to the door.

5

Sticking his head out of the office, catching Margaret pretending to work in order to avoid his stare, he says, "I thought I told you NEVER to put my ex-wife through."

"She sounded so—"

"Crazy? Yes, she is," he interjected. "That's why—"

"That's why you're no longer with her. I know, I've heard it a hundred times."

And they both let out a little laugh at this, as only two people who have spent countless hours together can.

"Please tell Bruce I want to see him. Thanks, Mags."

She motions with her head toward his desk. "You better get back before she realizes you're gone."

Picking up the receiver again, the droning sound of buzzing fly wings grows louder until it manifests into intelligible words.

"And another thing—Jonathan, are you listening to me?"

"I'm listening, Hannah!" *Caught it at just the right time,* he thinks, having done this a hundred times before. He knew precisely when she would realize no one was responding and question his presence.

"Did you hang up on me?" she asks, unaware of the irony of her question.

"No, Hanny. I'm still on the phone." This was another one of her annoying traits he grew to hate, knowing full well she could never change. This time, he expresses his thought, hoping to make one last desperate attempt to get her to see her mistake. "How could I answer you if I hung up the phone?"

"Don't take that attitude with me, Jonathan, and don't call me Hanny! You know how I hate that!"

Bruce knocks on the glass divider and Jonathan waves him in. "Not everything has to be a battle, Hannah. I didn't hang up on you before, but now I'm going to. Goodbye, Hanny."

A string of antagonistic words are suddenly silenced as the receiver comes to rest in the phone's cradle. *That's what divorce allows you to do,* Jonathan muses with a smirk, *piss off your wife without hearing about it for the rest of your life.* "Forty thousand dollars for a lawyer, a generous settlement, and half my 401k. I don't know why more men don't do it! Instead of buying a new car, you buy your freedom."

Jonathan walks halfway across his office to meet his long-time partner and friend. He slaps Bruce on his shoulder as he passes. "Thanks for coming in. Take a seat. I'll be right with you."

He peeks out the door, not waiting for a reply. "Margaret, can you come in for a moment. Thanks."

As she enters the room, he closes the glass door behind her, "Please, sit down."

Margaret moves to take her usual place, a small chair and table set aside for her to take notes.

"No, no. Not today. Please sit next to Bruce," he says, motioning to one of the two chairs facing his desk.

Margaret joins Bruce and shoots him a *'What's going on?'* kind of look. Jonathan only asked the two of them together on matters of extreme importance.

Jonathan moves to face them and leans back on the desk, taking an uncharacteristically casual stance. "I don't know how to say this, so I'll be blunt. I'm leaving."

Bruce looks perplexed, but jokes, "Sure, sure. I mean, the week just started, but hey, you're the boss, and if you want to knock off and get an early jump on the weekend, go ahead." His lightheartedness quickly vanishes when he sees the expression on Jonathan's face.

"Oh, you're serious." He raises his voice as he rises from the chair. "Are you sick? You never take a day off, much less three."

"I'm fine. I just need some time away."

Jonathan glances over at the worried and frightened look on Margaret's face. He motions to her that everything will be alright as Bruce turns and paces the floor.

"Is this some kind of a joke, Jon? I mean, you need some time away? What the hell? You're leaving? For how long? You can't leave; it's your company. Hell, *you* are the company!"

7

"Bruce, calm down." Jonathan uses the same *please don't jump, come back inside* tone he used earlier with Hannah. "Everything is going to be alright." He looks at Margaret, "We ... are going to be alright." He turns back to Bruce and adds, "The company is going to be alright, and you, *you* Bruce, well I think it's time we make some changes."

"What does that mean? ARE YOU FIRING ME?"

Jonathan shakes his head.

"Are you selling the company? Are we filing chapter 11?" His eyes widen and his face goes pale. "Are you going to jail? HAVE YOU BEEN STEALING MONEY?" He falls on the leather sofa in the corner. His silk suit wrinkles on the couch like ice cream melting on a hot summer day as his whole body slumps and goes limp. "I'm ruined." Then his face turns from despair to horror, and he bolts upright, "AM I GOING TO JAIL TOO?!"

Jonathan can't help but laugh a little as he sits next to his worried friend. He rests his hand on Bruce's knee. "No one is going to jail. You're gonna take the reins, and me, I just need to ..." Jonathan stops and thinks. *I just need to ... WHAT? Take my family on a journey around the world, trying to find a person I saw in my dreams, only to have it end with my demise? Boy, that does sound crazy.* "... to spend some quality time with the kids. I'm going to take them on a journey."

Place: North America
Year: 1657

In another part of the world at another time, a man prepared for a journey of his own. And there, too, was someone who did not wish to see him go. His wife, Makawee, made her protest. She spoke in a Munsee dialect of the Lenape people, one of the Algonquin languages. Her language was different from that of ours today, but in any language, her argument itself was timeless.

"Takoda, why must you go?" she pleaded with him.

"Makawee, we must make a better life for our people. This is the only way. Besides, I need to see what's out there." He turned his back on her, and continued to pack small items in a deerskin pouch.

"But you don't know what you will find ..." She paused as strange and terrible thoughts invaded her mind, and then escaped her, leaving her with nothing. "If you find anything at all."

He turned back to her. "I don't like leaving any more than you, but if this is what the elders want, if this is best for our people, I must go."

Takoda, from the Shinnecock tribe on the Easternmost tip of Long Island, was chosen as one of 13 men from his village to travel across the great sea in search of a better land for his people: a land where hunting would be plentiful and the soil would yield an abundant harvest to keep them fed throughout the near-endless winters. He knew the journey would be a long and dangerous one, but he was a good sailor and the other 12 men were strong and far more experienced at making such journeys on the open seas. But still, fear lived within his heart. What if he never saw her again? Or his children? What if he never made it back home?

That night, he went into the forest and found a black-sky tree. The wood was the hardest and the strongest known to his tribe. He watched his father use it to make wall carvings for the great lodge; they looked the same today as when he was a boy. He cut a small portion and began to shape the wood. He worked all night cutting, trimming, shaping, and grinding until it was just the right size. He polished it just as his father had shown him, until it was as smooth as a motionless morning lake.

With the craftsmanship of a woodworker, he began to carve 'Takoda' deep into the hardwood. His tribe gave him this name, which means *friend to all*. When he finished carving his name, he turned the piece of wood over and began to inscribe another word, an unfamiliar word of unfamiliar letters, but somewhere in his heart, he knew it belonged to him. Blowing the wood shavings from the tablet, he looked at the word.

$$AET\mathcal{E}r\mathcal{N}\parallel M$$

He was proud of the work he accomplished, and in the morning, he would give it to Makawee—something for her to remember him by—in case something should happen.

The next morning, he presented the small token to his mate.

"You must keep this safe," he told her, placing it in her palm and wrapping his large hands around hers. "And should I not return, tell the children who I was."

Staring into her eyes, he climbed into the boat. All around him, the sounds of crying women filled the air. He looked one more time into her eyes. It was the last time he would ever do so. She did not weep for her man, not then, and not in the days that followed. She already knew his fate. She only wept the following winter when the men finally returned and told her how he was swept overboard in the midst of a terrible storm. She cried deeply that night, clutching the small tablet to her heart.

PLACE: NEW YORK CITY
YEAR: PRESENT DAY

"It's right up here on the left," Jonathan calls to the driver.
"Dad, I thought we were going to the airport?" Cassandra asks him.
"We are. I have to pick up something first." He opens the door of the limousine and gets out, still talking to her. "This is important."

Jonathan waits to hear the buzzer before pulling the door open. "Giorgio!" he calls, greeting the well dressed elderly man behind the counter. "Thank you so much for doing this on such short notice."

"Mr. Taylor, always a pleasure to see you." Giorgio shakes his hand with all the vigor of a young man. "It was nothing. You have been so good to us over the years, the least I can do is to expedite a request for you."

Giorgio sets a leather viewing mat on the glass showcase. "Frankly, I was worried when you said you needed it today, but when you described the item, it took no time at all to create it. But may I ask, why such a ..." Giorgio searches for the right word so as not to offend his long-time customer. "... modest request?" He lays an ordinary piece of metal on the mat.

12

Jonathan picks up the small object and examines it. Two inches tall by three inches wide, polished to a high gloss and engraved on both sides, as instructed. On the front, three words above an eight-digit number. The first two digits, a hyphen, two more digits, another hyphen, then the last four. Below that, another four digit number. On the back, only one word.

"I love the subtle beveled edge you added," Jonathan remarks as he turns the object over in his hands. "How much do I owe you?"

"Oh, it was nothing, really," Giorgio says, taking pride in his work no matter how small the task. "Why don't I just add it to your next bill?"

Jonathan pulls out a small bankroll from his pocket. "Better settle up now, Giorgio," he smiles. "You never know what tomorrow brings. Like my priest used to say, if you want to make God laugh, tell him your plans for tomorrow."

At the airport, Jonathan and Cassandra wait at the ticket counter. Trevor sees them and waves. Cassandra rushes to meet him.

"Hey, sis." He kisses her on the cheek. "What's this all about? I thought you said you wanted to try a new deli or something down in Soho or maybe the Village, but then Dad said to make sure I had my passport, that you two were going to meet me at the airport. Cazz, what the hell is going on?"

When Jonathan joins them, his lips curve upward, causing his cheeks to dimple. "Trevor. I'm so glad you could make it." He gives his son a huge hug, lifting him off the ground.

"Dad?" Trevor chuckles in a boyish kind of way, forgetting why he came. His father hasn't shown him this kind of affection since he started high school. For a brief moment, feeling the warmth of his father's face, Trevor is seven years old again. Memories of his father's coarse, razor-stubble cheeks mixed with the aroma of long-forgotten aftershave, awaken images of being carried from the car into the house after falling asleep late at night. He closes his eyes and allows the fleeting childhood memory to engulf him for a moment, but as his feet touch down against the hard marble floor, he is transformed back from an innocent youth to a 27-year-old man, standing in a crowded, bustling airport.

"Okay, I was able to get three tickets to New Delhi, First Class." He grabs both their arms with excitement. "This is going to be great!"

"Dad! WHAT?" Trevor feels his momentary childhood euphoria replaced by sheer confusion. "NEW DELHI! As in INDIA?!"

Jonathan nods enthusiastically.

"I'M NOT GOING TO INDIA, Dad! I just flew five hours to New York because *you* told me you were dying." He looks at his sister, then back to his father. "You were babbling about taking a trip and she was telling me you're leaving your company. Now you want us to travel to India with you?!"

"Trevor, lower your voice." His father calmly takes him by the elbow and guides him to a row of seats where people are waiting to board their flight.

Trevor stops abruptly. "I'm not going anywhere. And I'm certainly *not* getting on a 15-hour flight to travel halfway around the world!"

"Trevor!" Jonathan's voice is forceful but still not louder than his first request. With his head bent, he motions with his eyes to the small group of airport security, dressed more for a deployment to Iraq than guarding Disney-bound passengers and senior citizens zipping by in motorized scooters. The handful of trained terrorist spotters take an interest in their conversation.

Trevor looks over and smiles politely, assuring the officers that he is not being kidnapped. Ever since 9/11, airports have been saturated with security officers, and after 21 somewhat years, he's betting a couple of them are just itching for one bad guy to raise his voice or start a commotion. Trevor feels his father's hand on his arm and allows himself to be led to the waiting seats.

"Alright, Dad, *what's* going on? I told my boss my dad was sick and I had to be with him. That bought me a few days, but India?

Really, Dad? We're not 10 anymore. You can't just pull us out of school because you and Mom ..." He stops himself and corrects the comment. "... because *you* want to take a family vacation."

"I can go," Cassandra interjects.

"You have school!" Trevor quickly shoots back.

"I have one class left, and it's creative writing. Besides, my teacher is always saying I need more life experience. I'll just shoot her an e-mail saying 'I'm going to get some life experience ... be back soon'." Cassandra playfully sticks out her tongue, contradicting Trevor's statement about not being 10 years old, which is not received well.

Trevor's gaze swings back to his father. "What about work, Dad?"

Jonathan opens his mouth to answer, but Trevor's not done. "Some of us have to work!" He realizes his son is not so much concerned about his father's company as he is with his own employment.

"Trevor," Jonathan starts with all the precision of a surgeon. "I *need* you to come with us." He takes a deep breath. *Maybe that wasn't the best way to approach it.* "I *want* you to be with us. This is something I have to do. For Christ's sake, I left my company for this! I didn't just take a vacation or an extended holiday. I left the firm. I left Bruce in charge." He stops for a moment, contemplating that decision. *Maybe Bruce wasn't the best person to leave in charge.* "Hell, I may never step foot in that office again."

"Dad, that's crazy," Trevor says quietly.

"Trevor, no one ever, and I mean *ever,* said on their death bed, 'Gee, I wish I had worked more'." He let his words sink in before growing doleful. "What I wouldn't give to spend one more day—no, one more moment, one more sunset with my father, if I was granted the opportunity." He looks at Trevor with pleading eyes. "We have that opportunity, and I'm asking for one more experience. Please, son. Give me that."

"Dad," Trevor starts, like a poker player calling a bluff, "you're not dying. Look at you. You're probably in better shape than I am."

"Trevor, we're all dying. It just takes some of us 85, maybe 90 years to get there. Some of us get there at 40, and it takes another 35 for them to get into the hole. Let's not be like one of those people. Let's seize *this* moment! What if there is no tomorrow? Like my priest always says, if you want to make God laugh—"

In unison, Trevor and Cassandra join their father, since they've heard him recite these words their entire lives. "You tell him what your plans are for tomorrow." Then they both laugh the same hearty laugh as their father. *God, I sound just like a carbon copy of my father,* Trevor thinks.

"Trevor, seriously," Jonathan returns to the delicate process of convincing his son to take a leap of faith with him. "I need you with me to make sense of all this. I want you there because, frankly, I don't know what's going on. And, I'm not too proud to say, I'm a little frightened."

"But why now, Dad? Why does it have to be spontaneous, at *this* moment? Why don't we plan this thing? I'll take a month off from work. Cassandra can finish school."

"NO!" Jonathan's response is firm. For the first time, he raises his voice. "It has to be now!" He places his hand on Trevor's knee, and his voice is once again tranquil and reserved when he speaks next, "Son, I can't tell you why I have to go, or where I have to go, or even for how long I have to go. I just know I have to go, and I have to *go* today." With a bowed head, Jonathan's voice gets even softer. "All I know is, the older we get, the faster time passes us by. I never really felt that before, but I'm starting to now, and last night, something awakened inside me." He raises his head. "I can't explain it. I just know something called to me. Spoke to me. Told me what to do, and if I don't do it, I'll regret it for as long as I live." Looking into his son's eyes, he adds, "I never felt more strongly about anything in my whole life, and I don't even know what I'm doing." A moment more passes before he says, "But I need you and your sister there with me."

Trevor's eyes start to tear. This man, a man who has always been his rock, is now looking to him for support. How could he say no?

"Okay, Dad. I'm in. I don't know where this is going, but I'm with you. Every step of the way."

In another part of the world at another time, Akal

Datta awoke before dawn as she had for the past 48 years. Only that morning, she awakened with a troubled heart and haunting images from a dream. It was not just any dream; it was the most vivid dream she had ever experienced, accompanied by a feeling of overwhelming dread, the dread that comes from knowing one's own death. With trembling hands, she wiped away the beads of sweat from her brow as her breathing slowly returned to normal.

Her husband stirred and she quickly exited the bed to make his breakfast. She made him idlis, a typical steamed rice-dough pancake, and a small dish of chutney. Her youngest son, Vijay, joined his father at the table as Arjun, her oldest son, ran past her, late for work at the market.

"Arjun! One moment!" Akal yelled, stopping him at the door.

She handed him 100 rupees, taking care to block the transaction from her husband's sight. She then kissed his cheek and said, "I want you to purchase a flat stone for me." She gave him the dimensions needed and

17

instructions on what the stone carver was to inscribe on the front. She then slipped him a piece of paper with a single word written on it. A word foreign to her. A word she saw in her dream on similar stones. She told Arjun to have the stone cutter inscribe that word on the back of the stone.

Arjun, bewildered, studied the piece of paper. The letters were neither Hindi nor Urdu; they were foreign to both son and mother.

"Be home for dinner," she told him as he ran from the house.

Her husband stood and announced that he too must leave for work. Another day began. For everyone else, it was merely the same old routine, as one day blurred into the next, but for Akal, haunted by the predawn premonition, it was anything but ordinary.

"I have to talk with you when you get home," she announced before her husband reached the door.

"Is everything okay?"

"Yes. It's nothing that can't wait until tonight." Her lie comforted her husband.

In the hour that followed, Vijay walked to school with his mother, who worked at the local poultry farm just across the train tracks from his school. She kissed her son goodbye, saying, "Be good, my little candlenut!" Her mind still preoccupied on this morning's dream, she proceeded to work. In the dream, Akal stood on the bow of a wooden boat. Her hand rested upon the neck of a great serpent. Its head rose from the front of the ship, guiding the vessel across a turbulent sea. Her body was strong, that of a man's. Icy water splashed on her long red beard. In her other hand, she grasped a small river stone she wore around her neck. Her fingers traced a strange word carved into it.

Akal, unaware of her surroundings, began to walk up the slight incline toward the railroad tracks. As she tried to remember the writing on the stone, she recalled a second dream, a dream in which she found herself in a cave surrounded by men of a much darker color. Her hand, also the same dark color, was placed on the cave wall. A spray of bright color filled the air, coating the wall and covering her hand. In this new dream, she was also a man, a young, slender black man.

What did it all mean? She remembered seeing herself give a similar stone to one of the tribe's elders. It too was inscribed with the same word as the red-haired sea traveler's stone. There was a low muffled sound that steadily grew louder until it was a deafening roar. One of the men in the cave placed a firm hand on her shoulder and pulled her backward. Suddenly, the cave was gone. She was ripped from a time long ago, back to her time where a wall of steel and glass sped by her. She awoke from her trance to find herself yanked back off the railroad tracks by a stranger. Mortified by the thought of what could have happened, she nervously thanked the man who saved her life, and banished all thoughts of the morning's nocturnal visions.

For the second time that day, her hands trembled uncontrollably. Arriving at work, it was clear Akal was unnerved. Her friend, noticing her pale complexion, asked if she was alright.

"I was almost hit by a train!"

"Oh, that train is the devil. So many people are killed every month by that thing. You must be more careful."

Akal took a deep breath and settled her nerves. She shook her head and remarked, "I see so many children walking on the tracks. They should never have built that school there."

That night, Akal's husband returned from work. She greeted him at the door and held him tight, something she had not done in years.

"My dear, what is wrong?"

"I had a terrible dream this morning, only," she started, still thinking about it. "I don't think it was a dream. I think—"

"What do you mean, you don't think it was a dream? What else could it be?"

"I think maybe—" She stopped, too frightened to say it.

"Maybe what?" her husband urged.

"I think maybe my soul from past lives was trying to come back and warn me?"

"Warn you of what?"

8

"Warn me that I may not have long to live in this life." A tear ran down her cheek. Several more followed, her eyelids unable to hold back the flooding tide.

"Oh, you're just being silly!"

Her hands clenched in rage. "I was almost KILLED today," she barked at her husband. "On the way to work!"

Just then, the door opened, and both Akal and her husband turned to see Arjun arrive home for supper.

"What's going on? Momma, why are you crying?"

"Your mother had a visit from her previous life," his father commented in a clearly mocking tone.

Wiping her face, she rushed to her son. "Do you have it? Do you have what I asked you to get for me today?"

He retrieved a small cloth from his pocket and unwrapped it, revealing a rectangular stone. She snatched it from his hand and examined it closely.

Akal Datta
February 29th, 1876

She turned it over. *Perfect,* she thought, and turned to her husband, thrusting the stone in his face.

"Do you see this? This is not a figment of my imagination!"

Now Vijay joined them, and both sons stared at their parents, watching the heated discussion.

Her husband took the stone and glanced at it. "This is a stone. How does it prove anything?"

She plucked it from her husband. "Do you see this?!" she yelled, facing it toward him as she pointed at the mysterious word inscribed. "Do you see this?! This was in my dream. Both of the men who I used to be had a stone like this one, with this exact word on it."

He took a closer look. "What does it mean?" he asked, softer now.

"I DON'T KNOW!" she screamed, "BUT I KNOW IT'S IMPORTANT! AND I KNOW IT IS WARNING ME!" She broke down. "I DON'T WANT TO DIE!"

He hugged his wife. "Akal, you're *not* going to die."

"You don't know that! I almost died today!"

Both children gasped then, looking on with furrowed brows as she continued. "Promise me! If anything ever happens to me, you will keep this stone. And keep it safe!"

"But it's just a stone—" her husband began.

"NO!" she screamed. "NOT TO ME! This is who I am! This is who I will always be—" She tried to catch her breath. "And if you forget about *this* stone, then you have forgotten about me!"

Vijay ran to his mother and hugged her tightly. "I will keep the stone. I will not forget you!"

Arjun quickly joined his brother and embraced her, all the time staring at his father. "I will *not* forget you either, Mother, and if you want me to keep the stone for you, I will!"

Akal's husband stood alone, feeling ashamed. A shy smile crossed his face and the loving man she married emerged before them. "We will keep your stone, if that is your wish, but nothing is going to happen to you, and we certainly are never going to forget you."

She embraced her family. That night, sleep did not come easily to Akal, fearful of her uncertain future.

The following day, the haunting dream still preoccupied Akal Datta's thoughts. This time, there was no man walking behind her to pull her from the tracks. She died on a Tuesday.

Her young son Vijay, the first of their family to reach her body, removed a small, flat stone from her pocket. He would be the one to keep the stone safe. She would not be forgotten. And one day, he hoped, she might return to claim it.

Place: In Flight Over the Atlantic Ocean
Year: Present Day

Approximately 36,000 miles above the ocean where

Takoda drowned centuries before, a commercial airliner cruises at 482 miles per hour. Cassandra, Jonathan, and Trevor sit in first class. One excited, one anxious, and one confused about why he is there.

"So tell me, Dad. Why India?" Trevor asks.

"I don't know? I mean, I can't tell you. I had a dream. I woke up and called out to your sister that we had to go to India."

Trevor looks at Cassandra sitting across the aisle. She shrugs with a confused look.

Jonathan proceeds to recount his dream, turning from Cassandra to Trevor who is sitting next to the window. "I told your sister I had to go home and see—" He pauses, trying to recall the dream. "My sister? My mother? Somebody close to me, a family member, I believe?"

"Dad, your sister lives in Wisconsin."

"And you didn't say anything about going to India," Cassandra adds. "You were scrambling around your office looking for photo albums."

"I know. That's the strange part," Jonathan continues. "As I said, I got up, had an entire conversation with your sister about why I had to go to India, walked all around the apartment, started to get my things together for the trip, when all of a sudden, I woke up!" He scans their eyes, his gaze darting back and forth between them, their faces registering only confusion. "It was a dream within a dream. I was so disorientated. I remember showering in a daze. I wasn't sure if I was still dreaming or awake; if I had talked to your sister or not. I wasn't sure of anything. Not even where I was!"

"Dad, that's the strangest thing I ever heard," Cassandra says softly.

"I know," Jonathan answers, looking back at Trevor. "Something in that dream was telling me to go to India and to go today!" That's when I actually yelled out to your sister, where she found me in my study searching through my things.

"A dream?!" Trevor yells out, drawing the attention of the surrounding passengers.

"Keep your voice down," Cassandra urges, noticing some concerned faces.

Trevor looks at his father and whispers through his teeth, "A *dream*, Dad? You had me fly from Arizona to New York and then get on a plane going to India because *you* had a *bad dream?* And NO, I'm not going to keep my voice down, Cazz!" he half shouts, looking at his sister. "You should have told me this over the phone!" He turns to his father, but his anger turns to concern as he sees the distressful expression on his father's face. Jonathan's mouth is agape, gasping for air.

"Dad, are you okay?! Are you choking?"

"He didn't eat anything!" Cassandra shouts.

Jonathan coughs and then coughs again. This time, a small amount of water spews from his mouth. Jonathan quickly covers his mouth and takes another gasp of air.

"DAD!" Trevor shouts, as Jonathan stands up and bangs his head on the overhead compartment. His hands search the ceiling of the plane, seeming to grasp for something above him.

Jonathan has all the hallmarks of a drowning man.

Again, Trevor shouts and Cassandra yells for a flight attendant to help. Jonathan hunches over and vomits clear water, coughing the entire time. Trevor, now on his feet, rushes to his father. Everyone in the first-class cabin is up in their seats, craning to observe the commotion.

Jonathan falls to the floor, calling out, "Makawee!" before more water gushes past his lips. "Makawee!" he cries out again, before collapsing on the cabin floor.

A loud voice resounds from the back of the cabin. "Make a hole, people. AIR MARSHAL coming through."

A mountain of a man bolts past the passengers, followed by several flight attendants. He kneels to assess the situation.

"How much has he had to drink?" the marshal asks Trevor, who is attending to his father.

"What?! Nothing. None. My Dad doesn't drink alcohol," Trevor lies.

The marshal turns his doubtful gaze to the boy for a second before turning his attention back to Jonathan.

In an attempt to correct his error he adds, "At least not this early in the day."

Jonathan, now on all fours, water dripping from his mouth, cries out faintly one last time, "Makawee," then suddenly, the violent seizure passes.

The air marshal steadies him as he tries to get to his feet. "Just take it easy, sir. We want to make sure everything is okay."

"I'm fine, I'm fine," Jonathan protests, placing one foot forward in order to straighten up. "Not sure what the hell that was. Salty, tasted like," Jonathan pauses, searching for the answer. Then it comes to him. "Sea water."

"Sir, have you been drinking?" the air marshal redirects the question to Jonathan.

"I told you my father doesn't—" Trevor begins.

"Its alright, son. The man is just doing his job." Facing the marshal, Jonathan says, "I want to thank you, but I can assure you, I haven't been drinking. Now if you'll excuse me, I need to wash this salt taste from my mouth."

Jonathan stands up. He looks at all the faces staring at him. Embarrassed, he says, "I think I'll go freshen up?"

The air marshal places his huge hand in the center of Jonathan's chest, "I think you should have a seat. Just until we make sure you're okay." The air marshal looks at the flight attendant. "Can we get him a drink of water?"

Jonathan sizes up the stronger, younger, mountain of a man whose hand spans his chest. Knowing the argument is pointless, he concedes. "Yeah, I think that's best," and returns to his seat.

"So what happened here?" the marshal turns to Trevor and Cassandra.

"He just started throwing up, officer," Cassandra explains.

"More like it was forcefully coming out of him," Trevor observes, adding, "He looked like a drowning man."

A flight attendant hands Jonathan a bottle of water. "I'll get some towels to clean this up." Other attendants reassure the passengers that all is well.

The Air Marshal leans down. "Sir, are you sure you're alright?"

"I'm sure whatever I ate has passed, Officer."

With not a hint of alcohol detected on Jonathan's breath, the Air Marshal smiles. "Then I'm sure there's no need to alert the captain. I'll have to make a full report though, but no need to make a special landing," a slight wink to Jonathan. "Right?"

"Rodger that," Jonathan nods and gives him a thumbs up.

"Oh, and it's Marshal, not Officer." He smiles at Cassandra. "We get that a lot." He turns to Trevor and leans in to whisper, "You're sure he hasn't been drinking?" He straightens, seeing Trevor's reaction. "Alright, I just have to be sure."

"The flight just took off; they haven't even come around with the cart yet."

Jonathan tugs on Trevor's shirt. "Son, they don't have carts in first class."

The air marshal and Jonathan exchange a polite glance. *Ah, to be young again.*

"Just checking since they're going to want to see that I asked in my review."

Trevor points to the cabin's soaked carpet. "Nothing but water."

The air marshal kneels down. Seagulls, sand, and endless summer days walking on the boardwalk fill the marshal's head. The strong salty scent of the Atlantic Ocean triggers long-forgotten memories of Mother's Day weekends down at the Jersey shore.

Cassandra turns away and makes a face. *Bet you don't get THAT a lot?*

Saltwater? The bewildered air marshal thinks to himself. He stands as the sounds of boardwalk arcades and sideshow barkers retreat to the memories of his youth.

Four hours into a fourteen-hour flight, Trevor asks his father, "Dad, who is Makawee?"

Wrestling with the same thought, Jonathan slowly answers. "I think she's someone I once knew?"

"You think? You mean she *is* someone you once knew, or you don't know? You can't *think* you once knew her. Did you know her or not?"

"I think, a long time ago, I knew her."

"Like before Mom? A college girlfriend? Or maybe in high school? How long ago is a long time ago?"

His father stares at the back of the seat. "Trevor, this is going to sound weird, but I think I knew her years ago, like many years ago."

"Like in elementary school?"

Jonathan shakes his head.

"Jesus, Dad, do you have Alzheimer's?" He looks at his father, glances over at his sister, then back to his father again. "Is this what this is all about? We're flying to India because you have dementia?" Trevor's foot taps rapidly as he continues with his inquiry. "I'm flying halfway around the world, stuck on a plane for an entire day, because you think your grammar-school crush lives in India, and you're having flashbacks from the '70s?'"

"I don't have Alzheimer's!" Jonathan snaps at his son. "And it wasn't just a dream. I don't know how to explain it. Something told me to go." He puts his hand on his son's knee steadying his foot. "I don't know. Maybe I am losing it? All I know is that I saw a place in my dream and I needed to get there as soon as possible."

"The same voice that told you that you were going to die, I suppose?"

"YES!" Jonathan rifles back. "Only it wasn't a voice. More like a feeling—" His voice trails off, growing so faint it's drowned out by the constant murmuring of the plane's engines.

"Well, news flash for you, Dad. You're *not* going to die! You're healthier than Cazz and me put together! You don't smoke. You don't eat crappy fast food. You don't drink. Well not like a college student, anyway. Hell, you're gonna outlive Grandma, and she's 95."

"Trevor, I can't explain the feeling I have. It's like an obsession, or a desire, or some overpowering urge making me do this."

"Do *what?*"

"I don't know. But I do know, if I didn't get on this plane, something horrible would have happened. That's why I need you and your sister with me."

"You mean you *want* us here to introduce us to your grammar school sweetheart, Makawee. Did you two rekindle over Facebook? Please don't tell me she's a mail-order bride. She probably Googled your bank account and—"

"Trevor—" Jonathan throws his son a curve ball, derailing his babbling. "I think Makawee was my wife." He sees his son's face turn to shock and then confusion as he clarifies. "My wife in a previous lifetime."

"YOUR WHAT?" Trevor stands as First Class passengers shoot the trio another look. A kettle of emotions comes to a boil, turning his pale complexion a deep crimson. He begins several sentences, spewing out one word at a time, stopping then starting anew, not making any sense. Finally, he looks at his sister. "Did you know about this?" He doesn't wait for a response. "We should have taken him right to the hospital. Clearly, he had a stroke or something." He begins walking down the aisle, mumbling to himself. "Lost *his* mind. I cannot believe I'm flying to India because Dad is having a mid-life crisis."

"Sir, is everything alright?" a flight attendant asks Trevor.

"Ask my father. He's the one having an affair with another woman in another life." He storms past her, pointing in his father's direction.

She stares at Jonathan and Cassandra.

"He gets nervous when he flies. He'll be alright. Just has to walk it off," Cassandra reassures the flight attendant.

Minutes later, Trevor returns after walking the aisles several times. Having nowhere else to go, he sits quietly for a long time. Many years ago, his father taught him that when sailing up wind, sometimes you have to take a different tack. Trevor decides to do just that, and with an open mind and calmer head, he turns to his father. "Alright, Dad. Tell me what makes you think you had a wife in another lifetime. This Makawee woman?"

During the course of the 14-hour flight, Jonathan tries to describe the images and feelings he's been experiencing ever since that morning, two days ago. Hours pass as he explains and corrects himself, uncertain of which images are feelings and which may simply be dreams. Questions and answers go back and forth. Finally, Jonathan lays out his case fully to explain to his children why exactly this matters so much to him. "And that's why I have to go to India," he concludes.

Trevor thinks for a long while before responding, then says, "Okay Dad, you've got four days. After that, we're going back to the States, I'm calling a doctor, and you're going for a CAT scan or an MRI. At the very least, you're sitting down with a therapist."

Jonathan smirks.

"And not just any therapist; I'm calling Mom, and she's going to find you a good one."

"Christ. Your mother will have me committed before the plane lands. She'll be waiting at the gate with a shit-eating grin, standing with two guys dressed in white holding out a straight jacket. *Welcome home, Johnny boy.*"

Cassandra laughs. "Dad, you know if there's one person who can find you the best therapist in the world, it's Mom."

"I suppose. She's like a bloodhound that way." It's the best Jonathan can muster as far as a compliment to his ex-wife. "Okay." He concedes, "You have a deal."

PLACE: NEW DELHI, INDIA
YEAR: PRESENT DAY

As the plane makes its descent, Jonathan tries to prepare his children for the complex, diverse, wonderful culture that is India.

"India is like no other country we have ever been to before." He tries to find the right words. "It's as busy as Italy, but instead of mopeds and traffic signs it has, well, it has—it's basically mass chaos. There are no traffic rules, and there are people and livestock everywhere. It's like the East Village, but with a billion more people and cows."

He thinks for a moment, "I really can't explain it. I guess India is just something you're going to have to experience." He looks at Cassandra. "Try not to be too shocked. At least *try* not to show it."

The plane touches down at Indira Gandhi International Airport at 1:30 p.m. The airport seems ordinary enough, but as soon as they walk through the terminal's main doors, the real India makes herself known to them. It was as Jonathan described, but a thousand times more. A thousand times more crowded, a thousand times noisier, a thousand times more colorful, and a thousand times more pungent.

The first thing they all notice is the oppressive heat. Trevor sheds his shirt, leaving only his tee-shirt to cover his perspiring torso. Cassandra begins to remove her outer layer of clothing, only to be stopped by her father, "You may not want to do that, Cassy. India is somewhat of a modest country."

She looks around and sees all the women covered with brightly flowing garments. None of them seems to be affected by the heat. "Okay, but I'm buying something lighter to wear first chance I get."

They left the bright, clear skies of New York, and like Dorothy, emerge strangers in a strange land. A fine mist of dust fills the air, and an ever-present fragrance of curry permeates their nostrils.

People, animals, and livestock roam freely everywhere. Cassandra's iPhone goes into overdrive as she begins documenting every nuance of this exotic new land. Green and yellow three-wheeled taxis, called auto-rickshaws, scurry in every direction along with the usual cars and trucks. People on bicycles, sometimes whole families balanced on two-wheeled frames, move past them. All manner of transportation moves in every direction with no street signs or traffic signals in sight. It's as if the entire population of Manhattan, all 1.6 million people, flooded the streets at once in search of someplace to go.

Cassandra stands with her mouth agape.

Jonathan waves off several men who attempt to negotiate a taxi fare. They smile and go about their business, moving on to other travelers departing from the terminal. "I had Margaret arrange for a guide to take us around," Jonathan tells them with a big smile. "I will say this. They are some of the nicest people you'll ever meet."

"For ripoff artists, that is," Trevor comments, as he listens to one man quote a price of 15,000 rupees for a fair that costs a third of that amount.

Jonathan looks at him inquisitively.

"What? It was a long flight. I did my research on the plane," Trevor shrugs. "I like to know a little about the country I'm visiting."

"Wonder where he gets that from?" Jonathan sneaks a comment to Cassandra.

"Mom," she playfully retorts.

"Mister Taylor?" A well-dressed Indian man asks.

Jonathan turns and extends his hand, "I'm Mr. Taylor."

The man takes his hand, but when addressing the children, especially Cassandra, he places his hand over his heart and bows slightly with a traditional greeting, "Namaste."

Cassandra presses her palms together, her fingers pointing upward, her thumbs close to her chest, and repeats, "Namaste."

This small act brings a wide smile to the man's face.

Trevor looks at her and half-heartedly mimics her actions, softly repeating, "Namaste."

Again the man smiles and bows in appreciation.

Trevor, still looking at his sister, asks, "How do you know about Indian customs?"

"It means I bow to the divine in you," she answers. "I learned about it in Yoga class. It's Hindi."

"Very good," the man says. "This gesture is called Añjali Mudrā or Pranamasana. And I am Mitra Dubashi. Please call me Mitra."

He glances at his phone and touches the shiny mirrored surface. "Your Miss Margaret made reservations at an Airbnb in the Panchsheel Enclave at Armán The Green. An exceptionally nice place. I just called for an Uber."

"You have Ubers here?" Cassandra asks.

"Oh, yes. They are much more—" He searches for the right word, trying not to give a bad impression of his country, "—honest, than the taxis."

"So, what does Mitra mean in Hindi?" Trevor asks, somewhat sarcastically.

But Mitra does not take it that way. He merely answers honestly, "It means *Friend* or *Very helpful friend.*"

"Well, I hope you're an extremely helpful friend and an excellent guide, Mitra," Jonathan adds. Surprisingly, his words are delivered not in English but rather in Urdu, one of India's least spoken languages. Only four percent of the population is able to understand it.

Mitra stands puzzled, as are Jonathan's children.

"What was *that?*" Trevor asks.

Jonathan looks at them all confused, unable to understand why they appear so shocked.

"Dad, you were speaking Hindi!" Trevor shouts.

"No, I wasn't," Jonathan protests.

"Yes, you *were*, Dad!" now it's Cassandra who's yelling.

"No, he's not," Mitra proclaims.

"He's *not?*" both children respond.

"No, I speak Hindi, and *that* was not Hindi," Mitra says.

"Then, what was it?" Cassandra asks. "And how is my father speaking it?"

"Mister Taylor, please say something else. Ask me where the hotel is located," Mitra pleads.

"Why do I need to know where the hotel is?" Jonathan responds in plain English.

"Alright! What's going on, Dad?" Trevor demands. "Is this some kind of a joke? First you get us to come to India; then you start speaking in some language you learned on YouTube, trying to impress us?"

"Trevor, I have no idea what you're talking about," Jonathan protests.

Mitra turns to Jonathan asking in Hindi, "Aap kaisa mahasoos kar rahe hain?"

Jonathan answers in Urdu, "I'm fine." An amazed expression covers his face, as he hears his own words in a foreign tongue.

"What the HELL, Dad?" Trevor yells.

"So, he IS speaking Hindi," Cassandra says.

"No. Your father understands Hindi, but he's responding in another language."

"What do you mean, another language?" Cassandra asks, puzzled. "We're in India. He's not speaking Portuguese."

"My dear child, India has more than 20 different languages with more than 700 different dialects. Most of the country can only communicate through English," Mitra explains.

A microbus pulls up to the curb and Mitra motions that it's their Uber.

"You've got to be kidding," Jonathan exclaims, his brow furrowed.

"I'm sorry, but there are not many big cars in India. You'll find the small ones get around much faster."

The Taylor family begins the arduous task of squeezing themselves, Mitra, and their luggage, like sardines, into the tin can with four wheels. When the last door is closed, the Uber bolts right out into the congested area, barely avoiding a major collision.

For the next 20 minutes, the Taylors are unable to focus on anything but the most terrifying car ride of their lives. As the driver weaves and swerves, accelerates and brakes, Mitra tries his best to call out points of interest in his city. Cassandra flinches and screams as rickshaws and motorcars jockey for dominance over small patches of the dusty road. Again and again she brushes the flies from her face, as the car stops next to a resting cow. The sound of horns honking fills the air in a concert of music only India can appreciate. New York City's taxi cabs seem like gentle leaves drifting down the rivers of Manhattan's tributaries in comparison to the insane traffic that congests India's streets in a relentless struggle to move from place to place.

As soon as the car stops, everyone's thoughts return to Jonathan's sudden and mysterious bilingual abilities.

"It's not like you just picked up an Indian language, Dad," Trevor says, continuing to hound his father while they check into their rooms.

Armán The Green B&B is one of the nicest places to stay in all of Delhi. The owners, Amar and Manini, who live on the first floor, show them to their rooms on the second floor.

"Just let me know what you want for breakfast, lunch, and dinner, and we will be happy to prepare it for you," Amar tells them. "My wife Manini shops at the market every morning, so everything is fresh."

For only $60 a night, the space is incredibly large, and having their own personal chef is amazing. After they settle in, the family joins Mitra in the common room. The conversation once again returns to Jonathan's sudden indoctrination into the Indian culture.

"It's just *not* done, Dad," Trevor says. "You don't just start speaking another language all of a sudden."

"Maybe he picked up a couple of words at the airport?" Cassandra offers.

"A couple of words maybe, but Dad was speaking in full, coherent sentences, and *not* even in the predominant language. We have no idea what he's speaking."

"Mr. Taylor, why did you come to India?" Mitra asks.

"I wanted to find—" he starts.

"He wanted to find his family," Trevor interrupts. "The only thing is, he doesn't have any family in India. They're all in the States."

"Maybe your ancestors came from India? Are you trying to find your roots?" Mitra asks.

"I think Dad's ancestors came from England," Cassandra answers.

"He always felt a closer connection with Scotland," Trevor adds, turning to Cassandra.

Mitra cocks his head to one side and asks again, "So tell me, Jonathan," he turns and looks at the children, "And only Jonathan, why have you come to India?"

"Something within me," he starts. "Some driving force woke me from a sound sleep. I had this urge, a powerful urge, that I had to come to India." He searches for some expression on Mitra's face, a subtle hint of skepticism or suspicion of insanity, but finds no such reaction. On the contrary, his words are received with understanding and reassurance.

"This urge that you speak of, was it a longing to return home?" Mitra asks.

"Yes," Jonathan answers.

"And did you feel like you were someone else, yet this person was also you?" he continues.

"YES!" Jonathan's face lights up. For the first time, he has made a connection with someone who has a glimpse of understanding.

"And did you see other people, a family perhaps, mother, father, maybe children that were your own, but not Trevor or Cassandra?"

"YES! Yes, I believe I had two children, both sons," he says, glancing sheepishly at Cassandra.

"Were you older or younger? Man or woman?"

"Man or woman?" Trevor asks, his head tilted quizzically, "What do you mean? Of course, he was a man."

"Woman," Jonathan answers firmly, stopping Trevor cold.

Trevor looks perplexed, unable to respond.

"And your house. You saw your house where you lived?" Mitra continues his interrogation, paying no attention to Trevor.

"Yes, I saw the house and a town. I saw the place where I worked. It was a poultry farm," he recalls, "And it was across from where Vijay went to school. Across the tracks!" Jonathan stops suddenly. "Oh God, my son's name was Vijay."

"Vijay!" Cassandra and Trevor exclaim in unison.

"The tracks?" Mitra inquires.

"Train tracks," Jonathan murmurs. "But I don't want to talk about that," he says in a stern tone.

Mitra appears puzzled.

"Dad has a thing about trains," Cassandra explains. "When I was little, and we had to take the subway, Mom would tell me, 'Never stand too close to the platform'. Right before the train came, it would get quiet; the temperature would change and the wind would pick up, pushing the stagnant air through dark, cavernous tunnels. There would be a deafening roar and papers would swirl everywhere on the platform. Then came the rhythmic, pulsating metal clatter of heavy wheels speeding past. Sparks ignited in the darkness as electric contacts were made and broken. I loved it, but Mom said Dad would never take the train. He was deathly afraid of it. I used to think a dragon was hurtling through his lair, spitting fire as it went. Dad said something about the subway one time. What did you say again, Dad?"

Jonathan stares at the ground, "At least you always know when the subway comes."

"Jonathan," Mitra asks, his gaze again fixed only on him, "what is the last thing you can remember about being this woman with two children?"

"I was going to work." Jonathan's leg begins to shake.

"At the chicken farm?"

"Yes." A bead of sweat runs down the side of his face.

"Across the tracks," Mitra continues with the questions.

"Yes," Jonathan runs his fingers through his hair like a guilty murderer who's just realized the detective knows where the body is buried.

"The *train* tracks?" Mitra presses on.

"YES!" Jonathan gets up, suddenly pacing the floor like a strung-out addict looking for his next fix.

"Mr. Taylor, don't you see it? This could be the reason you don't like trains," Mitra says.

"Why? What about the train tracks?" Cassandra asks, wondering why her father hates trains so much.

Like all the other memories that have flooded Jonathan's mind, he now realizes why he is deathly afraid of trains.

"It's the last memory you had as this other person, because when you were going to work, the person you used to be was struck and kil—"

"I said I don't want to talk about it!" Jonathan shouts, silencing Mitra with a very uncharacteristic outburst.

The whole room falls silent. A strange stillness fills the air, the kind that comes upon hearing the news of a loved one's death.

Finally, Trevor asks, "Mitra, what's going on? It was just a dream. Shouldn't we get Dad to a doctor, or maybe a therapist?"

"I'm not sick!" Jonathan barks.

"On the contrary," Mitra offers. "I'm not sure if it was a dream at all. Mr. Taylor, you may have had a glimpse of a life you once lived." Then, turning to Trevor and Cassandra, he adds, "I think your father has had an actual past-life experience."

"Oh, come on," Trevor scoffs. "You don't really believe that, do you?"

Mitra laughs. "My young friend, you are in India! You will find that almost everyone in India believes strongly in reincarnation. It is the central tenet of the Indian religion. And not just Hinduism. 25 percent of all Christians also believe that the soul returns to earth.

Native Americans as well as the indigenous people in Australia also share similar beliefs. Even Plato, in the 4th century, believed in an immortal soul that participates in infinite incarnations."

"Are you saying I may have lived before? Here, in India?" Jonathan frantically points downward.

"As a woman, Dad," Trevor adds.

"I think you may have. Isn't that why you *really* came here?"

Jonathan nods. "I think it is."

"Okay, wait. So how do we find out if Dad had one of these past life thingamajigs or just some incredibly vivid dream?" Cassandra asks, addressing the room.

Again the group of four grows quiet.

Initially, no one speaks, then Trevor has an idea. "The answer lies within what Dad was saying, or, more importantly, in what language he was saying it in."

"But there are over 20 languages spoken in India. And I have no idea which one I was speaking," Jonathan says.

"And you said there are how many dialects spoken in this country?" Trevor asks, looking to Mitra.

"More than 700," Mitra answers. "In fact, you can often tell where someone is from by the language they are speaking."

"Say that again," Jonathan says.

"There are more than 700?"

"No, the other part!" both Jonathan and Trevor exclaim together.

"You can often tell where someone is from—" As Mitra recites the phrase, he hears the connection, "—by the language they are speaking."

"So we just have to find someone who can understand what Dad is saying, and then ask them where they're from." Cassandra smiles as if she's the only one who has solved the mystery.

Mitra smiles. "I know just the place."

In another part of the world, it's autumn in New York City. Howard Convery, a 63-year-old Professor of Archaeology, awakens in his west side apartment and begins his weekday ritual.

"What are you doing?" his wife stirs and asks with a yawn. "It's Saturday. You don't have to go into the office today."

He falls back in bed and rolls over to kiss her on the forehead. "Good morning, my love. Big day today. Marcus said it may come today." He gets out of bed and heads toward the shower.

"My love? Ha. The only thing you love is that museum of yours." Her voice follows him into the bathroom.

Professor Howard Convery is the Head Curator of the Archaeology Department at the Museum of Natural History in the greatest city in the world. He's been putting together an exhibit for a long time, and today, the crowning jewel for that exhibit is due to arrive from Africa.

He peeks out from the bathroom door. "You know you're the love of my life, and I would give it all up if you asked me to." He ducks back into the bathroom, brushing his teeth.

"Honey," she yells from the bed, "can you give up your job and come back to bed, please?"

His head quickly peeks out again. "Nope," he answers, then promptly retreats to the security of the bathroom, his face covered with shaving cream.

By the time he's finished showering, she's out of bed and making coffee. He quickly dresses and joins her in the kitchen. She sits at the table in her bathrobe drinking coffee, completing The New York Times crossword puzzle. "I've poured you a cup."

He stops and looks at a picture of his two grown daughters. "I can't believe my college roommate still calls them Peanut Butter and Jelly. I mean, it was cute when they were small, but they're in college now."

She smiles. "The girls still think it's cute."

"Speaking of cute—" He joins her at the table, taking a sip from his mug. "You look adorable in that robe."

"I looked even better in bed, but that didn't entice you enough to stay home," she says, not looking up from the paper.

"Big day today," he says again. "Big day." He gets up and grabs his hat from the wall hook. He leans down and kisses the top of her head. "You could come with me."

"Why? To be your love slave?" she says, and they both laugh at an old inside joke.

"I really *do* love you."

"I know. Hey listen, don't forget—" she starts, and he finishes in unison with her, bobbing his head from side to side with every word. "We have the Fausners tonight."

He heads toward the door. "I know, you've only been telling me for the last two weeks."

As he steps out of his brownstone into the bright morning sunlight, crisp air fills his lungs, the first evidence summer is ending and winter will soon be descending upon New York City. He squints upward between the towering skyscrapers; the sky is a deep sapphire blue with but one solitary white cloud perched in the heavens. *It's going to be a great day,* he thinks to himself, and heads toward the museum. On such a beautiful day, one can't help but walk in the city. Even on an early Saturday morning, the city streets swarm with activity. Taxi drivers race among slow-moving buses and passenger cars, their eyes and ears scanning for outstretched arms or short halting whistles. People scramble in the concrete canyons like ants on the move in the Serengeti. Lean marathon runners jog past, making their way to Central Park to join strangers united in their health-crazed crusade.

Howard makes his way up Fifth Avenue. Passing the New York Public Library, he yells out to the two majestic stone lions guarding its entrance. "Good morning, Patience! Good morning, Fortitude!" As he reaches 58th Street, the park comes into view. Just in front of Grand Army Plaza, a beautiful courtyard with the Pulitzer Fountain emerges, greeting guests to the iconic Plaza Hotel. Howard decides it's such a beautiful day that a scenic stroll through the park is better than fighting the weekend street vendors peddling their charcoal caricatures and NYC trinkets. He travels the footpath as it winds to the left and then to the right, up hills and down inclines, before cutting across Sheep Meadow, passing the world-famous Tavern on the Green. He takes the footpath up to Central Park West, past Strawberry Fields where he wonders, *Why are the good ones taken much too soon?* He stops at the circular black and white mosaic memorial to John Lennon, bearing his iconic one-word statement to the world, *IMAGINE.* He exits the park at 72nd Street and crosses Central Park West, passing in front of The Dakota where John Lennon drew his final breath. He turns right onto Columbus Avenue, stops at Starbucks on the corner for two coffees, then continues to 79th Street and the museum's employee entrance.

As he passes the loading dock to the warehouse, Marcus from Receiving comes toward him with a big smile. "Hey Doc! I got an awfully big-box delivery for you today!"

Howard's face lights up. "I was kind of hoping you would!" He hands Marcus one of the coffees and asks, "Why do you think I'm here today and not back home in bed with my wife?"

Marcus laughs. "I have no idea. Hell, I'd rather be back in bed with your wife than here unloading boxes."

"I'm here because of what's in that crate. Oh, and I'll tell my wife you said that!" Howard jokes.

"Don't you dare, Doc. I'll bring it down to your office as soon as it clears inventory. And hey," he tips the cup saluting Howard, "thanks for the coffee."

"I appreciate it if you could ..." Howard clears his throat and adds a wink, "expedite it in any way. I've been waiting a long time for that package." Howard jokingly slaps him on his arm as he heads out. "Oh, and hey, thank you!"

Howard takes the elevator down to the research level of the museum and walks to his office. He inserts the key and turns the lock, opening a glass door that reads:

PROFESSOR HOWARD CONVERY

HEAD CURATOR

ARCHAEOLOGY DEPARTMENT

Only took half my life to get here, he smiles. It's a good life.

As Howard enters, cold, blue-tinted lights flicker before turning the room an eerie white. A low hum fades into the undetectable white noise. Spanning the length of the entire room is a massive three-dimensional map of the world. On the left side, Alaska's westernmost point of Little Diomede Island in the Bering Sea. On the right side, the easternmost point of the island, Big Diomede in Russian territory. Just a little more than two miles separate these two great superpowers, now separated by an entire wall. It's become Professor Howard Convery's life work. Dwarfed by the size of the map in front of him, he wonders, *Has it been worth it? Have I spent more than 40 years on this one project and still haven't gotten any closer to figuring it all out? What the hell does it all mean?* He throws his coffee into the wastebasket with such force that the lid pops off, sending most of the nearly-full dark-roasted Caramel Macchiato spouting up into the air like Moby Dick's tell tale blow-hole spray. He lowers his head. *Is there a meaning to all of this? There has to be.*

The sound of a door closing interrupts his thoughts. Anthony, his assistant, crosses the room. "You okay, Professor? I would have thought you'd be happy, especially on this day?"

"Ah, yeah. You know how I hate it when they get your order wrong," Howard lies, looking at the mess around the trash basket.

"Yeah," Anthony mumbles, not paying any attention to Howard's momentary outburst as he makes his way to the wall. "This really is quite the map you've constructed, Professor. I do believe you broke the record for the world's largest topographical map."

"Wait a moment, Anthony, what are you doing here today?"

"Are you kidding? The biggest find in what? A couple hundred years? Maybe even a thousand years? Is probably arriving today from Ethiopia, and you think I'm going to sleep in?" Anthony stops, bends at the knees and turns his hands up looking like he's about to catch a falling child. "It did come today, didn't it?"

Howard nods with a boyish smile.

Anthony spins around and claps his hands together. "HOT DAMN! I knew it would. Ever since I got here, all you've had me doing was working on this project."

Professor Convery smirks. "Since you got here?" he chuckles, "It's only been a year or two since you joined my team."

"It's been five years, Professor," he corrects him.

"*Five* years!" He looks at Anthony. The young boy who stumbled into his office half a decade ago, announcing he was the new hire, has transformed before his eyes into the young man now standing before him. "It's been *five* years since you graduated college and started working for me?"

Anthony nods his head. "Time flies, Professor, when you're having fun."

"It certainly does," Howard says, "I started working here, let me see," he tilts his head back, looking up, trying to remember the date. "Forty-one years ago, it was May of 1981. I was 22-years-old and just graduated from Brooklyn College. I had never been out of the city before. It all started with this one, right here." He points to a small town in South Dakota. "With Mr. Joseph Kehm."

"Not another car ride," Cassandra whines.

Jonathan, his two children, and Mitra squeeze into an oversized, three-wheel rickshaw.

"It's not far," Mitra reassures her. "We are going to Dilly Haat," he calls to the driver.

"What's Deli hat?" Cassandra asks with just enough of her New York accent to mispronounce the name.

"It's an open-air bazaar run by The DTTDC," Mitra recites to the entire cab.

"And the DTTDC are who?" Jonathan asks.

Mitra chuckles. "Not a who, a what. The Delhi Tourism and Transportation Development Corporation," Mitra answers. "It sits on six acres of land, salvaged as part of a reclamation project, and transformed into a plaza. Unlike other markets in Delhi, this one is permanent, but vendors can only stay for fifteen days. So there are always new people coming from all over India."

Twenty minutes later, the four of them emerge from a rickshaw at the bazaar. "There are more than 60 vendors," he adds, turning back to thank their driver before he pulls away.

"Yes, thank you for *not* killing us," Trevor says under his breath.

Mitra walks to the entrance. "Since the government runs it, there is a fee that helps maintain the grounds."

Jonathan opens his wallet. "How much is it?"

Cassandra spies the five purple 100 Rupee bills her father takes from his wallet, and Jonathan sees the confused look on his daughter's face. "I exchanged some money at the bank before we left."

"It's 100 rupees each," Mitra answers, so Jonathan hands him four bills.

"What! A hundred dollars to go into a flea market?" Cassandra screams.

"A hundred rupees," her father corrects her.

"Rupees … dollars … I don't care what you call it. Nothing in there is worth a hundred of anything."

"Cazz," her brother says, "a hundred rupees is like a dollar forty."

"A dollar forty? As in one dollar and forty cents? You're kidding?"

All three men nod their heads.

"God, how much is a cheeseburger around here? Like 1,000 rupees?"

"Well, that would be like paying fourteen dollars for a hamburger, if you could buy a hamburger," her father informs her. "Unfortunately, you can't buy a hamburger in all of India."

"What? WHY? There are cows everywhere."

"The cow is sacred in India," Mitra tells her. "We believe the cow is a symbol of life that should be protected and revered. In the Vedas, the oldest of the Hindu scriptures, the cow is associated with Aditi, the mother of all the gods, and for this, no harm can come to them."

"Can I eat chicken? Or is the chicken the father of all gods?" she jests, half-smiling.

"No. It is okay to eat chicken. In fact, we have some delicious dishes made with chicken. Tonight I will take you to Moti Mahal. It's where butter chicken was invented in 1947. Your Gordon Ramsay went there to learn the recipe." Mitra smiles and bows as they enter the bazaar.

Once inside, Cassandra forgets all about hamburgers. Bright, colorful fabrics and garments, handbags, and shoes overload her senses. She runs from stand to stand, touching and feeling the material, draping scarves and shawls over her shoulders and head. The vendors swarm to her like honeybees to a flower, disregarding the three men who seem to be immune to the shopping fever Cassandra has contracted.

"Very beautiful, very beautiful and for you, only 350 Rupees," the shop keeper entices, seeing her fingers dance over a bright, turquoise shawl.

She looks at her brother, who does a quick calculation, and mouths the words *five dollars* holding up one hand with all five fingers extended.

Her eyes widen, but before she can ask her father for the money, Mitra takes it from her. "Three hundred and fifty Rupees is way too much. I know a place down here for half that." He starts to hand it back to the vendor.

Her face doesn't have time to change from joy to anger as she hears the shopkeeper counteroffer for 200 Rupees. Mitra shakes his head, examining the garment, pushing it back to the merchant.

"One fifty," the desperate merchant cries out, pushing it back to his formidable opponent. Mitra thrusts his hand into his pocket, pulls out a 100 Rupee note, and holds it out to the shopkeeper. The man snatches it from his grasp, and the transaction is complete.

Mitra hands it to Cassandra. Jonathan takes out his wallet. "No, no, sir," Mitra says. "A present for your daughter." Jonathan smiles and puts his wallet away.

"How do you say *thank you* in Hindi?" Cassandra asks.

"Dhanyavaad."

Cassandra repeats the word as best as she can, and they both bow.

"Let us not forget why we're here," Jonathan says, and they begin the task of finding someone who can understand Jonathan's mysterious language.

Booth by booth, vendor by vendor, Mitra takes Jonathan around, having him repeat the rehearsed phrase only to receive the same response again and again. Trevor stops to get some chicken on a skewer, while Cassandra refines her haggling skills in order to acquire a new wardrobe suitable for the torrid climate.

Forty vendors in, Jonathan repeats the phrase like a parrot, "Do you know what language this is?" when he hears a passing gentleman speaking to his companion in the same mysterious tongue.

"That man doesn't even know what language he is speaking." They both laugh.

Jonathan quickly spins around, searching for them in the sea of people.

"Mitra!" he cries out, pointing to a casually dressed man. "That man there! He understood. He knew what I was saying!"

Catching up to the two gentlemen, Mitra stops them and asks, "Excuse me, sir. Sir! Do you speak Hindi?"

The men appear confused.

"English?"

"Ah ... English, a little," one of them responds.

Mitra puts one arm around Jonathan's back, and with the other, pats Jonathan's chest. "This man here. Can you tell me what language he was speaking?"

The two friends look at each other. "Urdu."

"Urdu?" the three Americans repeat in the form of a question, but Mitra says it as if missing the final answer on Jeopardy. "Urdu!"

"Please tell me, sir, what part of India are you from?"

The two men look as if they are on a game show, but answer in unison, "Madhuban."

"Madhuban?" Mitra repeats.

"Yes, Madhuban, Uttar Pradesh."

Hearing the words Uttar Pradesh jolts Jonathan's memory, and images flash within his mind. People's faces, buildings, and images come at him faster than he can process.

He shouts out, "Yes, Uttar Pradesh, I know this place. I lived there. I grew up there." His words are foreign to all but the two men from Madhuban, who understand just a little.

They look at Mitra. "It's Urdu, but a different dialect. Perhaps a surrounding village, such as Ibrahimabad, Awadhuteswar Shiv Mandir, or Ghosi."

"DAD!" Trevor shouts as Jonathan's legs go weak and he stumbles to the ground.

The mention of the town Ghosi cripples Jonathan, and he falls as though shot. The four men rush to steady him. Jonathan starts crying. It is more than a dream that brought him to this place. These are not the memories he read about in books or suppressed memories of some film he watched as a child. These are *his* memories. The memories he had growing up here, raising a family here, taking a husband.

"Oh my God!" he says. *I had a husband.*

"Dad, are you alright?" Trevor asks, helping him to his feet.

"Yes, yes. I'm alright." Jonathan turns to the men and asks in Urdu, "How far away is Ghosi from here?"

One of the men answers him quickly, "Two days drive."

"Two days drive?" Jonathan repeats in English.

"What? What's a two days drive?" Cassandra asks.

"The town where we have to go!"

"We can go by car or by train," Mitra suggests.

"NO! No trains!" Jonathan cries out.

"Oh, right. Sorry, I forgot. Anyway, it's true. The trains are extremely dangerous in India," Mitra says, looking at the children. "It's all quiet and then out of nowhere, *swish!* A locomotive will speed by. Hundreds are killed every year."

He looks at Jonathan. "We will go by car."

PLACE: DEADWOOD, DAKOTA TERRITORIES
YEAR: 1876

In another part of the world at another time, a tall, lanky

man with long hair and a wiry mustache rode into the town of Deadwood in the Dakota territories. The year was 1876, and one year earlier, miner John B. Pearson discovered gold in a narrow canyon in the Northern Black Hills.

In the months that followed, every broke, desperate, out-of-work dreamer for a hundred miles away flooded into the small valley, all hoping to make their fortune by digging in the ground or growing rich off the poor saps that did. And where the men were, the women followed. Saloons, dance halls, gambling parlors, and brothels all sprung up almost overnight to handle the thousands of miners and prospectors that swarmed to the upper northwest hillside.

Even though the calendar read July 24th, the entire country was still celebrating its centennial 20 days later. But this tall, lanky man who rode into town hadn't come to celebrate. He hadn't come for the women. And he certainly hadn't come to wallow in the dirt, searching for gold. He had come to forget; to forget a lifetime of killing, blood, and death. At

49

times he felt like he'd become the angel of death as foretold in the Book of Revelation.

"And I looked, and behold a pale horse: and his name that sat on him was Death, and Hell followed with him."

All around the town, men were busy building structures out of wood, or canvas, or any combination of both. Deadwood grew at an alarming rate.

The tall man stopped his horse and addressed an old man sitting outside what looked to be a hardware store of sorts, a makeshift hut constructed of canvas tarps draped over a wooden structure held together by knotted ropes.

"Morning," the man said, looking down from his horse, and he received the same for a reply. "You got a lotta dead trees lining the canyon coming into town."

"They don't call it Deadwood Gulch for nothing." The words fell from the old man's mouth as he spit out a wad of dark black tobacco. An ugly trickle of leftover slime hung from his lower lip.

"You wouldn't happen to know where a man can get a drink, perhaps play some poker, maybe a place to stay?" the long-haired stranger asked.

"You can try the Old Style Saloon No. 10 for poker and the drink, but Mindy's is the only place left in town with a bed. I'd head there first. Spaces getting snatched up pretty darn quick, Mister."

"Much obliged." And with a brief nod, the stranger tipped his wide-brim hat in gratitude.

Rooms at Mindy's were 50 cents a night. The Baldwin Hotel in San Francisco charged a dollar a night, but that was a five-story building that took up an entire city block with bellhops and room service. Seeing how there was a line waiting for a room at Mindy's though, the stranger considered himself lucky, and paid a week in advance for two rooms, then made his way over to The Old Style Saloon No. 10.

As soon as he walked into the saloon, he knew he was going to like it there. He didn't care what the outside looked like; this saloon, like any other town west of the Missouri River, didn't have to be refined for him to feel at home. As long as the music was playing, the drinks kept flowing, and the poker earned him money, he would happily call this place home. He walked up to the bar and ordered a whiskey, the only thing he would drink in this Godforsaken shithole.

"What brings you to town?" the bartender asked. "You don't look like the mining type."

"Why, cause I ain't got shit all over me?" he asked, taking a sip.

"Well, yeah! That and on account a' those fancy clothes you got on."

"Is it a crime to look good around here?" he asked, loud enough for everyone in the room to hear, before finishing his whiskey and ordering another.

"No, sir," the bartender continued as he poured a second drink. "I don't mean any offense. It's just we don't get many men of your caliber in here, is all."

"None taken." He took the bottle from the counter and dropped a couple of coins on the bar. "I'm waiting for a friend of mine, a real loudmouth; you'll know her when you hear her. She goes by Jane." He motioned over to the poker table. "Tell her I'll be over at the tables, will ya?"

"Sure thing, mister." The bartender wiped down the top of the bar and spied the silver pieces. "And *thank you*, sir," he added cheerfully.

The stranger wasn't there more than two hours when a grungy-looking young man flung open the doors and yelled to the bartender, "Whiskey, my good man. Freddy, I'm feeling lucky tonight!"

The caramel-colored liquor burned as it slid down his throat and warmed his belly. The rot gut, appropriately named, made him a little queasy as he headed toward the poker table.

He addressed the three men at the table, "Mind if I join ya's." It was more of an announcement than a question.

The dealer tipped his head and motioned to the empty seat.

The tall stranger looked up, immediately repulsed by the smell of the unkempt interloper. *Digging in the dirt all day is no way to make a living,* he thought, but nodded graciously, happy to take the tin pan's money.

"Joseph Kehm," the loudmouth said, flopping down in the chair. "Most people just call me Joe. No sense wasting formalities on me."

The two other men at the table introduced themselves, but when it came time for the tall stranger, he just stated in a quiet, no-nonsense voice, "James Butler," then lit up a smoke to cleanse his nostrils of the offensive man's odor.

Joe took a single dollar from the pocket of his mud-covered pants, and pushed the lonesome bill over to the dealer for some chips. James noticed the dirt under his fingernails, another reason to dislike the young wanna-be poker player.

"Have you guys heard?" Excitement got the better of him, and he leaned forward as if to whisper, but gushed out, "Wild Bill Hickok is coming to town!"

"Son, that man is wild—" the fat man across the table started.

"I'm WILD about playing cards!" snapped James Butler, interrupting the pot-bellied man and throwing him a look that would stop most men's hearts. Never relinquishing his death-stare upon the pot-bellied man, James addressed the dealer, "Are you going to deal those cards or are we gonna sit around here all day like a bunch of old ladies gossiping?"

The dealer quickly threw seven cards to each of the four players, and the night carried on. They played a couple of hands, and young Joe even won a few. After a while, the tension faded, and the game returned to civil discourse. Joe tried for a second time, "Boy, I sure would like to meet Wild Bill Hickok."

James looked up from his cards, his gaze fixed on young Joe. There was clearly no getting around the annoying topic of conversation. "I take it you don't know what Wild Bill Hickok looks like?"

"Why no," Joe answered, calling for another card. "I hear he can kill a person with a stare though."

James locked eyes with Joe and time froze. Then James tossed his cards into the center of the table, conceding the hand to the young conversationalist. Joe remained in good health. "I tell you what," James said, a genuine smile crossing his face for the first time since Joe sat at the table. "If I see him, I'll point him out to ya."

"You've *seen* Wild Bill?" Joe slipped right back in to his former state of excitement.

"I've seen him. A couple of times."

Joe sat back, trying to concentrate on his cards. For a brief moment, the nagging cackle of his hyena voice was gratefully absent.

The tall, long-haired stranger thought to himself, *How long will it be, before he starts flapping his lips again?* James picked up his cards. A stream of smoke rose in front of his eyes. He looked around and studied his opponents. Confident in his assessment, he threw a chip into the center of the table.

"Can I ask you a question?" Joe said, matching his bet.

And there it is, lips flapping. "Can I stop ya?" he asked, and Joe took it as a joke, even if that's not how it was intended.

"Where were you born?" he inquired. James looked mildly amused.

"For a moment, I thought you were going to ask me something stupid, kid," he said with a smile. "Illinois."

"So you must have seen lots of different places, mister."

"A few. I reckon," James answered, trying hard not to get annoyed.

"And you had a few jobs along the way?"

For the first time in a long time, James thought of his past employment. A fugitive from justice, a stagecoach driver, a lawman in the Kansas and Nebraska territories. He fought and was a spy for the union army during the Civil War. And after the war, he was a scout and a marksman. Even an actor—for a brief time—before trying his hand as a professional gambler; which brought him here, to this shithole, listening to this asshole, which he now regretted.

He took the rolled-paper cigarette from his lips, exhaled slowly, and allowed a cloud of white to float across the table. When next he spoke, it was firm, as if to say, *you're getting on my nerves.* "What's this about, kid?"

"It's just that—" Joe paused, not wanting to sound stupid, as if he couldn't help it if he tried, "You ever feel like you been someplace before, but you haven't?" he asked.

James sighed, "Yeah, kid, lots of people feel that way."

"Do they?"

"Sure," he said once again, feeling relieved, tossing another hand into the pot.

"I've been to Nebraska once," the pot-bellied man said, not comprehending what Joe was trying to say. "Don't reckon I ever been there before?"

James threw the man another look, which could only be interpreted as, *Why don't you shut the fuck up?*

The pot-bellied man stood up. "I think I'll call it a night," he announced, and walked to the bar.

"Smart man," James muttered, through his wiry mustache.

The dealer shuffled the cards and dealt another hand. The remaining three players each threw a chip into the center of the table.

"You ever feel like you're gonna die?" the kid asked.

James straightened up, rigid with practiced fear at the question. His right hand perched on the stock of his old friend strapped to his hip and his eyes focused on the young Joe like a rattlesnake before it strikes.

"Oh, I don't mean you, Mister. I was talking about myself." He sensed that James must have had a brush or two with death. The nervous young pan handler tried to put the tall man's mind at ease, quickly adding, "A couple weeks back, I got the strangest feeling I was going to die."

The tall man sat back, concluding that Joe's inquirer was no real threat. His hand surrendered its grip on the gun and returned to the cards. "Yeah, I get that feeling a lot."

"You do?"

"Every day, kid." *I just got one a few seconds ago.* He conceded his hand to Joe. "Fold."

"I had this made," Joe said pulling a small rectangular piece of blacksmith's metal from his pocket and tossing it on the table. It landed with a thud.

The other man sitting at the table leaned forward and examined it. His long beard, hanging below the top of his vest, draped the green velvet table with pepper-colored whiskers.

James wasn't sure what this other man did for a living, and he didn't care. All he knew was the man played cards and, until now, kept his mouth shut.

"What the hell is that?" the man asked, retracting his chin hair from the stack of chips in front of him.

"I don't know. I just had the urge to have it made."

"Did Walter make that?" the bearded man asked.

James squinted his eyes at the man as if to say, *now don't you go pissing me off too.*

"Yeah, when he got done shoeing a horse."

The man leaned in, looking closer, not reading the signs James was throwing his way. "It's got your name on it?"

"Godamn it! Is this show and tell or a god damn poker game?" James barked, his fist slamming down hard on the table, making the chips jump.

The pot-bellied man, who had several drinks at the bar, walked back over to the table and looked at the piece of metal. "And what's that date there?" he asked.

James looked at the pot-bellied man as if to say, *I told you to walk away.* Unlike the bearded man though, pot-belly read his eyes loud and clear and walked back to the bar.

"It's my birthday," Joe said, and turned it over. "And here's the strange part. I had him chisel this on the other side."

"What the hell does that say?"

Joe studied it in his hand. "I don't know. It just came to me, so I asked Walter to 'scribe it on this here piece of metal."

"Looks like a goddamn headstone kid. Now get the fucking thing off the table; it's bad luck."

Joe quickly put it back in his pocket, seeing how annoyed Mr. Butler was getting.

"It's just ... I feel like I have to do something before I die, Mr. Butler."

"How about playing some fucking poker?" James snapped. *I wish someone would put a bullet in my brain right now, if that would stop this goddamn talking.*

"I never thought about dying before, but for the last few weeks, I feel like I'm not long for this earth," Joe said. His eyes danced from card to card as he fanned out his hand.

"I can help you along with that, kid, if you don't start playing some goddamn poker," James said, and no one at the table thought he was joking.

As the night moved on, young Joe's luck took a turn for the worse. His hand traveled to his pocket and retrieved more and more dollars that slid across the table for more chips. On the other side of the table, Mr. Butler's stack of chips kept growing. Joe became resentful and belligerent with the dealer, which only increased the tension as the poker chips grew tall in front of the stranger.

"It's not the dealer's fault, kid. Sometimes your luck just runs out," James said. "Better to walk away while you still have some money in your pocket. There'll be other nights."

Joe remained at the table.

A few more hands and a few more chips favored Mr. Butler.

The night grew late, and hand after hand went to the tall stranger. The bearded man finally dropped out and joined the pot-bellied man at the bar to drink away what little money they both had left.

Only James Butler and Joe remained. They sat across from one other like a pair of gunfighters at a high-noon showdown. James, armed with a mountain of chips; Joe a dwindling pile of less than five dollars. His pockets depleted, he sat broken, on the verge of being penniless; his heart full of malice.

The dealer shuffled and fanned seven cards to the two remaining players for what was sure to be the last hand of the night. James picked up his cards, but instead of studying them, he watched the kid's eyes as they looked at the hand the dealer just dealt. They grew wide, and he quickly placed the cards on the table: a sure 'tell' that he had what could be a winning hand. James diverted his gaze, stealing a glimpse at the cards in his hand. Three kings, an ace of diamonds, and a seven of clubs. A truly excellent hand, which made him wonder, *what does Joe have that he thinks is so good? Aces? He could only have three at the most, and what are the odds of that? Queens. Has to be queens. Even three of them and he would still lose.*

James checked and asked for one card, discarding the seven black clover.

The dealer slid a single card across the table and turned his query to Joe.

"Two," Joe said a bit too loudly, drawing the attention of the patrons in the saloon.

The dealer counted out two cards. One … two … and slid them to Joe, retrieving his discards.

Joe snatched up the cards and, upon a quick glance, tried to hide his delight, to no avail.

James lifted the single card from the green felt table. Unlike his opponent, his face remained stoic and unchanged.

James threw in a safe amount of chips, knowing Joe would raise.

Joe walked the path that James and fate had laid out for him. He matched the bet and threw a generous amount into the center of the table, hoping not to frighten off his patsy.

James matched his bet, but to Joe's delight, raised again. Only this time, a substantial amount.

Joe was taken aback. *What's he doing? He must know I have the better hand.* A bead of sweat trickled down the side of Joe's temple. *He's trying to bluff his way to the pot.* Joe's eyes strained as they tried to focus on the cards trembling in his hands. He looked at his adversary: no movement, stone-cold eyes as dead as a corpse.

Joe swallowed as his mouth went dry. *If I call, that's all my money.* He looked at the pile of chips in the center of the table. *That's more money than I make all year.* He looked up at the long-haired, wiry mustached man. His pose never changed. He sat like a statue across from him. *How can he be so calm?*

"Are you going to play cards, or shit yourself?" James taunted.

Joe's anger grew fast and out of control. *How dare that pompous piece of shit!*

The entire saloon now stood around the lone table. No one made a single sound. They watched as Joe made his decision.

He threw the rest of his money in the center of the table. "Okay, Mister, I'm all in! I call!" he said in a loud, committed voice.

An audible gasp came from the crowd and then fell silent again, waiting to see the hand on which Joe risked an entire life savings.

He turned over the cards. Three aces and two sixes.

"A FULL HOUSE!" he yelled, jumping up from the table as the saloon erupted in cheers.

Joe looked around the room and waved his arms in the air. He couldn't believe it! All that money, it was all his.

All night long, Joe had to take shit from this long-haired, wiry mustached out-of-towner. This wandering poker player thought he was so good with his *goddamn this* and *goddamn that!* This would show him! This would show him he couldn't come to Deadwood and blaspheme in Joseph Kehm's town!

Joe was still celebrating when he suddenly noticed the entire saloon was as quiet as a cemetery after midnight. Not a sound came from the more than twenty people who had just been cheering like John B. Pearson when he struck gold, cheering so loudly that it would surely wake the entire town of Deadwood.

Joe turned slowly and looked down at the green felt table. Behind the stack of chips in front of James, present for all the bar to see, were four kings and the last remaining ace.

"YOU CHEATING BASTARD!" Joe yelled.

James stood. "I know you're mad, kid, but I don't take kindly to anyone calling me a cheater!"

"YOU PIECE OF SHIT!" the ranting continued as James tried his best to calm Joe.

"It happens, kid. That's why they call it gambling."

"I'LL KILL YOU!" he threatened.

"Now watch it, kid." James got real serious and his voice dropped an octave. "Don't do anything stupid."

Everyone in the saloon feared for Joseph's life, but he was too angry to see what the rest of the saloon just witnessed. James, the quiet, ill-tempered poker player, turned into a deadly gunfighter right before their eyes.

"YOU NO GOOD PIECE OF SH—" and Joseph went for his gun.

A cigarette dropped. Time stopped. A single shot rang out!

A shower of tiny ambers erupted from the barrel, peppering Joe's face. A cloud of white smoke engulfed his body, like the breath of an exhaling dragon. What took a half heartbeat to transpire appeared to stop time for everyone watching. Joe never felt the hot sparks kiss his cheek, stinging him with the touch of hundreds of bees. Nor did he smell the charred scent of gun powder that violated his nostrils. Joe never saw, felt, or smelled anything. Along with all of his senses, a bullet from James's gun snuffed out Joe's life from existence.

Joe's hand never even got the gun barrel past the leather holster.

James acted out of instinct. His basic survival reflex took over. Kill or be killed. He had pulled one of his two 1851 Navy Colt revolvers worn around his waist, and shot Joseph right between the eyes. The instrument of death was returned to its resting place, the barrel still hot, before Joe's body hit the ground.

"I told you I would point out Wild Bill Hickok if I ever saw him, kid," James said, looking across the saloon where the bartender stood with his mouth agape.

James raised his hand and pointed with his trigger finger. "Well, there he is."

All occupants turned and looked to see Wild Bill Hickok. Even the bartender turned and looked, knowing there was no one behind him except a large, ornate, decorative mirror.

James stared at his reflection, pointing back at him. "Ladies and gentlemen, I give you Mr. James Butler Hickok, also known as WILD BILL." James donned his wide-brimmed short-crown hat and collected his money.

The smell of burnt gunpowder snaked its way through the saloon and out the doors, where a rough-looking woman breathed in the all too familiar scent.

"GODDAMMIT, BILL!" A loud voice shattered the silence as she entered the saloon. "I TOLD YOU NOT TO KILL ANYONE!"

The small, shocked gathering of twenty or more people turned and looked to see an infuriated Calamity Jane.

"That kid was getting on my last fucking nerve, Jane. But I gave him every opportunity to walk away." Wild Bill looked down and noticed the small metal name plate that had fallen out of Joe's pocket as he hit the floor. Bill picked it up and placed it together with a few coins on the bar. "Here. Bury this with the kid. It's the only thing he had left in the world. Seems only fitting he should take it with him."

Bill then turned back to his only friend in town. "Come on. I got us a nice little place over at Mindy's." He walked past the crowd, still traumatized by the sight of Joseph's body, blood slowly pulsating from the center of his forehead.

A month later, Wild Bill's body would be lying on the same floor, staining its wood with his blood as he clutched a pair of aces and a pair of eights.

It takes two days to drive from Delhi to Ghosi,

a total of 14 hours by car. For Mitra, a citizen of India, it's just another day, another drive through his country, but for Jonathan, Cassandra, and Trevor, it's 14 of the most hair-raising hours the three American passengers have ever experienced. They leave Delhi early in the morning and drive for three hours to the city of Agra.

"Mitra, would you mind if we make a small detour?" Jonathan asks.

"Really, Dad?" Trevor complains. "Can't we keep going? We're making good time."

"There's nothing *good* about this car ride," Cassandra mumbles.

"I thought you wanted to get life lessons for your book?" Trevor reminds her, the sarcasm clear in his tone.

"Yeah, I can title it, *'Dad and the wild goose chase'*."

"Seven Years in India?" Trevor counters.

"Seven Years Trapped in a Sardine Can?" she retorts, and they both laugh.

61

"Trust me, kids. You're going to want to see this!" Jonathan and Mitra exchange a knowing smile.

Mitra takes the exit off Route 62 and maneuvers his way down small streets, navigating the labyrinth of thoroughfares until he can go no farther.

He parks and announces, "We have to walk from here."

"Where are we going?" the children ask.

"To chār bāgh," Jonathan answers. "It means four gardens."

"We're stopping to see gardens?" Cassandra asks, sounding disappointed.

"Not just any gardens. These are the most famous gardens in all of India," Mitra proudly boasts. "People line up to get inside."

"I thought India was only famous for one thing," Cassandra says, half serious.

As they walk down the stone avenue, enormous red stone gateways come into view. Lines of people wait to enter the courtyard.

"Wow, you weren't kidding," Trevor says.

Jonathan suggests they get in line while he purchases tickets. The line moves swiftly, and once they're through the stone archway, the sheer magnitude of the complex unfolds before them. A crenelated terra cotta stone wall surrounds the gardens with entranceways on the east, south, and west sides. On the north side, a beautiful grand entranceway with two octagon turrets capped in white marble on its flank with an iwan— an arch-shaped doorway—stands guarding their treasure.

"Oh my God, it's beautiful," Cassandra exclaims. "Are the gardens through there?"

"Just you wait, my dear," Mitra says with a smile. "What is it you Americans say? You haven't seen anything yet."

Through the darkness of the ingress, a ghost of a building stands in the distance. Becoming increasingly visible in the bright sunlight, the four iconic pillars and domed roof of the most famous building in India emerges. Two rows of perfectly manicured Cyprus trees line the reflecting pool that welcomes visitors to Mumtaz Mahal's final resting place.

"Oh my God! That's the Taj Mahal!" the kids exclaim in amazement. "Simply beautiful!" Jonathan remarks.

The ivory marble building is almost blinding against the blue sky; lush, green grass blankets the garden's grounds.

"Who lived here?" Cassandra asks.

"Not a soul," Mitra says. "It was built as a mausoleum."

"A tomb?" Trevor asks.

"Commissioned by Emperor Shah Jahan in 1632 to house the body of his favorite wife, Mumtaz Mahal."

"He built that just for her, and she wasn't even alive to see it?" Cassandra exclaims. "Boy, *that's* love!"

Designated as the trip's photographer, Cassandra takes group photos and selfies from every angle of the incredible building. She snaps picture after picture of her father and brother: in the gardens, in front of the building, looking out over the Yamuna River. Mitra takes a photo of the three of them with the magnificent architectural masterpiece in the background. For Jonathan, the building is a work of art, one that every living person should see at least once in their life. It is absolutely breathtaking. They spend two hours walking around, marveling at the structure, before getting back on the road.

"*That* was amazing!" Cassandra beams as she swipes through her many photos.

"Yes! Thank you, Mitra, for sharing that with us," Trevor adds.

In four hours, they make their way to Lucknow, the capital of Uttar Pradesh. They reserve three rooms at the Hotel Ranjee's. Six hours of driving remains; tomorrow, they will reach Ghosi.

That night, Jonathan has another vivid dream, but not of India.

PLACE: AUSTRALIA
YEAR: 1685

In another part of the world at another time, an

Aborigine man returned home to his tribe after a five-months-long walkabout in what would later become known as the Northern Territory. The year was 1685, 102 years before the Europeans would arrive on the shores of Australia. His people had lived this way for more than 40,000 years. He was just one in a long line of men in his family who had made this journey.

This was not his first walkabout either. As a rite of passage, the males of his tribe, prior to reaching manhood, would leave their tribe and walk in the wilderness for as long as six months at a time before returning home.

Kilara was 14 when he first 'went walkabout'; his parents worried because he stayed away for seven months. There are many things in the Australian Outback that could kill a small boy. Several members of the tribe never returned home, and every year, the chieftain would warn those going that it was not a trip to be made lightly. For the first few nights, Kilara considered returning home, but to do so would have brought shame upon his father and his father's father, all the way back through his line. This was something he could not do. If the land wanted to claim Kilara for its own, then that was meant to be.

Fourteen years later, Kilara once again had a strong desire to go walkabout. But this was for another reason. For the past year, he had been having dreams of a faraway land. The elders of his tribe called this Dreamtime, a time going back to the beginning when the spirits first created the land and people. They made everything: the rivers and streams, rocks and hills, plants and animals. The Aborigine people understood the Dreamtime was a beginning with no end. They held the belief that the Dreamtime was a period on a continuum of past, present, and future.

One evening later at night, Kilara awoke and went outside. The sky was a blanket of stars, and he searched the heavens, wondering why he felt as though he was in another land. Below his feet, instead of the orange rust-colored earth, he stood on streets of marble lined with ivory white buildings supported by massive columns. The people were clothed in white flowing robes with one shoulder bare. His skin had faded from its dark brown coloring to a pale, slightly pink tone. His name was hard to pronounce, and the language was foreign to him, even though he understood what people discussed. All along the front of the building, there were stone figures frozen in place: some clothed with laurel wreaths around their head, some naked, and some engaging in acts of war and battle.

By morning, the vision faded but the memories remained. His body returned to its former self; he was once again Kilara. But he was also someone else. He had lived a life unknown to him, and now retained all his former life experiences. It was as though he had two childhoods, was two adults living within one body, and two cultures, cultures that could not be further apart from one another. He spoke with the elders and told them how he felt. He didn't tell them, however, that he had another feeling, a stronger, more sorrowful one filled with dread and quietus.

Perhaps, they suggested, the spirits were simply showing him what his next life would look like. It was these words that persuaded Kilara to go walkabout.

Before he left, his mother gave him a powerful protection stone. These scarce stones were said to absorb and transfer negative energy and help preserve one's own energy. Kilara thanked his mother for the black stone, kissed his family goodbye, and set off on his journey.

Five months passed, and the visions, once contained to his sleep, now abandoned his dreams and invaded Kilara's waking days. What he once thought to be images of that which awaited him in his next life, he now believed were glimpses of previous lives. In one life, he had hair the color of fire, long and wildly blown by the ocean winds. He had long facial hair, woven into braids. His skin was the color of ivory, drained of color. He was a strong, muscular warrior who crossed the sea in a long wooden boat. At the foran båtenas, which the men in his dream called the front of the ship, the head of a serpent rose high above the crescent waves. These men sailed from their homeland, a cold, rocky forest land, to the shores of a place that had green pastures where farmers tended their sheep. They made war against these peaceful people who seemed defenseless. Kilara recalled the peaceful farmers prayed to a man nailed to a cross by his hands and feet.

On some days, he returned to the place in his mind where everyone wore white robes and sandals, and read strange markings made with ink on a flat sheet called papyrus.

Other days he found himself in a different part of the world that had the same colored soil as his homeland, but the trees and animals were strange to him. He saw great creatures the size of the Boab tree with gray skin and huge ears. Large white horns grew out from the sides of their mouths. Their nose hung down and could act as a hand. He saw other large prowling animals with hair all around their heads, and was told they could kill a grown man as easily as swatting a fly. In this strange land, his skin was much darker; a much deeper tone than that of his present skin.

There were many more places and many more lives, but in all these visions, each person he had become carried a small marker. Some were made of wood, others of stone or clay. But all of them had the name of the person inscribed on one side; some had numbers, some didn't. Kilara did not know what the numbers represented, but all the markers had one more thing in common. On the opposite side of the names, they all had the exact same letters arranged in a way that spelled a word unknown to most of them. A single word was constant throughout every life.

AETERNUM

In the months away from his tribe, Kilara had an ever-growing, persistent feeling that he did not have long in this life, and soon it would be time to move to his next life. It was this feeling that made him carve his name into the black onyx stone. He shaped the rock like the others he'd seen in his waking dreams—a small, flat rectangle. He worked for months. Every day he scratched his name deeper into the stone's surface, so deep it would never wear away. And, just like his spirit ancestors had, he carved A-E-T-E-R-N-U-M on the reverse side.

He returned to his village, hugged his father and thanked his mother for the protection of the black stone. He showed them the tablet and said it had been around the world, through time and back.

That night, the village gathered and danced in celebration. As the fire crackled, sending bright glowing embers high into the night sky, merging into the pure white glow of the stars, Kilara sat with the elders. He told them of his journeys and the places he visited. He told them of the things he learned and the strange languages he spoke in his past lives. Though the words had a peculiar sound, he was always able to comprehend them.

Kilara told them of the far-off lands and the strange animals that walked on four legs, marked with black and white stripes; animals with long necks that reached to the skies, that ate leaves from the tallest of trees. He told them of the city created of white stone; of goddesses wrapped in white flowing cloths who drank wine made for their gods.

He even told them of one barbaric life and how they killed unarmed men. Perhaps, he mused, it was because they nailed one of their own tribesmen to a cross made of wood?

He told them how the color of his skin would change from a deep dark ebony to pale ash, devoid of any richness. In one life, his hair was wiry black and in the next, soft, straight strands of golden wheat, even one with a bright blaze of wavy, fiery rust in another.

The elders listened and thought, *thanks to Altjira, for our simple life, and to the spirits who have given us all we need to live.* They convened in a circle and agreed to bring Kilara to the holy place. As the people in the village danced and sang, the elders led Kilara to the base of a mountain, where an unprotected cave stood. No one would enter this sacred place without the permission from the chief elder, who kept it forever safe. As the elders walked to the cave, they gathered stalks from nearby bush, then ushered Kilara inside. One of the elders carried a torch, and he went in first. The small glow in the darkness grew bright as several torches, placed all around the cave, were lit. On the bright red walls of the cave, illuminated by flickering torchlight, Kilara saw drawings and markings left by ancestors long past.

One of the elders gestured to Kilara to leave his mark. He was confused, so an elder took Kilara's hand and placed it against the wall. Then, each of the elders dipped one end of a hollowed-out stalk into a clay pot that held a paint-like substance. As each elder joined Kilara at the wall, they pointed the painted tips at Kilara's hand. Blowing through the dry end of the stalk, a bright-colored mist sprayed the wall, covering Kilara's entire hand and arm. When Kilara removed his hand, a perfect silhouette remained on the wall, hopefully for all eternity.

Kilara showed the elders his black stone marker. He explained how he carved his name into the stone. Turning the stone over, he showed them the strange word. In the Dreamtime visions, he told them, this word was carved into all the other markers as well.

"One day, a person may come," he told them. "They may be a man or a woman, a child or an elder. They may be pale, or dark, or even yellow-skinned. They will find their way here and have one of these markers," he said. "It may be clay, or wood, or stone, or some other material not yet known to us."

The elders listened solemnly as he continued, "That person will be me. Tell your sons and their sons—and their sons after—what I have told you, so they will know me when the time comes. It may take many lifetimes, but one day, I will return."

"How will we know for certain?" asked one of the elders.

Kilara looked at the rust-colored wall covered in handprints marked by elders and chieftains. "Have him come into this holy place. If he can place his hand within my hand, you will surely know it is I." Then Kilara dipped his finger in the paint-like substance and marked the center of his palm print with an inward spiraling circle.

All the elders agreed. Kilara handed them his stone, and asked them to keep his marker safe for him until the day he returned.

That night, as the flames of the fire burned away and extinguished, leaving only a bed of glowing embers to twinkle and fade away, just as the last member of the tribe drifted off to sleep under the Empyrean celestial sky, Kilara joined the spirits in a place of supreme peace.

The next day the elders placed his black stone marker within the cave and waited ... waited for his return.

PLACE: GHOSI, INDIA
YEAR: PRESENT DAY

It's just after two in the afternoon when the car finally

makes its way into Ghosi. As Mitra drives down Varanasi-Gorakhpur Highway, sights and landmarks start looking familiar to Jonathan, but the buildings and shops are all so different.

"I think I worked at a chicken farm," Jonathan says.

"There's a poultry farm coming up on the left," Cassandra says, referencing her iPhone.

"Norman Poultry farm," Trevor adds, also navigating with the GPS app on his phone.

"Why don't we pull over and walk around," Mitra suggests, stopping the car in front of a shop. "Maybe something will come back to you." The four of them exit the vehicle, and the smell in the air immediately triggers Jonathan's memories of a previous life. He looks around, tries to get his bearings, turns around several times, and suddenly takes off down the street like a bloodhound hot on the trail of an escaped convict.

"Yes, yes, I know this place." He walks, then stops, then walks again.

"I think your farm should be on the other side of those railroad tracks," Cassandra says, motioning to a slight incline in the road.

Jonathan hesitates to cross as the others walk past him. Dismissing the haunting feeling, he eventually follows the group.

Turning to ask a question, Trevor goes completely pale when he sees his father standing between the tracks. Jonathan's face is frozen in terror, and then he yells out, "Rajmund!"

Then Trevor witnesses the most frightening thing of all. His father is thrown several yards from the tracks, rolls down an embankment, and comes to rest, lying motionless in the grass.

"DAD!" Trevor screams, running to his father.

Cassandra and Mitra are quick to follow. By the time they reach him, Jonathan is getting up, dusting the earth from his pants and shirt.

"What the hell happened?!" Cassandra screams.

"I fell," Jonathan answers.

"The hell you did, Dad!" Trevor rebuts. "It looked like you were hit by a train!"

"It was nothing, but I think we should go this way," Jonathan points back to town.

"I'm calling Mom."

The band of three follow Jonathan without saying a word as though watching a sleepwalker, afraid to wake him. He turns left down a road, then points to a building. "This is new." Then he points to another one. "This was a shop that repaired bicycles." He frantically moves through town, recalling places he once knew. "That was a small grocery shop where I used to buy milk and rice. Over there was where we mailed letters. And over there was where Rajmund and I met."

Rajmund? the group wonders.

"Over there you could buy fabric," he continues, entwining English words with Urdu.

A few people on the street take notice and become curious. As they walk through town, a small crowd of local businessmen stop to watch the strange American give a guided tour of their town.

Jonathan continues a bit further down the street and then stops.

71

"Dad, are you okay?" Cassandra asks.

He points to a small housing complex.

"There. Right up there, I believe, is where I lived," Jonathan says, his voice shaking.

One of the shopkeepers calls out to Mitra and inquires about the nature of their business. Mitra, unable to understand the gentleman speaking Urdu, looks to Jonathan for interpretation.

"He wants to know what we are doing, if he can help," Jonathan says. "We are looking for someone who used to live there."

The man walks up to Jonathan, impressed that he speaks Urdu so well.

"I know most of the people in the town," he says in Urdu. "Maybe I can give you some assistance?" Then, in English, he offers to the group, "I also speak English quite well."

"A woman lived there. She had two boys," Mitra explains, pointing to the building complex.

The man begins to shake his head.

"Maybe several years ago?"

"More like 100 years ago," Jonathan adds.

The man cocks his head, baffled by Jonathan's comment. "Anybody who lived there a hundred years ago would surely be dead by now."

The obvious statement hits Jonathan like a freight train. "My boys are dead?" he says softly in Urdu. But it is not Jonathan who makes the comment, it is the part of Jonathan that was Akal. Instantly, he feels the tremendous sorrow of a mother's grief for the loss of her children.

"Your boys?" the shopkeeper asks, bewildered.

Through his tears, Jonathan replies, "Arjun and Vijay."

The shopkeeper is respectfully quiet, leaving Jonathan in a void of darkness. Desperate to help this man struggling with grief, the shopkeeper searches for any thread of hope to comfort Jonathan. Finally, he offers, "Do you mean Vijay Datta?"

Jonathan's eyes light up. "Yes! Yes, Vijay Datta! Did you know him?"

"I believe Sachi had a grandfather named Vijay."

"Sachi?" the four of them repeat.

"Sachi Agrawal. She's a school teacher. She used to be Sachi Datta before she married. I believe her father is still alive, Ranvir Datta. He must be in his 80s by now, although I believe he is still quite healthy in his mind. His father's name was Vijay."

I have a grandson? Jonathan's heart swells with pride. But then a new thought overwhelms him and he chuckles to think of it. *And he's 30 years older than me!* Out of nowhere then, a look of terror appears on Jonathan's face. What he previously thought were mere dreams may now *actually* be a reality.

"So, can we speak with Sachi Agrawal? Do we know where she is?" Trevor asks.

"I believe she is still at the school," the man says. "I can show you the way."

Jonathan looks at the man. "That won't be necessary, I think I can still find it after all these years," he says in Urdu.

The four of them thank the man and follow Jonathan, this time in quiet reflection.

As they approach the school, hoards of children hurry through the streets, making their way home. They reach the school with apprehension, wondering how they will be received.

Several teachers, leaving for the day, walk out in groups of four. In the fourth wave exiting the building, Jonathan spies a woman in her late 50s talking with two other women. Immediately he knows she is Sachi.

He quickens his pace and approaches the women at the front gate. The party of three stay behind so as not to frighten the women.

"Excuse me, Ms. Agrawal?" he asks.

"Yes," she replies inquisitively. "May I help you?" She looks at Jonathan and sees something vaguely familiar.

Jonathan searches for words. *What am I going to say? I think I'm your dead great, great grandmother?* Before he can say anything, Cassandra emerges, greeting the teacher and shaking her hand.

"Ms. Agrawal. Hi, you don't know us, but my father was here years ago, and was friends with a man named Ranvir Datta. We were told that you might be related to him?"

"Oh! Yes, he's my father. But you must have been a boy when you knew him. I don't remember ever meeting you."

"It was a long, long time ago," Cassandra adds.

"I don't know if your father will remember me," Jonathan answers.

"He's 82, but his mind is as sharp as a tack."

"And his father? Is he still alive?"

"Oh no, Vijay passed in 1979. He was—"

"Only 71," Jonathan finishes her sentence.

"Yes," Sachi says, looking confused.

"My Dad is something of a math savant," Cassandra answers quickly.

"But how did he know when he was born?"

"Your father! He must have mentioned it to my Dad," Cassandra lies.

"You must have one great memory, Mister—umm?"

"Mr. Taylor, Jonathan Taylor," Jonathan replies, taking her hand in a formal introduction. "This is my daughter Cassandra." He points to his son. "My son Trevor." He introduces Mitra as their friend and traveling companion.

"I'm on my way to see my dad for afternoon tea. You're welcome to join me."

When they walk through the door, Jonathan's heart drops in his chest. Only days ago, these were all just foggy images in a disturbing dream, not someone's distant memory. Now, seeing these images manifest into reality, Jonathan is not sure he's prepared to meet his 82-year-old grandson, who sits in a recliner watching TV. Sachi walks over and turns the set off.

"Papa, this man is Jonathan Taylor. He said he knew you when he was young?"

Jonathan steps into the room. A frail old man, dwarfed by the soft leather recliner, sits and turns his eyes toward the stranger in his home. Jonathan sees a little of Vijay in those eyes and wonders if this is what his son would have looked like when he grew old. The man searches Jonathan's face for any sign of recognition.

"I'm afraid I don't remember him," the old man utters in Urdu.

Jonathan moves a chair from the table and sits, facing the grandson he didn't know he had. He leans forward, rests his elbows on the armchair and clasping his hands, he allows the man to study his face.

"I'm sorry, maybe my memory is failing me," the old man says, apologetically.

Jonathan takes a deep breath, as if preparing to leap from a great height. He begins his conversation with the man, speaking in Urdu.

"You have no reason to apologize. It is I who should apologize to you and your daughter. This is going to sound crazy. I hardly believe it myself. When I am done, if you wish me gone, my family and I will quietly leave and never bother you or your daughter again."

The older man sits motionless.

"About a week ago, I woke from a dream, a dream so real I gathered my family and came here. In this dream, I was a woman married to a man named Rajmund, Rajmund Datta. I had two sons, Arjun and Vijay—"

The man's eyes widen.

"What is this?! What are you saying?" Sachi interrupts, growing increasingly angry with every word coming out of Jonathan's mouth.

"I don't think it was a dream," Jonathan pleads. "I believe I lived in this village. We walked around the town this morning, and I remembered buildings and places—"

"I want you out of my house!" Sachi yells.

"I believe my son, Vijay, was your father. I know it sounds insane, but I think I was your grandmother, Akal Datta."

"I'm calling the police!" Sachi finally screams.

The old man raises his hand. "Wait," he commands, looking at Jonathan. "You came from America?"

"Yes," Jonathan answers.

"You took your family and flew from America to India?"

"Yes."

"And then you traveled here?"

Again Jonathan answers in the affirmative.

"And you learned Urdu?"

"No," Jonathan says.

The man looks puzzled. "But you're speaking it now?"

"I was unaware of a language called Urdu before a few days ago. When I landed in India, I just knew how to speak it. I can't speak Hindi, or Bengali, or Kannada, or any other language in India."

"Because Akal could not speak any language other than Urdu," the old man says. "My father said his mother always used to call him by a nickname. Do you know what that name was?"

Jonathan closes his eyes, recalling the last day of Akal's life when she walked Vijay to school. As she did every day, she kissed him goodbye and told her little candleberry to be good.

"Candleberry," he says softly. "I used to call him my little candleberry."

"Sachi, call your brother right away. Tell him to come here. And tell him to bring me the thing I gave him last summer when I went into the hospital."

He then turns back to Jonathan. "Tell me everything you remember."

Jonathan shares stories of Ranvir's father when he was a boy; how he and his brother, Arjun, would torment their father. He told them of the day Vijay was born; how proud her husband Rajmund was, how he told the whole town how excited he was to have two sons. He told them of Akal's job at the poultry farm, and how she hated the railroad tracks. He also told them of the day she died.

"I was on my way to work. My mind was wandering as it had been the day before. I heard people shouting, then I heard nothing, and I don't remember anything else after that."

"It was a train," the old man interjects.

"A train?" asks Cassandra.

"My father lost his mother when he was seventeen. She was hit by a train on the way to work."

"I remember being so frightened. The day before I—" Jonathan can't bring himself to say the word 'died'. "I had Arjun purchase a stone for me in the marketplace." Jonathan touches the small tablet in his pocket and lowers his head. Closing his eyes, he continues, "I wanted to keep that stone, for some reason I can't explain. I just know it meant a lot to me, but I must have lost it after … the accident."

Ranvir's son enters the house and joins the two men, now talking for some time.

"Mr. Taylor, this is my son, your great-great-grandson."

The old man sees his son is confused, then asks, "Did you bring it?"

Ranvir pulls a small stone from his pocket. "I kept it safe just like you have done, Papa."

The old man motions for him to hand it to Jonathan. "The owner has returned for it."

He watches as the tablet, which had been passed down from father to son, and to son again, is now passed back to its original owner.

"I believe *this* is yours. Welcome home Akal," his grandson says.

Jonathan looks at the name on the stone. He turns it over and looks at the word inscribed. He pulls the tablet Giorgio made for him from his pocket, and holds the two markers together.

AETERNUM

That night, Jonathan helps Sachi prepare a traditional dinner for the family. She smiles as he uses all the right spices to make the family's special curry. He shows her how her great-great-grandmother used to prepare meals and, for the first time since arriving in India, Jonathan feels at home. They stay at a small hotel in town.

The same dream, the one he dreamt the night before, returns to Jonathan: a vivid vision of an Aborigine man in a cave and a stone as black as tar. Another marker with another name. And on the reverse side, a single word, the haunting word that is on both tablets in his possession.

In the morning, as he relates the dream to his children, Jonathan is confident they must travel to Australia. It takes some persuading, but during the two days on their drive back to Delhi, Jonathan makes a compelling argument.

77

Before saying goodbye to Mitra, Cassandra finds a store to print out photos. She selects an image of the four of them standing in front of the Taj Mahal. "I wrote our number on the back. I do hope you'll stay in touch," she says with a kiss on his cheek.

Mitra studies the photo. A turquoise shawl wrapped around Cassandra's neck is draping her shoulders; it's the one he purchased for her at the market. "I will keep your father and your family in my heart." He smiles as he bids them a safe journey, "I will keep in touch. I want to see how this story ends."

That night, the three of them find themselves on a 13-hour flight to Darwin, Australia.

PLACE: NEW YORK CITY

YEAR: 1981

In another part of the world at another time, Howard
Convery, a 23-year-old Brooklyn College graduate, returned home to
the humble East Village apartment he shared with his college girlfriend,
Christine, a 21-year-old accountant who vowed that one day, she would
marry Howard.

"Christine!" he shouted as he entered the small dwelling. "Christine!"

She looked up from the petite four-burner stove, watching the pasta
water boil as she stirred the sauce. "You don't have to shout," she said.
"I'm not on the roof."

In four short steps, he was next to her in the combination kitchen,
living room, dining room, partial bedroom. Grabbing her by the waist
and spinning her around he said, "You'll never guess what happened
today." He kissed her hard on the lips, holding his lips against hers extra
long tonight.

"What happened today?" she asked when he finally released his hold.

"They want me to go to South Dakota! Can you imagine it?"

He twirled around the room, almost knocking over lamps and chairs.

79

"To live?" she asked, sounding worried. "You're leaving me … and you're *happy* about this?" She slammed the wooden spoon down, and tomato sauce splattered everywhere.

"No! No, not to live. On a brief assignment. For work. It's a good thing!" he said, trying to calm her down. "It means they're giving me more responsibility." He grabbed her waist again. "You can come too!"

"What would I do in South Dakota?" she asked.

"You would be assisting—" he started, pausing to kiss her again, "the assistant." Then another kiss, causing her to smirk, "to the assistant," and one more kiss as her smirk turned into a giant smile, "to the curator of the Museum of Natural History."

"Oh, so in other words, I'd be your love slave?" she asked, pushing him away with a laugh. "No thanks. I already have that job here," she waved her hands around. "And as can you see, I'm being paid exceedingly well." Bursting out in laughter, she quickly asked, "How long will you be gone?"

"Hard to say," he responded, turning his back to her, rubbing his face where his beard would be.

"You didn't ask?"

"Well," he said sheepishly, "I was so excited they asked me, I didn't think—" He spun around quickly then. "But don't you see what a great opportunity this is for me?"

"What will you be doing?"

"They want me to go to South—"

"Yes, you said, South Dakota," she interrupted him.

"Not just any place in South Dakota. Deadwood!" he practically yelped, waiting to see her excited reaction, which never came. Instead, she stood there, arms crossed, one eyebrow raised, with a *this better be a hell of a lot better than Disneyland* expression on her face.

Finally, she asked, "What is so great about Deadwood?"

"What's so great about Deadwood?" his voice raised just loud enough to make his point. "What's so great about Deadwood?"

"Yeah! What's so great about Deadwood?"

He thought for a long moment. "I guess nothing, really?" and they both laughed until the smoke detector went off.

The burnt sauce on the bottom of the smoldering pot sent streams of black smoke billowing toward the ceiling. They both ran—all of two steps—to the kitchen. Howard grabbed the blackened pot and raised it above the stove as Christine extinguished the circle of blue flames that danced around the burner. She snatched a dishrag and fanned the smoke detector until it ceased its dreadful squawk.

Almost immediately, there came a loud knock on the door. Christine yelled, "It's okay, Miss Schneider! False alarm!"

Howard added, "Again!"

She turned to Howard. "Chinese?"

He already had the phone in his hand. "Yes, so that's one order of sweet and sour chicken and two egg rolls. Thank you, Mr. Ng."

Later that night, as the last of the uneaten chicken bathed in the thick, reddish glaze of the sauce, she asked him once again, "So what *will* you be doing in Deadwood? And why is it so famous?"

"Well, this town, Deadwood, it sprung up overnight after a guy, I forget his name, found gold in the Northern Hills of the Dakota territory."

"You mean South Dakota?" she corrected him.

"Well, there was no North Dakota or South Dakota; it was just called the Dakota territories."

"How do you know all this?" She was amazed at his knowledge.

"It was 1876. Right after the war—" Howard paused, noticing her puzzled face. "The Civil War," he explained, hoping for some recollection, "between the North and the South—" He continued until a spark of high school history lit up her face. "Anyway, something like a thousand people rushed into Deadwood to get rich."

"A thousand people?"

"Maybe more! They all came flooding into this little area that wasn't even a town yet. A lot were just ordinary people, but some were famous!"

"Like movie stars?"

"Well, no. There were no movies in 1876. Actually, the first motion picture was invented just two years later in 1878, when a man named Eadweard Muybridge made a series of photographs of a horse, and—"

"Howard!" she said sharply, stopping a long train wreck of facts she didn't care to hear. "I swear you should go on a game show! Anyway, if they weren't movies stars, who were these famous people?"

"Oh, people like Wyatt Earp and Doc Holiday, Wild Bill Hickok and Calamity Jane, Buffalo Bill Cody, Texas Jack, California Joe, Poker Alice, Potato Creek Johnny Colorado—"

"Potato Creek Johnny? Come on. Now you're just pulling names out of your—"

"I'm serious. Lt. Colonel George Armstrong Custer. You know him? Not a favorite with the Native Americans." Pretending to be shot by multiple arrows all over his body, Howard played dead with his eyes closed and his tongue sticking out.

Christine giggled.

"They even had *The Painted Ladies of Deadwood Gulch.*"

"Well, there better not be any '*Painted Ladies*' there now, or you're not going," she said sternly.

He nuzzled at the side of her neck. "You're the only lady I want to see wearing paint."

She pushed him off, repeating her original question, "So what exactly what *will* you be doing in Deadwood?"

"Oh, yeah right, well, it seems they uncovered a gravesite that no one knew about."

"Yeah?"

"And they need a group of us to go out there and unearth the graves."

"Yuck. You're going to dig up dead people?"

"Dig them up, photograph the remains, and try to identify them, yeah, if we can. They've been in the ground for over 100 years."

"Geez, how disgusting. And you want *me* to go? No thank you, the place would give me the creeps. Oh!" She grabbed his arm with excitement. "What if these ghosts haunt you for disturbing their rest?" She raised her arms over her head like a cartoon ghost. "Whooooooo." He chuckled. She got up then, cleared the table, and said in a more serious voice, "Don't be bringing any funky-ass ghosts home with you. This place isn't big enough for us as it is. We can't have a ghost walking around here all night too."

"Unless they want to share the rent?" he suggested.

"I'm serious. And there better not be any female co-workers going on this trip, either."

It's a strange thing to go to sleep at night in one place and wake up the next morning in a completely new and different country. But as the Taylor family slept, with the constant hum of the plane's engines combined with gentle air currents lulling them into a peaceful slumber, they leave the overcrowded country of India behind them, and awaken to the tropical paradise coastland of the Australian continent.

Shortly before landing, the captain's voice fills the plane's compartments, announcing the time, date, weather, and gratitudes on behalf of AirAsia. The bright, green coastline surrounded by clear turquoise water comes into view as they descend through the clouds.

The earth rises to greet the aircraft's landing gear. A loud chirp, matched by the engine's sudden deceleration, thrusts the passengers forward as their seats shake and shudder before slowly returning the cabin to normal as the plane taxis to the terminal. Passing through the airport, Cassandra remarks that it resembles Long Island's MacArthur Airport with its blue carpet and less crowded check-in areas.

"I spoke with Margaret before we left India," Jonathan tells them. "She's making arrangements for a pilot to fly us into the Northern Territory." He hesitates. "I'm just not sure where yet?"

Jonathan approaches the General Aviation Contact counter. "Excuse me, could you tell me where we would go to charter a flight?"

"Certainly, ya want to exit the main buildin' and tyke a short walk ovah to the Carter Hangers. Someone there should be able t'help."

Trevor and Cassandra look amused by the beautiful woman speaking with a Crocodile Dundee accent.

They make their way to the hanger, a row of clean, white corporate jets are parked wing to wing, each emblazoned with the name *Pearl Aviation*. Beyond them, the twin-prop planes of *Fly Tiwi* are parked, and further along, the single prop planes of *Jandakot Flight Centre* sit.

One of the mechanics, eying them from the hanger, calls out, "Cahn oy help ya?"

Jonathan calls back, "We're looking for *Outback Extreme?*"

The man sighs and points to the last hanger bay.

They walk down the row of planes. The low, unmistakable California drumbeat of The Beach Boys' *Surfin' Safari* grows louder with every step. An older model single prop plane with oversized tires and appearing to be held together with duct tape and glue, is being nursed back to health by a slightly younger version of Jimmy Buffet, complete with a Hawaiian shirt, Bermuda shorts, and flip-flops. A worn and frayed bright yellow baseball cap is perched on his head, with the words *Outback Extreme* stitched in blue thread across the front.

"Is this, uh, Outback Extreme?" Jonathan inquires, hoping the man is just restoring an old junker, perhaps a pet project for the air museum.

"It certainly is," the man says, switching a wrench from his right hand to his left as he turns to extend a proper greeting. "Ya must be Jonathan Taylor."

Jonathan robotically shakes the man's hand.

"And family," he adds, looking at the kids. "A real nice sheila frawm New Yawk rang up and said ya'll be needing a roid."

"Sheila?" Cassandra asks, looking at her father. "Dad, do you have a Sheila working for you?"

The man lets out a short hoot of laughter. "A woman. Oy loike t'call women sheila."

Cassandra smiles and thinks, *I wonder if the women like it?*

"Oy believe she said her nyme was Maggie?"

"Oh, Margaret." Trevor corrects him.

Jonathan just nods, still shaking his hand, hoping Margaret was playing a joke on him.

"Rande Cooper." He introduces himself, laying the Australian accent on thick, "Moy mytes call me Coop."

As he cleans up the tools, Jonathan introduces Trevor and Cassandra.

"So Maggie wasn't sure what the destination was, just said ya nayded a plyne for a couple of days. Whoy don't we head into moy office."

They follow Coop, all three casting looks back at the flying machine that will carry them into the wild blue yonder.

"Is that the plane we'll be using?"

"Yup. *The Laura Belle,*" Coop says with pride in his voice. "Gawt the idea frawm that movie, *The Memphis Belle.*"

"That explains the World War II pin-up girl on the side."

Trevor nudges his sister. "Remember the scene in Star Wars when they hire Han Solo, and they see the Millennium Falcon for the first time?"

Cassandra laughs. "You came in that? You're braver than I thought."

Trevor chuckles. "Yeah, that was Princess Leia when she saw it. Luke said, *What a piece of junk.*"

Coop sits behind an old wooden desk that must have come with the building, because no one would have moved a piece of crap like that into their office. "Sao, where ahh we hayded todye?"

The kids look around the office for a place to sit, but opt to stand on account of the mess.

"Ah, we really don't know, and to be honest, I think we're all a little jet-lagged and tired," Jonathan starts.

"Oh. Oy'm sorry, Oy didn't mean we had to leave right now. Oy'm in no hurry."

"It's just, well, we just got off a long flight and—" Jonathan stumbles, trying hard to avoid sounding like he's trying to back out of the deal.

"Hey, Oy totally understand," Coop says, standing and stretching. "Yaw probably hungry and tired. Oy geh' it."

"Yeah. Hungry," Cassandra blurts out.

"And tired," repeats Trevor.

"Why don't we get a bite to eat, maybe check into a hotel and meet later to discuss a destination?" Jonathan says, taking charge, sounding more like himself.

"Nao worries myte, sounds good. Oy still need to myke a couple of minor adjustments on old Laura Belle."

The kids exchange looks. *Myke?* Cassandra thinks. *Adjustments?* Trevor wonders.

"Can you recommend a place to eat?"

Coop walks to the door, and they follow him outside. "Oh shooah, ya could geh' a cab back at the terminal. Just tell'm ya want to head down to the Mindil Beach Market area. It's about 12 minutes awhy. It's Wednesday, so half the town should be there."

Coop scratches the back of his head and looks up. Unaware that they just spent the better part of a week in India, he begins, "Now let's see, there's the *Nirvana Restaurant* if ya like Thai, Indian or Malaysian food?"

The kids vigorously shake their heads.

"Okay. There's *Darwin Tandoor* or *Magic Wok* but, personally, Oy would go to *Tim's Surf & Turf.* It's a great styke house, and the lunches are reasonable. It has seating outside, which is noyce on a day like today. But if ya want a good burger, Oy would head over to *Good Thanks Burger and Bar.* There's even *Frying Nemo Fish and Chips.* It's kind of a ply on the whole Disney thing, but thy have really good shrimp, size of moy thumbs." He gives two thumbs up in a final gesture.

"Okay, I think we got it," Jonathan says. "Why don't I give you a call in a couple of hours?"

"Grite!" Coop says, then adds, turning back, "Oh whyte," he yells, and runs back into the office. He comes jogging back, holding a business card. "Ya gonna need moy number."

"Right," Jonathan agrees, taking the card and staring at the graphics. *Outback Extreme* appears in skywriting smoke on a blue field. The type reads, Rande "Coop" Cooper, Owner and Pilot of the *Laura Belle*.

Jonathan shakes his hand. "We'll be in touch," he says dismissively as he turns to leave.

"Tyke your time, ya got me faw a week."

Got you for a week, the phrase snaps Jonathan's head back like a rabbit punch. He turns, "All week?"

"Yeah, Maggie booked me faw the week. Said she didn't know where ya were going or how long ya'll be. Sao Oy'm here whenever ya want to geh' going."

The whole week? Jonathan hears the words over and over in his head. *Why would she do that?*

The three of them head back to the terminal. Jonathan prays his children won't start laughing before they are out of earshot of the Owner, Pilot, Mechanic, Flight Coordinator, and one hell of a good up-seller. *I should have him come work for me.*

"Where do you want to eat?" Cassandra asks, snickering.

They decide on *Tim's Surf & Turf.* Jonathan comments that if it's going to be his last meal, he's going to have steak.

"What do you mean you already paid him?" Jonathan yells into the phone.

Trevor makes a face at his father and pans his head around the dining room at Tim's, observing the other patrons. Jonathan leaves the table and moves to the outside bar area.

His voice, significantly lower as he paces the bright sun of the courtyard, "but all week, Margaret? The plane looks like it will fall apart in a strong breeze!"

Cassandra and Trevor sit staring at each other, waiting for their food. Cassandra finally says, "It has to be safe to fly, right? I mean, he couldn't take us up if it wasn't safe?"

But before Trevor can answer, Jonathan throws Coop's business card on the table and announces, "Well, I guess we're stuck with him."

He sees the disappointment on his children's faces. "Apparently it's cheaper if you book him for the whole week and you have to pay for the fuel upfront." Jonathan shakes his head in disbelief. "He came *highly* recommended." He mocks Margaret's voice and rolls his eyes on the word highly. "Anyway, it will be alright; we just have to figure out where we're headed."

"Maybe we won't need him at all?" Cassandra suggests with optimism in her voice.

"Yeah, maybe where we need to go is within driving distance?" Trevor adds. "Hell, we just spent four days driving across India! What's a couple of days in the Australian Outback?"

Cassandra asks timidly, "Dad, just how are we going to figure out where we need to go?"

"I have a vision of a cave and some beehive-shaped mountains that look like they were tiger-striped."

"Oh great, that could be anywhere in the Northern Territory," Trevor says, shaking his head.

"We'll just have to drive around till we see something that Dad recognizes."

"Cazz, Australia's huge," Trevor says. "The whole continent is the size of the United States. The Northern Territory is almost twice the size of Texas. We could be driving for weeks before we see anything, or worse, we could pass right by it and never even notice."

Jonathan continues, "There were also huge termite mounds rising from the orange earth. And waterfalls, beautiful waterfalls, but I think I saw those when I was on walkabout."

"Walk-a-what?" Cassandra asks, but before her father can answer, the server interrupts, placing the plates on the table.

"Here we go—" He notices Coop's business card. "Ya guys booked a flight with Coop? He's the best. Knows every square inch of these parts."

"You know Coop?" Cassandra asks, looking up.

"Oh shooah, almost everyone in the Top End knows Coop. Great guy! No better flyer down under."

"Top End?" asks Jonathan.

"Oh, that's what we locals call Darwin, on account of it being sao far north.

"And that plane of his—is it safe?" Trevor asks.

"What, old Laura Belle? Safer than that taxi ya got out of. That plane will still be mykin' trips to Sydney and back long after those fancy plynes are sold off faw scrap."

Jonathan begins to feel better about Margaret's decision. The server turns to leave, but Jonathan stops him. "Excuse me, one more question. If we wanted to talk with some Aborigines—not the ones in town—maybe the tribe's elders, who could arrange that for us?"

The server points at the business card. "Nobody better, myte. As Oy said, Coop knows almost everyone, including the elder tribesmen. He moy be the only white man to participate in their rituals."

"I bet he gets a kickback for sending people here," Trevor comments after the server disappears through the kitchen doors.

"Taylor family!" a loud voice resounds throughout the dining hall. "Oy knew oy would find ya here." Coop makes his way over to their table, shaking hands and waving at Darwinians enjoying lunch. "The usual, Joey," he calls out to the server.

"I knew it," Trevor mumbles under his breath.

He joins the family at the table, "Oy knew ya were a meat-eater, Johnny! Have you tried the Wagyu? Fraykin awesome."

"Coop? I thought you were fixing the plane?"

He laughs. "Fixing? Nao, just mykin' some last-minute adjustments."

Trevor leans over to his sister, "I swear that's exactly what Han Solo said about the Falcon. Only not in a Steve Irwin accent."

She giggles, remembering, *mykin'*.

"Rande, look, I think I misjudged you, and I need to apologize."

"Please, call me Coop, everyone does. And hearing ya call me Rande is like dressing a gator in a suit. Ya can do it, but it just doesn't seem right."

Jonathan smiles and laughs, "Okay, Coop. I didn't think you were the right person for the job, but—"

The server sets a juicy cheeseburger down in front of Coop.

"But after talking to your friend here," Jonathan motions to the server, "I think you're the perfect person for us."

Staring at his burger, Coop says, "Thynks myte!" Jonathan can't tell if he's talking to him, thanking the server for the talk-up, or just acknowledging the service.

"Coop, we have a problem, and I think you're about the only person who can solve it."

"Ya know, a problem is just a solution that hasn't revealed itself. How can Oy help?"

"I'm looking for a place. It may be a sacred place for the Aborigines."

Coop takes a huge bite out of the cheeseburger, and despite the food in his mouth, mumbles, "Go on."

"Tell him about the termite mounds and waterfalls," Cassandra jumps in.

"Termite mounds?" Coop asks, scooping up a couple of french fries.

"And waterfalls," she adds.

"That's easy," he says, taking a sip of his cola. "Sounds like Litchfield Park, home of some of the largest termite mounds in the world, some reaching more than three meters tall."

"Three meters?!" Trevor interrupts.

"Oh, little more than nine feet," he continues, "and there's Wangi and Tolmer Falls. Both magnificent in their own right." He looks at Jonathan. "Buh ya could have looked that up on any YouTube video on your way here." Coop cocks his head. "Those aren't Aborigine places, and they certainly aren't sacred, so moy question to you, mate, is where is it ya really wanna go?"

Quiet fills the restaurant, like a scene from an Indiana Jones movie right before Doctor Jones announces he's looking for the lost Ark.

"I'm looking for a holy place, a place the Aborigines would have guarded for thousands of years, a cave where painted handprints decorate the walls and elders have passed stories down from generation to generation."

"Why do you wanna find this? Are ya a reporter or a journalist?" Coop asks. But there's a hint of recognition in his voice that suggests he has either heard about the cave or knows someone who knows about it.

"I'm looking for something," Jonathan says, feeling the markers against his leg through the thin material of his pants.

Coop laughs. "Like buried treasure? Oy assure ya myte, the Aborigines don't have any of that. They live off the land and give everything back to the land. They're what ya call, uncommonly non-materialistic." Coop takes another huge bite of his burger.

"No. I'm not a journalist looking for a story or a treasure hunter looking to get rich, I'm looking for my people." He takes a deep breath, then adds, "I'm looking for my home."

A small amount of burger falls from Coop's mouth as he stares, motionless, at Jonathan. The man's words paralyze him.

"Mr. Cooper?" Trevor slowly says, placing one hand on his back. "Are you okay?"

"Your people?" he asks, looking back and forth between Jonathan and his children.

Jonathan nods.

"CRIKEY! YOU'RE FROM NEW YAWK!" he drops his burger on the plate. "Oy mean, look at ya people! Yaw NAWT Aborigines! Yaw NAWT even black!" He continues his rant, and customers' heads start to turn. "What did ya do? Take one of those genetic tests, and it came up one-tenth of one-tenth of one-tenth of a percent native Australian, so right away ya thought, hey, let's go discover moy roots?"

"Mr. Cooper, Rande, Coop. Please, calm down. We're not playing a game of wild exploration into genealogy." Jonathan's voice is stern, but holds a hint of compassion. "You are maybe the only one who can help me."

"Is this some koynd of joke?"

"I assure you this is no joke. I flew halfway around the world, and well, what I found in India scared me. And if I find what I'm looking for here, if I find the same thing, I'm not sure if it will be a blessing or a curse."

Coop contemplates the expressions on their faces. What he sees worries him. "Just what are you looking faw?"

Jonathan pulls out the tablet from India. "I went to a village, a village in India, a place where I've never been before." He hands Coop the stone.

"So they gave you a rock? Big deal." He looks at it. "Seems an awful long way to go for a souvenir rock."

Jonathan then takes out the tablet his jeweler, Giorgio, made for him, and hands it to Coop. "I had this made right before I left New York."

He studies both tablets in each hand. Turning them over and noticing the same word carved into both markers.

AETERNUM, Coop reads to himself. *Okay, that's a little odd.* He turns the markers over, looking at Jonathan's name, then looks at the name on the other stone. "So who's this Akal Datta?"

Jonathan waits a long time, debating whether or not he can trust Coop. *Will he think me mad? I could possibly get my clock cleaned.* He looks at his children, who are nodding their encouragement and approval, and takes a leap of faith, deciding to trust that Australians are understanding people.

"I told you I had this one made for me in New York before I left," Jonathan raises his right hand that holds the tablet with his name. Then he slowly raises his left hand. "And I had this one made for me in India, before I died, more than 75 years ago."

Coop cranes his neck, his brow furrowed.

"Akal Datta was me," he shakes his head. "*Is* me. Listen, Rande, this is all terribly confusing for us too. Hell, I don't even think Trevor believes it, so why should I expect you to. But I'm telling the truth, no bullshit. When I told you I have never been to that village in India, it's true. I've never been there, *not* in this lifetime, but I think I've been there in another lifetime, in a previous life."

Coop's face changes; Jonathan can't tell whether it's understanding or doubt.

Jonathan continues. "I think," he starts. "No. I *know* I've been here in a past life, and I think I left one of these tablets here too, somewhere in Australia. Simply put, we need your help to find it."

Coop unexpectedly takes a bite of his cheeseburger, then sips his drink. He scratches the back of his head. "So, these things?" he says motioning to the tablets lying on the table. "These belonged to ya? Oy mean, at one tyme?"

Jonathan looks at his daughter, who is nodding her head. Trevor just smiles. "I'm starting to believe they did."

"And ya left one somewhere here in Australia?"

"I believe I did," Jonathan answers.

"Australia's a Moyty big place, myte!"

"I'm pretty sure I left it in good hands."

"Hell, better be excellent hands," Coop says, bursting into such a hardy laugh it startles half the customers, including the Taylor family. "Oy wouldn't even leave the *Laura Belle* with me own Mawm," and laughs even harder.

He picks up the last of his burger and yells to the server to bring four cold Fosters. "Now tell me, where do we start looking?"

"So, you believe me?"

"Let's just say, Oy have some first-hand knowledge of the lives of the people whose ancestors walked this continent long before, well, long before Christ. According to them, your story doesn't sound so far-fetched."

Jonathan starts to explain his visions, trying to remember every last detail. Coop hands him one of the glasses of beer; Jonathan continues to describe the beehive, tiger-striped mountains, waterfalls, and the towering termite mounds. He recalls to them all the rich, orange dirt at the entrance to the cave where the elders took him. He recounts every last detail of his visions, then waits to see Coop's reaction.

Coop drinks in Jonathan's vision and sits quietly before finishing his third beer. "I think I know someone who can help you."

He stands and announces, "But we're gonna have to hurry. I want to get there before the sun sets."

"Before the sun sets?" Trevor blurts out.

The sun doesn't set for three hours, Cassandra thinks.

Coop looks at Trevor. "Harder to land in the dark."

"We're not going to fly, are we?" Jonathan asks, sounding concerned.

Coop smiles, "Ahhhhhh, hell yeah!"

"But you just drank three huge glasses of beer!"

16

PLACE: DEADWOOD, SOUTH DAKOTA
YEAR: 1981

One week later, 23-year-old Howard Convery was
in Deadwood, South Dakota to work at the dig site. He was accompanied by two female co-workers from the archaeology department, Samantha and Nicole, or, as Howard referred to them when speaking to Christine, Sam and Nick.

"We took scans and readings of this entire area," the project leader briefed the new recruits. "So, basically, any gravesites we could detect were marked with flags. We need you, and I can't stress this enough, to *carefully* dig down until you reach a casket, then slowly and gingerly unearth the delicate remains. Did I mention, *carefully*?"

He looked at the first-year hires. "These sites are extremely fragile," he added, picking up what looked like a dirt-covered stick. "Most of them have been in the earth for more than a hundred years." As he closed his hand, the rotted sample crumbled to pieces. "That was a human femur. A thigh bone for those of you who slept though anatomy class. Some may not be intact, while others, we're hoping, may have held up pretty well." He referenced his clipboard. "Okay, you have all

96

been assigned plots. Samantha, you'll take the areas marked with green flags. Nicole, you have the areas marked with red, and Howie, why don't you take the blue ones."

"Why, because I'm a boy?" he whispered to Nicole, who giggled.

"Howie, if you need help with your body, just ask Samantha or me," Nicole flirted, walking away and turning her head, watching him with her best *I'm so cute* smile. She caught up to Samantha and they both giggled, strolling away arm in arm like a couple of high schoolers.

Howard stood, shovel and gloves in hand. "Hilarious, ladies!" he shouted after them.

Samantha was the first to unearth a casket. "I reached one!"

Everyone on site immediately ran over to carefully and meticulously help move the dirt away, using both their hands and some small brushes.

"Careful. Be extremely careful, now," the project leader instructed.

It was a plain pine box, obviously treated with some type of lacquer, which preserved it remarkably well. Two men approached, each carrying a large, L-shaped pole. They slid one down on either side of the coffin and rotated the poles 90 degrees, moving the arms of the poles underneath the casket.

"Okay, just like the last one. Nice and easy. 3 … 2 … 1!"

The men lifted the dirt-covered box out of its resting place and onto what appeared to be an oversized wheelbarrow.

"What do we do now, Professor?" Nicole asked.

"Well, the rest of you can go back to work. Samantha will accompany this subject all the way to relocation."

Sam looked at him, perplexed. "Relocation?"

"The final stage," the project manager explained. "First, we bring the subject to the *studio tent*. That's what we like to call it. There we photograph anything and everything we see to catalogue and assign a case number."

"Then what?" Howard asked.

"Well, we first determine gender. Sometimes that's easy, sometime not so easy." He frowns, as if to show them it's often very difficult. "Then we take x-rays to look for any distinguishable marks or items that can give us some insight into who the person was."

"Distinguishable marks?" Sam asked.

"The x-rays can tell if the person died from a gunshot wound, knife injury, if they had a broken bone anywhere; all this can be used to identify the body."

"Okay and items?" Nicole asked.

"Pocket watches, old jewelry such as a brooch or a locket with an etching inside of it can be very helpful." The professor smiles, thinking back. "One cowboy was buried with his guns; his name was inscribed right on the barrel. After everything is photographed and archived, our research staff will search through birth records, death records, even journals in order to connect this individual with their name. It's painstaking, but we do whatever it takes to make a match."

"And if you don't … identify them?" Nicole asked.

"We give them a number, and they become a case study. The photos are sent to research labs all across the United States. We usually get a hit within a month or two." He turns to Sam. "You ready to take your new friend to the studio?"

"Sure." She walked with the other men as they transported the fragile cargo.

An hour later, Nicole yelled from her plot, "I reached one!"

The entire process began again, however this time, the site did not hold up as well. With every brush of dirt, the box crumbled and caved in on itself.

"I'm afraid you have a lot more work than Sam," the project leader advised, as the men with the poles returned to the tent and came back to the plot carrying five-gallon plastic buckets.

"You're gonna have to retrieve all the soil around the immediate site.

98

Then we'll sift through it looking for bones, clothing, jewelry—anything that could lead to an identification." He handed her a bucket. "Welcome to the glamorous life of an archaeologist."

She grunted her reluctant acceptance, then began her long, tedious task.

Finally, it was Howard's turn. "I got one!" he yelled, *and it looks good,* he thought.

Just as Sam had done earlier, Howard accompanied his casket to *the studio.*

"Nice job, Howard," the project leader said. "Nicole, why don't you wrap up for the day and catch up to Howard in the studio. That way, you can experience what happens in there."

More than happy to stop filling buckets with dirt, bone, and wood, Nicole headed for the studio tent. Moments later, she joined Howard and the other men as they moved the casket to a metal gurney. Next they wheeled the gurney under a suspended camera structure and the photographing began.

An overweight, under-groomed, pony-tailed technician sat in front of an oversized computer monitor emitting a ghoulish green glow. Flash bulbs fired in succession, illuminating the dark tent, reminiscent of a creepy laboratory in an old black and white horror movie.

"Why aren't there any lights on in here?" asked Nicole.

"I asked the same thing," answered Sam. "I was told it had something to do with exterior light interfering with the quality and details of the photos."

The camera moved on two overhead rails, photographing every inch. State-of-the-art equipment recorded every detail associated with this individual's final resting place.

"Okay," the technician said, "Time to open her up and see who's inside." Howard's hands trembled. A bead of sweat trickled down his forehead, not from the heat but from anxiety. "You ready for this, champ?" the technician asked him. "It's your find."

"Sure," Howard lied, lifting a crowbar from the table. He gently wedged the tip into the space between the lid and body of the coffin. A slight tap with the hammer, and the wood crumbled.

"GENTLY! Gently!" The project leader hollered from the tent's entranceway. Howard jumped as an involuntary scream escaped his lips.

The girls laughed and Howard turned bright red. Even the technician laughed as the project leader joined them. He slapped Howard on the back, "Sorry, Howie, didn't mean to startle you there."

Howard looked at the girls, who were still laughing but now looking devilishly sympathetic. "You two are never going to let me live this down, are you," he asked.

"Oh, we're going to let everyone at the museum know about this," Nicole said.

"Great," Howard said, looking at the project leader with a half smile. "Thanks, thank you very much."

"Okay, enough joking around. Let's get this lid off and see who we've got." The project leader grabbed a crowbar himself and walked to the other side of the gurney.

The two of them wedged the tips of their crowbars into the wood. Picking up a rubber mallet, the project leader waved it at Howard. Flush returned to Howard's cheeks, only not so noticeable as he picked up his own rubber mallet, and ever so delicately, they both began tapping on the end of the crowbars. With minimal pressure applied, the lid began to lift. Moving the crowbars down, working their way from the top of the casket to the base, all nails pulled out cleanly. The men placed the tools down on the gurney and carefully worked their fingers under the lid. Howard smelled the foul air as it escaped from the coffin. He looked into the project leader's eyes, which conveyed confidence as he counted down.

"3 … 2 … 1 …"

Both men lifted slowly. The girls immediately covered their mouths and pinched their noses, repulsed by the rancid smell. Howard and the project leader walked the lid to a side table and laid it down. The two men then returned to the gurney, stopping to gather five surgical masks.

The project leader handed them out before peeking in on their unearthed guest. Howard looked inside, as did the girls. The filtered masks did little to suppress the terrible stench.

Inside, a male corpse lay in a state of decay. His hands rested on his chest, and he appeared to be clutching a small metal plate.

The five of them stood over the casket and studied the remains.

"Mm," said the project leader, breaking the silence. "It looks like you just unearthed the remains of Mr. Joseph Kehm." He straightened up. "Congratulations, Mr. Convery. This just may be the easiest case we had all year."

"Joseph Kehm?" Howard asked, already retreating from the open casket so as to avoid the pungent odor emitted by the deceased Mr. Kehm. "How do you know?"

The others turned to look at the project leader. Dumbfounded, they waited for the answer. He removed a pair of latex gloves from a small rectangular box marked large, and slid his hands into the gloves. Fumbling with the latex, he worked until the glove snapped snug around his fingers. Reaching into the coffin, he pried open the brittle fingers and released a rectangular piece of metal with a name chiseled on the front. Being careful not to drop the piece of steel into the exposed chest cavity, which lay on the bony ribcage, the professor handed it to young Mr. Convery.

"He left his calling card!"

Howard felt the weight in his hands and examined the small metal marker.

Joseph Kehm

March 3rd, 1855

"Besides," said the leader, "that hole in the center of Mr. Kehm's forehead?" They hung on his every word, as if Sherlock Holmes was about to reveal the killer. "I can almost guarantee you an 1851 Navy Colt revolver made it." *Extraordinary, Holmes, but how did you know?* "In fact, it wasn't a bullet, but a ball-and-powder shot," he added.

"What?! You don't know that?" protested Samantha.

"Come on! How can you possibly know that?" asked Howard.

"He's good," the long-haired technician assured them.

"I can even tell you who fired the shot!" the project leader boasted.

"No way!" exclaimed Nicole incredulously, "I'll buy the first round tonight if you can actually tell us that."

"And I'll buy the second round!" Sam added. "But you have to prove you're right."

"How about you, Howard? Want to buy the third round?" the project leader taunted.

"Don't do it, kid," the technician warned.

"Sure," said Howard. "I'll call."

The project leader smiled. "Funny you should use that turn of phrase. Okay, I'll expect three rounds tonight at —" He paused and began to laugh. "Oh, this is so appropriate," he continued, laughing even louder. "You're not going to believe the irony of this!" His laughter escalated, almost out of control. "Let's say three rounds tonight on the newest recruits at the Saloon No. 10!"

"Did we miss something?" Nicole asked, looking back and forth at everyone.

"Yeah, what's so funny about the Saloon No. 10?" Howard asked. "Are drinks like $20 a beer there or something?"

"Why do I feel like we just got hustled," Sam sighed.

"No kid, the beers are regular price, but when I explain it to you, you'll really get a kick out of it."

"So," asked Nicole, "who killed this guy?"

"The person who fired that shot was none other than—"

"YES?!" Nicole shouted.

"Who is it?!" Samantha echoed.

"The notorious gunfighter, wagon master, lawman, and gambler, most famous perhaps for how *he* was killed—" He can't help but build the suspense.

"Oh MY GOD, just say it already!" Howard yelled.

"The one and only Wild Bill Hickok!" he announced. "I'll see you three at the saloon tonight at eight o'clock. Don't be late and don't forget to bring cash!" He beamed in triumph at the smiling technician. "Because like the ad says, they don't take checks, and they don't take American Express! Ha, ha, ha, ha." Gloating, he bowed with a parting smile. *My God Sherlock, you've done it again,* he heard the little voice recite inside his head.

"Wait!" the three of them called out.

"How do we know Wild Bill shot this man?" Howard asked.

"For the answer to *that*, my young associates, I'll have to have at least three beers purchased by each one of you." Again he bowed triumphantly and bid them all good night.

"We still need a complete set of photographs of the body," he instructed the technician on his way out, "and don't forget that metal tablet. And you," he added, addressing Howard. "I'm sure you're gonna want that piece for your museum, Professor."

"Professor?" Howard turned to the technician. "Why did he call me Professor?"

"Perhaps he sees something in you?" the technician replied, turning the tent, once again, into a cheap haunted house attraction, as he began snapping photos.

Howard stood motionless, studying the metal object. He slowly turned it over and felt something scratched on the surface. *What the —*

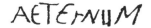

Rande "Coop" Cooper adjusts the tiny dials and

knobs on the dashboard, checking his instruments, as the Taylor family sits crammed in the small cabin of the *Laura Belle*. Jonathan sits next to Coop, while Trevor and Cassandra are snug behind them, rubbing shoulders. The hum of the engine vibrates the plane and Jonathan notes the rattling door frame and pale-gray duct tape scattered throughout the interior.

Coop yells into the headset's microphone, "You're lucky I have some knowledge about the indigenous philosophy. Any other bloke would have had a go at ya, thinking ya were pulling his wanker."

Jonathan nods and feigns a smile, more concerned about air travel at the moment than a bloody nose. "I assure you, Coop, I have no interest in pulling your wanker!"

Coop lets loose a hearty laugh and slaps Jonathan on the knee. "Oy knew Oy liked ya, mate."

Jonathan smiles, then asks, "Indigenous philosophy?"

"Aborigine philosophy! Like Oy said back at the bar, Oy have some first-hand knowledge. Ya see, the aborigines believe in Dreamtime, a state where dreamers, or spirit beings, are messengers that communicate with the living and introduce new knowledge to us humans."

Jonathan scans the empty runway.

Coop continues, "Maybe one of these dreamers was sending you a message."

Cassandra raises an eyebrow, as if to say *maybe,* but instead shouts, "What are we waiting for?"

"Gotta get clearance. We share the runway with the Royal Australian Air Force."

Unrecognizable chatter comes over the headset followed by numbers and letters, then Coop answers back, "Okay! We're clear for takeoff."

"Where are we headed?"

"CLARAVALE!" he shouts, before pushing several knobs against the dashboard. The cockpit convulses as the engine screams; the plane taxis to the runway.

Cassandra types the word 'Claravale' into her phone's GPS app, and her eyes widen. "It's over 15,000 square miles and there are *only* 10 residents!"

"My friends, Terry and Matt, have a place there. I called and told them we were coming for the night."

"Let me guess, the Dorisvale Homestead?" Cassandra yells, as the plane turns 90 degrees onto the runway.

"YEAH! How'd ya know?" Coop laughs, yelling back as he throws another nob forward, sending the plane roaring down the tarmac.

"It's the only place there!" Cassandra wails into her headset, feeling her body becoming almost weightless as the small plane takes to the sky.

Within minutes, the city of Darwin grows small and becomes a cluster of white and tan rooftops, connected by a spiderweb of roadways. The land takes on a velvet texture as the plane climbs high into the cobalt-blue Australian sky.

The Taylor family watches in amazement as the Australian flying machine remains airborne. Coop sways with the gentle movements of the airfoils, lulling the plane. Never has a man seemed more at peace. He makes some minor adjustments with the instruments and settles in for a short flight.

"About 40 miles to the left is Kakadu National Park. I believe that's where Terry's going to tell us we need to go."

Moments later, Coop noses the plane downward and begins to descend.

"Are we here already?" Jonathan asks. "We could have driven!"

"No! I'm taking you over Litchfield National Park." He levels out the plane. "I thought you would want a better look!"

Words cannot describe the beauty of this country. The park explodes with living color. Everywhere, bright green vegetation grows out of fertile umber soil. Blue sky and white clouds reflect perfectly in green, turquoise, and aqua-colored pools of water, cascading down from snaking rivers high above.

Even from the air, ancient rock formations become strangely familiar, as Jonathan remembers traveling this land on foot. Coop dips the plane lower, "You have to see this up close to appreciate it."

The top of the tree line breaks and the lush green leaves give way to a speckled-brown plateau. Gray and white headstone-like monuments rise from the earth. Jonathan's eyes widen as he plasters his face against the glass.

"What are they?" Trevor asks.

"Termite mounds!" Jonathan yells back, then softly adds so no one else can hear, "I've been here."

"Not just any termite mounds. Magnetic termite mounds," Coop recites in tour guide fashion.

"Why are they called magnetic?" Trevor asks. "They don't attract metal, do they?"

Coop dips the wing and circles around. "Ya see the shape? Kinda wide on one side and narrow on the other."

"Yeah, they're all pointed in the same direction," Cassandra observes, her face now pressed against the window too.

"They construct every mound pointing toward magnetic north. So if ya ever lose ya wye in the bush, just find a termite mound and ya'll know where ya are."

Coop pulls back and turns the yoke, banking the plane and making her climb. The majestic trees turn into small bushes; orange roads turn into brown strands of thread, criss-crossing the landscape of the northern outback. An hour later, just before the sun sets and twilight takes hold, Coop touches down on a small patch of dirt, just south of the house that sits on Dorisvale Homestead.

Now I know what the oversized tires are for, Trevor thinks.

Coop brings the plane to a halt, just shy of a 55-gallon steel drum, with a makeshift pump perched on top, an accommodation to bush pilots who, when in need of fuel, can land and refuel. It also provides Terry and Matt with extra cash. The doors of the cockpit open, but before the family can disembark, a rich, earthy aroma of herbs and wildflowers triggers Jonathan's memories. He steps out onto the orange soil, bends down, and scoops up a handful of dirt, rubbing it between his palms before bringing it to his nose. He breathes it in deeply, as every nuance of this rich land welcomes him home. Closing his eyes, all memories of a life once lived take their place alongside his other memories.

An ATV approaches as Matt rides out to greet his long-time friend. "Coop! How the hell are ya?!"

"Can't complyne. Oy want ya to meet some friends of moyn!"

That night, Jonathan recounts every detail of his past life to Terry and Matt.

"Well, the waterfalls and termite mounds are definitely Litchfield park," Terry comments.

"Ya, we figured that one out," Coop says.

"Now, the beehive-shaped mountains with tiger stripes, that's gotta be Bungle Bungles in Purnululu Park."

Matt and Coop agree.

"But Oy'm pretty sure the plyce ya looking faw is Kakadu, a plyce sacred to the aborigines," Terry continues.

Jonathan looks bewildered as Cassandra asks, "Cack-a-what?"

"Kakadu National Park," Coop says.

"Isn't that the first place you pointed out to us?" Trevor asks.

"Ya, the Bininj and Mungguy people have been taking care of Kakadu for more than 50,000 years."

"Why don't we just fly back in the morning, so Dad can walk around and see if he remembers anything?" Trevor suggests.

The three Australians burst into laughter as the three Americans appear mystified.

"Did I say something amusing?"

Coop pours another round of beer for Terry and Matt; Jonathan waves him off, still nursing his second pint. "Son, Kakadu is half the size of Switzerland. It would take ya forever to trek from one side to the other."

Matt looks at Terry. "They're gonna need your help."

Coop clinks Matt's glass with his own, "That's why Oy brought them here. Whata ya say, Terr, ya think ya can contact the elders?"

"Is Terry friends with the Aborigines?" Jonathan asks.

"Friends? She's family." Matt looks at his wife who nods in the affirmative as he continues. "It was back in 1974, worst storm I ever lived through. Cyclone Tracy leveled the entire city of Darwin. More than 25,000 people were evacuated from Darwin airport. That's when I met Coop. We were both scared little boys, but Coop said it would be okay. We sat next to each other on the plane and Coop kept me talking during the entire flight; he took my mind off everything."

Coop jumps in to add, "It was then that Oy knew Oy wanted to become a pilot."

Matt takes a swig of his beer before continuing. "Yeah, Coop took to the skies like an Osprey, a real natural. We were the lucky ones." He motions to his wife. "Terry wasn't so lucky. Her family was hiking in Kakadu when the storm hit. Roads flooded, the ground became unstable, flash floods raced through the canyons. It was terrible. She became an orphan that day." He glanced at Cassandra. "Imagine your whole family taken from ya?"

Cassandra closes her eyes and a shiver runs down her spine.

"A tribesman named Jandamarra found Terry. He was part of the Bininj tribe. He sheltered her, and when the storm was all over, he saw her safely returned to her grandparents. Any chance she had after that, she returned to stay with the tribe, sometimes for a week, sometimes longer. Jandamarra became her adopted father and she became the tribe's ivory child."

Matt gives his wife a long look and says, "So if anyone can help ya, she can."

"Don't give me those big puppy-dog eyes, ya big shyt." Terry throws a dish towel at her husband. "Ya know damn well Oy'm gonna help him."

Coop smiles and Terry's eyes shoot daggers his way. "And *you*. You knew Oy was gonna help them right from the start. That's why you brought them here."

"I wasn't sure until I heard that part about the cave with the handprints. Other than the elders, yaw the only other person on this continent Oy heard talk about that cave."

She glances at the clock in the living room. "It's a bit late. I'll contact the elders in the morning."

Puzzled, Trevor asks, a bit snidely, "And how do you do that? Smoke signals? Carrier pigeons?"

"I'll call him on his cell phone. Just cuz we ain't got skyscrapers doesn't mean we ain't got technology. Crikey, it's the 21st century, not the 1800s." Terry smirks and after a long pause, the whole room erupts in laughter.

The following morning, the Taylor family readies to leave. Terry packs some sandwiches and kisses Coop on the cheek before turning to Jonathan. "I spoke with Minjarra, the tribe's elder. He wants to meet with ya."

Jonathan thanks her and says, "So it was the part about the cave that persuaded you to help?"

She nods. "You know, Jonathan, you may be the only other white person who will see the inside of that cave."

"You mean you've seen it?" Jonathan asks in amazement.

"When I was little, Jandamarra took me in, showed me the wall of hands and told me of their history. He may have even told me of you. There was a young Bininj who came back after going walkabout, telling of the lives he saw in Dreamtime. His name was—"

"Kilara," Jonathan somberly speaks his name out loud for the first time.

"Yeah!" She looks at him with a bright new wonder in her eyes as her jaw drops open. "Ya know, Jonathan," she finally says once she shook off the amazement enough to speak, "the aborigines believe the Dreamtime is a complex and comprehensive concept that embodies the past, present, and future. I wouldn't be surprised if the closer you get to the things you remember from your past life, the stronger your memories will grow. You myte even start reliving many of them."

"Did Jandamarra mention how long ago Kilara went into that cave?"

Terry touches his elbow, much like a nurse consoling a patient. "Jonathan, that was more than 300 years ago."

Jonathan removes his tablet from his pocket and hands it to her. "I woke up one morning and something told me to make this." From another pocket, he removes the tablet from India. "This one was given to me in India. The same feelings I experienced there, I have now."

She looks at the tablet. "This one is from 1876. A hundred and—"

"Forty-four years ago. I believe I was this woman, Akal Datta, some 144 years in the past. Now I'm starting to think I may have been this *Kilara* person as well."

Terry turns the stones over. The same word appears on both. "How can this be?"

"I don't know, but I think this is what I'm searching for, a tablet like these. I suspect I left one of these tablets in the cave more than 300 years ago." He hangs his head.

"Cheer up, Jonathan. If Oy learned anything from Jandamarra, it's that we are all connected, and not just with one another, but with all living things on this planet. Hell, even with the planet itself! It's like we're a series of islands: they look disconnected, but if you remove the water, you'll see the land is joined. That's what we are on this planet; we're all somehow connected—islands, but not really alone. Ya just have to wait for the water to go down before ya can see it. Oy know that sounds a bit strange, but we're all put here for a reason, Jonathan. Ya just have a better advantage than most to figure it out."

"How so?" Jonathan asks.

"You're leaving yourself proof."

Jonathan feels a surprising sense of optimism wash over him.

"Maybe it took you all these lifetimes to figure it out. If Oy were you, Oy would start to leave more than a stone. Oy would start writing a blah-dee book."

"Who's writing a book?" Cassandra asks, joining them.

"Terry was just saying that, if we're going to all these places, we should write a book."

"Mm, not a bad idea." Wheels start turning in Cassandra's head. "Oh. Dad, um, Coop says he's ready."

Terry returns the markers to Jonathan. "Think about it, Jonathan." She kisses him on the cheek and smiles. "I hope you find what you're looking for, if for no other reason than so I don't have to tell you the same blah-dee thing 50 years from now when you come back around in your next life."

Howard, Sam, and Nicole left their hotel and walked down Main Street.

"I've asked some people around town about this Saloon No. 10," Samantha said. "Apparently, it's been here since the town was built."

"Ugh, it's that old?" Nicole asked. "I bet it's a dump."

"I wish you would stop using that term!" Sam said.

"What term? Dump?" she asked.

"No! *I bet!* Stop saying, I bet," Sam snapped.

"Yeah," Howard agreed. "Last time *you* said that it cost me a round of drinks."

"Me too!" Sam added.

"Oh my God! Look at this place!"

As the three of them strolled past Lee Street, the dark wood bar came into view on the right: a two-story brick building, the facade of the first-floor resembling a log cabin, rather than the town's watering hole. Four huge, black, wrought iron lanterns—more appropriate to the French Quarter in New Orleans than to Deadwood, South Dakota—

threw an eerie yellow light on the front of the building. Four blood-red wagon wheels, actually windows, stood out against the dark brown paint of the logs.

"Are we sure we want to go in?" Sam asked.

"We could go back to the hotel and play strip poker?" Nicole suggested.

Howard smiled. "I'm not playing any kind of poker in this town. It doesn't end well for people around here. But if I did—" He briefly glanced down at Nicole's tight sweater and then at Samantha's T-shirt. "I'd bet you two would lose more than your shirts." He gave them a goofy smile and then held the door. "After you, Nicole. *You* got us into this mess."

She walked past him. "I'm a pretty good poker player, but I've been known to lose a hand—" and with a playful wink, "—or two."

They found themselves inside what looked to be an all-in-one old-time hunting lodge, trading post, gambling hall, museum, and saloon. Nothing had prepared these three Manhattanites for what awaited them inside. Animal heads and pelts decorated the dark wood walls together with pistols, rifles, antique photographs, and portraits of famous men from the old west. Turn of the century glass lanterns illuminated the walls while ornate chandeliers hung from the ceiling; tables and chairs, fashioned from whiskey barrels, were scattered about the sawdust-covered floor. People everywhere were talking, drinking, laughing, and smoking. The aroma of spilled beer and whiskey from the previous night—or probably, more accurately, the past hundred nights—permeated the air. The ever-present smell of cigarette and cigar smoke was thick and choking. All scents conspired together to call this saloon 'home'.

"I did not expect *this!*" Nicole exclaimed.

"Me neither," Samantha and Howard agreed in unison.

With so many things screaming out for their attention, they stood baffled and confused, uncertain where to look or how to proceed. Stuffed pheasants and birds of all species were frozen in flight or perched among the dark wood rafters overhead. Animal heads weren't the only things on display in this macabre museum from Deadwood's past. Over the bar, displayed in three glass cases, were the busts of Wild Bill Hickok, Calamity Jane, and Wild Bill's executioner, Jack McCall. Underneath them, mounted on wooden boards, were three pistols: two facing right and one facing left.

"Oh my God, this entire bar is a shrine to Wild Bill," Howard said, looking around. *Christine is never gonna believe this.*

Black-and-white portraits lined the walls with Wild Bill in various poses: some with other people seated in wooden chairs; others by himself, with a stoic death stare. Five playing cards, two aces and two eights, all black suits, with a bright red nine of diamonds, fanned out on a green velvet cloth, were framed as a wall decoration—Bill's final poker hand. They even had Wild Bill's chair, with his guns in a gun belt slung over the backrest, and built into the wall in its own glass display case, a sign in bold letters read, "WILD BILL'S DEATH CHAIR."

"Do you see—?" Howard started yelling over the noise in the crowded bar, when the project leader shouted from the back of the saloon, "Hey guys! Back here!"

The threesome walked the length of the long bar, past a row of slot machines. On the mirror behind a section of the bar, the words *WILD BILL BAR* was stenciled in gold lettering. A turn-of-the-century ornate gold cash register sat unused against the wall.

"They really love Wild Bill!" Howard commented, bringing his lips close to Sam's ear, so as to be heard over the commotion.

"What? You really love who?" she shouted back.

"Never mind!" He shook his head. A waitress passed by in an old-time bustier carrying a tray of drinks. Howard's gaze followed her chest.

"Well, at least we know he's not gay," Nicole called to Sam.

"Here he is!" yelled the project leader. The back room erupted in applause and people started to shake Howard's hand and slap him on the back. Sam and Nicole were pushed aside as a sea of people attempted to greet Howard. The waitress who'd passed by a few moments earlier made her way to him as well, tossing her long blond hair out of her eyes—her second best feature.

"The owner wanted to buy you a drink," she said, handing him a shot. Leaning in closer, she placed her cheek against his and whispered in his ear, "The next one's on me!"

The sweet, honeysuckle aroma of her perfume permeated his nostrils and went straight to his brain, impeding all rational thought. She smiled with her eyes—as only a girl wanting to be noticed could—and she lingered a few seconds longer, letting her words marinate.

Seeing this, Nicole turned to the project leader. "What the hell is going on here?"

"The kid's a rock star! And *you* owe me a drink!" He smiled at Sam. "And *you* owe me a drink, after hers."

"Yeah, yeah, I know," Nicole uttered dismissively, still fuming over the blonde waitress in the purple bustier.

"But why *him*? He's never even been here before," she asked.

"Are you kidding?" The project leader's tone implied he was mocking her for being so oblivious. "In case you haven't noticed, Wild Bill Hickok is kind of a big thing around here." He waved his hands around the bar, pointing out photographs and pictures. "A hundred years ago, Wild Bill sat at a poker table right here in this saloon and shot Joseph Kehm right between the eyes." Having already downed a couple of drinks before they arrived, he playfully poked Nicole in the center of her forehead. She shook her head and grimaced at their tipsy leader who kept talking. "Young Master Convery over there found the very first person Wild Bill killed right here." He pointed at the ground several times to drive the point home. "In this very saloon!"

"Ew, right here!" Nicole said, looking down at where he was pointing and stepped over an invisible body to stand behind Samantha. "I was standing on a dead person!" she yelled in Sam's ear.

The project leader laughed. "Well, not this very spot. Most likely back by the poker tables! They even have a photograph of his body in the coffin. He spun around in place, attempting to get his bearings, then pointed to the side of the bar that displayed several wanted posters and gruesome photos. "Over there, I believe."

Nicole crossed her arms and pretended to take in the décor, secretly searching for her busty new nemesis.

"Now, how about that drink!" he clapped his hands together and the three of them headed to the bar. Howard was left to enjoy the praises of the crowd, and some more attributes of the cocktail waitress, particularly her long blonde hair and purple corset.

After a while, Howard joined them in a booth at the back of the saloon.

"Did you have fun with 'Little Miss Big Boobs'?" Nicole asked.

Howard looked confused. "Oh, you mean Heather?" he asked, connecting her derisive comment with the cocktail waitress. "She's nice. I think she likes me."

"It's her *job* to flirt with the customers!" Nicole shouted. "It's how *she* makes her money!" Slamming her hands on the table a bit more harshly than she intended, she exited the booth. "I need a drink," she exclaimed, throwing a dead stare right at Howard. "A very strong, tall, handsome, drink!" She turned, getting her bearings before walking away.

"Why is she so angry at me?" Howard asked Sam, still within earshot of Nicole.

Overhearing this, Nicole spun around and yelled, "Because some of *us* went to college and have to dig around in dirt looking for dead people to make our money! Argggg," she grunted, and stormed off to the bar.

Sam got up. "I better join her before she gets into a knock-down, drag-out with Little Miss Big Boobs," she chuckled.

Howard and the project leader heard her laughing as she made her way through the sea of people.

"What did I do?" Howard asked.

"My dear young friend. You have a lot to learn about women but, more importantly—" He waved Heather over.

"Professor? No, please, I think I'm in enough hot water already."

"Relax, Romeo. I'm thirsty," he said as Heather leaned over the booth, presenting her best assets to Howard.

"Is there something I can get you gentlemen?" She stared at Howard's distracted eyes.

"Yes, another round of drinks. Jack Daniel's for me—" He pried his gaze from two of Heather's best forward-facing traits and looked at Howard.

"I'll just have a beer," Howard said, lost in her mesmerizing sapphire blue eyes.

"One Tennessee whiskey straight up," *for the pervy old guy,* she thought, "and one beer with a whiskey chaser for the handsome gentleman." She smiled. "Yours is on me." *Hopefully not the only thing that's 'on me' tonight.* She stared at Howard like a hungry lioness eyeing a porterhouse steak.

"Oh, and put that on the handsome man's tab," the project leader yelled after her as she walked away.

"Professor, can I ask you something?" Howard asked.

"You want to know if you should go home with the blonde, blue eyed cocktail waitress or Nicole?" The project leader fired back. "Personally, I try not to get involved with co-workers, but Nicole really seems to like you. Then again, the *body* on that waitress! Son, women like that only come along once in *your* lifetime," he smirked, "twice in mine. And she *really* wants you!"

"No. No, not that, this!" Howard reached into his pocket and pulled out Joseph Kehm's death marker.

"Where did you get that?" He sat up quickly as if Howard had just produced the very gun Jack McCall used to kill Wild Bill.

"It's from the site, remember? Geez, Professor, how much have you had to drink?"

"You can't just walk off with evidence!"

"I didn't," Howard said. "I signed it out. I know the procedures." He turned over the metal marker. "I wanted to discuss this with you." He pointed at the haunting word. "What do you think it means?"

"AETERNUM," the project leader read. "It means—"

Howard interrupted him. "I *know* what it means, Professor, and I know *you* know what it means. But I seriously doubt Joesph Kehm *knew* what it meant. Think about it. A down-on-his-luck panhandler who ended up on the wrong side of Wild Bill's Colt revolver in the 1800s, you really think he knew Latin?"

"I think it would be improbable." The project leader looked around for his drink.

"So, what *does* it mean? What made him chisel *that* into a piece of metal?" His mentor shrugged as Howard continued. "How would a guy like that even know that word? And, why inscribe it on a piece of metal?"

Another shrug from his half inebriated leader.

"And why would he chisel his name and, what I can only assume to be his birthday, on a piece of metal just to carry it around? And why—"

"Okay, that's one Jack Daniel's for you." Heather placed the drink in front of the professor and turned to Howard. "And one beer, extra cold, and one very strong, independent, totally available, shot of whiskey for you, stud." She placed his drinks down and ran her finger around the rim of the shot glass, gathering a drop of the caramel-colored liquor. Bringing her finger to her lips, she teased her lower lip, opening it slightly before sliding her finger into her mouth with eyes closed. "Mmmmm," she moaned, smiling playfully before she walked away.

The project leader, eyes transfixed and mouth wide open, followed her ass as she paraded through the crowd and disappeared.

"She *really* wants you, kid!" he exclaimed, not taking his eyes off the spot she'd just occupied.

"Professor, can we talk about this tablet? Please!"

"Howard, there is *definitely* something wrong with you." His gaze returned to the marker Howard held in his hand. "The truth is my young, naïve, foolish apprentice, I haven't got a clue." He picked up his drink and took a sip. "But, if you like, I'll have that little piece of metal assigned to you, and when you get back to that fancy museum of yours in New York City—" He'd said it like it left a bad taste in his mouth. "—You can work on it all you like. And when you solve the mystery of Joseph Kehm's sermo familiaris vocabulary, I hope you'll let me know, because I am so throughly riveted." He ended on a sarcastic note, but Howard didn't care. All that mattered was keeping a mysterious souvenir from his first ever archaeological dig.

"Really? You'd do that for me?"

"Sure, kid. Now drink your beer and relax. You're the shit in here tonight! Drink up and get yourself laid already!"

Nicole teetered at the end of the booth, her words slurring. "Did someone say they're getting laid?" Samantha stood behind her, arms at the ready.

Sam mimed like she'd been drinking too much, and then pointed to Nicole.

"Maybe we should get you back to your room," Howard suggested. He stood and put the tablet in his pocket.

A smile appeared only on the left half of Nicole's face as her eyebrows lifted even while her eyelids remained tiny slits.

"You kids have a good time!" the project leader yelled as they walked away. "Oh, and hey, thanks for the drinks, suckers!"

With Howard holding up Nicole on one side and Sam on the other, they maneuvered her through the crowd. Howard spied Heather and flashed her an *I'm sorry* expression. He nodded toward Nicole and said, "We have to get her home. She had way too much to drink."

Heather frowned, but handed Howard a slip of paper as he passed.

Nicole's head fell back. She craned her neck, trying to focus on Heather as a stream of incoherent babbling flew from her mouth. "You hear that, Missssss Biiigg Booooobs, he'shhh taaaking me 'ome."

"And you thought we weren't going to have fun tonight?" Sam joked.

Howard laughed. "There's still time. How are you at poker?"

"I thought you said nothing could get you to play poker in this town?"

Howard smiled with a little wink. "I was bluffing."

An innocent yet devilish grin creeped across Sam's face.

After a long plane ride, and what felt like an even longer hike through Kakadu National Park, the Taylor family is moments away from their destination. As Jonathan walks along the forest trail, he realizes Terry's words were a hundred percent correct. From the moment he set foot in the park, his former life started becoming more and more evident. Vegetation and trees had changed, but rock formations and canyons were as familiar to him as walking through Times Square.

"Up ahead is a gorge," Jonathan calls out, "and, beyond that, a waterfall." A moment later, all is as predicted. "And further up ahead is Namarrgon, the lightning man, who split the sky open with his ax to produce rain for the crops." Jonathan sounds like a tour guide all of a sudden, as if conducting a private excursion through the park for his family.

Several yards up the path, they encounter a group of people taking pictures and studying a strange drawing painted on the rock. Jonathan informs the small group that the drawing dates back thousands of years. Namarrgon was responsible for spectacular thunderstorms, and when he approached, it meant the coming of wet season for the Top End of the Northern Territory, a time for the Aboriginal people to harvest the Kakadu Plum.

Cassandra snaps picture after picture. Two young tribesmen approach from another path. When they see Coop, they make their way to him.

"Mister Coop, so good to see you. Is this Jonathan Taylor?"

"Jiemba, Daku!" Coop guides the family over to the two young men. "Yes. Allow me to introduce you to Jonathan Taylor and his children, Cassandra and Trevor."

They exchange greetings, and moments later the tribesmen lead them back down the trail from which they came. Observing their surroundings, Jonathan is certain he's walked these paths before. Thirty minutes later, they arrive at a clearing where tribesmen stand outside several small huts constructed of sticks and branches.

"Minjarra wishes to speak to Mister Taylor alone," Jiemba says, walking Jonathan away from the group. Daku welcomes the others into a circle around a fire, where members of the tribe sit and talk among themselves.

"Are all of you family?" Cassandra asks.

"We are kin," Daku answers as the other men smile and nod. "You see, young Miss, the Aboriginal people inhabit a universe of kin. We use the word 'kin' with the people we interact with during the course of an ordinary life."

"So you and the other gentleman who brought us here—" Trevor hesitates.

"Jiemba," Daku says pointing to the man walking away with Jonathan.

"Yes, Jiemba. You're kin?"

"Jiemba and I are of the same 'band'."

"A band? Like musicians?" Cassandra's back straightens like she thinks she's just correctly answered a question in class.

The men sitting around the fire laugh among themselves, whispering and mimic playing instruments. Cassandra slouches as her face turns red.

Daku shakes his head, "No, no, no. A 'band' consists of two or more families that regularly travel together and interact on a daily basis. Our two families have been traveling together since we were small." He looks towards the sky. "I have known Jiemba my whole life. I am as close to him as my own brothers."

Trevor cranes his neck, "And the man my father is going to see?"

"That is Minjarra. He is the eldest of the kin or estate group. He is a guardian of our sacred sites and objects. If anyone can help your father, it would be him." Daku smiles a reassuring grin.

A man half the size of Jonathan with skin wrinkled and aged by time, sits smoking a long pipe. "Please, Mister Taylor, have a seat and tell me why you have come."

Jonathan sits next to the man. "I've come looking for something."

"And you believe we have it?" A small orange glow in the well of the pipe intensifies as the old man inhales.

"Yes."

Long trails of smoke float effortlessly upward from the corner of his mouth. "What could we possibly have that you would want?"

"A stone." A familiar aroma teases Jonathan's nostrils, pulling long-forgotten memories from the far reaches of his mind.

"We have many stones." Minjarra gestures toward the ground. "Please, help yourself."

"This is a sacred stone." Jonathan studies Minjarra's eyes. "A black stone."

Minjarra's face lights up and not from the glow of his pipe. Still he asks, "And, if we have this stone, wouldn't that make it ours?"

"I believe I left it with your—" Jonathan wants to say great, great grandfather, but he doesn't know how far back nor how many 'greats' he needs to add. He settles for the simple choice of words. "Your ancestors."

"My ancestors?" Minjarra asks with curiosity. "How can this be?"

"I'm having trouble believing it myself," Jonathan starts. "Maybe this will help—"

Everyone around the fire falls quiet and listens to Jonathan's story. Jiemba and Minjarra cannot believe their ears. His children and Coop hear the words, but they are totally unfamiliar to them. The group around the fire stands and draws closer to listen to their language, spoken by a white man. Jonathan is telling his tale in Kriol. Now thought to be a dead language, Kriol was the first language spoken throughout the Northern Territory.

"I am Kilara. I have walked these paths and traveled these lands long before your father's father's father. I have traveled to the dreamland and back. I have seen many lands and many strange animals. I have trusted the elders to tell my story through the ages. I have placed my hand upon the sacred wall and I have left my mark. I am here to reclaim the black stone. I am Kilara, and I have returned."

No one moves, and no one dares to speak. Even the surrounding forest seems to take notice. The only sound comes from the occasional crackle of the logs in the fire. Trevor looks at Cassandra, who frowns her concern.

Coop stares at both of them. "Eh, did ya know ya pawp could speak their language?"

"He's been doing a *lot* of strange things lately," Cassandra answers.

"That's it. I'm calling Mom." Trevor threatens and storms away from the fire.

Minjarra stands and embraces Jonathan. "If you truly are Kilara, and I do not doubt that you are, you know you have one more task to perform."

"I am ready. Shall I lead the way?" Jonathan asks.

Minjarra motions for him to go first and follows, together with four other elders. The youngest retrieves a burning stick from the fire and carries it like a torch.

Jonathan leads them down a winding passage that brings them close to the base of a rock wall. He follows the wall north until he comes to a large patch of over grown vines. He moves the vines aside, revealing the entrance to a hidden cave. The youngest of the five men, the one who carries the torch, enters first, lighting the way. He ignites the torches scattered about the cave, illuminating the inside with flickering yellow and orange lights that dance in the shadows. Hundreds, perhaps thousands of handprints of all sizes and colors are imprinted on the walls. Centuries of generations have left their mark, a record in time, for future generations to remember and join them.

"It was you, Kilara, who created this test. Do you know what you have to do?" Minjarra asks, throwing down the proverbial gauntlet.

"I do," Jonathan answers, and he moves farther into the cave. The four elders follow.

Upon seeing the walls, Jonathan can't believe how many more impressions have joined the 'brethren of hands'. He wonders if he will remember where or even if it's still here. It may have faded with time, or perhaps the pigment dried and flaked off the stone. Or it might have been covered by another. Maybe—but just then, Jonathan stops and picks up a torch mounted on the wall. Gingerly, he makes his way along the length of the wall, a stone here, an outcrop there. Remembering, he walks closer to the wall and shines the light. He looks up—an ancient memory ignites—and he reaches out instinctively. A small handprint, silhouetted by red paint with an inward spiraling circle in the center, catches his eye. His hand slaps the stone, blocking out his old handprint, engulfing the faded, painted handprint.

The elders stand amazed. One picks up a small tube that lies in a bowl of paint. The others follow. One by one, they take turns, spraying the paint around Jonathan's hand until an entirely new silhouette forms. He removes his hand. For the first time in a millennium, it is permissible for a handprint to completely cover another. The two are almost identical. Among the elders standing witness in the cave, there is absolutely no doubt that the man known as Jonathan, and the man once known as Kilara, are one and the same.

Minjarra walks over to Jonathan and examines the handprints. He bends down, and on a small rock shelf scattered with artifacts and trinkets, he finds a small wooden box with a metal clasp. He picks up the box and undoes the latch.

"My father told me a story when I was just a boy." He opens the wooden box. "I didn't believe the story as a boy, but as I grew to manhood, I began to have more faith in the old legend." Gazing intensely into the blackness of the box, he says, "I would come in here and look upon this stone. My heart would fill with hope that one day Kilara would return."

Gently, he retrieves the small rectangular stone, disturbing its years of tranquil repose. "Others would tell me of their journeys, of visions they encountered on their trek through sacred valleys and lands once rich with our people." A shimmer of light reflects off the polished black surface now held in the palm of his frail hand. "As the years passed, I grew disappointed, and I'm ashamed to say, my faith weakened. How many centuries would pass before someone would come to claim the stone? Was yet another generation of Bininj or Mungguy to be the one to witness a miracle? Was the old legend just that? A fairytale told to children?"

Minjarra turns to look at Jonathan again, his face shining brighter than any torch within the cave. A smile cuts deep into the creases of his cheek and his eyes behold all the joy of a father on his daughter's wedding day. He holds out his hand and presents the black onyx stone to Jonathan.

"Not only have you made me so very happy, Jonathan Kilara Taylor, you have renewed our faith and our belief in our culture and our way of life. The story of how Kilara of Bininj, who left a marker with his elders hundreds of years ago, has returned to reclaim it—*your story*—will be told around campfires for generations to come, long after my children's children's children have joined me in the earth."

That night, Jonathan, Trevor, Cassandra, and Coop are granted the highest honor bestowed on any non-aborigines. They join with the Bininj and Mungguy people, eating, drinking, and dancing in celebration of Kilara's return. Coop spends most of the night drinking and laughing.

Cassandra and Trevor watch in amazement as their father, previously only known to them as a jaded if still open-minded New Yorker, dances around the fire in perfect harmony with the tribesmen. Remembering every step from long ago, Jonathan jumps, spins, and circles the flames, long into the night, as though he has been performing the sacred ritual since childhood.

As the night wears on, Jonathan recounts stories of life hundreds of years ago. He tells the tribe how their ancestors hunted for food, and how, in the wet season, when Namarrgon split the sky with his ax, they moved to areas that had the best hunting grounds. He shares stories of the tribe's legends, as told by the elders of Kilara's time. Stories like the one of Nabulwinjbulwinj, a dangerous spirit who struck females with a yam before devouring them. Throughout the evening, as news of Kilara's return spreads throughout the area, tribe members, both men and women, arrive to hug Jonathan and welcome an old friend back home. At peace with his new family, his life back in New York feels more and more like a distant dream. Part of him—the Kilara in him—is home. He has multitudes of cousins, aunts, and uncles. In this small area of land, on the smallest continent of the planet called Earth, Jonathan feels loved. Loved by every member of his newfound family.

A blanket of stars fills the heavens as the day ends. A huge reddish-yellow moon rises over the towering banks of the valley's orange walls, shining a ghostly bluish hue on the nocturnal gathering. Jonathan sits with the elders as they pass the pitch-black rock among themselves.

"And you carved this?" one of them asks. "I mean, you remember doing it?"

Jonathan nods. "As if it was yesterday." He takes Akal Datta's marker out of his pocket and places it in Minjarra's hand. "I went to India before coming here."

Minjarra looks at the stone. He turns it over, taking note of the word written on the other side, before passing it down the line of elders.

Jonathan continues, "And I had *this one* made before I left New York." He gives it to Minjarra, who examines it before passing it along.

Each elder in turn studies the tablets, paying particular attention to the strange word before handing it to the others.

"To the average person, they're just similar objects in shape and size, inscribed with different people's names. But I know you see the same thing I do."

Minjarra nods as do the other elders. "The word."

"Yes! What does it mean?" Jonathan searches their faces for a glimmer of understanding.

"It means, my son," Minjarra begins, "your soul has walked across the sands of time and has journeyed on this earth for many, many years. It probably will for many, many more." He leans forward, his face profoundly serious as a deep silence falls on the crowd. "You are the Soul Keeper. You will walk this earth until the very last soul is born, and then you will be one with all humans on this planet."

Without warning then, he reaches a bony hand out and seizes Jonathan by the arm. "But beware! If the Soul Eater finds you first, it will feed upon you, consuming your soul, and if that happens, all mankind is doomed, for after it devours your soul, no more souls will ever be born again."

Jonathan swallowed his fear and nodded, then asked Minjarra or anyone else whose eyes might be able to answer him, "What does this Soul Eater look like?"

The tribe of elders shakes and grimaces. "Oh, it's a horrible creature," Minjarra says. "Long, razor-sharp fangs, yellowish eyes that burn with the fires of hell, twisted fingers with long, pointy nails, fur running down the length of its twisted, distorted, grotesque back."

Immediately, a thought enters Jonathan's mind. *I think I married it.*

"Or it can take the shape of a beautiful woman."

"Great," Jonathan exhales. The entire counsel of elders laugh. "So there's no way to break this cycle?"

One of the elders timidly offers a solution. "It was written long ago, long before Kilara went into the cave—" He closes his eyes and recites the well-memorized passage, "And the first broke a limb of the forbidden tree and set forth upon it: the first mark. From that day and in all the days that follow, the one has kept the word. Only when the first reunites with the one may he finally be set free." He stops and opens his eyes

"But what does that mean?" Jonathan asks. "Reunite with the first. The first what?"

"Maybe if you find the very first marker, your soul will be complete, and you can move on? In a sense, reuniting *you* with your very *first* soul."

The others all nod their heads in agreement.

Quietly, Jonathan exhales. "How am I going to do that? Where do I begin looking. And how long is that going to take?"

"We have waited over 300 years for Kilara to return, but here you sit," Minjarra says. "It may take several lifetimes, or perhaps, even hundreds before you find that for which you are searching. But you will find it one day."

Jonathan's head hangs low.

For the longest time, the tribe elders sit with Jonathan in complete silence. They are happy for their son's return, but sad knowing the pain and suffering he has experienced and will continue to go through. They hope that one day, his soul will join theirs in a place of rest.

As the celebration dies down, Trevor approaches to talk with his father.

"Dad, I got in touch with Mom earlier. I asked her to look up a doctor for you." Trevor prepares for a battle. "Now I know what you're going to say—"

"Good!" his father quickly replies.

"I'm going to have to insist—wait, did you say, good?" Trevor asks, confused.

Jonathan stands and guides Trevor away from the elders, not wanting them to hear. "I think I need to see someone. A professional."

"A professional?"

"A psychologist. A therapist. Maybe a specialist."

"Dad, I don't think you're crazy!"

Jonathan laughs, "I don't think I am either, at least I hope I'm not; however, I'm pretty sure there are people who specialize in this sort of thing."

"What sort of thing?"

"Past lives, reincarnation. Regression or something? I don't know? Tell your mom I want the best and turn her loose. She loves this kind of shit. She's like—"

"Trevor smiles and stops him. "Don't say it, Dad."

"She is—you *know* she is."

"Yes, we all know how—*focused* she can be," Trevor concedes.

Jonathan smiles and breaks into laughter, hugging his son as they walk toward Cassandra and Coop. "She's like a bloodhound when it comes to finding doctors."

"You *must* be talking about Mom," Cassandra chuckles.

The stars fade in the early dawn. Long after the last of the celebrators have gone to sleep, Jonathan sits alone, with only the dwindling fire to keep him company. He stares down, intensely pondering the three small tablets resting on the orange soil—three lifetimes spanning centuries.

Trevor joins his father. "Morning, Dad, what'cha doing?"

Jonathan points to the markers. "Terry told me Kilara went into that cave over 300 years ago, sometime in the 1600s." He points to the middle tablet. "Akal Datta's tablet is dated 1876." His finger moves to his tablet. "And mine."

Trevor shrugs, missing the connection. "Have you been up all night?"

"What if, roughly every 150 years—"

"What, you return to walk the earth? Destined to search the world for what? To find tiny little markers? Like some kind of sick game, like *Where's Waldo* or trying to find a needle in a haystack on a planet of haystacks?"

Jonathan gazes at his iPhone's screen. A Google search reveals the meaning of the word inscribed on all three tablets.

"What if this thing is a curse? What if—"

"I don't buy it, Dad." An electronic ringtone breaks the quiet stillness of the morning. Trevor quickly retrieves his phone. A picture of his mother flashes on the screen. He places it against his ear. "Hi Mom."

He slowly saunters away as Cassandra and Coop join Jonathan.

"Hell of a party last noyght. Hey Johnny."

"Morning, Coop. Morning, sweetheart."

"I don't suppose there's any coffee?" Cassandra asks.

"Quoyte the headache, hay?" Coop comments. "Yeah, me too."

Trevor rejoins the group. "Well, Mom found someone for you."

The bloodhound does it again, Jonathan thinks. "Great. Coop, if you wouldn't mind getting us back to Darwin, I believe we have a plane to catch to the States."

"Yeah, we have to catch a plane, but it's not to the States." Trevor hesitates. "The therapist is in London."

"England?"

Cassandra chuckles and thinks, *If Dad was drinking, that would have been one hell of a spit take.*

Her father shoots her a look.

She responds quickly, "Well, where else would it be? London, Connecticut?"

"Actually, there's one in Ohio. London, Ohio." Jonathan fires back.

"Oh, and there's one in Arkansas," Coop offers, immediately receiving questionable looks from the Taylor family. "What? Oy have a brother who lives in Arkansas."

Minjarra strolls over. "There's also a London, Kentucky. Good morning, Jonathan-Kilara."

And now everyone looks puzzled, waiting for an explanation.

"Good morning, Minjarra." Jonathan says softly, still confused.

Minjarra looks up as the sun breaks through the clouds. "Going to be a beautiful day." He walks past Cassandra. "There's coffee in the main tent along with breakfast. I hope you'll join us before leaving." Then, as he walks to the main tent, he repeats, "London, Kentucky. In Laurel County. It is the second-largest city named London in the United States and the fourth-largest in the world."

Jonathan watches the old man stroll away. *Never judge a book by its cover* comes to mind. "Well, if your mother found him, he's gotta be the best."

"Actually Dad, he's a *she*," Trevor corrects him.

Jonathan shakes his head and bends over to pick up the tablets. "Your mother *would* do that. She knows how much I hate women doctors."

"Wait a second, Dad," Trevor says, bending down next to his father. With phone in hand, he snaps a few pictures of the tablets. "Okay, thanks." He starts typing.

"What are you doing?" Jonathan asks, watching him text furiously on the phone's keyboard.

"Sending your relics over the internet. Maybe someone on the web may know what this is all about."

"Smart boy!" offers Coop. "Let's get breakfast before we say our goodbyes."

Over breakfast, Jonathan reminds Coop to thank Terry and Matt for all their help. "They're great people."

"And good friends!" Coop adds. "They've always been there for me. 'Got my back' as you yanks would say."

"You know, Coop, I have a friend like that back in the States. He got me into rock climbing back in my college days." Jonathan slaps his belly. "I'm a bit out of shape, but back in college, I was quite a different guy."

Cassandra laughs. "Yeah, that's why Mom fell for you, Dad. Your six-pack abs."

131

"May I continue with my story?" Jonathan makes a face at his daughter. "Anyway, one day we're up in New Paltz—" He stops, noticing Coop's perplexed expression. "Upstate New York." Coop nods in recognition. "Shawangunk mountain range. They call it the Gunks for short. Some of the best climbing on the east coast—"

"Gunks, Oy like that. Sounds like someplace here in Australia."

"Is this Uncle Yuss?" Trevor asks.

"Who's not really our uncle, we just call him that," Cassandra adds.

"You know how I hate that," Jonathan barks back. *Another annoying thing their mother encouraged them to say.* "Yes, Yuss Simon, who's really not your uncle, just a college friend. Now may I please finish?"

Jonathan directs his attention to Coop. "As I was saying, I was on this rock face some 75 feet up when I felt my hands slip. Nothing but solid granite below me."

Coop focuses intensely on Jonathan's words.

"Yuss is belaying me from down below, but I don't know if he can see me. So I start yelling, *'I'm slipping!'* My arm tightens and I feel my legs go weak, so I yell again, *'I'm slipping! I think I'm going to fall!'* Still, I hear no response."

Coop leans forward.

"So as my hand begins to slip from the rock, I start yelling at the top of my lungs, *'I'M FALLING! I'M FALLING!'* My other hand desperately clutches the cliff's face; my legs press hard to the narrow ledge that's the size of a gnat's ass on which I'm balanced." It's deathly quiet; everyone in the tent hangs on Jonathan's every word. "I feel my body pull away from the rock's face … my fingers slip from the small crack … I'm off-balance and I know for certain, any second, I'm going to fall. And, if that happens—" Jonathan slaps his hands together with a loud clap. "Bam! 75 feet straight down. I'd be road kill!"

"What did ya do?" implores Coop.

"I yelled louder, *'I'M FALLING! I'M FALLING! OH GOD! I'M FALLING!'* The entire Gunks knew I was falling." Jonathan pauses, and no one in the tent breathes. "Then, I heard my friend yell back, *'Just fall already, I got you!'*

Well, my hand slipped from the rock and the rope pulled tight. I came off the wall and dangled like a pendulum, inches from the ledge where I was moments ago. My dearest friend—75 feet below me—was absolutely secure in the knowledge that no harm would come to me because he wasn't going to let me fall!"

Coop exhales a sigh of relief.

Jonathan continues, "I was terrified. I knew I was going to fall and hit the rocks below. I was convinced of it. But Yuss wasn't scared, he knew I was safe. He wasn't going to let any harm come to me. And that's my point. I tell that story to everyone who has a good friend. If you have friends like Terry and Matt, you can rest easy knowing they're always going to catch you when you fall. Those *are* good friends. And, *you* should let them know every day how much they mean to you."

Coop smiles. "As soon as Oy drop you off in Darwin, Oy'm heading back out there to tell'em. Maybe bring a steak or two."

Rande *Coop* Cooper does just that. After dropping off the Taylor family at Darwin Airport, he fuels up Laura Belle, picks up a half-dozen steaks, a cooler filled with shrimp, and a stash of Foster's. Once in the air, Coop calls his friends Terry and Matt and tells them to fire up the barbie, 'cause he's bringing them dinner together with something important to share! When asked about Jonathan, all Coop said was, "It's one hell of a story! I can't wait to tell it!"

With a quick phone call to Margaret in New York, all the arrangements were made. In 22 hours, the Taylor family would touch down in London. Just when Trevor thought they'd keep heading east till they once again returned to the United States, they were heading back west. Not to London, Ohio or London, Arkansas, or even London, Kentucky. To the original: London, England.

PLACE: VÉRINES, NÉRY, FRANCE
YEAR: 1940

In another part of the world at another time, a young
French girl, Camille Dumont, played in an upstairs nursery. Scattered
around the room were toys from years past, seldom played with but
which still held memories of innocence and wonder. Recently, most of
Camille's playtime had been preoccupied with Antoinette, an antique doll
with a porcelain face whose long locks of curly blonde hair, according to
Camille's Grand-mère, needed constant attention.

A floorboard creaked as Camille's older sister Clara entered the
nursery, her gaze intensely fixed on a small block of wood in her hand.
"Bonjour, Camille."

"Bonjour, Clara. Have you come to play with me?"

Clara, who was two years older than Camille, had just turned 16.
Their father said she would soon be able to work in his jewelry shop in
Néry. Her family lived in a small town called Vérines in the north of
France, a short walk to Néry. In the afternoon, Clara often walked with
Camille to visit their father in his shop and bring him the lunch their
mother had prepared.

"I am too old to play with dolls, Camille," Clara said, even though, unbeknownst to Camille, she still loved having tea parties with her dolls. "Besides, I have other things to attend to."

"Like carving your name into that stupid block of wood?" Camille hissed back.

A week before, Clara had asked her father for a block of wood.

"You can use some of the old scraps from my tool shed out back, but you need to be very careful when carving, Clara," her father had said.

"I need a piece of wood exactly seven-and-a-half centimeters long by five centimeters wide, Papa."

He smiled at his daughter. "So precise, my little angel. Okay, I'll go out to the shed after supper and cut you a piece of wood." Bending down, he kissed her forehead. "Precisely to your measurements."

"Thank you, Papa!" For the next week, Clara was completely consumed with the small block of wood. Every minute of every waking hour, she was sanding, carving, then sanding some more, until she finally finished. That was the day Camille asked her to play.

"All finished!" she announced to Camille. "Would you like to see it?" She presented it to her sister with an outstretched arm.

Camille placed Antoinette's hairbrush next to the well-groomed doll, then took the block of wood from her sister.

Clara Marie Dumont
March 29th, 1924

She examined it, running her small fingers in the depressed letters that formed the words. "Smooth as glass." She turned it over and tried to read the word, stopping halfway through her pronunciation.

"A-E-T-E-R ... what is this word?" Camille asked. "This isn't French!" How do you expect anyone to read that?"

Clara shrugged.

"Do you even know what this means?" Camille asked, sounding more like Clara's mother than her younger sister.

Clara stared blankly back at her sister.

Camille thrust the wood back into Clara's hand, disgusted with her sister. "Don't let Papa see that … *that* piece of English wood!"

She picked up Antoinette's brush and turned away. "Is that what you've been working on for an entire week?" Not waiting for an answer, "Waste of time if you ask me."

Clara turned and stormed out of the nursery. "No one asked you!" she shouted.

Running up the stairs and into their bedroom, Clara slammed the door and threw herself on the bed, crying, clutching the small wooden block close to her chest.

Downstairs in the kitchen, the children's parents were discussing matters of a much more pressing nature. A bold headline on a newspaper thrown on the table read:

GERMANS INVADE FRANCE!

"Jacqueline, we must prepare to leave. They could be here any day!"

"You don't think they will come here?" she asked, looking around the kitchen. "We have nothing!" She waved her arms around the room. "Nothing they would want!"

"The whole town is talking. They could be here in a day or two!" Holding his wife, he spoke sternly, trying to convey the severity and urgency of the situation, but then his voice turned soft so as not to upset her. "Maybe sooner!"

"Surely, the Americans will stop them?" Jacqueline looked at her husband for an answer, but he just turned away. "Charles, please tell me the Americans will do something?!"

The thoughts of a worried husband manifested in a quick pace around the small kitchen. "They talk and talk, that's all they do is talk and make treaties, while our countrymen are dying and people are being marched off to God knows where." His face grew distant and still. "They are even saying there are camps where people are being led into—"

Upstairs, a door slammed so hard it shook the house, stopping Charles from describing the horrors of a madman named Adolf Hitler.

He looked up at the ceiling. "Sounds like Camille made Clara angry again."

Jacqueline started for the stairs, but Charles stopped her. "I'll go. Clara wanted to show me what she's been making." He paused to share a kiss on his wife's cheek, "It will be okay. As long as we are together, we will be okay." As he left the kitchen he added, "We'll stay with my sister Marguerite in Orleans."

Jacqueline shook her head. "I'd rather have Germans over for Sauerbraten."

"I heard that!" Charles called as he made his way up the stairs.

"Knock, knock," Clara's father announced, gently tapping on the door and opening it slightly. "May I come in?"

Clara, eyes red and watery, nose running, sat up in bed.

"Oh, my little cacahuète, why so sad?"

"Camille is so mean!"

"What did she do this time?" Her father waited and listened, having heard countless stories so many times before.

"She's so stupid. I showed her what I've been working on. I finally finished it and she took one look and said it was a waste of my time."

"May I see it?" her father asked.

"No, Camille said you'd be mad at me." She moved the small object behind her back.

"Please? I promise I won't be angry. I'm just glad you still have ten fingers," he added with a smile.

Slowly, Clara revealed the week-long project.

Her father took the object and turned it around in his hand once, then twice. He tossed it into the air several times. "Not bad. Not bad at all!"

"Do you really like it?"

"I do! I do. It shows real craftsmanship." He smiled, but then his expression turned to bewilderment. "Um, what exactly is it? Why did you carve your name and birthday on it?"

"I don't know," Clara responded. "I don't know why I did that. I woke up one morning and something told me this is what I had to do."

With the nimble fingers of a jeweler, Clara's father turned the block of wood over in the palm of his hand. His face scrunched, his gaze focused as he ran his thumb over the letters on the reverse side. "And these letters? Is this English? Are you learning English in school?"

"No, I don't know why I had to add those letters, Papa. I don't even know what they mean."

Charles looked at the strange foreign word. "Well, whatever it is, you carved it beautifully. You should be very proud." Then with a kiss on Clara's forehead, he handed it back to her.

"I wanted to talk to you. You're the oldest and I think you should know. Your mother and I have been discussing it; we may have to go and stay with your Aunt Marguerite for a while."

"Because of the Germans?"

"How do you know about the Germans?"

"Papa, everyone in the village has been talking about them. It's everywhere. Did you think I was so preoccupied I didn't hear what the people were saying?"

He wrapped his arms around her and held his daughter tight. "I don't want you to be frightened. We'll leave tomorrow and this whole nasty business will soon be over."

"It's okay, Papa, I feel like I've been through war before."

He thought nothing of this last comment, attributing it to the constant battles she had to endure from her younger sister. He rose and said, "I'm going to talk to your sister now."

"Are you going to beat her?" Clara asked, jokingly with a smile, knowing full well their father had never raised a hand to either of them. His way had always been a subtle yet firm, and often lengthy conversation.

He walked to the doorway and shouted down the hallway. "Oh yes, I'm going to take her out to the stables and beat her with a horsewhip for making you cry!" He turned to Clara and winked, happy to see the big grin on her face.

As her father stomped extra hard on the wooden floorboards above the nursery, he bellowed down the stairs, "Camille Paulette Dumont, I would like a word with you!"

Clara smiled, studying the small piece of wood. *How is it that Papa always makes everything better with just a few words and a smile?*

The sadness and anger she felt just moments earlier were replaced with happiness and pride. But as she looked out the window, those feelings were suddenly torn from her. Advancing down the road, a battalion of German soldiers marched toward the village.

"PAPA!" she screamed, running down the hall. "PAPA! Germans! Germans are outside!"

She met her father coming up the staircase. Pointing at her bedroom, she screamed, "Germans! Coming here!"

Charles grabbed his daughter by the arm and rushed her into his bedroom. Looking out the window, he assessed how much time they had. *Not much,* he realized.

Pulling out dresser drawers, he quickly removed handfuls of jewelry and a small black pouch, one used to carry diamonds. He emptied the jewelry into the pouch, and then tucked it into a tiny wooden crate-like box on the bed.

"Clara, you must do something for me." Wrapping the little wooden box in a cloth, "I need you to hide this in your room."

"Papa, I'm so frightened!" she cried.

"I know, Clara, we all are, but you need to listen to me and listen carefully! Under your dresser in the corner of your room, there is a loose floorboard. Hide the box in there."

"Under—?"

"Under the floorboard!" he roared.

For the first time in her life, her father raised his voice to her. Clara's heart beat rapidly as though it would burst from her chest, not from her father's lashing out, but from the monsters approaching their doorway.

"I'll go downstairs and distract them," her father instructed, holding her arms with his hands.

"Charles!" his wife screamed.

"Hide this!" He handed Clara the cloth-wrapped box. "Then I want you to take your sister and run as fast as you can to Mr. Boutiette's farm." He hurried her to the door. "I'm coming!" he reassured his wife. "Clara, do you understand what you have to do?"

"Yes, Papa!"

"Good," he said, kissing her. "I love you, my angel." Hugging her for the last time—a wooden box between them—he added, "Watch over your sister, and if anything happens, run Clara. Run as fast as you can into the fields!"

"I will, Papa!" Tears welled up in her eyes.

He wiped her tears with his lips as he kissed her face. "Go!" And she ran to her bedroom. 'Go', unbeknownst to her, would be the last word her father ever spoke to her. She moved the dresser and heard the loud pounding on their front door. Clara searched the floorboards; one moved. Her fingers tore at the unfastened board, prying it loose. Loud German voices filled her house and she shook uncontrollably but managed to place the wooden crate in its sanctuary. Her father's small voice was beaten down by the aggressive tone of the German commander. Clara fumbled with the floorboards, working frantically until the loose board slipped back into place. Forceful militaristic German words overpowered the sound of her mother crying. Replacing the heavy dresser, Clara raced to the end of the hall as fast as her feet could carry her. Working her way down the stairs and into the nursery, she found her sister crouched in the corner, her knees pulled tight to her chest, clutching Antoinette and rocking. Tears streamed down her cheeks.

"Camille, we have to go!" Clara yelled.

"No! Papa said to stay here," she shouted back.

Remembering how her father's voice grew soft and low whenever he wanted to make a point, Clara used her most delicate voice to persuade her sister. "Camille, we have to go. Papa asked me to take you to Mr. Boutiette's farm, but we have to leave now." Whispering she added, "We have to be very, very quiet."

Clara released the clasp of her necklace—a gold chain with two intertwined hearts, given to her by her father on her 16th birthday—and removed it from her neck. She placed it around Camille's neck and closed the clasp. "This will keep you safe. It is our two hearts entwined forever. Nothing can change that."

Camille looked at her sister and saw the sincerity in her eyes. Slowly she rose. A small puddle where Camille sat had already begun seeping into the wooden floorboards. Clara was too frightened to notice the pungent odor. She took her sister by the hand and led her to the back staircase. They heard men yelling and their father pleading. As quietly as possible, trying not to make a sound, they made their way down the staircase. One of the floorboards creaked. They both stopped, as did the yelling.

Clara's breathing was shallow and rapid. She gripped her sister's hand tightly and heard the crass voice, once again shouting something in German, before he continued to interrogate their parents. They took another step, then another; soon they reached the bottom landing. Clara could see the back door through the kitchen.

Clara's gaze fixed intensely on her sister's eyes. "We're going to run as fast as we can to the door and then outside."

Her sister nodded in agreement.

She held up her hand and raised her fingers, one ... two ... and as she raised her third finger, they began to run. They took three giant strides. Out of the corner of her eye, she caught the gray-green uniform of a

German soldier. He stepped in front of her path, cutting off their escape. Clara collided with a wall of muscle. Her forehead hit the rifle strapped across his chest. Her sister crashed against her, pushing Clara even harder against the soldier.

Grabbing the girls like they were two sacks of discarded trash, he walked them into the living room and threw them at their mother's feet. Jacqueline dropped to the floor and hugged her children, trying to shelter them from the circle of invaders.

"I ask you one more, and then I shoot your children," the German spoke, butchering the French language.

Clara stared at her father. Her mother's grip tightened. Her father's face was bruised and bleeding, one eye swollen shut. His left arm hung limp.

"I don't know what you want—" Charles began.

Clara heard a deafening crack of thunder, and her father fell to the floor. A thick, red liquid spilled from his head, pooling on the carpet. His eyes stared motionless ahead.

Jacqueline screamed, leaving her children to blanket her husband's lifeless body. Clara remembered her father's words. *'Run Clara, run!'* She got to her feet, and focusing on the door, pushed the murderous soldier aside and ran. Her mother screamed for her to stop, but she had already thrown open the door and was outside. She saw German soldiers littering the streets. She saw Mr. Boutiette, standing outside his house with hands raised. She saw the blue skies and white clouds covering France. She saw the fields of her country shrouded in green grass. And then she saw nothing, ever again.

Place: London, England
Year: Present Day

The Taylor family arrives at Heathrow Airport on Saturday, a little over a week since they'd left New York. *The weather is so different in this part of the world,* Jonathan reflects. They take the Heathrow Express, and in 36 minutes, arrive at Paddington Station. Margaret had made reservations for them at the Mercure London Hyde Park Hotel, a short five-minute walk from the station. They make their way up Praed Street, where Cassandra is surprised to see a Burger King on the corner. As they turn right on London Street, however, she is taken aback by the three-story white and tan facades of the brick buildings lining the street. She always pictured a typical London street looking this way. Spending most of her time in the East Village in Manhattan, this street reminds her of home with its coffee houses, pubs, and restaurants. The Dickens Tavern, with its Irish green and gold trim exterior, catches Trevor's attention first and foremost. Stenciled in white on the window, it boasts 'Famous Fish & Chips since 1860.' Since he never had authentic fish and chips, what better place to indulge than a pub named after his favorite English author.

143

"You want to get something to eat?" Trevor asks.

"Sure," Jonathan responds. "Why don't we check into the hotel first though; it's right around the next corner. Then I'll treat you to the best dinner in London."

"I'm in!" Cassandra quickly agrees.

"I can definitely go for some fish and chips," Trevor announces, cleverly dropping a hint as he cranes his neck in the direction of the tavern.

Cassandra looks across the street. The Sawyers Arms, a pub with a deep green, almost black facade has wooden park benches out front placed on an artificial green carpet. Further down, on the same side of the street, Cassandra spies The Sussex Arms.

"What's with all these *Arms* places?" she asks. "Are they like a suit of armor?"

Her father chuckles. "No, in this case, the word 'arms' means a *hall* or *court,* as in a place to eat." Wrapping his arm around her shoulders, he gives his daughter an affectionate one-armed hug. "Loosely translated, it means, 'come in, sit down, and we'll feed you'." Jonathan smiles. "Only in England."

They turn right onto Sussex Gardens. "Dad, Mom made your appointment for 9 a.m. tomorrow," Trevor reminds him.

"Your mother," he begins, directing them right onto Talbot Square. "She certainly is good at finding doctors, I'll give her that." *Lawyers too,* he thinks.

A small park with green grass lined with tall trees occupies the left side of the street. A row of beautiful flowers stand at attention behind a black wrought iron fence. Along the right side, a row of off-white five-story buildings stand side by side, forming one long massive structure. Outside each doorway, two columns support a small balcony with ornate railings. Halfway down the block, hedges adorn the tops of four of the balconies with two small shrubs flanking each side. Just below those balconies, fastened away from the building, steel lettering declares they've found the Hotel Mercure.

"Here we are. Let's check in and then get something to eat."

The following morning, the family enjoys breakfast at Mimos Cafe—a small local establishment reputed to have the best English breakfast in all of Paddington.

"Three orders of bangers and mash," Jonathan cheerfully requests of the gentleman behind the wood countertop.

"Um, I'll just have a croissant," Cassandra says. "And I'd like to try an Espresso Doppio. Please," she adds in a girlish kind of way. Jonathan has come to interpret this as, '*Thank you, Daddy, for treating*'.

"And I'll just have a coffee and some toast, please," interjects Trevor. "I'm not very hungry this morning."

The previous evening, counter to Trevor's earlier wishes, they had dined at The Victoria, which the hotel concierge had referred as "a lavish Victorian boozer". This had immediately appealed to Cassandra and Trevor, who both indulged in one too many orders of fish and chips.

With a roll of his eyes, Jonathan says, "I wonder why? How many fish and chips did you end up eating last night?"

"Way too many, but oh, they were so good," Trevor replies. "I'll never eat at an Arthur Treacher's again!" The others laugh, knowing exactly what he means. Once you've had the real deal—.

As the server places their order before them, Trevor and Cassandra observe their Dad's delighted expression. Jonathan's meal, in comparison to their cups of coffee and bread selections, is a bona fide banquet. His gaze travels to the plate, where two sunny-side-up eggs, two fat sausage links the size of hotdogs, three slices of ham that resemble pork chops, two pieces of toast plus another two buried under the eggs, a ladle full of sautéd mushrooms, a sea of baked beans, and a half grilled tomato stare up at him.

"Unbelievable, Dad," Cassandra protests as though he himself created the concoction.

"What? It's delicious!" Jonathan's says, before devouring his breakfast.

"But a tomato? Really?" Cassandra pokes it with her knife. "I'll never understand English cooking."

"The tomato?" Trevor asks. "You're objecting to the tomato? What about the baked beans or the mushrooms?" You don't have a problem with those?" They giggled quietly so as not to offend the owner.

By 8:45 a.m., all three sit in the waiting room of Elizabeth Davidson, Psy.D. Jonathan confides to Trevor that her impeccable credentials, specializing in past lives and reincarnation, are the only reason he agreed to the appointment. Apparently, Trevor's mother—Jonathan's ex-wife—discovered the foremost world-renowned therapist in past-life regression hypnotherapy lived and worked in London. Apprised of the circumstances surrounding Jonathan's *episodes*, and fascinated by the details, Dr. Davidson agreed to see him before his return to the States.

Her office door opens, and Dr. Davidson steps into the waiting room. Extending her hand to him, she says, "Good morning, Mr. Taylor. May I call you Jonathan? I'm Dr. Davidson, but you may call me Elizabeth."

Jonathan stands and shakes her hand. "Jonathan's fine. Is it alright if my children join us?"

"Of course," Dr. Davidson replies, turning to shake Trevor's hand. "You must be Trevor. Your mother spoke of you on the phone." Extending her hand, she turns to Cassandra next. "And you are?"

"This is my daughter, Cassandra," Jonathan says.

"Apparently, Mom didn't talk about *me* on the phone," Cassandra says rhetorically, her tone more hurt than annoyed.

"The conversation concentrated primarily on your father, but we can focus on that in another session if you'd like?" Dr. Davidson gives Cassandra a kind, reassuring smile to convey there is no malice in her response. "Please, all. Come in."

Jonathan takes a seat facing the doctor, and the children sit on the couch.

"So, Jonathan, what brings you here today?"

My ex-wife, he thinks. "Well, my son thought I should see someone," he starts. "No, that's not fair," he corrects. "Sorry, I shouldn't put that on him. *I* wanted to see someone."

"That's good," Dr. Davidson says. "That's a good start. Accepting responsibility. Excellent. Now, why do you think you need to see someone?" She picks up a legal pad, prepared to take notes.

"I … I'm remembering things. Things I should not be able to remember."

"Things such as where you put your car keys?"

"No. More like, where someone might have put their car keys 200 years ago, if car keys were around 200 years ago."

"I see, and do you hear voices?" Dr. Davidson asks.

"No. I don't hear voices. I'm not crazy, Doc."

"No one thinks you're crazy." She smiles at his children. "We don't like to use the term crazy these days," she says with a wink, before turning her attention back to Jonathan.

"Well, maybe I am? I have these visions, more like memories of someone else's life, but they're mine, if that makes sense?"

"Perfect sense to me. Please go on," she urges.

"Doc, I know everything they knew or did or said, or even felt!"

"Please call me Elizabeth or Beth if you prefer." She places her hand on his knee. "I believe you. When you're these people, are you still in control of your body? Or does this other person or personality take over?"

"It's not as if they take over. I'm aware of what I'm doing. I'm just doing it as another person. Do you think you can help me?"

"That's why you're here, and I'm here to make sense of everything you're going through. Now, tell me, do these other people want to do you harm?"

"No." Jonathan shakes his head, suddenly worried with her line of questioning, but Trevor lets out an involuntary "Ha!" which captures Dr. Davidson's attention.

She turns to face Trevor. "I'm sorry, do you want to add something?"

"My dad almost drowned."

"Were you swimming when another personality took over?" Dr. Davidson asks, looking at Jonathan.

Before his father can speak, Trevor answers for him. "He was 30,000 feet in the air! In an airplane!"

"So, you were drinking, and you choked?" Dr. Davidson poses to Jonathan, attempting to find a reasonable answer.

"Nope," Trevor continued, still answering for his father. "We were in the middle of a conversation when all of a sudden, Dad began gasping for air like a fish out of water. He even spit out seawater, and I'm putting it lightly. He coughed up volumes of salt water out of nowhere as though it was coming right from his lungs." Then Trevor adds, standing to face his father, "Tell her what happened in India, Dad. That's the main reason I wanted him to come here."

"What happened in India?" Dr. Davidson inquires, documenting all the details quickly on her notepad.

Jonathan makes an attempt to recount the story, but Trevor interrupts him again as he paces around the office. "I'll tell you what happened. He was hit by a train."

Dr. Davidson stops writing. Quite alarmed, she exclaims, "Oh my God, are you alright?"

"Oh, he's fine. Because there was no train!"

Dr. Davidson looks confused. "No train? I don't understand?"

"Dad was walking around, speaking to people in the town in whatever strange language they were speaking." Trevor waves his arms in the air making hand gestures. "He told us where he grew up, where he worked, what he was doing, and then he stopped right there on the train tracks. Mind you, no trains have run through that village in years, and when I say years, Dr. Davidson, I'm not talking 4 or 5 years ago. I'm talking 15, maybe 20 years. All of a sudden—" Trevor pauses, thinking it out. "How do I put this? Something that wasn't there struck my dad, causing his body to go flying through the air, and it wasn't as if he jumped backwards or threw himself down. He was *hit* and *pushed* through the air, then he tumbled down the embankment and flopped, lifeless, on the ground."

Frantically, Dr. Davidson jots down Trevor's words as fast as she can write. She looks at Jonathan when she asks, "Is this all *true*?"

"I'm afraid so," Jonathan answers, looking down like a dog who's just been scolded for wetting the carpet.

Dr. Davidson turns to Cassandra then. "And you witnessed these events as well?"

Cassandra nods. "Yeah, I thought he was dead when I saw him laying there."

Elizabeth blinks a few times very quickly, turns back to Trevor, then glances at her notes. "A moment ago, you said he was speaking in *'whatever language they were speaking'*. Your father was speaking *their* language?" She looks up from her notes. "He wasn't speaking English?"

Trevor shakes his head.

"He spoke in a different language?"

"Several," Trevor answers.

"He spoke to them in several languages?" she asks.

"No. Dad has spoken several languages since we left Manhattan," Cassandra jumps in, almost annoyed at her brother's lack of proper explanation.

Dr. Davidson turns her attention to Cassandra. "And he was fluent in these languages?"

Cassandra nods. "He spoke as if he was born in India."

"Fascinating." She jots down more notes. "Is your father fluent in other languages? French perhaps?" Dr. Davidson asks.

She shakes her head. "I don't think so. But I didn't think he knew Urdu either."

The doctor writes the word 'Urdu' down and then asks, "How about Spanish?"

"How about an Aborigine language no one born in Brooklyn would know," Trevor adds.

She looks at Jonathan. "You were speaking an Aboriginal language in India?"

"No, I didn't even know Kriol when I was in India. That was a different past life."

"What do you mean, 'different past life'? How many lives do you think you had?"

Trevor again answers for him. "Well, so far we know he was a mother in India and a black man in Australia. If you count what happened to him on the plane too, when he almost drowned, I would say three lives so far, not including this one."

Dr. Elizabeth Davidson leans back, staring at the wall. "Interesting!"

"Interesting?" Trevor repeats.

"Usually, patients come to me because they have a glimpse of *a* past life." She holds up a finger. "A *single* past life. A person rarely has two past-life experiences, let alone multiple past lives. That's highly unusual."

"Dr. Davidson," Trevor interrupts, suddenly with grave concern in his voice. "I'm afraid one of these past lives is going to kill my father."

Dr. Davidson turns to look at Trevor, now standing by the window. "Oh, that's not how it works. He's simply re-enacting the moments of his death, or in this case, his past lives' deaths."

"There's nothing simple about this," Trevor states emphatically. "What if there are more people in there? What if one of those people committed suicide by jumping off a building? Who's to say that one day Dad won't decide to take a swan dive out the window of his 67th-floor office?!" He nods at the window for effect.

"I see how that could be a concern," Dr. Davidson nods slowly in deep thought, then walks over to Trevor and casually closes the curtains. "Okay. Let's try something." Addressing Jonathan again, she says, "If you don't mind, I'd like to try hypnotherapy."

"You're not going to turn me into a chicken, are you?" Jonathan asks with a grin. He'd wondered if she might say this and had prepared the joke just in case.

She returns his smiles. "You have to trust me here, Jonathan." Then looking at the kids, she adds, "I only did that once. At a party in college. It was pretty funny, but the clucking got annoying after a while."

In another part of the world at another time, five
wooden longships traveled across the North Sea from what would later
be known as Scandinavia; their destination was Britannia. The year was
794. Bjørn Gudmund stood on the bow of one of the warring vessels.
The cold North Sea spat icy water in his face, but he was no stranger to
harsh weather. As a boy, he grew up on the rocky shores of what would
later be called Norway. The rough country and cold winters forged Bjørn,
molding him into the giant man he became. Easily one of the strongest
men in his village, he would become chief one day. His people called him
Stor Rød Bjørn, the *Big Red Bear,* because of his size, his long red hair,
and his over-grown scarlet beard.

As for his people, they were known as Norsk men or Norsemen,
meaning *from the North.* History would later rename them Vikings. For
some, it was a term to describe any seafaring pirate, however the name
'Viking' originally meant king of Viks. In Old Norse terminology, Viks
means creeks or rivers. And that's why they became known as the river
kings or Vik-Kings.

This was not the first time Bjørn had made this journey. Five years earlier, he was part of a raiding party that landed on a small island located off the northeastern coast of England. There they ransacked and killed everyone in a lonely monastery at Lindisfarne.

As he looked out on the stormy gray skies, with the sea cascading water over the sides of the boat, his mind wandered back to his village, a great fear in his heart. He wasn't afraid of the voyage or the threatening conditions, nor his ability to navigate. He was frightened for his pregnant wife he'd left behind. Five years earlier, she was by his side, fighting just as fiercely as he did. Now with their first child on the way, his mind was consumed with thoughts of his family, and fear that he might not ever return home to welcome his newborn infant into the world.

Three days prior to his departure, while lying in his bed under the warmth of animal skins, Bjørn confessed to his wife that he had an uneasy feeling, a premonition of his approaching death.

"Are these like the stories you have made up about your life as other people?" Revna jokingly asked. But then she saw the seriousness in his eyes.

"They are not stories, woman," Bjørn said sternly. "I have seen my life. I have seen who I was in another part of the world, in another land. I know not where they are, but I have known I have lived *there* in *that* world."

"Oh, and you have another wife there too, I suppose?" she asked, folding her arms across her chest. "And you are fathering a child *here* and living with another woman *there!*" She began to get out of bed, but he pulled her naked body back to him. "I suppose you are a father to *her* children as well?"

"It is not like that Revna, I told you. My life there ended, and now I am here, but I *was* there. It is not a dream. I saw it. I felt it. I knew things when I awoke," he tried to explain. "How do you explain how I can speak different languages?"

"What? *That* dribble you make up? How do I know if it is even a language?"

"Because I know it is! Just like I know—" He stopped.

"Know what?" she asked, searching his face for the answer. "Know what? That you are going to die?"

He hung his head low, his thick, red beard blanketing his chest.

"My big bear of a man," she whispered, touching him tenderly. "You are the strongest, bravest, most skilled warrior in the whole village, in all of the great Norse clan. Not since Beowulf has there been a stronger man."

"Then why do I feel like my time here is coming to an end?" He looked deep into his wife's blue eyes, hoping she had an answer.

"These are normal feelings every man experiences when he is going to be a new father. You are suddenly aware of the passing of time. You have taken your father's place, moving from husband to father. You have seen your father grow old and perish, therefore you feel it will soon be your time to join your father in the halls of Valhalla."

"It is not that, Revna. I do not feel that my life will end because I will be a father. I feel that my life will end and I will not be a father, or a husband, or a chieftain, or even remembered for that matter!" His huge arms engulfed his wife tightly, her body made diminutive within his embrace. "Revna, I am going to die. And I am afraid I will not be here to raise our son."

She hugged her man, trying to comfort him against his impending future. Comfort, unfortunately, did not come. Finally, she joked, "Who said it is going to be a boy?"

Reaching down, his immense hand cradled her belly. He lowered his head to her stomach, tenderly bringing his lips below her breasts. "I will always be watching over you, little one," he whispered. "No matter who you are," he added, laughing with his wife.

She smiled and pushed her man down on the bed as she straddled him. "Now let us see if I can take away some of your worries."

"What about the baby?" he asked anxiously.

She laughed and teased her husband. "You are not *that* Stor!"

23

Dr. Elizabeth Davidson points to the couch. "I know it sounds cliché, but please, lie down."

She directs Cassandra to Jonathan's vacant chair. "You can sit there." Then she pulls her chair from behind her desk and moves it over to the couch. "Now, Jonathan, this will only work if you are completely open to it." She turns her head to the others, "And I'm going to require complete and total silence from both of you." She raises an eyebrow and looks at Trevor especially.

He makes an *okay* sign with his index finger and thumb, then crosses his lips like he's sealing them with a zipper.

"Okay, Jonathan. I want you to close your eyes and surrender yourself completely. Listen to the sound of my voice and focus all your attention on your breathing."

Surrender yourself completely. He hears the words and thinks, *I did that once and it cost me a fortune!* Nevertheless, he does as he is told.

"Just breathe in and out normally. When you breathe out, I want you to let go of all the stress you're feeling and release any negative thoughts you have. And when you breathe in, Jonathan, I want you to think positive thoughts and keep an open mind."

The kids can actually see their father becoming more and more relaxed.

"Now, Jonathan, you're going to enter a dream-like state. With every new breath, you're going to go deeper and deeper and become more and more relaxed. Your body will grow tired and your mind will be temporarily unaware of your surroundings. Are you ready?"

"Yes. Just don't turn me into a chicken, Doc."

She smiles. "Let's begin. I'm going to count down from ten. When I do, you will relax more and more. Ready?"

"Yes." Jonathan's breathing starts to slow.

"Okay, ten. Just breathe. Nine, your mind is at rest. Eight, your arms and legs feel completely weightless. Seven, your cares are melting away. Six … five … you're almost there. Four … three … you're now completely relaxed. Two … one."

Jonathan lies motionless on the couch.

"Jonathan, can you hear my voice?"

He nods his head.

"Good. I want you to focus on my voice. Let it guide you. You will feel no pain. Nothing can harm you, and you'll never be in any danger. Do you understand?"

Once again, Jonathan nods his head.

"You are only an observer in this world. Your sole job is to apprise me of what you see. Is that clear?" she instructs him.

Again, he nods in the affirmative.

"Good. I want you to go back … back to a time in your life when you were the happiest … go back and tell me, what do you see?"

He takes a deep breath and smiles. "My daughter is being born. I'm in the hospital … the doctors and nurses are all around my wife."

"What day is it, Jonathan?"

"It's Sunday."

"What's the date, Jonathan?"

"It's December 14th, 1997."

Cassandra smiles and her eyes fill with tears.

"I want you to go further back. Back to another time when you were happy," she instructs. "Where are you now, Jonathan?"

"I'm watching my son being born. I have a son!" he says, and they watch as fresh tears roll down his cheeks.

"And what is this day?"

"It's Wednesday."

"And the date?"

"May 17th, 1995." Trevor and Cassandra exchange a smile.

"Okay, Jonathan. Listen to me. I want you to go back further ... I want you to play back the events in your life as though you're observing the highlights ... kind of like a movie of your life. I want you to tell us what you see as it plays backward. Do you understand?"

"Yes," he agrees, and recalls moments from his life. "I'm getting married. It's my wedding day. I'm so happy. She looks so beautiful. I'm on my first date with her, so nervous. I'm graduating from college. I'm presenting my final project, redesigning four city blocks. My professors are impressed. Drinking at McManus Pub. I hope she likes me. Wendy, beautiful long red hair."

"Mom doesn't have red hair," Trevor whispers to Cassandra.

Dr. Davidson looks at Trevor sharply and holds her index finger to her lips. Embarrassed, Trevor's head sinks into his shoulders.

Jonathan continues, "It's my first day in the dorms. My parents are taking me to Manhattan ... to college. It's a week before I leave for college, I'm at Lake George with my family. I'm in high school. I hate school. I'd prefer to hang out with my friends, especially my best friend, Mike. We ride bikes everywhere. I am going to middle school. All the girls think I'm ugly. I'm going to see Star Wars. We're walking to elementary school. The teachers are so tall. I hate homework. I just want to hang out with friends and draw buildings. We play stoop ball; sleep out in the backyard. Going to the first day of school ... playing on the see-saw, I split my chin. My mother takes me to the hospital. I need eight stitches. I'm in my room, holding my soft Jets football player doll. My older brother got a Giant's football player. He had to go to the hospital. Someone threw a rock and hit him in the eye. My parents are so worried. My dad carries me into the house from the car; I fell asleep … I'm sitting in the back of my dad's Chevy; my grandmother is there. She looks so young. I'm looking up at a hospital window. My mother is waving at us. My younger brother is born."

At this moment, Dr. Davidson stops him. "Jonathan, can you hear my voice?"

He nods.

"What day is it? The day your younger brother is born?"

"It's a Saturday … May 20th, 1967."

"And what day are you born?"

"It's also a Saturday … February 29th, 1964."

"Do you remember that day?" she asks.

He nods his head, "It's cold."

"What are you doing?"

"I'm crying as I lay on my mother's chest. The doctors just handed me to her."

"Listen to me, Jonathan; I want you to go back further …"

Cassandra quietly slaps a hand over her mouth in shock. She looks at her brother who returns her gaze with an expression even more surprised than hers.

Dr. Davidson continues, softly and slowly. "You're going to go back a little further. Tell me what you see."

"My hips are stuck. The doctor is supporting my back. My shoulders are moving in, my head, there's a light … it's warm and I'm at peace."

Suddenly, Jonathan sits up screaming. His arms flail, slapping every part of his body.

"ARRRRRRRR!" He gasps for breath. "FIRE! Fire everywhere! I can't breathe … Skin tightening. My hands burning, melting, clothes on fire!!!" He shouts uncontrollably.

"Jonathan, LISTEN TO MY VOICE," Dr. Davidson screams above his cries. "Listen to my voice and only my voice!"

Cassandra grabs her brother's arm. Just as Trevor is about to demand the doctor stop, Jonathan falls back on the couch.

"Jonathan! Jonathan, can you hear me?" Elizabeth repeats over and over until he finally nods his head.

"Jonathan, remember, nothing can hurt you. You feel no pain."

But Jonathan did feel pain—the pain of a burning man.

"Jonathan, where are you?" She turns to Trevor and snaps her fingers softly for his attention. She points at her desk to the notepad, making a gesture as though she's writing.

Trevor quickly retrieves the pen and pad from her desk and gives them to her.

"I'm in a school," Jonathan answers. His voice is deeper all of a sudden, with a distinctly Scottish brogue.

She scribbles the words *school* and *fire,* then asks, "What are you doing in a school?"

"There be children in there." His accent becomes thicker. "The building is on fire. I've run in to rescue them," he says. "I got two of the wee lads out and have gone in for a third."

Elizabeth writes down '*Scotland, kids saved, one dead?*'. "Jonathan, we can't understand your accent. From here on, you're only going to speak as Jonathan Taylor. Is that understood?"

Jonathan nods.

"Jonathan, you are no longer in the building. There is no fire. You are safe, and the children are safe, do you understand?"

Again Jonathan nods.

"Can you tell us your name?" Elizabeth asks.

"Daniel. Daniel MacNaughton."

She writes the name on the top of the sheet and circles it several times. "How old are you, Daniel?"

"Twenty-three."

"You're so young. Can you tell us what day it is?"

"It's February ... the 29th day in the year of our Lord, 1964."

She stops for a moment and writes in capital letters:

'INSTANTANEOUSLY!!!' The kids are now both covering their mouths in shock. She looks at them and then back at her patient. "Jonathan, where are you, what town are you in?"

"Oldshoremore. In the highlands of Scotland."

"Jonathan," she begins, but corrects herself. "Daniel, I want you to go back to a happier time. A time before the school and the fire, and tell me what you see."

"My bonny Moira." He smiles. "She's beautiful, hair like fire and eyes as green as emeralds."

She writes the name on the pad next to his. "And she's your girlfriend?"

In a stern highlander voice, he answers, "She's me wife!"

Both Trevor and Cassandra turn to each other and mouth *'wife'*.

"Tell us about your life, Daniel?"

"I love my life … I love my town. I was born here, met Moira at the beach when we were wee little things. I knew I was going to marry her one day. She took my heart the very first day, and she'll have it long after I die." And with that, his face changes.

"What's wrong, Daniel. What is it?"

"The day I die." He repeats. "I'm going to die! I know it."

"How do you know it, Daniel?" Elizabeth makes some notes.

"I don't know. I have to … I have to …" He stops. His mind searches for something. "I have to leave my mark and find the rest of them."

"The rest of what? What do you mean by *them?*" She writes down, *mark* and *them*.

"The rest of them. My markers … every time … I have to leave one and find the others."

Elizabeth crosses out the word *them* and changes *mark* to *markers,* not understanding exactly what Jonathan means. "And have you found *them?*" she asks.

"Yes. Well, not all of them. I'm not sure if I'll ever find *all* of them." Ever so slightly, his face droops.

Cassandra and Trevor both move to the edge of their seats.

"Where were they? Where did you find *them?*"

"I went to France. That was my strongest memory. I lived in a house outside of Paris, but they sent me away, thought I was crazy."

"Who sent you away, Daniel?"

"My niece, living in *my* parents' house."

"Daniel, do you remember where in France you lived?"

"Deux Rue de l'Église Vérines, near Néry France." His voice changes. It grows soft, more feminine, with a Parisian accent.

Cassandra makes a mental note, *Number 2 Church Street Verrines, in Néry France.*

Dr. Davidson quickly scribbles the address on her pad. "Then what did you do?"

Daniel continues, "On the way back to Scotland, we stopped in Copenhagen. I had the strangest feeling I had been there before. The closer I got, the more I started to remember my life there in a little town south of Copenhagen called Dragor. It's a small fishing village. The houses are all small and everyone knows everyone else. I went to the house where I used to live and explained to them that I lived there before. I told them my name at the time I lived in their village. I told them my father's and mother's names and the names of my brothers. Immediately, they brought me to a house. Moira stared at me, shocked because I was able to speak their language. As far as she knew, I had never been outside of our village. When I entered the house, everyone hugged and kissed me as though they knew who I was. The oldest member of the household—my distant relative—said they had been waiting for me for almost four generations. They were sure, however, I would come. He said the person I used to be left something extremely important and would return one day to claim it. Then they presented me with a wooden box."

During this entire time, Dr. Davidson frantically wrote down every keyword: *Copenhagen … Dragor … fishing village … Wooden box.*

Trevor finally interjects, breaking Dr. Davidson's connection with his father, "I think we should end this!"

She turns to them, ready to shush him again, but she's caught between Jonathan's stories and their worried faces. She seems to think about it for a moment.

"Okay," she agrees. "Just let me ask one more question." Turning back to Jonathan, she asks, "Daniel, what did you do with the box?"

"I put it in my rucksack and we took it back to Scotland."

"Who has the box now, Daniel?"

"Moira. I told her to keep it safe should anything happen to me." He pauses. "The fire was the next day. Somehow I knew I was going to die, but I had to save the children."

"Okay, Daniel, I need you to listen to me. I'm going to count to ten. As I reach number four, I want you to rest and let Jonathan take over. Do you understand?"

Jonathan nods, or perhaps it is Daniel, Dr. Davidson can't be sure.

"Jonathan, as I approach ten, you're going to slowly wake up. You will feel completely refreshed and well rested. Understood?"

Once again, he nodded.

"Okay. One, you're feeling lighter. Two, you're at peace. Three, you're surrounded by love. Four, I'm speaking to Jonathan now. Five, you're waking up. Six … seven, you're starting to feel your arms and legs. Eight, take a deep breath. Nine, feel your body return to you. Ten, you're wide awake."

Hearing the number ten, Jonathan opens his eyes. "Well? Did I cluck like a chicken?"

"Dad!" Cassandra runs over and hugs him so hard he falls backward a bit on the couch.

Dr. Davidson smiles. "This has been very enlightening, Mr. Taylor … or should I say, Mr. Daniel MacNaughton."

"Are you serious?"

"Serious!" Trevor shouts from across the room. "Dad, she just had a conversation with some Scottish fireman who married a redhead!"

"Apparently you have a thing for redheads," Cassandra adds, glancing at Dr. Davidson's auburn ponytail.

"Mr. Taylor, you don't remember anything?"

"Not really, no, but I feel great."

"Jonathan, I've conducted hundreds of these sessions with people who claim to have lived before. Your ex-wife may have told you, I'm the leading expert in England, perhaps the world. I have to tell you though, I have never had a clearer, more concise session than the one we just had."

"So I'm not going crazy, or whatever you want to call it?"

"No, Jonathan. You're *not* crazy!" the doctor assures him with a smile. "But I have to ask about these markers you spoke of while under hypnosis."

"Markers?" Jonathan asks.

"Your word, not mine." She smiles, then clarifies. "Well, actually, Daniel's word. Some kind of object he had to find. He would leave one and look for another." She searches her notes for accuracy.

Jonathan pulls the small metal tablet from his pocket. "You mean something like this?" He places it in her palm and she turns it over several times, studying it.

"He has two more. He was given one in India and another in Australia," Cassandra interjects. "The one from Australia is extremely old."

A-E-T-E-R-N-U-M

Hmm, Dr. Davidson ponders. "Interesting. Apparently, these *markers,*" she makes air quotes with her fingers, "are the things your past lives have been searching for."

She hands the tablet to Jonathan. "Guard it well. You wouldn't want to lose any of them." A moment later she adds, "I'm pretty sure you'll find more of them in a wooden box in Scotland. That is, if you can find a Mrs. Moira MacNaughton."

"Mrs. who?" he asks, putting the marker back into his pocket.

"Your hot redhead from a former life, Dad." Trevor teases.

Dr. Elizabeth Davidson touches her patient's arm, perhaps unconsciously holding on to the most important case of her entire career. "I would really like to have more sessions with you, Jonathan. Perhaps three or four to fully understand—"

Jonathan's gaze falls to her hand. "I'm afraid we're heading back to the States. London was just a side trip on the way home to determine whether or not I've lost my mind."

"What?" both children cry out.

Elizabeth releases her grasp but holds his attention with her gaze.

"Dad, we can't stop now!" Cassandra begs.

"Yeah, Dad, we have to see this thing through!" Trevor insists. "You're the one who dragged us on this roller coaster around the world. Now when we're finally getting some answers, you're throwing in the towel?!"

Jonathan cannot believe the small revolution taking place in the presence of a perfect stranger by his children.

"I thought you wanted to get back to work," he says to Trevor. "And you," he adds, looking at Cassandra, "I thought you were tired of schlepping around strange countries."

"Dad, you *have* to find these markers!" Cassandra pleads.

"Work can wait, Dad," Trevor says. "What's important is you finding these things. We want to go with you! Who knows how many of these tablets are out there. If there's even a small chance of finding a few more and solving this thing, we have to try."

"I guess we're going to Scotland," Jonathan says, looking at Elizabeth.

"Or Paris!" Cassandra cries.

"Paris?!" Jonathan turns and looks at Cassandra with confusion. "I thought you said I lived in Scotland."

"You did—*and* France!"

"France too?" *Just how many places have I lived?*

"It appears so," Dr. Elizabeth Davidson agrees. "Daniel told us he went to France, because that's where he had a strong memory of a past life *he* had." She hesitates. "I believe I detected a woman's voice with a French accent in one of your answers."

"Yes, the one where you asked if Dad knew the address." Cassandra's face lights up. "We have an address in Paris! All we have for Scotland is a woman's name."

"And the name of the town in Scotland," adds Dr. Davidson, checking her notes. "Could be Old Shore More, or two words, Old Shoremore, or, possibly, knowing the Scotts, one word, Oldshoremore."

"Oldshoremore, all one word," Jonathan confirms without hesitation.

"Are you sure?" Elizabeth asks.

Jonathan smiles, recalling a memory from Daniel's childhood. "Yes."

Trevor looks at his father. "So what shall it be, Dad? The highlands of Scotland or the vineyards of France?"

"France, France! Let it be France!" Cassandra cheers.

Jonathan looks at his therapist. "Any preference, Doc?"

She smiles. "I do love a man with a French accent." A slight blush fills her cheeks, leaving Jonathan unsure if that particular secret was meant to escape.

"Paris it is."

Cassandra jumps around the room, dancing as if she just scored the winning touchdown at the Super Bowl.

"Okay," Trevor agrees. "But, we should also go to Scotland! It may be the best chance we have to find a lot of those markers."

"Let me make a copy of my notes," Dr. Davidson suggests. "You may need them while in France. And if you go to Scotland, there may be something in them that helps you find Mrs. Moira MacNaughton, and, hopefully, the box of markers Daniel received."

With a smile, she crosses the room to a small office copier in the corner. "I'd like to review your case with some colleagues too, if you don't mind?"

"Of course," Jonathan agrees.

The machine spits out a perfect copy. "Everything you need to find Moira MacNaughton is here." She hands him the photocopies of her notes. "Are you sure you can't stay a day or two longer? You have no idea how much we might discover if we regress one, two, maybe three lifetimes back." She stares into his eyes.

Jonathan shakes her hand and leans in toward her. *He's going to kiss me on the cheek,* she thinks. Instead, he whispers in her ear, "I'm not sure how much time I have left, Doc." He stops and corrects himself. "Elizabeth." He draws back, but still holds her hand. "Maybe next time around."

Elizabeth looks puzzled. *Is he even aware of the double meaning?*

"So you said you have the address in Paris where I used to live?" Jonathan asks half-jokingly.

Both Cassandra and the doctor reply in unison, "A town call Néry." They look at one another and laugh.

"Well, I guess we're headed to Néry tomorrow!" Trevor announces.

Place: Jarrow, England
Year: 794

In another part of the world at another time, Bjørn
Gudmund stood on the deck of his ship and laughed, remembering the
'big' comment made by his wife.

His childhood friend joined him. "What is so funny, Bjørn? Do you
take pleasure knowing a storm is almost upon us?"

"No. I take no pleasure in anything on this trip. The only pleasure I
take is when my woman is in my arms and in my bed." His hand takes
hold of a small rectangular stone he wore around his neck. A band of
braided yellow hair emerged from a nest of red. It looped around his neck
and through a small hole in the stone.

"You finally finished that thing, have you?"

"Ja," he replied in the affirmative. "Before we left, Revna cut her hair
and braided a necklace."

His friend cupped the stone in his hand, a paltry piece compared to
the size of his palm.

"I asked her to go to the shore and find a river stone, flat as an ax
blade and square in size, not rounded like most."

"Ja. She did a good job," his friend agreed. "And you finished it well. Some fine craftsmanship." He admired the stone's surface.

The name Bjørn Olavi Gudmund was inscribed on one side, adorned by a Viking ideogram. He turned the stone over. "And this? What be this?"

Carved on the reverse side were letters foreign to Bjørn's kin. "Are these some markings you saw in one of your dreams?"

"I believe it is an ancient word," Bjørn replied. "A driving force told me to etch it on the stone's surface. The same driving force told me we would find great riches in this new land."

"I will drink to that!" his friend exclaimed. "I long for the day when we can sit in the halls of Valhalla, feast with Odin, and see my father again!"

"I also long for that day, my friend. I only hope to see my son grow to be a man before that day comes," Bjørn said, placing the stone close to his heart.

"Who said it is a son?" his friend joked, and walked away laughing.

"Why does everyone say that?!" Bjørn yelled to the back of the boat.

He turned back, watching the sails fill with wind, and spied the dark clouds behind them. As the ship cut through the icy water, a fierce storm was coming to England. Bjørn feared it was an omen of the worst kind.

In two days, the five boats made their way down the coast of Great Britain to an inlet that led to a river the English named Tyne. A short distance from there, they came to rest on the shore. A band of savage marauders prepared to descend on St. Paul's Monastery in the small town of Jarrow. But unlike the raid of five years earlier, this one was destined to be met with resistance. The villagers, remembering the attack on the monastery of Lindisfarne and fearing the Norsemen's eventual return, have been preparing their defense for years.

The ground was wet and soft beneath Bjørn's feet as he jumped from the ship to the bank of the Tyne. *This land is so richly fertile* he thought. The smell of wildflowers and herbs permeated his nostrils. The sky, once a tranquil blue with billowing white clouds, grew dark and ominous. Within an hour, no less than 150 invaders trampled the lush green grass, turning it brown with the mud carried from the river's shore. Like a slug leaving a slimy trail behind it, the band of slaughtering invaders moved across the meadow's landscape, crushing and killing anyone and anything in their path.

As they came up over the hill, Bjørn was the first to spy the small church. Before he could signal his kinsmen, a woman working in the fields spotted the invading horde. Her scream broke the silence of the peaceful countryside, raising the alarm throughout the entire village. Screeching blackbirds took to the air.

Moving as one well-organized force, the band of savages raced toward the church. All 150 invaders ran screaming, banging their weapons against their shields as though driving frightened cattle toward the slaughter.

Most of the villagers made it inside the monastery's walls. Only a few fell prey to the arrows of the well-trained marksmen. Like a swarm of locusts, the Vikings descended on the large stone structure, searching for its most vulnerable point. A wooden door on the far side of the monastery proved to be its Achilles' heel. Within minutes, the threshold was breached and the horror began.

Lightning flashed and thunder crashed as if God himself objected to the raid on his people. Heavy rain began to fall, turning the ground sopping wet and slippery under the Vikings' feet. The villagers fought back, but they were no match. For every five inept farmers, there was one skilled Norseman. Still, they fought back anyway with all they had, and ultimately, their years of training coupled with their sheer numbers inside the compound turned the odds in their favor.

All around, Bjørn saw his outnumbered countrymen battling bravely. Slowly, however, his kinsmen were taken down by the poor, inexperienced, simple peasants. The marauders began to retreat, but

Bjørn battled on, severing limbs and thrusting his sword into the chests of fathers and sons. He fought with no shield; a broad sword in his left hand and a double-headed battle-ax in his right. Both were equally dangerous, no matter which one Bjørn wielded.

Without the aid of his countrymen, Bjørn stood in the center of the church's courtyard. Most of the horde, chased by well-armed peasant farmers defending their land, disbanded and withdrew to the safety of the field.

The rain, combined with the salty sweat dripping from his brow, stung Bjørn's eyes, making it difficult to see. His arms ached from brandishing the heavy iron weapons. Exhaustion finally overcame him and his foot slipped: a chink in his armor that gave the villagers a distinct advantage. A frightened farmer swung his sword—perhaps for the very first time in his life—aiming at Bjørn's chest. Bjørn leaned back. The sword fell short. The tip of the blade merely caught a tiny wisp of Bjørn's braided red beard, severing the fine strands from the rest. Lucky for Bjørn, but unlucky for the poor farmer, who felt the hard steel of Bjørn's sword plunge upward into his soft belly. It would take six days for this humble landowner, a man simply trying to defend his community, to die a slow, painful death.

Another villager, not waiting for Bjørn to withdraw his sword, moved in with his spear to the Viking's left side. Bjørn released his grip on the embedded sword and smacked the spear from the man's hands. It fell behind him. Instantly, Bjørn grabbed the peasant by the throat. He felt the man's vertebrae with the tips of his fingers as his thumb closed tightly around the man's windpipe.

The man thrashed, swatting at Bjørn to no avail. As Bjørn kept him at arm's length, another man charged from the right. The would-be attacker raised his sword high, exposing his chest. Bjørn lifted his battle-ax, swinging it in an arching motion, catching the ill-prepared peasant's exposed torso. As the crescent blade of the ax cleaved through skin, muscle, and bone, it severed the man's stomach, liver, and lungs. He tried to scream, but no air passed through his throat. Instead, a great mist of red blood sprayed from the open gash.

Just as Bjørn felt victory was at last in sight, a searing sting erupted in the center of his back. The burning sensation ran through his core, ultimately bursting from his chest. He looked down. The tip of a spear—the one he'd swatted away—now protruded from the center of his chest. The burning intensified as the spear withdrew from his body, only to reemerge for a second fatal thrust.

Bjørn dropped to his knees, his red hair matted and disheveled from the rain. He watched fresh, clear water run down his chest, mixed with the crimson fluid from his open wounds. Pooling at his knees, his life's blood drained into a half a dozen flowing scarlet streams. All around him, the rich, fertile soil was tainted with the blood of his sins, just as Abel's blood, spilled by Cain, had once stained the earth as well. He smelled the sweet fragrance of the wildflowers one last time and thought, *this would have been a nice place to raise a family.*

His body fell to the ground. The last thing he saw was a river stone suspended from a yellow braid, fashioned from the hair of his unborn child's mother, and the word, AETERNUM.

After the terrible battle, the villagers wondered what to do with Bjørn's body.

"We shall give him a proper funeral within the Church walls," the priest said. "If we could not save the body, perhaps we can still save the soul." He bent down and examined the small stone the Viking carried around his neck. The marking on the side with Bjørn's name was unrecognizable, but on the other side, the priest knew this word all too well.

Strange, a barbarian wearing THIS, the priest mused. Recognizing the word, he snatched the stone, breaking the braided blonde strands from the corpse.

He then instructed the congregation. "Place this in the church library as a lasting reminder of the events of this day."

The Viking horde retreated to their ships, where before leaving, two vessels sank in the fierce storm. The villagers killed those who made it back to shore. When the three surviving ships returned to Scandinavia, Revna was told of her husband's death. Holding their newborn son in her arms, she wept.

The following morning, the Taylor family boards the

underground from Paddington Station to Victoria Station, then Jonathan
purchases three bus tickets on the southeastern line to Dover.

"Dad, I thought we were flying to Paris?" Cassandra asks.

"I thought this would be a little more nostalgic," her father answers.
"Besides, I want you both to see the white cliffs of Dover. Everyone
should see them before they d—" he stops mid-sentence. Perhaps not the
best turn of phrase, he considers, remembering the reason for this trip.
"Well, you guys really need to see them."

"Nostalgic?" Trevor asks.

"Yeah, your mother and I backpacked around Europe years ago
before we even thought of having a family. It seems like a lifetime ago,
as though it happened to someone else."

They board the bus and take their seats. "I don't remember much
about the bus ride. I was jet-lagged for most of it. Your mother had to feed
me yogurt raisins the entire time." He smiles and chuckles fondly. "It was
the only snack we packed and the only thing I could keep down. Anyway,

171

when we got to Dover—I'll never forget the sight of those white cliffs. Some images will be forever burned into my memory, those being one of them."

Some two hours later, the bus pulls into Dover, and Jonathan purchases tickets for the next ferry to Calais, France. The morning is gray and overcast—a typical English morning, as the locals would say—but the clouds start to break, allowing small rays of sunshine to illuminate the shore. As the ferry makes its way out of the harbor and past the breakwater jetty, Cassandra, Trevor, and Jonathan stand on the stern, marveling as the morning sun radiates off the ivory banks. Jonathan observes the look on his children's faces and thinks, *that was my exact expression more than 35 years ago when I was their age. For thousands of years, these cliffs have stood, and they'll stand for a thousand more. In the overall scheme of things, we really are here for just a blink of an eye.*

So many people worry about their jobs, or worry about having the latest technology, if their children have the latest iPhone. We spend so much time on trivial things, when all that really matters are the people in our lives and the happiness we should try to give them. So many people hold on to anger and resentment, living years—lifetimes—without speaking to one another. If they only realized that this life will end before they know it, would any of them waste a single minute holding on to such inconsequential worries and emotions?

By the time the ferry pulls into Calais Harbor, the sun is shining and it promises to be a beautiful day.

"How are we getting to Néry?" Cassandra asks.

"We could take a car straight there," Jonathan says, before holding up three EuroRail passes to Paris. "But we're in France! And you can't go to France without seeing Paris!"

Cassandra throws her arms around her father's neck. "I always wanted to see Montmartre! Oh, and the Louvre, can we go there?"

"I guess that little incident in India cured you of your fear of trains?" Trevor asks.

"I think it did." Jonathan smiles.

Trevor scans the train schedule to see what time they arrive in Paris. "Well, sis. Looks like you have approximately two-and-a-half hours on the train to plan everything."

As they board, Cassandra whips out her phone and starts Googling places to see.

Jonathan finds an empty compartment and slides the door open. As they enter, memories from 35 years earlier come rushing back to him. He laughs lightly, remembering how he and his carefree girlfriend—his wife-to-be—made their way to Paris, neither of them knowing where they would be staying. *A simpler time.*

"You know," he says. "When traveling at night, these seats fold down into a bed." Jonathan bursts into such a hearty laugh out of nowhere, the children jump.

"What's so funny?" they both ask.

"Your mother and I, well, she wasn't your mother at the time—that is to say, we weren't married at the time—"

"Yeah, yeah, Dad, we get it," Trevor interrupts. "What happened that was so funny? You guys had sex on the train and got caught?"

"Ewww, Yuck!" Cassandra blurts, "Dad, please don't tell us anything like that happened?"

Jonathan shoots her a puzzled look, "You know, your mother and I were young once, little lady, and very much in love, I might add. But no! We never—" he pauses, then, "got caught." He looks at Trevor. "And that's not what I was laughing about."

"So what was it?" Cassandra asks.

"I was going to say, your mother and I took the train from Paris to Florence." Jonathan begins to get giddy as he always does with a story he thinks is funny. "It's a 13-hour train ride. Your mother was very good at planning things. Maps and travel books, timetable, train schedules; she had everything worked out to the very last minute. It wasn't easy back then. I'm talking about a time before smartphones and Google or even the Internet, if you can believe that. Anyway, she planned it so we would leave Paris at night, sleep in the berth, and wake up in Italy." Jonathan starts to laugh. "What she didn't know though," he continues, his laughter growing, "is that as we crossed into Italy, the train stopped." Now, unable to contain himself, he laughs even harder.

Both Cassandra and Trevor start nervously laughing along with him.

His eyes begin to water. His uncontrollable laughter continues, and as he gasps for breath, he continues, "We didn't feel the train stop, because we were both sound asleep. The Italian police had to check passports, so the conductor slid the door open with a loud bang!"

Jonathan's hand moves to his side, suppressing a stitch from laughter. "Behind him stood two Italian soldiers dressed in black, both carrying Uzis and yelling, *Mostraci i tuoi passaporti! Mostraci i tuoi passaporti!*"

By this time, Jonathan is laughing so hard his children can barely understand him.

He looks at them with a confused expression as though they've missed the punchline. "Show us your passports! They were asking to see our passports!" he translates for them. "Well, your mother woke up, thought they were robbing the train, and threw her hands in the air, yelling 'Don't shoot! Don't shoot! We're Americans!' As if that was going to stop them." Jonathan's tears stream down his face. "The two police officers and the conductor began to laugh. I heard one of them say, 'Americans', and the other two laughed even harder." Jonathan laughs and laughs until he winds down to a slow chuckle, shaking his head back and forth.

"Then what happened?" Cassandra asks.

"Well, we showed them our passports and they moved on."

Just then, the door to their compartment slides open and a well-dressed French conductor announces, "Passaporti, per favore." Then he repeats in English, "Passports, please." The three of them burst into simultaneous laughter.

The conductor checks their tickets and mutters to himself, "Americans," which only makes all three of them laugh even harder.

They stay at the Hôtel Eiffel Trocadéro, a narrow building set between Rue Vineuse and Rue Benjamin Franklin. The front of the building appears no wider than a moving truck in Manhattan. The seven-story white building with a gray slate roof sits at the very end of the street. Its bronze and glass lanterns decorate the front and sides of the building; its beautiful glass doors, etched in art nouveau flowers, beckon guests into the lobby. At night, the ornate lanterns give the building a golden glow, while vibrant hues of cobalt blue and purple illuminate the top floors.

Cassandra's room is small compared to her father's, but less whimsical. The unembellished white room is accented with sea-foam green watercolor lilies painted on the wall. Driftwood lighting fixtures create an ambiance more akin to California than the heart of Paris.

Trevor's room is approximately the same size as his sister's. It boasts a luxurious wood floor and beige striped walls; otherwise, it offers no color. A modest writing desk sits in the corner.

By far the most amusing room is Jonathan's. It has a turquoise blue sky mural on the wall, and a small diorama of the Parisian cityscape on another. A creamy, sand-colored comforter and matching pillows rest on the king size bed. Best of all, a wrought iron portion of the Eiffel Tower, an imitation anyway, serves as the bed's headboard. Trevor comments that the décor is more appropriate for Euro-Disney. One absolutely indisputable fact, however: the view is magnificent! Gazing out the windows, Paris' magnificent iron structure calls to them, proclaiming, 'welcome to Paris!'

They dine at small cafes along the boulevards. Afterwards, they wander through the streets of Paris, drinking in the city of lights where strangers become friends, and friends become lovers. They stroll up the Champs-Élysées and circle the Arc de Triomphe. Jonathan describes the details of the amazing stone architecture and its embellishments, enhanced by the beautiful flowing lines of the city.

"This is the reason I pursued architecture," he explains. "Many of these structures are hundreds of years old, their craftsmanship and beauty as exquisite today as it was back then."

They discuss the Louvre and the Rodin Museum. They meander among the gardens, eating croissants, and speculating what it must have been like during the French Revolution.

As they tour the city streets, Jonathan resists the urge to explain what used to be. Instead, he focuses on the present, hoping to help his children experience the city just as he first did.

You can't help but fall in love with Paris. The city wraps you in love and embeds itself into your soul. It makes every man a poet, every woman a muse. There is no mad rush like in Manhattan. No neon techno glow like that of Tokyo. Paris is simply romance wrapped in a warm blanket, sitting by the fire, drinking a glass of wine.

Jonathan's thoughts take him back 30 years. At night, the whole city sparkles, illuminated by the glow of a thousand electric candles. He recalls the pitch black River Seine with tiny sparks of twinkling lights dancing across its surface. He remembers a girl. He recalls a feeling the two of them shared as they walked through the city streets at night. They spoke of dreams and promises that were never meant to be broken. *When did those dreams end? When were those promises broken? And why did love die?*

If only we could live but one single moment of our lives, would we truly be happy? Maybe that's our curse. We only get one moment in time to embrace such happiness. Then time moves on, happiness fades, and we've outlived our moment. All we have left is death, and so we must die.

After dinner, the Taylor family returns to the hotel. Instead of heading to his room, Jonathan arranges a time to meet for breakfast in the morning and bids his children goodnight, before heading out into the Paris night.

As tired lovers all across Paris whisper their final goodnights, one last embrace before slumber takes hold, and the city of lights bids a bonne nuit to the passing day, Jonathan walks the empty boulevards alone, rekindling the love affair that now lives only in his memories. Like so many marriages, Jonathan's was on life support for too many years before it succumbed to a terminal illness. Time of death: October 14, 2010.

The next day, Jonathan rents a car and they make an hour-and-a-half drive to Néry. They stop in Senlis so Jonathan can marvel at the Cathédrale Notre-Dame de Senlis and the Château royal de Senlis et prieuré Saint-Maurice, partially destroyed during the Second World War. The small, winding, stone-covered street is right out of Victor Hugo's novel, *Les Miserables*. They continue Northwest on highway D1324. Miles and miles of flat farmland roll by. The green and golden fields sleep under a blanket of gray clouds. The landscape looks more like Kansas than France.

They continue for some 30 minutes before the electronic voice of Cassandra's iPhone GPS instructs them to 'make a left in half a mile onto Highway D113'. As Trevor drives on, their electronic copilot informs them that D113 turns into D98, the Rue des Peuliers, where a sharp right turn is required. A small, rectangular, mustard-colored signpost on the corner reads D98; below it are two signs. The bottom sign bears the number four in front of the name TRUMILLY; the top sign has the number one in front of VERRINES.

"One mile," Cassandra says, as they pass the sign.

"Kilometer," Jonathan corrects. "Distance is measured in kilometers in Europe."

Jonathan's stomach quivers. There's something about this town he doesn't want to remember, but he doesn't know what. Telephone poles span the left side of the road, and up ahead, high-tension towers can be seen on the horizon.

"These weren't here before," Jonathan says. "This was all farmland."

Trevor follows the road that bends to the left; an oasis of trees comes into view.

"It's up here, halfway through the town, on the right," Jonathan calls out.

As they enter the town, a small white sign with red trim welcomes them to VERRINES, with the words C ne de Néry. A separate white sign, circled in red, indicates a speed limit of 50 kph. A small stone wall constructed before WWII extends along the right side of the road. Trevor slows the car to 30 kph, as the next sign indicates, and they continue down the road. Buildings appear on the left and right. Stone structures, weathered by time, their walls thick with ivy, make up this small hamlet. Trevor veers to the right and then the left following the bends in the road.

"You passed it!" Jonathan shouts.

"Where?" Trevor calls back.

"That stone building on your right, the one you just passed."

Trevor slows and makes a U-turn at a fork in the road, in front of a white stone structure with wooden shutters that looked more like a horse stable than a house. He brings the car to a slow roll as they move through town, so they don't pass the house again.

"There seem to be more street signs than houses heading this way," Trevor comments. The stone building, passed just moments ago, comes into view.

"On the left! That's it! That's it!" exclaims Jonathan.

Trevor brings the car to a halt. In front of them stands a majestic old three-story stone house. Two dog-house structures with windows sit on a moss-covered, red-slate roof. Two chimneys rise from the center of the roof. Four windows line the front of the first floor; three more are positioned above, on the second floor. One window, on the left side of the entrance, is bricked over—perhaps destroyed during the war. In order to gain access, the front door is three steps down, giving the illusion of a smaller half door from street view.

Trevor parks the car in the cobblestone courtyard in front of the house, wondering why Jonathan is suddenly motionless in observation.

"Well, we're here, Dad. Are we going in?"

Howard finishes telling the story of how he discovered
Joseph Kehm's body almost 40 years earlier in the town of Deadwood,
South Dakota.

"So is that what started all this, Professor?" Anthony asks, waving
his arm across the landscape of the map positioned on the back wall.

"Well, yes and no. Initially, I brought Joseph Kehm's marker home
with me as a souvenir of my first important find. I wanted to brag to
Christine that I was good at my job. I never suspected I would ever find
out why Mr. Kehm possessed the marker in the first place, let alone
why *that* word in particular was scratched on it. It was simply a small
souvenir, one that sat on my desk and reminded me of a nice night out
in Deadwood." A smile crosses Howard's face as he recalls the waitress
with the purple bustier and amazing eyes.

"Then, one day, a friend and colleague, Mike Bodnar, came to my
office to join me for lunch. He noticed the piece of metal and asked me
about it. Examining it, he said, 'That's interesting?'"

Anthony raises an eyebrow.

179

"So I asked, 'What's so interesting about this little three by two inch piece of metal?' And you know what he tells me?"

Anthony shrugs.

"He said that Professor Mintz from Early Native American Studies has one just like it. 'Mike saw it in her office last week' he says. The same size, different name carved into the surface, only hers was made of wood. Here's the eerie part. He said hers had the word AETERNUM carved on the opposite side as well!"

"Two markers with the same word inscribed on them?" Anthony asks, confused. "So what did you do?"

"I didn't go to lunch, I can tell you that!" Howard jokes, "I ran right down to Native American Studies trying to find Professor Mintz. That marker was sitting on my desk for almost two years and then I learn that someone else in this very building has a similar one? Well, I just had to see it."

"What are the chances, Professor?" Anthony interrupts. "I mean, two tablets having the same word! Maybe they were common artifacts among Native Americans? Maybe this Joseph Kehm saw a Native American with one and copied the word, not knowing what it meant? Or maybe—"

"That's a lot of maybes," Howard says, interrupting Anthony this time. "Anyway, I found Donna—I mean Dr. Mintz, and I asked to see her tablet so we could compare the markers. The two were almost identical in size and shape. The only differences were their mass and material."

"The metal one was heavier," Anthony surmises.

"Of course. Dr. Mintz told me she unearthed hers at a dig site on the East Coast. The tribe was called Shinnecock."

"Oh yeah, I've heard of them. We studied them in high school, even took a field trip to the end of Long Island."

"Well, here's what's really significant. The Shinnecock tribe spoke Munsee, a dialect of the Lenape people, one of the Algonquin languages. And the Lenape kept records using wooden tablets, tree bark, and stone."

Howard catches the perplexed expression on Anthony's face. "Don't you see? They kept *records*. On *wooden tablets*!" He enunciates each word very slowly. "Dr. Mintz had one of the records! The wooden tablet! Donna's tablet was discovered with the skeletal remains of a Shinnecock woman. Tribe historians tell a story of a husband who left on a fishing journey, or an expedition to find new lands or whatever. Before departing, fearing he might die, the husband gave a wooden talisman to his wife so he could be remembered."

"So what happened to him?"

"He died, of course." Howard looks at Anthony in disbelief, as if it was the dumbest question ever asked. "Anyway, my point being, this was a small Indian tribe—" He falters. "Sorry, Native American tribe, and on the East Coast, not the Apache Nation."

Again, observing the confused look on his assistant's face, Howard explains, "The Apache Nation was huge, and spread out over Oklahoma, Texas, Arizona, and even New Mexico. Joseph Kehm was from Sioux City and traveled to Deadwood, I'm guessing for the gold. He wouldn't have had any interaction with a Native American tribe on the easternmost coast of Long Island. I doubt he came in contact with The Apache Nation either. He might have encountered members of the Sioux tribe. I think they settled in the Dakota territories back then, or maybe a small part of the Cheyenne. But he definitely wouldn't have had any interaction with a small tribe from Long Island. Hell, I doubt most people even knew of Long Island back then."

"So, how—"

Howard runs to the map on the back wall and points to South Dakota before Anthony can finish his sentence. "So how did Joseph Kehm, from the West, and a Native American on the East Coast—" He takes several steps to the right and points to the elongated island jutting out from New York. "End up with similar tablets no bigger than the palm of your hand? What's more, how is the exact same word inscribed on both of them?" He shakes his head. "That's the real question."

"And, how would a Native American know Latin?"

"That's an even bigger question!" Howard agrees. "Did either one even know what the word meant? Was it proof of some kind of earlier

European influence in North America? We simply don't know. Not yet, anyway."

"So anyway, after collecting dust on my desk for almost two years, I discover, thanks to Professor Mintz, there are two almost identical artifacts, in shape and size, bearing the same word. These tablets, or markers, if you will, became my obsession. I asked Professor Malher, Head Curator at the time, if I could work on this project. I spent months researching and dispatching inquiry letters to museums across the country, asking if anyone had information regarding a stone, wood, or metal tablet the size of a playing card, with names inscribed on them. More importantly, did any of them bear a Latin word on the back?"

"Why didn't you just Google it, Professor?" the naive apprentice asks.

"It was the 80s, Anthony!"

"Oh, right. Google wasn't live yet."

"The internet wasn't live yet! We had nothing! We had to rely on what you call snail mail, writing everything on paper with a pen. You know, a good old-fashioned letter!" He smirks. "Okay, so I used a typewriter, but you still had to mail it with a stamp."

"Geez, like back in the Civil War era?" Anthony's eyebrows raise.

"I'm not that old! That was over 150 years ago!" Howard snaps, taking offense.

Anthony laughs. "I'm just pulling your leg, Professor. So then what happened?"

"Nothing," Howard chuckles, still amused by the implication of his age compared to a Confederate soldier.

"Nothing?"

"Absolutely nothing. Nothing at all came from it." He paused, allowing a solemn beat of silence to sit between them before he continued. "Nothing for over two years. Then, finally, one day in 1983, Professor Malher entered my office and threw an envelope on my desk. I can safely say that envelope changed the next 40 years of my life."

"What was in the envelope?!" Anthony could hardly contain his curiosity.

PLACE: VÉRINES, NÉRY, FRANCE
YEAR: PRESENT DAY

Jonathan timidly knocks on the door of number two
Church Street. Seconds later, a woman in her early forties answers.

"Bonjour?"

To his children's surprise, Jonathan unexpectedly begins speaking
perfect French. "Bonjour, mademoiselle, Êtes-vous le propriétaire de
cette Maison?"

"Oui," the woman replies.

Trevor looks at Cassandra. "Did you teach Dad French?"

"No."

"Here we go again," Trevor says. "What are they saying?"

Cassandra translates, "Dad just asked if she's the owner of this house;
she said yes."

"Have you lived here all your life?" Jonathan asks the woman, the
two still conversing in French.

"Yes. My family has owned this house since before the war. What is
this about?"

"I apologize for the questions. I lived here, briefly, as a small child, after the war. Is it alright if I come in and show my children where I stayed?" he lies.

The woman considers his question for a moment, then motions for them to enter.

"Voici ma fille, Cassandra et mon fils, Trevor," her father introduces them.

"This is my daughter, Cassandra, and my son, Trevor," Cassandra continues to translate for Trevor.

"Bonjour. Bonjour," the woman greets each of them.

Trevor tries his best to repeat the greeting. Cassandra delivers an adequate pronunciation, thanks to three years of high school French.

The woman turns to Jonathan. "I'm sorry, Monsieur. My mother once told me that her mother took in many children during that time. Our house was one of the few left standing after the attacks."

Jonathan's gaze moves around the room, drinking it in. The smell of the furniture and antique wood takes him back to a different time, a time when he was a sixteen-year-old girl. It was just as he remembered. "Is your grandmother alive?"

His hopeful expression fades as she answers, "No. She passed in 1998 at the age of 72. But my mother is still alive."

"May I speak with her, please?" his eyes implore.

"Wait here. I'll see if she is up for visitors."

Trevor bombards his father with questions. "Dad, who is this woman? Do you know her? Does she know you? Are you related? Were you related? Did you know you could speak French? How are you doing this?"

"I lived here," he says quickly. "I grew up here, as a teenager before the war. Then one day—" He stops, suddenly horrified as the memories take hold. "The entire village was talking about Germans invading. Oh, the Germans!" Jonathan puts his hand to his mouth in a girlish gesture. "The monsters. They came to our house. I had to hide my father's—I had to—" He starts to cry. "They shot my father." He stares at the floor.

"Right here! Right here in front of me, and I—" Jonathan sits, for fear his legs will give out and he will collapse. "I had to get away, so I ran. I ran outside and, and I can't remember anything after that."

The woman returns, escorting her mother into the room. "Pardon, Monsieur, my mother, Mrs. Emma Beaulieu." She introduces her mother as though she is royalty.

Jonathan stands and wipes his eyes. He can barely believe the vision before him.

The woman leads her mother to a chair and helps her to sit. When she looks up, she sees a look of astonishment on Jonathan's face.

"Forgive me, Madame, you are the perfect image of your mother, Camille Dumont."

"That was my mother's maiden name, Camille Dumont. She married my father, Edward Beaulieu. My daughter told me Camille took you in after the war? You must have been a baby. How could this be? You look barely 50 years old."

"Madame, please don't think me mad. I told your daughter I lived here. That is true. I know every inch of this house." Jonathan sees the confused look on her face.

"As a small child, I played in the upstairs nursery with my sister—" He hesitates, wondering if he should say it. "My sister Camille. Your mother."

"What's this all about?!" her daughter snaps. "I want you and your children out of my house." She violently waves her arms at them.

Trevor has no idea what the woman is saying, but apparently whatever his father said upset her terribly, to the point she is now frightening him.

Cassandra—still interpreting—rises from her chair. "Ahhh Trevor, we should go. She's throwing us out of her house. Dad just announced that he's her dead grandmother's sister."

"Mademoiselle, please, I beg of you, please hear me out." Jonathan pleads.

"Out! Out! I'll have none of this in my house. And take your children with you!" The daughter flails her arms resembling a mother goose protecting her nest.

But then, unexpectedly, her mother raises a hand to silence her daughter's rant.

"Francis, please. Let me speak. About 50 years ago, a Scottish man arrived on my doorstep and claimed the same thing," she speaks softly. "I reacted as you did, and sent him away." She lowers her gaze. "I questioned, how could this be? This man claims to be my mother's sister? He remained outside the doorway, screaming that he needed some kind of tablet, a small marker left in the house. I had no idea what he was raving about."

Jonathan reaches into his pocket right away. His fingers touch the metal tablet. Slowly, he removes it. "Something like this?" he asks, presenting it to Emma Beaulieu.

The woman is both shocked and confused. "I don't know? As I said, I had no idea what he was talking about. I never saw a tablet. My mother never spoke of one. For all I know, the damn Nazis took it. They took everything my grandfather had, including his life. The bastards shot him right here in this room."

Suddenly, Jonathan remembers what Clara hid. The Germans *didn't* take it. It was his job—her job—to hide it. Her mother and father were downstairs. Her sister was in her room. She was able to hide it, but then they came, the Germans, barging into the house. She ran, but before she could tell them, she ran outside, and—and then Jonathan was lost in the memory. *Why can't I remember anything after that moment?*

"Mademoiselle, I know this sounds absurd, but I can prove it," Jonathan says, using the same persuasive tone he used with Trevor at the start of their journey. "Your great-grandfather was a jeweler. He was always giving us worthless pieces he couldn't sell in his shop. Go to your mother's bedroom. Bring back three pieces of jewelry; one piece belonging to your mother when she was a young girl. The other two pieces, something perhaps you may have purchased recently, but nothing new. They all have to look as if they're from before the war. If I'm able to tell you which piece is hers from long ago, then I hope you'll believe me."

Emma instructs her daughter to collect the pieces. Francis leaves, muttering, "I don't see how this will prove anything." Moments later, she returns with some old photo albums and items wrapped in a cloth. She places them on the table.

As she unwraps the items, Jonathan moves to the table. He stares at the three necklaces of the same shape and size. His eyes widen.

Immediately, he picks up a gold chain with two intertwined hearts. A tear runs down his cheek. "This was not your mother's," he says. "It was mine. I gave this necklace to your mother when I heard those bastards break down our door."

Emma nods, confirming his choice is correct. "My mother often told of that day. How her sister, Clara, fastened that necklace around her neck for safekeeping."

"This proves nothing," Francis objects. "You expect us to believe you are my dead grandmother's sister because you picked out her necklace?" Emma walks to the table. She opens the scrapbooks containing the family's old photographs, yellowed by time.

"Stop!" Jonathan places his hand on the page. "This is my father!" He points to a well-dressed man. "And this," he says, pointing to a woman, "this is my mother!" he cries. He flips the pages. "This, this is Camille!" He's aflutter with excitement as he sees his life, a life that once existed only in his dreams, is now becoming a reality through these black and white photographs. "And this!" He yells out, pointing to the page. "This is me! Clara. I am Clara Dumont!"

Emma's mouth falls agape in a state of total shock.

Jonathan continues, pointing to the dog. "This is Doodles, and this is Miss Penelope, our cat!"

Francis looks at her mother. "How could he know about the cat?! That fucking cat has been dead for over 90 years!"

Jonathan turns the page and beholds a photograph of his entire family. "This was the last time we were all together. It was my birthday. I had just turned 16." Jonathan, still clutching the necklace, looks down and opens his hand." My father gave me this on my birthday. It was his mother's, and he said she wanted me to have it when I was of age."

With thin, fragile fingers, Emma slowly reaches out to Jonathan, and taking his hand carefully, closes it around the necklace. "Then you should have it."

"Mother! That's the only piece of jewelry we have from your family!" Francis protests.

Jonathan's face lights up. "No! No, it's not!" He looks at Emma. "Your grandfather was a jeweler. He had many pieces in the house, and diamonds too. That's what the Germans were demanding when they broke down the door. They shot him to force my mother to tell them where they were," Jonathan speaks as Clara. "But she didn't know where they were. I hid the valuables. Papa gave them to me to hide."

"The Germans searched the entire house. My mother and her mother searched every inch of this house for years. They found nothing. Either the soldiers found Granddad's jewelry and left or maybe they found nothing. Either way, our family never recovered financially." Emma hangs her head low.

"If you allow me," Jonathan says. "I'm pretty sure I know where to look."

"What's going on, Cazz? What are they saying?" Trevor looks at Cassandra who continues to monitor the unfolding events, translating as much as she can to Trevor.

"I think Dad hid something in the house, something of value that the Nazis wanted."

"Nazis?" Trevor's neck jerks. "How could Dad hide something in this house? He's never been here before."

"Trev, I think Dad thinks he's this woman's dead aunt." She pauses, looking at her father. "No, what I mean is, I think he *is* this woman's aunt!"

"This is insane," Trevor says, throwing his arms up. "This whole trip has been insane! I think that doctor screwed up Dad's head or something."

Francis agrees in perfect English. "Yes, this *is* insane." She then reverts to French, "Mama, are you really going to let this charlatan rummage through our home?"

Emma looks at her daughter. "Do you want another person to show up 50 years from now, claiming *he* or *she* is Clara Dumont? Regardless of whether or not this is some sort of trick or this person is actually the reincarnation of Clara, I'm tired and I want to get to the bottom of this. After all, what could it hurt?"

She turns to Jonathan. "Alright, Monsieur, you have the run of the house. And when you're done with your little parlor trick, I'll kindly ask you to leave."

Jonathan bows his head—an acknowledgment of respect. Then he focuses his gaze on the banister. "It's upstairs, in my bedroom. My sister and I slept in the same room. There are two beds separated by a window. Mine was on the right. That's how I knew the Germans were coming. I saw them from my window, where the road bends up the hill. I ran to my father's room and told Papa. He gave me a box and told me what to do. There's a dresser in the corner of our bedroom. Under that, there is a loose floorboard. After I replaced the dresser, I ran to find my sister." Jonathan faces Emma. "Your mother. I gave my necklace to Camille in the nursery to protect her. I remember her sitting there shaking in the corner of the room. I heard those animals enter our house. So many people were yelling and screaming. A deep, gruff voice shouted at Papa. He was answering calmly saying he didn't understand what they wanted. My sister and I tried to sneak out the back. A soldier grabbed us as we tried to escape. Then they shot Papa right in front of me. A single shot, and I heard Mama scream. I couldn't stop crying. I pushed past the guards and ran out the door, and—and—and that's all I remember."

All who understood French are shocked. Only Trevor stands speechless in a state of confusion. "Could someone please say something in English."

When Cassandra looks at her brother, he sees she's got tears in her eyes. "I think Dad just told us how he died."

Jonathan stands silent, alone in a world long past, mourning a death of long ago. The room is as quiet as a gravesite just before the coffin descends into the earth. Everyone reflects on the words he just spoke. Jonathan finally breaks the silence. "What you've been looking for is upstairs in the corner of the bedroom under the floorboards. You have to move the dresser, the one with crystal knobs." Jonathan wipes the tears from his cheeks.

For a long moment, no one speaks. Then, Emma clears her throat. "Francis, why don't you and Mr. Errrrh? What is your name, sir?"

"It's Taylor. Jonathan Taylor, madame."

"Why don't you and Mr. Taylor go upstairs and put this whole thing to rest once and for all."

Francis and Jonathan climb the stairs. When they reach the landing, she asks him in a snarky, sarcastic tone, "Which room was yours, Mr. Taylor? Or should I call you Clara?"

Ignoring the comment, Jonathan answers, "My room was on the top floor, together with our parents. These rooms were where Papa worked, and sometimes had morning tea. The nursery was over there, where my sister would play with Antoinette,"

"Antoinette?" she asks.

"A porcelain doll my Grand-mère, Marie Dumont, gave her," Jonathan continues. "Marie was my middle name. She would have been your great-great-great-Grand-mère."

He proceeds down the hall and stops at a door blocked by a small table displaying various books and pictures. Francis had never opened that door; she had no idea what was behind it.

"Help me move this, please." Jonathan places the picture frames on their faces, careful not to break them. After sliding the small table to one side, Jonathan opens the door, revealing a flight of stairs.

"My room was up there," Jonathan says in an *I told you so* tone.

When they ascend to the landing, four doors greet them.

"That was my parents' room and that was the bathroom we all shared."

Francis opens the door to a small water closet housing a white porcelain sink and toilet. Rust stains line the bowls of the old fixtures frozen in time. She moves down the hall opening the door to the parents' room. As children, Camille and Clara never went into this room. There was something sacred about it, and though so many years have passed, Jonathan still cannot bring himself to cross the threshold. Francis enters the bedroom and moves around the sheet-draped furniture. White sheets, like Halloween ghosts, cover the chairs, dressers, and an armoire. She stops at the small double bed and imagines her great-great-grandparents sleeping there. After resting a moment in silence to show respect, she makes the sign of the cross and leaves the chamber, quietly closing the door. Slowly, she begins to believe Jonathan might be telling the truth.

"So which door was your room?" she asks.

"The one on the right. The other opens to a small closet."

Francis turns the doorknob to the small closet. A cabinet with shelves holds old linens neatly folded and tucked away.

"How could you possibly know all this?!" she asks, astounded.

"This is my home." Then he corrects himself with respect, "This *was* my home. It's as clear to me today as your room downstairs surely is to you."

She motions for him to open the last door. "It's your room. Entrer."

Jonathan turns the handle and opens the door. A small room with two beds separated by a window comes into view. Francis holds her hands to her face and begins to cry. Above the left bed, written in pencil, was the name Camille. Clara's name decorated the wall above the bed on the right. A small rag doll is draped across Camille's bed. Jonathan enters his long-forgotten bedroom, his fingers tracing the bed frame. He remarks how tiny they look.

"I remember this room being a lot larger," he says, picking up a child's drawing, one he drew some eighty years ago: a crayon figure of a big sister holding hands with her younger sister, a doll with yellow curly hair hanging from the small figure's other hand. Red misshaped hearts float above them. Jonathan returns the drawing to the desk and rests his fingertips tenderly upon it.

They turn their focus to the corner of the room. A four-drawer dresser with crystal knobs stands vigilant, guarding a family's long-kept secret. Years of dust blanket the surface, akin to a forest's ground covering undisturbed on a winter morning. It doesn't seem proper to disturb its slumber, but Jonathan knows he must. He takes one side of the dresser and Francis the other. Without too much effort, they move the fragile antique off to the side.

Pointing to the wooden floorboard, Jonathan says, "That's the one."

Francis kneels slowly, her hands shaking, and she pries the floorboard up with her fingernails. She stares inside and is shocked by what she sees. A small box wrapped in cloth lays undisturbed.

Carefully, she removes the box from the floor and shakes her head. "You have got to be fucking kidding me," she says in English. Quickly she apologizes though, returning to French. "Pardon my French," she says. Despite the tension, Jonathan laughs.

For the first time since he arrived, both of them feel at ease. They leave the room and start downstairs. Jonathan takes one final look at his small bedroom and smiles. *For sixteen years, I was happy here. As a family, we were happy. My father was a good man. My mother was loving. We believed nothing could destroy our happiness. We were wrong.*

Jonathan catches up to Francis on the second floor and they make their way downstairs carrying the cloth-covered box.

"Mama!" Francis calls out, "It's true. It's *all* true. I don't know how he knew, but the rooms up there are just as he said. He knew everything, right down to the smallest detail! And look! Look what we found, right where he said it would be! In the corner of the room. We moved the dresser, and it was right there under the floorboards." As she places the cloth-covered box on the table, Emma stares on in disbelief.

Trevor is still perplexed, waiting for Cassandra to translate.

"They found it, Trevor!" she exclaims. "Right where Dad said it would be."

"So Dad is this woman's aunt?" Trevor asks, baffled.

"Shhhh," Cassandra waves her hand for her brother to be quiet.

Emma carefully unwraps the delicate fabric. An antique wooden box is slowly revealed. As she opens the lid, she begins to cry. Necklaces, rings, and jewelry of all shapes and sizes swim in a sea of gold, silver, and precious stones. She retrieves a small black-velvet pouch and opens it. Diamonds pour into her palm.

"Papa was a jeweler," Jonathan repeats. "He trusted me to hide these from the Germans."

Emma rises and gives Jonathan a hug. "You did well, Clara," she whispers in his ear. "Trés bon. Now you can rest."

For the first time, Jonathan hugs his niece. The two of them begin to cry. Emma can feel the love of her mother's sister embracing her. Jonathan feels the love of a niece he never knew.

The two warmly embrace for the longest time, refusing to let go of this special moment. Finally, Jonathan takes Emma's hands in his and kisses them. "I'm sorry I wasn't there for you or your mother. I would have liked to watch you grow up."

Francis peers into the box and removes a small 3 inch by 2 inch block of wood, and hands it to Jonathan. "Is this what you've been searching for?"

Clara Marie Dumont, March 29th, 1924 is carved into the block. Jonathan hesitates to turn it over, fearful of what he will see. The small, wooden block tumbles in his palm and there it is—the word that haunts him—the word he knew would be there.

AETERNUM

"You mentioned a man from Scotland who came here years ago, ranting about a small tablet?" Jonathan asks Emma.

"Oui."

Cassandra turns to her brother. "That means—"

"I know what Oui means," Trevor snaps. "I have no idea about anything else they said."

"Do you think you were also that man?" Emma asks.

"I don't know." Jonathan stares at Clara Dumont's name on the tablet. Lost in his own thoughts, he repeats, "I don't know, but I think it's time I found out."

She smiles sympathetically, imagining the long journey that awaits him.

"Come on, Trevor," Jonathan nods toward the door. "I'll explain everything on the plane."

"Plane?"

"Looks like we're going to Scotland," Cassandra says, smiling at her brother.

Jonathan gives Emma a kiss on the forehead and hugs Francis goodbye. A fleeting smile betrays the promise of staying in touch as Jonathan knows this is au revoir.

"No one is ever going to believe this," Francis says, watching as Jonathan and his children leave the house.

The three of them head down the stone walkway. They get no more than ten feet away, before Jonathan arches his back and falls to his knees.

Francis rushes from the house.

"Dad! Dad!" both Cassandra and Trevor cry.

Jonathan's head snaps forward, and he falls to the ground, his arms limp by his side.

"Dad!" Trevor screams, convinced his father is having a stroke.

"Call for a doctor!" Cassandra pleads.

But before the two women move, Jonathan stirs, then gets to his feet. "No, no, I'm fine! Don't call anyone!" They help him to his feet as Emma watches from the doorway.

"What the hell was that?! Trevor blurts out. "Dad, did you have a seizure?"

"That wasn't a seizure," Jonathan assures him.

Once she's convinced Jonathan is in no need of medical attention, Francis returns to the house.

"There is now absolutely no doubt in my mind," Emma says to her daughter. "That man, Jonathan Taylor, is the reincarnation of my Aunt Clara!"

"How can you be sure?" Francis asks.

"The reason he can't recall anything after running from the house. Your Great Aunt Clara was shot by a German soldier no more than ten feet from this very doorway, right there." She motions to the spot where Jonathan fell. "They put one bullet in her back and then another in the back of her head." As Francis closes the door, Emma whispers under her breath, "Nazi bastards."

PLACE: ROMA
YEAR: 169 BCE

In another part of the world at another time, a

condemned poet sat in a dimly lit cell on a cold, dirt floor. His name was Quintus Ennius. Outside, he heard the roar of the crowd as one by one, Roman centurions pulled terrified men from around him and ushered them into the arena. Many walked out without uttering a word, all hope already lost. Others had to be dragged off screaming. This was the third day of a celebration commissioned by Titus Quinctius Flamininus to commemorate the death of his father. The games were to continue for one more day, and by Quintus's count, four dozen men had already been slaughtered.

Sundown fast approached. Quintus prayed to stay alive at least for one more day. All around him, frightened men strewn across the floor or huddled against cold stone walls waited to die. Their hands cupped over their mouths, blocking their nostrils from the stale air which retained the thick, pungent odors of men's bodies mixed with rotting food and human waste. The smell was unbearable. Flies buzzed constantly around their faces, adding to the intolerable conditions. After three days, even the strongest-willed man had to concede to the annoying assault, and cease brushing them away.

Using a small metal nail he found on the floor of his cell, Quintus frantically scratched letters into a hard clay tablet. Other frightened slaves and condemned prisoners looked on in morbid curiosity.

"You, little man," a large Galilean demanded. "What are you doing there?"

Quintus continued to work, focusing on the task at hand. One more letter, one last character to etch into the hard-baked clay, and it would be finished. His fingers clutched the rusty nail tightly as he carefully applied pressure to create the downward stroke of the letter '*M*.' Suddenly, a foot kicked him on the thigh.

"I said, what are you doing?"

Quintus looked up to see a giant standing over him. Ignoring the titan would not be wise, so he responded simply, "I'm making a tablet."

"What is the purpose of this tablet? Why are you working so hard?" the behemoth asked. "For three days now, you've scratched away on that tiny stone."

"I am hoping it will survive me when I am gone from this earth," Quintus answered the man, adding, "And it's clay."

"Clay, stone, same difference to Juzif."

Quintus continued with his task.

"What are those symbols you scratch into the *clay*?"

Dismissively, Quintus says, "Letters."

"These letters make words?" the man questions, squatting next to Quintus.

"Usually," he replied curtly.

"Usually Juzif crushes man's head who makes Juzif mad."

Quintus realized it would be prudent to appease his inquisitive guest. Stopping mid-stroke, he turned his attention to the curious man and took notice of his incredible size. Choosing his words more carefully, Quintus said, "It was not my intention to anger you. It is just—I am almost finished, and the guards may be back any minute." He raised his eyebrows, his gaze darting back and forth between the big man and the clay tablet. "Would Juzif mind if I continue to work while we talk?"

Juzif waved his hand with a touch of flair, "Please continue. I doubt they will come for anyone else today. The sun is almost set and—"

Trumpets blew out in the arena above them, interrupting Juzif, signifying the end of events for the evening.

"See, we live for another day," the giant said, sitting next to Quintus.

In the cell, everyone breathed a sigh of relief. Quintus brought the clay tablet to his lips and blew the dust from its surface. He studied the etching and made small refined strokes to remove any imperfections. Again he blew on it, retouched it, and inspected his craftsmanship as Juzif looked on.

"What is that word you carved? Is that your name?"

"AETERNUM," Quintus answered, "and no." He turned the tablet over. "Here is my name." *Quintus Ennius.*

"May I see it?" the giant requested, holding out his hand.

"Please be careful. It's the only thing I have left in this world." Quintus laid the fragile marker in the man's enormous hand.

The small clay tablet looked minuscule when cradled in the palm of the giant. Gently, he inspected the tablet, struggling to understand the words scratched into its surface. Tenderly then, he handed it back to Quintus.

"This piece of clay will outlast you?" he asked.

Quintus looked defeated. "A piece of moldy bread will outlast me, I'm afraid, but yes, that is the idea. After I am butchered, this little tablet will live on. Hopefully, one day someone will remember me."

The giant chuckled as he rose. "Not if you bring that into the arena with you," he said, and then walked away. A small group of slaves arrived soon after, carrying a heavy black pot filled with slop. Dinnertime in the pit. A well-armed centurion opened the cage, allowing them to enter before locking the thick metal bars behind them again. They began to dish out the foul-smelling gruel. Juzif made his way to the servers.

The men at the back of the line stepped aside and let him pass. He returned with three bowls—one in his left hand and two grasped in his right.

He extended a bowl to his newfound friend, "Eat. They want us to be healthy when they slaughter us."

"Thank you," Quintus said, timidly taking the bowl from the man's hand.

The food wasn't good, but it was hot and contained some leftover shreds of meat. It warmed his stomach. Juzif devoured both of his bowls by the time Quintus had eaten half of his.

"It is better warm," Quintus remarked. "Thank you. By the time I get some, it is cold and almost never has meat."

"I know, I have watched you scratch on that tablet for days, often going without food."

"I do not see the point in staying healthy," Quintus said, slumping his shoulders and peering into the bowl.

"You never know. You might fight bravely, and if the gods favor you, they will let you live."

"Gods. The gods certainly favored *you*! If anyone comes out of this tournament alive, it will be *you*, my friend. The gods have blessed you with both strength and wisdom."

"Juzif is not a smart man or he would not be in here," the giant said.

"Why, what was your crime?"

"I strangled a man who tried to be with my wife," Juzif answered, staring at his open palms. "Now I am here and my wife is unprotected." Silently, still regretting his actions, he asked, "Why are you here?"

"Me? I am here because I slept with a woman," Quintus confessed, tossing his bowl to the ground. The flies descend quickly and begin feasting on the last remnants of the disgusting ration.

The big man laughed. "If that was a crime, I would have been in here years ago, many times over."

"Apparently, it is a crime when the woman is married to a member of the Senate." Now it's Quintus's turn to laugh.

Juzif joined in the laughter, and both condemned men released days of pent-up anxiety. For the first time since he was thrown in there, Quintus found some small comfort in the hellish place.

"What did you mean when you said I should not bring the tablet into the arena?" Quintus asked as their laughter subsided.

"Let us just say you are killed tomorrow," Juzif said, tilting his head and making a doleful face. "I am not saying it will happen, but it might."

Quintus smirked and shook his head. "It is a good possibility."

Juzif continued, "Well, then they drag your body out, strip you naked, and either hack up your body to feed to the dogs or throw your remains in a pit for other slaves to cover you with dirt. If they find that clay tablet, they will either smash it to bits or throw it in the pit along with your body. Either way, that will be the last anyone will ever see of you or that little tablet."

"What?! It has to survive me! I need someone to find it. Someone needs to know I was here."

The giant held out his hand. "Give it here."

"What if you die too? I know your chances are much better, but what if—"

The giant gestured with his fingers, beckoning the condemned poet to trust him. Quintus surrendered to the request. For a second time, he laid the fragile tablet in his new friend's hand. Juzif scanned the room until he spotted what he was looking for. In the back, where the wall met the ceiling, a small exposed brick jutted out from the rest. He moved to the back of the cell, and making sure no one was looking, reached up and pulled on the stone. The brick moved slightly. His large finger brushed the space between the stones; the mortar crumbled and gave way. A few more wiggles and the brick pulled free. Juzif brought the tiny tablet to his lips, kissed it, then reached up and laid it in its final resting place. There it would remain for hundreds of years.

Juzif tossed the brick to the other side of the cell. "One day, hopefully, someone will find it and you will be remembered. Now get some rest. Tomorrow we die."

He thanked his giant friend. "Maybe I can make you one?" The cold, damp floor chilled Quintus's body even as he spoke the words.

The Galilean folded his arms, making them appear even larger as he propped himself up against the stone wall. "If we live tomorrow, you can make me one. But I do not think the odds are in our favor."

Quintus's eyes slowly scanned the men remaining in the cell: all of them frail, feeble, half sick or half dying. If not for Juzif, Quintus would be the predominant male in the cage. They will surely fight tomorrow, maybe even matched against each other. And if that happened, Quintus knew, his life would at least end abruptly. For this night, however, Quintus was grateful to call Juzif a friend.

PLACE: VÉRINES, NÉRY, FRANCE
YEAR: PRESENT DAY

Jonathan's phone rings as the family heads back to Paris. Glancing at the caller ID, it reads *Dr. Elizabeth Davidson,* so he passes it to Trevor.

Trevor answers, putting it on speakerphone. "Hello."

"Hello, Jonathan? It's Elizabeth Davidson."

"My Dad's driving. We're on our way back to Paris. You're on speaker though," Trevor informs her.

"Oh, okay. Did you all go to Néry?"

"Oui," Jonathan answers. "Yes," Trevor needlessly translates.

"Is he speaking French? I didn't know you spoke French, Jonathan?" she inquires, then adds, "I don't speak a word, but I'd love to learn."

"He is, and no, he doesn't," says Trevor.

"Wait? What? I'm a bit confused."

Trevor lets out a little chuckle. "How do you think *I* feel, being the only person in the room who can't speak French? Especially when you father is holding an entire conversation with a woman and speaking as though he was born in Paris."

"Woman? What woman?"

"If you believe all this, she's my grand-niece," Jonathan says, with some uncertainty in his voice, only for the specificity of the ranking. He looks at Cassandra for confirmation.

Cassandra nods.

"Oh, so you're related to her?" Jonathan detects a hint of relief in her voice. Dr. Davidson then inquires, "So what did you discover?"

"Well—" Jonathan begins, but Trevor interrupts.

"Dad was shot."

"*What?!* It sounded like you said your father was shot?!" her alarmed voice shrieks through the receiver.

"Yup, twice!" Trevor replies nonchalantly.

"Oh my God! Twice?! He's been shot! *Twice!* And *he's* driving?!" Her voice resonates hysteria. "Why isn't he in hospital?"

"It wasn't me, Elizabeth," Jonathan quickly clarifies, "I'm fine. It was Clara who was shot—"

"Clara? I thought Trevor said it was you? Who's Clara? Is *she* alright? Is *she* in hospital? What happened? Why were people shooting at you?"

Jonathan laughs. "Elizabeth, calm down."

"I don't think this is anything to laugh at. A girl has been shot," she begins to argue, becoming quite defensive.

"Clara Dumont was shot almost 80 years ago," he explains. "Apparently, I was a 16-year-old girl named Clara Dumont who was killed by a Nazi soldier—"

"Wait!" Elizabeth stops him, urgency in her voice. "What did you say her name was?!"

"Clara Dumont. Why?"

"Jonathan, you're not going to believe this. The reason I'm calling you—I've been talking to some colleagues about your case. I wanted to know if anyone else had cases where the subject recalled such vivid memories—"

"I'm a subject now?" Jonathan interrupts.

"Yes, Jonathan, you're my subject." She sighs. "Anyway, if I may continue. One of my colleagues knows a doctor in Italy who's currently treating a patient who claims to be a French woman, a woman named Camille Dumont!"

"That's Clara's sister!" Jonathan yells at the phone, swerving the car unconsciously as he looks at the phone. "If I could somehow talk to her—"

"I'm already on it, Jonathan," she interrupts. "I'll call you right back."

Silence fills the car as the phone indicates the connection has been terminated. The hum of the tires murmur as the passing wind joins the chorus of anticipation. Aside from Jonathan's raised eyebrows, there is no movement whatsoever inside the speeding car. All three are thinking the same exact thing. *This thing keeps getting weirder and weirder.* Suddenly, Jonathan's phone rings again, startling Trevor. His arm jerks, tossing the phone in the air.

"Answer it!" Cassandra screams.

Dr. Davidson's voice fills the car again. "Hello, Jonathan?"

All three respond, "Hello!"

"I've just spoken to Dr. Macaluso, the therapist who's treating—"

Waving one hand off the steering wheel, willing the words to come faster, "Yes, yes?!" Jonathan's impatience can't be bridled.

Elizabeth cuts to the chase. "We can meet with him in two days. In Florence."

"We?" asks Jonathan.

"You don't think I'm going to miss this, do you?!" she argues. "Jonathan, I'm a psychotherapist specializing in reincarnation. This is like finding the Holy Grail! Where are you staying? At what hotel? I'm booking a flight on the next plane to France. I'm coming to Paris!"

Jonathan gives Elizabeth the information and says goodbye. Trevor hits the small red circle on the face of the phone, ending the call.

"I guess we're going to Italy too," Jonathan says. The hum of the tires and passing wind return for the next 30 minutes. Finally, Jonathan says, "So there's a doctor treating a patient who claims to be Camille Dumont. That's weird."

Cassandra appears puzzled as Trevor bursts out, "Oh, that's weird? You think *that's* weird? *Really*, Dad?"

Jonathan turns and gives him a 'look.'

"How about someone spontaneously speaking in different languages? You don't think *that's* weird?"

Cassandra nods from the back seat.

"Lots of people suddenly ... unexpectedly ... speak in foreign languages. It's called Xenoglossy," Jonathan informs them. "Well, not a lot, but it does happen," he mutters to himself.

Trevor continues, completely ignoring his father's attempt to justify his spontaneous linguistic episodes. "I'm not talking about broken Spanish picked up on the subway on the way to work. I'm talking tribal languages spoken on continents and countries halfway around the world, countries where the residents themselves can't even speak the specific language."

Jonathan raises a single eyebrow.

"That alone would be a cute trick, Dad, but what I'm really worried about is, and maybe you haven't noticed this, but some of these past lives of yours are trying to kill you!" Trevor raises his hand to count. "Let's see now. So far you almost drowned, in mid-flight over the Atlantic." Trevor raises a finger. "You were run over by an invisible train in India." He raises another finger. "And, this here is my favorite, you've been shot. Not *once*, but *twice*. In France. By frickin' Nazis!" Two more fingers pop-up, and he waves them all at his father.

"I can count, Trevor, thank you," his father says dismissively, trying to keep his eyes on the road.

"And if that's not weird enough for you, you're also carrying around miniature headstones of all the people you used to be! In past lives!" Jonathan opens his mouth to speak, but Trevor isn't quite finished.

"Dead people, Dad! Dead! That's *not* weird, but another person who has similar experiences is what *you think* is weird?!"

Again, the car falls silent for a long time.

"Look," Jonathan says, speaking in a low, quiet voice. "I'm just saying it's a bit weird to me that two people from the same family have been reincarnated and are both actively speaking to professionals."

"Maybe it's like playing an instrument?" Cassandra offers. "You know, like when one person is talented in the family, usually the whole family is talented." She smiles. "Like the Jackson 5. Only one of them is more talented than the others."

"Oh, great!" Jonathan exclaims, feigning anger. "So does that make me Michael?!" Jonathan waits a moment and then grins. The two siblings erupt with him in a chorus of laughter.

PLACE: ROMA
YEAR: 169 BCE

That night, Quintus dreamt he was performing one of his

plays on the great stage in front of his countrymen. He delivered every line with tender emotion, captivating his audience and bringing them to tears when he was sorrowful, and making them laugh when he played the fool. When he recited his final lines, the crowd erupted in applause, throwing roses at his feet. He took bow after bow as the cheers grew louder and louder: Quintus! Quintus! Quintus!

"Quintus!" Juzif shouted, shaking him from his dream.

The stage faded and turned into a dirt floor, littered with mud and puddles of piss. Noble ladies and esteemed gentlemen transformed into desperate, condemned criminals and thieves.

"Get up! The games have begun, and they already took away two of the men."

Quintus rose to his feet with the aid of his giant friend.

"So the day has begun. Today we die," he said, looking up into the eyes of his only friend in the world. "If we are to fight one another, I will not raise a sword against you. Promise me you will strike me as swiftly and painlessly as possible, as painless as death by a piece of metal thrust through your body can be."

"No!" Juzif protested. "You can not just surrender. We have to 'put on a good show' or your body parts will be hacked off while you are still alive, and fed to the beasts for amusement. The crowd will laugh as your screams fill the arena."

"Juzif, I am not incredibly huge like you. I am no gladiator. I am a poet! I have never even held a sword."

"Look at me!" Juzif ordered. "There are only four strikes."

The two men stood facing each other.

"An overhead strike—" As he recited the strikes, he demonstrated it several times. "The backhand, the cross hand, and the forward step, which is the hardest to block." Juzif moved behind Quintus, his immense body blanketing the small poet, and he grabbed one of his wrists.

"Juzif, what are you doing?"

"Hopefully, I am saving your life. If nothing else, I am giving you a fighting chance."

He moved his hand, and like a rag doll, Quintus's body responded. He grasped his shoulder with his free hand and positioned his body in a warrior's stance. "Now, you stand like this. Not too far forward." He bent his body forward, pushing Quintus off balance. "And not too far backward." He pulled on his shoulder, arching his back, causing Quintus to stumble backward.

"You want to be like this," he raised Quintus's arm, "with your sword hand raised high, anticipating the attack."

"Remember the overhead strike?" he asked.

Quintus nodded.

"You block it like this." He thrust his arm up, locking it in place. "You must make your arm hard! Harder than stone! The sword will strike your blade, and if your arm holds, the strike will fail!"

"If it does not hold?" Quintus asked.

"Then his blade will drive down, propelling your blade into your shoulder or chest, while his blade cleaves your skull in two."

"Let us hope I can make my arm like a stone."

"Let us hope," the big man continued. "Now the second attack, you block like this."

Juzif went through all the attacks and all the blocks. He showed Quintus how to defend and then counter-attack. "With every attack you block, you must quickly strike! Never give your opponent a chance to attack again. If you are lucky, and he underestimates you, *your* attack may just land a fatal blow. And if that happens, you may just win your freedom today."

"Do you really think so?"

The big man sat. "This is the fourth day of fighting. After four days, the arm of a man grows tired. Steel is very heavy and the days are very long. There is a reason why only the old and the weak are left now. No offense."

Quintus waved it off. "But what about you? You are the strongest one here. Why did they not take you first?"

"I am unsure of this myself. It is possible they are waiting for a grand finale, three against one, so the crowd will not leave."

Slowly as the day went on, the cell seemed to double and triple in size, until only a handful of forgotten souls remained.

Quintus refused to allow any hope to fill his heart, and his expectations manifested into reality when four centurions marched down the corridor and opened the cell doors. No words were spoken, only a disinterested finger pointed toward him, Juzif, and one other man.

They were led to a small room containing various battle gear and weapons, and instructed to choose one weapon and any protective armor they desired. Audible chuckles emanated from the three centurions.

Quintus picked up a sword from the table. The weight of the steel overwhelmed him right away and it crashed to the dirt floor, dragging Quintus down along with it. It was as though the godly hand of Pluto himself had reached up from the underworld and snatched the sword, pulling it to the earth. Quintus gripped the sword tightly, this time with both hands, and raised it over his head, trying desperately to defend himself against an imaginary attacker. He envisioned a powerful gladiator standing before him wielding a sharp steel blade. The phantom gladiator attacked. The invisible blade collided with his, sending it backwards. His arm gave way. The blade came to rest between his eyes, splitting his head wide open. Quintus imagined the unbearable pain he would suffer as he lay on the arena floor dying, and he shook with terror. The thought of surrendering crossed his mind next, and another image of his body, slowly hacked to pieces and fed to hungry animals, replaced the former scenario.

"Here!" Juzif said, thrusting a smaller, more maneuverable sword into his hand. "And wear this." He placed a helmet on his head. "This way they will have to work extra hard to split your skull." Quintus couldn't tell if he was joking or not.

A voice called down the hall. The time to die was upon them. As they walked down a long corridor, a bright light could be seen in the distance; the threshold to the arena. Quintus suddenly experienced a *'familiar'* feeling, and in an instant, memories of past lives came rushing back to him. Confused by centuries of scenes playing out within his head, he thought, *this must be what happens before you die.* With a forceful shove, he was pushed outside into the blinding sun and quickly shielded his eyes. For three days he had been in a dark, dank cell, but now the intense brightness of the sun's light burned his retinas. Slowly, the arena came into focus. Hundreds of his countrymen cheered and shouted applause for the three men about to die. All acclamation fell on deaf ears. The gritty, white sand beneath his feet was hot. It warmed the cold within his toes and ankles. His lungs filled with fresh air, and he felt the sun on his face. The sweet smell of wild flowers intoxicated him. He felt joy for the first time since the centurions broke down his door and dragged him away. He closed his eyes and imagined he was back in his garden. Slowly, the faint sound of a bee buzzing grew louder and louder, crescendoing into a howl. The pleasant hum was replaced by deafening cheers from the crowd, snapping him back to reality.

Four well-protected, heavy-armed gladiators stood facing the grandstand where Quinctius Flamininus and his wife sat, both of them quite bored. The four shouted something up to them, in unison, and then saluted the emperor and his wife.

Quintus wanted to cry out, apologizing that his wearisome death would not be exciting enough for the illustrious couple. But before he could, the four gladiators turned to the three sacrificial lambs and assumed an aggressive stance. The battle had begun.

Juzif jumped to readiness. Two of the gladiators marked him for their own. Quintus saw Juzif and made ready just as he was taught. The third man turned and ran. One of the gladiators took chase.

Cautiously, the three gladiators made their way across the arena toward the waiting men. Two flanked Juzif, and he took precautionary measures not to make it an easy kill. Quintus came face to face with his would-be executioner. His hands trembled as he waited for the first strike. Both men sized each other up. Quintus heard the clash of steel and stole a glance to see Juzif engaged with both men. His newfound friend frantically wielded his swords, deflecting blows and countering, desperately trying to strike a blow of his own. Quintus looked back just in time to see his opponent charging with his sword overhead. Quickly, he recalled the first block Juzif taught him. He raised his sword high above his head, horizontal to his opponent, making his arm as stiff as possible. The strike was tremendous. It came down with a crash of thunder against Quintus's sword. His wrist gave way, and the sword swung like a pendulum. But the strike was deflected. Quintus tightened his grip and prepared for another attack. His opponent came at him with a cross-hand strike. Quintus responded with the appropriate defense. Only this time, he immediately countered, catching his attacker off guard. The small poet's sword made contact with his opponent's massive breastplate. A resounding clash filled the arena. If not for the protective armor, his blow would surely have been fatal.

The crowd cheered for the underdog, infuriating the heavily clad warrior. His eyes widened, conveying the depth of his hatred for his inept foe. Both men were incredibly cautious as they now circled one other. Quintus recalled the words of his friend, who taught him how to fight. *'Remember, you do not have to kill him. If you inflict any major wound, he will be out of the fight, allowing you to defend yourself against other opponents.'*

Armed with these words, it was now Quintus who attacked, thrusting and slashing his sword again and again at the well trained gladiator. Much like a lion toying with a mouse, every attack made by Quintus was easily deflected. Quintus knew the skilled killer was merely waiting for the right moment to strike.

In the distance, the man who ran away cried out, and the crowd roared. Quintus feared it was Juzif, but remained focused on his opponent, who seemed fueled by the roar of the crowd. The muscular adversary brought his sword down. Quintus readied for the blow. He reinforced his grip on the sword with both hands and steadied his arms. Nothing could have prepared Quintus for the incredible strength the gladiator drove down upon his blade. The force crippled Quintus to his knees, burying the tip of his sword into the soft sand.

The crowd erupted in screams and shouts. Victory was within Rome's grasp. The triumphant gladiator again raised his sword high, intending to split his defenseless prey in two.

Quintus saw his chance. He pulled his sword from the earth, but instead of defending, he lunged, slashing wildly at the unprotected legs of his enemy. His sword buried deep into the upper thigh, and sliced open the meaty quadriceps of the gladiator's left leg. A shower of red sprayed forth, painting the white sand as deep crimson blood flowed from the gashing wound. The crowd cheered, but all Quintus could hear was the agonizing screams of the fallen warrior that laid just out of reach of his blade.

He looked over at Juzif in triumph. His friend was down on one knee, blood-covered, and badly hurt. One gladiator's body laid mangled in the sand, but the other was preparing another assault. Quintus got to his feet and ran toward his friend. The well-armed gladiator grasped his sword with both hands and hoisted it over his head. Quintus thrust his sword between his friend and the downward motion of the sword. The two instruments of death sang out in a clash of metal. The blow was deflected, but the attack did not stop.

Quintus felt another man's hand wrap around his throat from behind, and lift him into the air. It was the fourth gladiator who had given chase and killed the third prisoner, now returned unannounced and unaware by Quintus and Juzif. Quintus felt a sharp sting on his right side just between his ribs, and then a burning fire entered his chest and run up to his heart. He tried to scream, but the crushing fingers made it impossible. All around him, the bloodlust cheers of Roman spectators filled his ears.

He dropped to the ground like a rag doll. Searing pain burned throughout his chest. He felt a warm, sticky pool of blood travel under his body as he laid in the hot sand. The last thing he saw was Juzif, his friend's fallen body lying next to his. He closed his eyes and heard the cheers of the crowd. He was once again upon the stage. A slow smile grew on his face. The curtain closed. Quintus Ennius took his final bow.

Nearly 2,200 years later, an overnight security guard, Bruce Douglas, patrolled one of Rome's most famous landmarks. Every night, he walked the stone corridors of the ancient arena, making his rounds and checking locked gates. He often wondered what it must have been like to sit in the stands and watch an actual gladiator event take place. *Not too good for the poor slobs that were killed,* he thought. Tonight, he was inspecting the lower area where the slaves were held. All was normal, and he usually never encountered any trouble anyway, which is why he took this job in the first place. On this particular night, however, he would come across something that would earn him a place in the history books. In one of the cells, as he pointed his flashlight on the back wall, a tiny metal object caught the beam and reflected back at him. He spied a soda can wedged into a small opening in the back wall where a brick should be. *Freaking kids. No respect.*

He walked to the back of the cell, where an eerie feeling overtook him. For nearly a thousand years, these cells held condemned men waiting to be brutally butchered. The ghosts of men slaughtered for Rome's amusement were especially strong down in these cells, and tonight, Bruce felt as if he was not alone. He turned and looked at the entrance. *To live out your final days here must have been unimaginable.*

Then he turned and proceeded with the task at hand. He reached up and pulled the aluminum can from the hole. In doing so, a small clay tablet slid forward from the rock wall, breaking the plane and hanging over the edge of the stone brick upon which it rested. Bruce carefully removed the tablet from its 2,000-year-old slumber and blew on it.

Centuries of dust flew through the air, causing Bruce to cough. He shone his flashlight at the small tablet in his hand, and eyes widened as he began to make out faint writing upon the tablet. He blew harder, removing the tiny pieces of grime that made their home within the small grooves carved into the clay. The name *Quintus Ennius* appeared. A cold breeze brushed against his neck, causing a chill to run down his spine. He spun around, quickly shining the flashlight all around the cell. Shadows moved, and voices of long ago whispered through the stone passageways. In years to come, when Bruce recapped the story, he would say he heard someone whisper in a faint voice, 'remember me'. But for now, his attention returned to the clay tablet. He turned it over, and on the side that laid upon the brick, free from dust and clearly visible, he saw the word *AETERNUM* carved into it. He shined the light into the gaping hole, hoping to find more, but to his disappointment, the small clay tablet was the only remnant of a time long ago.

It will be added to the Colosseum Museum exhibits, and will forever be known as *The Douglas AETERNUM stone.* Circa 169 BCE.

Quintus Ennius (/ˈkwɪntəs ˈɛniəs/; Died c. 169 BCE) was a writer and poet who lived during the Roman Republic. He is often considered the father of Roman poetry. He was born in Rudiae, formerly a small town located near modern Lecce in the heel of Italy (ancient Calabria, today Salento). He could speak Oscan as well as Latin and Greek. Although only fragments of his works survive, his influence in Latin literature was significant, particularly in his use of Greek literary models.

His famous quote: "Let no one weep for me, or celebrate my funeral with mourning; for I still live, as I pass to and fro through the mouths of men."

That night, leaving the hotel on their way to dinner, Jonathan spots Dr. Davidson getting out of a taxi.

"Doc! Hey, Doc!" he calls out, waving to her. "I mean Elizabeth," he corrects himself as he approaches her. "What timing, the kids and I are going to get dinner. Did you eat yet?"

"Oh? Well, no actually. I came straight from the airport."

"Great!" Jonathan says. "You'll join us. We'll make it a foursome. Whattaya say?"

Taken off guard, she responds slowly, "I guess so, but I have to check in first."

"Nonsense." Jonathan takes her overnight travel bag and leans into the window of the cab. "S'il vous plait, attendez une minute," he says, once again in perfect French, asking the driver to wait a minute as he runs into the hotel.

Dr. Davidson looks at Trevor and Cassandra. "Is your father always this controlling?"

"No, he's just a take-charge kinda guy. I guess he's excited to see you," Cassandra says, adding, "I guess he likes you."

"Why do you think that?" she asks, but before Cassandra can respond, Jonathan comes jogging back out from the hotel lobby.

"Okay, we're all set." He holds the taxi door open for the three of them to enter.

As the kids settle into the taxi, she asks him, "You checked me in? That was fast!"

"No, no, I just asked the bellhop to place your bag in my room."

"Hm. Quite presumptuous of you," she murmurs, stepping into the taxi.

Jonathan's brain tries to decipher her last statement before the suggestive implication of his innocent action finally dawns on him.

"Oh! No, I didn't mean—" But it's too late. She's already sitting in the back seat. He looks in. Seeing how there's no room for a man his size to fit comfortably, he walks around to the front passenger side door and gets in.

They dine at the Café de l'Homme, an outdoor restaurant attached to the Homme Museum. The museum houses the most extensive anthropological exhibits from around the world, but what's more impressive is the view of the Eiffel Tower at night. It's absolutely breathtaking. Jonathan and Elizabeth drink wine and share stories of their lives, unaware twilight is descending on Paris. All around them, the City of Lights comes alive like fireflies dancing throughout the city streets. He talks of architecture and his love of famous buildings as the rose-colored sky turns a majestic purple before fading to a deep slate blue.

Over dinner, she shares intimate details of her life that some might say cross the boundaries of patient-doctor relationship. But there's something about him, she thinks, something comforting. Something in this handsome man's eyes sitting across from her, listening intensely to her stories, that makes her want to share her life story with him. *This is the closest thing I've had to a date in almost a year. Not that this is a date.* He smiles. *Is this a date?*

"I was dating a guy named Noah, but I broke it off months ago," she says. "I was searching for something, am searching for something, unforgettable." And she wonders if Jonathan can take a hint.

"I knew a guy named Noah once," Jonathan says, setting up a joke.

"You did?"

"Nice guy. Loved animals." He giggles. "Lots of them." He laughs as the kids join in.

She's puzzled, but then it sinks in and she smiles. "Oh, very funny!! Ha, ha!"

"He had a crazy idea about building a really big boat," Jonathan continues. "I read that in a book somewhere."

She playfully slaps his arm, then rubs the spot tenderly.

Cassandra looks at Trevor. Is she the only one who can see what is happening?

As dinner winds down, the kids grow tired and want to go back to the hotel.

"Okay," Jonathan says. "We'll meet tomorrow in the lobby for breakfast and discuss Italy, say around 8 a.m.?"

"Oh my God," Elizabeth blurts out. "We haven't talked about Italy! How are we getting there? When should we leave? Where will we stay?"

"It's okay," he says as the kids leave. "We can talk about it now. Unless you want to get back to the hotel? I mean, if you want to go to bed?"

She laughs. "That's the second time you've tried getting me into your room tonight."

Jonathan's face turns scarlet. "Oh, no. I meant if you wanted to get some sleep." He fumbles his words. "I meant, you must be tired." He looks up, relieved to be rescued by the server with the bill.

"Please, let me—" she reaches for the check, but Jonathan snatches it from the server's outstretched hand.

"No, no. I invited you to join us." As he pays the check, he adds, "Besides, I enjoyed our conversation."

"So, if you hadn't enjoyed the conversation, I would be paying?"

Again, he blushes. "Boy, I can't say anything right to you tonight."

"I don't know. I think you've said a lot of right things tonight." She laughs as they leave the cafe and head to the park. "You know," she says, trying to pronounce the name of the museum in her best French accent, "The Musée de l'Homme, has some of the finest studies of man's social and cultural development in the world."

"Perhaps I can discover why this is happening to me?" he replies.

"Do you mean bumbling your words? Then turning red in the face and ears?" She smirks. "Or the whole 'Hey I've been here before' thing?"

He chuckles. "Yeah, the last thing."

They turn onto the Avenue de New York and Jonathan looks at the sign. "I travel halfway around the world just to find myself back on a New York street."

A tiny voice inside her head tells Elizabeth, *Don't start, Beth. He's a patient.* She glances up into his eyes. *Okay, an incredibly good-looking patient, but he's still a patient, and you're not here for pleasure, you're here on business.*

"Whatchya thinking?" Jonathan asks. "I can see the wheels turning up there," he adds, pointing to her head.

I'm thinking the hell with professional codes of conduct. We should definitely get to know each other better. "Just enjoying the night," she answers with a smile, slipping her arm around his. "Do you mind? I'm a bit cold."

"No, I ... uh ... sure ... yeah, it *is* a little cold."

Maybe it's the wine. Maybe it's the allure of Paris with romantic music playing in the distance, or the candle-lit storefronts and cafés. Or maybe, just maybe, it's this handsome man walking beside her that makes her wonder, *How bad can it be? What's the harm? Maybe he's not even interested in me. I'll drop some hints, and if he's not interested, he won't pursue it.*

She struggles with her next sentence. *'Don't say it,'* a tiny voice warns her. She knows if she utters this one sentence, she could go down a path she may not be ready for emotionally. Blaming the wine, she chooses to ignore the tiny voice inside her head. *After all, this is Paris.*

The music starts, she kick off her shoes, and walks onto the dance floor of romance. "I think I know why you've been fumbling your words all evening—" The dance has begun.

"Elizabeth, I want to clarify something," he interjects. "Before you share your thoughts."

There it is! He stopped the music! He's pulling me off the dance floor. He's rejecting me.

But one rejection isn't going to stop her, she decides. She doesn't want to give up that easily, and if anything, she's going to try even harder, "Yes, Jonathan?" she says a little too girlishly.

The music starts. She waits on the dance floor.

"Back at the hotel, I didn't mean to imply that you were going to share my room tonight—"

Not a rejection, she thinks. *He's just new to the dance.*

"No?" she replies, with just a hint of disappointment to keep him off balance. In her mind, she performed a perfect pirouette.

"I was merely asking the bellhop to place your bag in my room," he says, ending the sentence sheepishly with, "until you were able to check into your own room."

A beautiful sidestep, she thinks. *I'll have to try harder.* "It's quite late," she says softly. "They may not have any more rooms available." She watches his reaction. "Then I would *have* to stay with you. After all, you sort of kidnapped me tonight. You wouldn't want me to sleep out in the cold, would you?" Her arm gently squeezes his, implying, *You can have me if you want.*

"No. No, we wouldn't want that."

She stops. "You wouldn't want me to stay with you tonight?" she asks, lowering her head. Her lower lip pouts.

"No. I mean about sleeping on the street."

She waits for the correct response.

"I *do* have a magnificent view of the Eiffel Tower."

Her head remains lowered, but she captures his gaze while raising her doe-like eyes to meet his.

"I mean, if there are no more rooms, I guess you would have to stay with me, but that's not what I had in mind," he reassures her.

A smile bright enough to rival the lights of Paris beams at Jonathan. *Don't say it! Please don't say it! Don't say it!!!!!*

She doesn't listen to her tiny voice though, and by now, the wine is drowning out her inner voice, making her carefree. Damn her emotions. Damn being safe. She wants this man. She wants to feel his arms around her, feel his lips against hers. She wants to know what it would be like to explore each other's bodies as they move as one. She wants him, but she wants him to want her too. On this night, destined for love, she wants to drink it all in, every romantic moment this night has to offer. After all, this *is* Paris. She *is* a woman. And he *is* one handsome man!

She takes a step. Then another. He follows, slowly trailing closely behind, watching her body move. She heads down the street, calling back over her shoulder, "What did you have in mind, Jonathan?" Her breathy voice trails off.

"I uh—" Jonathan suddenly realizes he's been on the dance floor the entire time.

"So, do you want to hear my theory as to why you're stumbling over your words this evening?" She tempts faith, beckoning him to release the sentence that will take her down the path.

"I'm very interested in your ... *theories* ... Doctor." *He begins his part of the dance.* He stops her under an Art Nouveau street lamp. The soft, yellow glow shines down, illuminating the red highlights in her hair, setting them ablaze. A long-forgotten memory, buried deep, awakens within him.

"Your daughter thinks you like me, and I'm beginning to think she's right. I think that's why you're fumbling your words."

He pauses for a moment, wondering how to proceed. *Has Elizabeth been sending signals this entire time, or is she just making conversation?* "What's not to like?" he plays it safe, but sends a hint of a signal back. "You're a beautiful, attractive woman."

"Beautiful and attractive, hm," she responds, smiling as he blushes.

I've got him, she thinks. "Back in London," she moves closer, "in my office," she feels his body, "when you whispered in my ear, I thought you were going to kiss me."

He leans in, pressing his body against hers, feeling her breast against his chest. "I wanted to."

"Why didn't you?" she asks, rising on her toes and looking deep into his hazel eyes, her lips coming close to his.

"What would you have done if I had?" Jonathan asks, moving his head slightly to one side as she tilts hers to the other.

"I would have slapped your face," she says softly, her lips so close to his she can feel their heat.

Not the answer he was looking for, and he recoils. "Seriously?"

"Seriously," she whispers, advancing anyway, leaning on him, closing the space between their lips once again.

"And now?" he asks as his hands move to her waist, pulling her hips against his.

"I'd still slap your face," she answers, pushing her hips hard into his, feeling him grow with excitement.

"Am I missing something here, Doc?" he whispers with a puzzled look.

"A woman must surrender herself, Jonathan," she says, moving her hands up his back, feeling his strong muscles under his shirt.

"Are you surrendering yourself to me, Doc?" he asks, running his large fingers under her strawberry blonde hair, capturing the nape of her neck, cradling it in one hand as the other moves to the side of her face.

Elizabeth moves slowly forward. Her lips touch his. She feels their warmth. She smells his scent. She feels his excitement and aches to be with him. She withdraws slightly and breathes out silently in a soft whisper, "Oh yes, Jonathan."

His strong hands pull her to him. This time, he kisses her. A gentle, tender, yet forceful and confident kiss.

"I'm ready to go back to the hotel," she whispers in his ear. "And I'm not tired, and I don't think they have any more rooms."

Jonathan and Elizabeth spend the rest of the walk back to the hotel arm in arm, stopping whenever they feel the urge arise to kiss each other's lips, neck, and skin. He holds the door open for her, and the night desk clerk watches them as they make their way across the lobby to the elevators.

The both of them, too enthralled with each other, never see the old man. He smiles, knowing his city, the City of Lights, has brought these two together, if only for tonight.

Jonathan opens his door with a swipe of the key card, and Elizabeth steps inside. *Are you sure you know what you're doing Beth?* she hears her voice say.

She turns and falls against him. They embrace in a kiss. Her runner's body pushes him back against the slowly closing door, causing it to slam shut in its final inches. *I have never been more sure,* she answers herself.

Kicking off her shoes, she crosses the room. Her hands unzip her pencil skirt and it falls to the floor as she reaches the bed. She stands with her back to Jonathan, allowing him to marvel at her ass. She stops, only for a moment, before unbuttoning her blouse and letting it slip from her shoulders, covering her ass, once again obstructing his view. She smiles a coquettish grin and tosses her shirt to the chair in the corner of the room. Turning to face him, Elizabeth allows him to drink in her body with his eyes.

She can tell he is not disappointed. She sits, and pushes her body in the center of the bed before lying back. She spreads her arms out full over the king-size comforter. Elizabeth Davidson surrenders herself like a sacrificial virgin.

Jonathan walks across the room, removing his shoes and socks before undoing his belt buckle. His trousers drop to the floor. He undoes his shirt, throwing it to the corner chair, where it joins her blouse. He kneels on the bed. His gaze falls upon her toes, her legs, her hips, and her breasts as he travels up her body. His lips touch hers.

She whispers, "Say something to me in French."

"Je voulais faire l'amour avec toi la momne que je t'ai vue," he whispers back.

"Oh, Jonathan," she moans soft and sweet as she feels his body melt against hers.

He kisses her neck, then slowly moves down to kiss her breasts tenderly, discovering every inch of her before slowly moving lower. He kisses her stomach and slowly, ever so slowly, he moves down.

Moments later, she cries out again, "Oh, Jonathan!"

The next morning, they awaken to a knock at the door. Elizabeth's eyes widen as Jonathan sits straight up. He jumps out of bed and makes his way to the door.

"Jonathan!" she yells in a silent whisper. He's halfway across the room before he realizes he's stark naked. Jonathan runs to the closet and puts on a robe as Elizabeth throws the blankets over her head and hides. He turns and looks, giving the hotel room a quick scan. Elizabeth's shoes, skirt, blouse, bra, and panties are scattered about, as if Dr. Elizabeth Davidson's wardrobe exploded in his bedroom.

Another knock, "I'll be right there! Coming!"

Elizabeth peeks out from under the covers, watching Jonathan race around the room, gathering her clothes and throwing them in the closet. A tiny laugh escapes her. He brings his finger to his lips, making a shhhh sound. She quickly ducks back under, covering her head with the warm comforter like some kind of naked adult whack-a-mole game.

Jonathan opens the door, but only a few inches. "Hey! Good morning," he says, clearing his throat like someone who's been drinking. "What are you kids doing here?"

"Dad, it's 8:45!" Cassandra snaps. "We've been waiting in the lobby for 45 minutes already!"

"I must have had a little too much wine last night."

Cassandra starts to push the door open, but Jonathan stops her and holds the door firm. "Um, I'm not dressed." He pulls the top of his robe closed with one hand. "Why don't you guys go to breakfast, and I'll catch up in about 30—no, make it 45 minutes. Okay?" A faint snicker comes from the bed.

Cassandra's right eyebrow raises.

"Okay," Trevor answers.

"Okay," Jonathan mimics, closing the door. "Or maybe go sightseeing?"

"Wait, how are you going to know where we'll be?" Cassandra yells, trying to steal a peek at the bed as the door closes.

"Text me!"

Trevor and Cassandra stand dumbfounded in the hallway.

Trevor looks at Cassandra, and she looks back at him. *Sightseeing?* they both wonder.

Jonathan runs back to bed, sheds the robe, and jumps in under the covers. Elizabeth, unable to contain herself, bursts out laughing as Jonathan hugs her and begins to tickle her.

"This is all your fault!" he says, still tickling. Her body flails beneath him and she begs him to stop. "You almost got us caught!"

Jonathan's fingers cease the assault and wrap around her back, holding her tightly. "I bought us 45 minutes. What do you want to do?"

She lifts her head off the pillow and kisses his lips. "The same thing we did last night." She smiles. "Only faster."

Thirty-five minutes later in the shower, Elizabeth runs her fingers over Jonathan's body. She stops at two scars in the center of his chest, scars she overlooked last night.

"How did these happen?" she asks.

"I don't know, I've always had them. Since birth." He looks down, running his fingers over her chest in return.

She embraces him, wrapping her arms around him and gently feeling his back, secretly searching for something, something she hopes she won't find, but in her heart, she fears she will. He pulls her close, feeling the warmth of her skin as the cool water flows down his back. Her hands move over his flesh and then she feels it. Located directly opposite the two scars on his chest, the skin feels different, as though something impaled him, years earlier.

She turns, standing with her back toward him so he won't see her face. "We have to get dressed."

Jonathan kisses the nape of her neck and marvels at her body one last time before she gets out and dries herself with a towel.

"I don't think I'll ever find another woman with a body as beautiful or as perfect as yours."

Elizabeth can't help the rosy glow filling her cheeks. "That's quite the compliment, especially seeing as how you may have *literally* searched lifetimes to find me."

She hands Jonathan the towel and walks to the bedroom wearing only a smile, teasing him with one final look of her ass before getting dressed. She can feel his eyes watching her. Her inner voice warns, *Be careful, Beth. You're falling hard for this one.*

PLACE: NEW YORK CITY
YEAR: 1983

Professor Howard Convery sits in thoughtful silence

within his office at the Museum of Natural History in New York City. For almost three years, he'd tried to solve the mystery of the tablets, nicknamed *The Mystery Markers* by his colleagues, with no luck. The wooden tablet acquired by Professor Mintz, and the metal tablet he found in Deadwood both remained much like Winston Churchill's famous definition of Russia, "a riddle, wrapped in a mystery, inside an enigma".

Frustrated by the amount of inquires he sent out to no avail, he mused, *I know things move slowly in the archaeological world, but this is ridiculous.*

"How's it going?" the curator of the museum asks, sticking his head into Howard's office.

"I don't know, Ross. Everything is going well with my other projects. I just haven't made any headway with the—"

"Mystery Markers?" Professor Malher interjects, smiling. "You've gotta admit, it's a catchy name." Ross entered Howard's office holding the morning paper along with a couple of letters and what looked like an oversized manila envelope.

225

"I sent out letters all over the country and nothing turned up. I even sent letters to all the major museums in Europe, Asia, the Middle East, and Africa. I still haven't heard a thing."

"Well, I'm sure something will turn up. Perhaps today." Ross tossed the manila envelope on Howard's desk.

"Are you kidding me?" Howard snatched the envelope. "You had this the whole time?"

The address on the front of the envelope reads:

Museum of Natural History
Central Park West at 79th Street
New York, New York, 10024
Attn: Mr. Howard Convery

Howard reads the return address.

National Archaeological Museum,
28is Oktovriou 44, Athina 106 82, Greece.

Howard watched as Ross moved to the window, sporting a huge smile. "Do you think it's in response to the markers?"

"Only one way to find out," Ross said, as he gazed out the window. *Beautiful day. God, I love this city.* He turned and leaned against the sill. Howard, too nervous to open the envelope, just stood there. "Oh, for goodness' sake, just open it," Ross bellowed.

Howard then retrieved a letter opener from his desk and in one quick motion, freed the contents of the envelope. Fishing through the collection of papers and photographs that spilled out all over the desk, Howard retrieved the cover letter and read it out loud.

Dear Mr. Convery,

I'm writing in regards to your inquiry about ... Blah blah blah. *We found your research interesting ...* Blah blah blah. *One of our oldest curators recalls a similar tablet to the one you described in your letter.*

Howard looked at his boss. "This is it!" He continued reading.

He remembered because he thought it especially odd. It had the word AETERNUM inscribed on it, just as the ones in your possession. It appeared to be in Latin, but some of the letters were askew. I have enclosed photographs.

Howard looked up. Ross joined him at the desk.

I hope these help. Please feel free to contact me.

Martin Charters
Head of Ancient Studies
National Archaeological Museum,
Athens, Greece.

Howard rifled through the enclosed photographs. Image after image revealed a small tablet in various positions photographed from various angles. Some had a ruler lying next to them for scale, while others were positioned with artifacts. All were set on the standard black velvet archaeologist's board. Howard came to one photograph and stopped. His eyes widened, fixated on what he saw.

As he handed the pile of photos to Ross, the curious curator asked, "What is it, my boy?"

Howard held in his hand a photograph of a worn and weathered tablet, edges cracked and broken, with a single word clearly visible on the surface.

AETERNUM

Howard threw his arms around his boss and screamed. "Woo-hoo!" Jumping up and down, he dragged his boss's body around the room along with him.

"What's going on here?" Mike asked from the doorway, watching in stunned bemusement as two grown men, entwined in each other's arms, hopped about the office like a couple of school kids.

"We did it!" Howard yelled, releasing Ross from his embrace.

"We found another one!" He grabbed Mike by the shoulders and pulled him close. "We got another one!" With joyous abandonment, he planted a big smooch on Mike's cheek.

"I have to tell Donna!" Howard suddenly exclaimed, pushing Mike aside as he hurried out of the office, leaving Mike alone with Ross.

"We have another *what*?" Mike asked, totally puzzled. "Because, whatever *it* is, I don't think *I want it*. Not if *it* causes *that* kind of reaction."

Ross just shrugged with a smile. "He didn't even want the rest of his mail," he said, looking down at the top envelope. A second letter, also addressed to Howard Convery, sat unopened with a return address of St. Paul's Monastery, Jarrow NE32 3DY, United Kingdom.

PLACE: PARIS, FRANCE
YEAR: PRESENT DAY

As Trevor and Cassandra step out into the bright sunlight of the Parisian morning, Cassandra suddenly stops and runs back inside the hotel lobby. "I'll be right back, I just have to check something with the desk clerk."

She throws her hands down on the counter, launching herself forward, stretching on her tippy-toes and invading much of the desk clerk's personal space. "Could you please tell me Doctor Davidson's room number?"

The clerk quickly taps his computer keyboard. "I am sorry, mademoiselle, but we do not have a Doctor Davidson staying here." He doesn't mean to sound snooty, but isn't doing a good job.

"How about Elizabeth Davidson?"

With an expression of annoyance, he keys in the new information. "I am afraid we do not have anyone by that name either."

Interesting, she thinks.

The desk clerk raises one eyebrow then, as if to say, *please go away.* "Will there be anything else?"

"I guess not." Turning to leave, she stops abruptly and turns around again to ask, "Oh, yes, is there a good place to have breakfast around here?"

"You might want to try Schwartz's Deli. I am sure you will find it to your liking," he suggests with a dismissive attitude, already going about his business.

"And how do I—"

"Avenue d'Eylau. Number 7. It is approximately a 6-minute walk," he blurts out as though speaking English offends his ears. "Just go around Place Du Trocedéro."

She thanks him, in perfect French, for his kind service. "Merci beaucoup pour votre aimable service."

As the door closes, she hears him grunt. Ten minutes later, she and Trevor sit in Schwartz's Deli and order breakfast. Cassandra texts the address to her father. She even *drops a pin* to his GPS app to help him find the location, knowing perfectly well he'll never use it. Instead, he'll just ask the concierge for directions.

Wanting to confirm her suspicions she has about her father and Dr. Davidson, Cassandra looks at her brother, who's fiddling with his phone. "Trevor, let me ask you, do you think Dad is—"

"Crazy!" he inserts into her sentence. "I don't know, Cazz, but what happened at that French woman's house yesterday? That was bat-shit crazy!"

She looks at him perplexed, realizing he's totally missing the point of her question as he continues his rant.

"I don't know if I'm buying this whole *reincarnation thing*," he says, gesturing with air quotes as he speaks. "But speaking French, and Urdu, and, and whatever he was speaking in Australia, Kriol I think he called it? That was weird."

She attempts to correct him, but doesn't get the chance.

"And finding that box of jewelry?! Talk about weird! Dad falling outside the house like he did? I'd swear he was shot in the back! Now that's crazy weird! And don't even get me started about the train thing in

India. I'm telling you, Cazz, I was looking right at him! *I tripped,* he said. Bullshit! Something struck Dad. Struck him so hard it knocked him to the ground. I don't care what this doctor says about reliving his past lives.

"Well about Dr. Davidson, do you think she's—"

"Sincere? Sure, as far as a therapist goes."

"No, do you think her and Dad are—"

"A good match? Sure. I think Mom found a great therapist for Dad. That's important, Cazz. You need a therapist who you can easily talk to. Like when Mom and Dad went through their divorce. I was seeing someone. I had a lot of anger issues. I probably still do."

"No! Do you think she's doing—"

"A good job? Yeah, she seems like she cares. I think she's doing a great job."

"No, you idiot! Do you think she's doing *Dad?!*"

"Dad?"

"Yes, Dad!"

Trevor points, "No, I mean, Dad! As in, here comes Dad! With Dr. Davidson!"

Cassandra's head spun so fast her hair whipped around, slapping her in the face.

"Dad!" she yells, jumping up so fast she hits the table, spilling coffee everywhere. "And Doctor Davidson! What a surprise!"

Cautiously, Jonathan joins his family, taken aback by the commotion his daughter unleashed in the cafe.

A server arrives with napkins to sop up the spill. "I will bring you a fresh cup right away," he says, smiling at Cassandra, who focuses on her father and Elizabeth.

"Dad! Doc! What are you doing here?"

Jonathan wrinkles his brow. "You texted me. Breakfast?"

She shakes her head, red with embarrassment, "I mean, Dr. Davidson. What are you doing here? I mean with my father? I mean together?"

Jonathan has that *don't be an ass,* look on his face. With calm composure, he lies to his daughter, "I sent Dr. Davidson a text when I got

231

yours and asked if she would join us for breakfast to discuss travel plans for Italy. She agreed, so I picked her up at her hotel and we took a cab over here together."

He holds the chair for Elizabeth. "Is that okay with you?"

"Did you use the app I sent you?"

"No, I asked directions at the front desk. That guy had a real attitude."

Cassandra laughs.

Jonathan watches Elizabeth slide into the chair. "Listen, I want to talk about Italy. I know it wasn't on our itinerary—"

"We have an itinerary?" Trevor interjects.

"Well, no, we don't have a set schedule. But I figured, since Dr. Davidson made arrangements, we might as well check it out. I mean, what if this person is my sister?"

"Dad, your sister lives in Wisconsin," Trevor fires back.

"You know what I mean. Clara's sister."

"You mean your alternate personality's dead sister?" Trevor looks at Elizabeth. "Do I have that right?"

"Trevor, what your father is experiencing—"

"What my father is experiencing is a mid-life crisis," he interrupts. "Brought on by an extremely stressful career, a failed marriage, years of guilt, piled on top of a desperate need to recapture some lost paternal vacation, together with an over-exaggerated Phileas Fogg complex. And let's not forget, a desire to solve a Sherlock Holmes-like mystery that he himself has concocted in order to avoid a nervous breakdown. I'm not buying this whole reincarnation thing. I have to admit, some of the things Dad has been doing are a bit out of the ordinary, but there's probably a reasonable explanation for everything."

"Trevor!" Jonathan raises his voice. "Don't be an ass!"

Trevor takes a moment, then apologizes to Elizabeth, "I'm sorry if I was rude, Doc. I'm just having a hard time with all of this. You have to understand, I believe that when you die, you're dead, and you stay dead, you don't come back in someone else's body and start a major architectural conglomerate out of New York City."

Elizabeth waves it off, but Cassandra comes to her defense. "Then, how do you explain the stones?!"

Trevor shakes his head. "I don't know, maybe Dad read about them in a book a long time ago, and he's just remembering them now?"

"Oh, come on!" Cassandra blurts out.

"Okay, listen," Jonathan brings the discussion to order. "We're going to Italy. I want to see if there's someone else like me. I mean, what if there's someone going through the same thing I'm going through? Maybe they can shed some light on why this thing is happening. Maybe it is a hoax, maybe it's not. Maybe it's something more. Either way, I want to find out! We're going to Italy and I'm meeting with this guy." He looks at Elizabeth. "It is a guy? Isn't it?"

She shrugs. "Dr. Macaluso didn't say who they were. He was very careful not to expose the identity of the individual."

"Okay, then," Jonathan continues in a stern voice, which Elizabeth finds very attractive. "We'll meet with this Dr. Macaluso and talk with his subject." He looks at Elizabeth when saying the word, *subject.* "Then we'll head up to Scotland to meet Miss What's-her-name."

"MacNaughton," both kids remind him.

"Moira." Elizabeth adds. And Jonathan detects a hint of jealousy.

"Right, Moira MacNaughton! After that, we'll put this whole cockamamie thing behind us and get on with our lives!" Jonathan finishes with all the enthusiasm of a high school football coach energizing his team at halftime.

Cassandra leans over, whispering to Dr. Davidson, "There's that take charge attitude you were asking me about."

Trevor, somewhat ashamed at his earlier outburst, says softly, "Yeah, okay, Dad, but I didn't pack enough clothes for all this."

"Me neither," adds Cassandra.

"Be like Jack Reacher," Jonathan evokes.

"Jack who?"

"You know, Jack Reacher from the Reacher series of the Lee Child novels. Come on, Jack Reacher?" Jonathan looks bewildered. His children stare at him with blank faces. "Nothing?"

233

"Oh, I love his books," Dr. Davidson comments.

"Thank you." Jonathan looks at Elizabeth and smiles. Then turns and explains to his children, "Reacher is this *huge* guy, a retired MP." His gaze falls to Cassandra. "That stands for Military Police."

"Oh! That's what it stands for? I always wanted to know," she says, rolling her eyes.

"Anyway," Jonathan continues. "He travels around the United States and only carries a toothbrush."

"So he's homeless?" Cassandra asks. "I thought you said he was a Military Police Officer?"

"Ex-Military Police. Ex, he's retired, but that's not important. The point is, he doesn't travel with any luggage."

"So he's homeless and a bum?" Trevor tosses in.

"No!" Jonathan's frustration mounts. "Jesus, you two should read a book once in a while. My point being, whatever town Reacher ends up in, he buys new clothes and throws the old ones away."

"He doesn't wash them?"

"No. It saves him the expense of doing laundry or carrying luggage."

"Geez, I don't know, Dad," Trevor says. "I think it's a lot cheaper to do laundry than it is to buy new clothes every day."

"I like my clothes," Cassandra adds, looking at Dr. Davidson. "I couldn't live like that."

Elizabeth chuckles, not knowing if the kids are playing with Jonathan.

He shakes his head in defeat and looks down. "My point is," he stresses for the final time, "we can *buy* more clothes in Italy if we need them. Be like Jack Reacher."

"Dad, he's a fictional character in a book!" Trevor shoots back. "This is real life. It's not just the clothes. At some point, I have to get back to work."

Jonathan looks at his children. "Wouldn't you rather look back on your life and say, 'I can't believe I did that', instead of saying, 'I wish I had done that'?" Then adding a bit of guilt, he says, "with Dad."

After a long pause, Cassandra breaks the tension. "I'm in, Dad. I could always use some new clothes from Italy."

"Okay, a quick trip to Italy, a short hop to Scotland, and then back to the U.S. before bedtime," Trevor says, allowing himself to smile.

Jonathan looks at Elizabeth.

"Do you even have to ask?" she says. "You *know* I'm going."

"This little adventure is beginning to look more like *The Wizard of Oz,* and I'm feeling a lot like Dorothy," Jonathan jokes.

"I have a pair of ruby slippers, but I don't think they're your size," Elizabeth adds, making the kids laugh.

"So we can take a flight and be in Florence in just under two hours or take a 10:43 train tonight, and be in Florence tomorrow by two in the afternoon. It's up to you guys."

"If it were up to me, I'd rather get to Italy as fast as possible and see the sights, Dad," Cassandra blurts out, not waiting to hear anyone else's opinion.

"I have to agree with Cazz on this one, Dad," Trevor says.

Dr. Davidson offers an alternative, "You Americans, always in a hurry to get somewhere. When are you going to learn it's not the destination. It's the *journey* that makes the adventure."

"Yeah, well, this little adventure has been traversing five countries on three continents in two weeks," Trevor says. "I was only supposed to stay on one continent, one state for two, maybe three days to look after my father," Trevor says. "The sooner we get this traveling circus back in its box, the happier I'll be."

"I don't know," Jonathan says, rubbing Elizabeth's thigh under the table. "Taking the train could be—" He wants to say romantic, but settles on, "Adventurous."

"I'm happy to concede the journey's adventure and fly, as long as I buy my own ticket," Elizabeth says.

"Nonsense," Jonathan answers. "This was your idea, Doc. All four tickets are going on *your* Amex card." He laughs as he watches her face go blank. "I'm kidding. I'll have Margaret make all the arrangements."

"Margaret?" Elizabeth asks, removing Jonathan's hand from her thigh.

"Don't worry, she's Dad's assistant," Cassandra replies. "He would be lost without her. For the past 17 years, she's been scheduling everything for Dad."

"Must be nice." She glances at Jonathan. "And I'm *not* worried," she adds quietly, so only he can hear.

Jonathan picks up his cell phone to call Margaret, but Trevor stops him. "Dad, it's 5 a.m. in the States!"

"What? She should be up." Jonathan glances at Elizabeth, who has a disapproving look on her face. "I guess it can wait an hour. Or two?"

"Better make it three," Elizabeth corrects him. "You know, you can always do it yourself?" With that, Trevor laughs, and Cassandra almost spits out her Pepsi.

Four hours later, the Taylor family plus 'guest' are booked on a 3:20 p.m. Air France flight from Paris, arriving at 5:05 p.m. in Florence, Italy.

"We have a reservation at Hotel San Gallo Palace,"

Jonathan announces as they disembark and make their way out of the airport to hail a taxi. "Reservations, I might add, which I made myself." He smirks at Elizabeth as he holds the taxi door open for her.

The cab weaves and swerves through the streets of Florence. All around them, small Fiats and mopeds dart past like herds of frightened animals. The entire metro community seems to be ignoring any form of traffic rules, and mayhem reigns supreme. It's an all-out, drive for your life, Mad Max Thunderdome arena known as the streets of Italy.

Jonathan takes pleasure in all the Italian architecture, pointing out the intricate construction and design as they go, all as the rest of them can't decide whether to fear for their own lives or pray for the lives of pedestrians in their path.

As the driver turns into the Piazza della Libertá, a beautiful Roman arch with magnificent Corinthian columns and ornate relief sculptures stands vigilant in the center of the ancient plaza. Directly in front of them, a long, four-story terracotta-colored building with an aqueduct-like column facade lines the piazza. Instead of following the traffic around the piazza, the taxi quickly veers right, and comes to a stop in front of a beautiful courtyard. They have survived the trip and arrived at the entrance to the Hotel San Gallo Palace.

Cassandra comments that the arch resembles the Arc de Triomphe in Paris and asks, "Do all European cities have an arch like this?"

Trevor laughs as the driver dismisses the question, attributing it to a failed American education system.

As they exit the taxi, Jonathan announces loudly, "I reserved four rooms."

Walking next to him, and catching his eye, Elizabeth tenderly touches his back and whispers, "To keep up appearances, I hope?"

He smiles. "Why don't we check in, get settled, and then all meet up in the lobby for an authentic Italian dinner?"

Cassandra chuckles, and Trevor shoots her a look. "Yeahh. Okay, Dad."

"What?" Jonathan asks.

"So, should we wait in the lobby or just head to a restaurant, where you two can catch up with us in about, oh, let's say 30—no, make it 45 minutes," she teases with a giggle.

"Did I miss something?" Trevor asks.

Cassandra glances at Elizabeth, whose head is buried in her chest as she holds back a chuckle. Then, unable to contain it any longer, the two women burst out laughing as the two men remain dumbfounded.

Jonathan hands two old-fashioned keys to the kids and passes one to Elizabeth.

"I think they're on to us," Elizabeth whispers to Jonathan. "At least your daughter is." Her cell phone rings just then, interrupting the awkward moment.

"Hello? Oh! Hello, Dr. Macaluso. Perfect timing, we just checked into our hotel. Yes. Yes, of course. Tonight? We were just about to get some dinner. Oh, hold on. I'll ask." She turns to the group. "It's Dr. Macaluso, the therapist. He wants to know if we can come by his office this evening."

"I thought we had plans to meet the doctor tomorrow," Jonathan says.

"We do, but he'd like us to stop by tonight for a short meeting."

Jonathan looks at his watch—5:47 p.m. "It's okay by me, it's a little early for dinner anyway, although I was hoping to—" he looks at Cassandra and quickly covers, "—take in the sights."

Cassandra averts his gaze, still smirking. "It's fine with me."

"Me too," adds Trevor.

"Okay, then. Get the address and we'll head over before dinner."

"Hello, are you still there? Yes, tonight is fine, say—6:45,—7 o'clock? Great! 4 Via dei Cerchi. Okay, we'll see you then." Ending the call, she asks the group, "Any idea where 4 Via dei Cerchi is?"

Jonathan turns to the desk clerk. "Mi scusi, sai dov'è la Via dei Cerchi 4?" A shocked expression grows on his face as he speaks, astonished to hear the Italian words flowing from his own lips.

Trevor throws his hands up. "Of course he speaks Italian too. Why wouldn't he?"

Elizabeth stares at him with her head cocked. "Amazing," she gushes.

The clerk at the front desk gives Jonathan directions, and they exchange the traditional formalities. "Grazie." "Prego."

"Okay, it's about a 20-minute walk." He smiles at Cassandra. "It's like going down to the East Village from our apartment. We take Via Camillo Cavour until we see the Hotel Spadai. We keep heading south and Camillo Cavour will turn into Via de Martelli. That will turn into Via de Calzaiuli. A quick left turn, and then a right, and we're there. Simple."

Cassandra nods in agreement, holding out her iPhone and pointing for her father to see a GPS map with a red line marking the route.

"Piece of cake," Trevor says. "Or, since we're in Italy, a slice of pie … pizza pie, that is." Everyone groans at the bad joke.

"Okay, we'll throw our bags in our rooms and head out to meet Dr. Macaluso. After that, dinner is on me," Jonathan announces, as if taking clients out after landing a big account.

Cassandra looks at Elizabeth. "There's that *take charge* thing again like we talked about in Paris."

The two of them laugh.

An hour later, after maneuvering through the narrow passages of the Italian streets, they arrive at number 4 Via dei Cerchi. Two thoroughly weathered solid-oak doors stand nestled between La Vera Pizza and a quaint little art store named Manzani. Directly above the doors, ancient wrought-iron bars cover windows that match the size and shape of the doors below. From the window sills above, lush green flora cascades down the building's facade.

To the right of the doors, below a large number 4 painted in blue, a bronze name plate reads, 'Michelangelo Macaluso, Clinical Therapist M.D., Psy.D.' Jonathan presses the intercom.

An abrasive chirp crackles from the box, followed soon after by a voice. "Ciao?"

"Dr. Macaluso, it's Dr. Davidson, Jonathan Taylor, and his family. You wanted to—"

Again, another horrible crackle, then an equally annoying buzzing sound as the large wooden door clicks open. "Entrare prego."

At the top of the stairs, the office door opens. Dr. Macaluso stands in the entranceway. "Scusarsi. Scusarsi. I apologize. At this late hour, my secretary has gone home for the night."

As they enter his office, Dr. Davidson shakes the man's hand and makes introductions. "Jonathan, Cassandra, Trevor, this is Dr. Michelangelo Macaluso."

"Oh please, call me Michael. My parents had 'delusions of grandeur', and with the name Michelangelo in this town, people expect great things from you." He laughs.

"Per favore," he gestures across the waiting room to his office. "Per di qua. Sorry, right this way." He smiles at Elizabeth. "Do you speak Italian, or do you prefer English?"

240

"English, please," she responds. "Although apparently Jonathan speaks Italian, but he wasn't aware of this till today?"

He turns to Jonathan. "Veramente, è vero?"

"Solo un po," Jonathan answers. "Just a little."

"Come sei arrivato a parlare italiano?" the doctor asks.

Jonathan responds, "Mi è appena venuto in mente. Come ogni altra lingua che viene da me quando sono in quel paese."

Dr. Macaluso faces the group. "I just asked Jonathan how he came about speaking Italian and he answered, it just came to him, like every other language that he can speak when he is in their country."

Jonathan shrugs his shoulders.

"Your Italian is very good. I detect an older dialect though, perhaps even Roman? What other languages have you spoken?" His excitement grows.

"In India, he spoke Urdu," Trevor says.

"He spoke to that aborigine tribe in Australia," Cassandra adds quickly.

"And French," Dr. Davidson says. "He speaks French very well."

"So it seems Jonathan can speak the language inherent to whatever country he visits. Would that be an accurate statement?" Dr. Macaluso assesses.

"Well, whatever country he once lived in," Cassandra clarifies.

Dr. Macaluso turns to Dr. Davidson. "I thought you told me in our telephone conversation that Jonathan lived exclusively in New York?"

"In this life," she explains.

"I'm confused. At first, you claimed Jonathan was the reincarnation of a young man who lived in Scotland?"

"He was," she answers, then corrects herself. "I believe he is!"

"Then later, when you called back, you said he was a young girl who lived in France, the sister of my patient?"

"It seems Jonathan has lived several past lives, four from what I can ascertain so far. He won't, however, allow me to examine him any further."

"I didn't say I wouldn't let you examine me," Jonathan protests. "I simply said we had to leave England in the morning."

"Fascinating. Do you realize how extraordinary this is?" Dr. Macaluso poses.

Elizabeth's eyes widen. "Oh, you don't have to tell me!"

"Well, thank you for meeting with me tonight." He motions to the chairs around the room as he takes a seat behind his desk. "The reason I am so eager to meet with you," he starts, fumbling with a file on his desk. "I don't quite know how to say this? When Dr. Davidson contacted me, I know she is outstanding in her field, but—"

"But what are the chances of two members of the same family being reincarnated who both show up to regression therapists at the same time?" Elizabeth completes his sentence.

"Yes!" Dr. Macaluso blurts out, relieved that he isn't the only one to question the unlikelihood. "I mean, what are the possibilities?"

Jonathan shrugs again.

"I've been working with this patient for a couple of months," Dr. Macaluso says, picking up a file and shaking it at them. "During that time, this individual has made certain details of their past life very clear to me." He looks around the room. "I am absolutely certain what they are telling me is true. I am, nevertheless, skeptical when I hear of another case coming forward with similar characteristics. Please, I mean no disrespect. I only want to be sure."

Elizabeth agrees with a vigorous nod as Dr. Macaluso continues.

"I have done extensive fact-checking. There was a woman named Camille Dumont, who lived in the village where my patient claimed to have lived."

"We went to *that* village!" Trevor shouts out. "My father recalled every detail, every inch of the house where he lived, he even reenacted getting shot!"

The therapist's eyes widen, and again, he asks Jonathan, "È vero?"

"Sì" Jonathan answers.

"In our last session, under hypnosis, I asked 'Camille' if she had any brothers or sisters," Dr. Macaluso says, addressing Elizabeth. "Camille answered in the affirmative, an older sister, but she died when Camille was young." His gaze moves to Jonathan. "But, what made me want to meet you, Jonathan, is that under hypnosis, Camille told me her 16-year-old sister died when the *Germans* invaded her village."

He drops the folder on his desk. "That was the one detail that captured my attention during our conversation, Dr. Davidson." He stands and walks around to sit on the front edge of his desk. "It is so very rare to encounter a person of mature age who claims to be reincarnated. It is even more difficult to prove it."

Dr. Macaluso sees the puzzled look on Jonathan's face. "Allow me to elaborate. Most of the time, our patients are children, as Dr. Davidson will attest. Children often remember bits and pieces of their past life, but it's highly unlikely the parents take them seriously, let alone consult a professional. Usually, the memories fade and the subject lives an ordinary life. It's only when these past memories start pushing to the surface and demand attention when they usually seek people like us out." He points to Dr. Davidson and himself. "When this particular individual came to me," he says, motioning to the folder behind him on the desk, still taking considerable care not to reveal the gender of his patient, "They became obsessed, and felt they were on the brink of madness."

Cassandra nods knowingly. *That's what happened to Dad that morning.*

"Even if some people *are* reincarnated," Jonathan inquires, "what is the likelihood of it happening with two members of the same family?"

"I don't know," Elizabeth replies. "We have much to learn about this field. How it works or why it happens is still all speculation. Hell, some people in our profession don't even take us seriously."

Trevor nods with a smirk.

"Yes!" Dr. Macaluso agrees. "But if we can prove these two people were related in a past life, it would be groundbreaking!"

"So let's get them together," Cassandra jumps in.

Dr. Macaluso slaps his thigh. "Precisely, my dear! And we will, but that is why I wanted to meet with you tonight. I propose a little experiment. It is my experience that people who have been reincarnated can actually recognize people from their former lives. There have even been reported cases where a subject, the reincarnated person, is able to recognize someone from a past life, in his or her present form." He shakes his head. "Even though the other person will of course have no recollection of the reincarnated subject." Dr. Macaluso folds his arms and looks up, speaking his next question slowly as he thinks it out. "What if a person, in the present, can also recognize the reincarnated subject?" He address the room again. "Have you ever been in a crowded place, or walked down a busy street, and suddenly you see someone … someone you never saw or met before? You have no recollection, no memory of this person, and there is no way you *could* possibly know this person, yet you suddenly lock eyes and experience an overwhelming feeling that somehow, you really do know one another."

"I get that sometimes," says Cassandra.

"Exactly, we all have," he continues, even more excited than before. "I believe that, in some cases, we really did know that person in a past life. Maybe it is your mother, or your sister, or your father, or perhaps simply a neighbor or a local shopkeeper from the village, but without question, we knew that person somehow."

Elizabeth nods in agreement.

"The people in India," Trevor says, still not understanding how it could be true, "seemed to recognize my father as one of their family members. And the tribe in Australia also seemed to recognize him."

"But not the people in France," Cassandra adds.

"Perhaps," Elizabeth suggests, "Clara was too young for them to remember?"

"Possibly," Dr. Macaluso says. "Maybe my patient, who claims to be Camille, and Jonathan, who we believe to be Clara, might recognize each other, even in their present bodies? And that is where my experiment comes into play."

"What are you suggesting, Doctor?" Elizabeth asks.

"I've arranged a dinner party tomorrow night. I instructed my guests to arrive before 7 p.m. If you come at 7:30—"

"But we didn't pack any clothes for a formal dinner party," Jonathan interjects.

"No need. It is—how do you Americans say—dress casual. Jeans and a T-shirt will be just fine. I will introduce you to my guests and observe if Mr. Taylor—"

"You want to see if Jonathan can spot his sister?" Elizabeth asks.

"Exactly!"

"And, if he can't?" Cassandra asks.

"If he can't, he can't. As I said before, at this stage, it is still simply a hypothesis." He turns to Jonathan. "And Jonathan, I am not suggesting Clara's consciousness doesn't live within you. On the contrary, from what Dr. Davidson has observed, I believe it does. And I am fairly confident Camille's consciousness does in fact live within my patient. I am merely proposing we conduct a little experiment to see if one past consciousness can detect another past consciousness."

"Is that what this is? My father's past consciousness?" Cassandra asks.

"Yes. I believe, and I think Dr. Davidson believes this as well, what makes us who we are *is* our consciousness. Some people call it our soul, but I prefer to frame the discussion within a more secular context. It is what makes us *who* we are. Our rights, our wrongs, our beliefs, and our awareness. Some people believe that we are aware of the physical universe, and *that* is our consciousness, but others believe we make up the physical universe *from* our consciousness."

"Come on, Doctor," Trevor says, scoffing. "We 'make up the universe'?"

"Yes, of course. The universe exists because we created it in our consciousness. I know it is a difficult concept to wrap your mind around. It involves both quantum mechanics and quantum physics." He looks at Cassandra briefly. "Some pretty heavy shit, you might say. Young man, there are many fascinating books on the subject. *Return to Life* by Jim B. Tucker, M.D. is one of the best." He clasps his hands together as if in deep thought before continuing. "I believe, if an individual's consciousness is strong enough, it can re-enter this world and take hold in another person's body, while the two shared consciousnesses inhabit one body together." He shakes his clasped hands at Trevor to illustrate the point.

"Like a split personality?" Trevor asks.

"More like a symbiotic relationship."

"I don't get it," Cassandra confesses with a strange grin on her face.

"Neither person owns the body. For instance, this is not you sitting here."

"Oh, it's not?" she asks.

"No, not really, this is merely a shell. The real Cassandra Taylor, that is, everything that makes you who you are, your memories ... your feelings ... the love you feel, the love you release, all of this only inhabits that body for a short time until your consciousness is released and moves on to another plane."

"So, you don't believe in heaven then?" Jonathan asks.

"Oh, I still do. It's just—not the pearly gates, harp-playing, halo heaven we were taught in Sunday School. Believe me, growing up in Italy with a Catholic church on every corner, it was extremely difficult to break free from that thinking." His voice raises several octaves then as his arms flail about, talking with his hands while mimicking his poor old mother. "Oh, Michelangelo, why can't you be a priest like your brother?"

Cassandra giggles at this, especially hearing him say this all in such a thick, Italian accent.

"I cannot tell you how many arguments I had with my poor mother about this very subject. I think she must still be praying for me in one of the churches out there." Now it's his turn to giggle, but then he glances at his watch. "I could discuss this all night, but I am sure you are all eager to get to dinner, and I have to get home to prepare for tomorrow night."

He accompanies them through the waiting room and shakes Jonathan's hand. "It was nice to meet you, nice to meet all of you!" he says, pausing to look at each one of them. "I expect to see the four of you tomorrow evening, and Jonathan, don't try too hard to spot my patient. Just let it happen. It is only a theory I have, so if it doesn't happen, it doesn't prove a thing. We may not have all the answers, but maybe one day!" He holds up his index finger. "One day, we may!"

"You all go ahead," Elizabeth tells them. "I just want a word in private with the doctor."

Jonathan and his family descend the stairs before Dr. Macaluso closes the door. "So, Dr. Davidson, how can I be of assistance? You have my home address, no? Number 2 Via Mazzetta."

"Yes. Yes I do, but there's another matter I wanted to discuss." Elizabeth clenches her jaw. "I noticed two significant scars on Jonathan— when I was examining him," she lies. "He didn't recall how or when he got them."

Dr. Macaluso closes his eyes as though searching for something. "I seem to recall an article written in the *Journal of Scientific Exploration*, something about 'Bodily Malformations Attributed to Previous Lives'." He opens his eyes and cocks his head in the affirmative. "They could be a remnant from a past life injury, or perhaps even a cause of death."

"Does your patient have anything like that on his or her body?"

"Well, I haven't done a physical examination, but if a person dies of natural causes, say old age or cancer, there wouldn't be any scars or marks. I believe Camille died well into her 70's, of old age, so there would be no marks. Whereas, Clara was tragically taken from this world at 16."

"What about a gunshot wound?" she asks.

"Well, yes. Something like that could surely leave a mark on one's self, perhaps even on one's soul." He feigns a smile.

Elizabeth shakes his hand. "Thank you, Doctor."

"Prego, dottore," he smiles. "You're welcome, Doctor."

"Oh, and can you recommend a good restaurant in the area?"

"Madam, this is Florence," he says, tilting his head. "Anywhere you go, the food will be amazing!"

"Right. Stupid question," she says with a smile.

"I would recommend Ristorante Il Granaio Firenze, if you want an exceptional meal. Turn right at the end of Via dei Cerchi onto Via dei Tavolini. Number 14. Cannot miss it, but like I said, anywhere you go will be a culinary experience."

"Grazie," she says, and he smiles. "See, I'm learning."

We have a saying here. "Nessuno è perfetto, ma puoi sempre imparare a parlare italiano."

"That sounds beautiful. What does it mean?"

He smiles. "Loosely translated, 'Nobody is perfect, but you can always learn to speak Italian'."

"After that," Howard said, "the letters slowly came in month after month, year after year, and with the creation of the internet, it was easier and faster to correspond with other museums. All across the world, curators contacted me with their findings. Many were discovered or unearthed in ancient ruins and I was immediately notified by email. I developed a reputation as the go-to guy whenever one of these tablets was found."

"But what does it all mean, Professor?" Anthony asked.

"Unfortunately, I still don't know. After 40 years, I'm no closer to finding out the answer to that question as I was back then when I first saw that metal tablet clutched in Joseph Kehm's dead, dried-out hand."

Marcus from Receiving taps his knuckles on the door frame of Howard's office. "Is this a good time, Professor?"

"It's a perfect time, Marcus. Please, bring it in."

Marcus props open the door and wheels a large crate into the room. "You have to sign for it, boss. You know how the curator likes everything nice and proper. He's a real stickler for following the rules." Marcus hands Howard a clipboard, giving Anthony a wink. "I hear he's a real pain in the ass to work for."

Anthony smiles back sheepishly, trying not to draw attention to himself.

"Marcus, I *am* the curator." Howard signs the document and hands the clipboard back to Marcus.

"Yeah, I know." He unloads the crate and pulls his handcart back. "Okay, it's all yours, Professor. Maybe now you'll stop pestering me." Marcus lets out a hearty laugh. "Every day for the last six months, *'Is it here? Did it come today? Is it here?'* Geez."

"Oh, come on. I wasn't that bad," Howard defends himself.

"Yeah, okay." He pushes the dolly to the door. "I still expect my morning coffee, boss." With a wave and a smile, Marcus disappears down the hall.

Howard turns his attention back to Anthony. "Hopefully the contents of this box will hold all the answers."

"In there?" Anthony asks, pointing to the wooden crate on the floor.

"I've been waiting for this package for two years, ever since I first read about the findings in, of all places, *National Geographic.*"

"Do they still print that?" Anthony asks. "You know they first published that magazine in 1888? My dad used to collect them, had a whole stack in the garage. I used to love looking through them. In fact, it was *National Geographic* that inspired me to pursue archeology."

"Interesting," Howard mutters dismissively before continuing his train of thought. "So anyway, Anthony, I was reading an article about Lucy, once believed to be the oldest living skeleton in the world. She dated back 3.2 million years. The article went on to say how anthropologists had discovered older, more complete fossil remains of an early human ancestor. Nineteen years ago, scientists in Ethiopia unearthed the remains of a 3.3 million-year-old Australopithecus afarensis baby dubbed *Selam.*"

"Geez, Professor. You don't have a baby skeleton in there, do you?" Anthony's face wrinkled in disgust as his head turned this way and that, examining the crate.

"No, no, Anthony," Howard chuckled, "but, if I did, you shouldn't be squeamish. It's all part of the job and the work we do."

"I guess. It's still creepy."

They move the crate to the desk, and with the aid of crowbars, they wrench the lid up. After a bit of tugging, the nails reluctantly surrender their hold on the wood, crying out with high-pitched screeches.

"At one of the dig sites close to where they found Selam," Howard continues, "an archaeologist laid an array of artifacts out on a table. These findings dated back some 10,000 years ago." He stops and retrieves a framed photo from the wall behind his desk, presenting it to Anthony. "Look what's lying on the table."

"Is that—" Anthony gasps.

"A marker!" Howard finishes. "Perhaps the very first one," he adds, his finger tapping on the top of the crate. "I've been trying to acquire this item for two years now, and today—today, my dear boy, we finally get to see it for the very first time."

"Professor!" a young girl shouts, flying through his office door.

"Oh, good. Kaitlyn, I'm glad you're here. It came! Marcus just dropped it off." *Has everyone decided to work on Saturday?*

"Dr. Convery," Kaitlyn said, panting as she tried to catch her breath. "I called your house—"

"Anthony and I were just about to—" He stops when he sees how flustered she looks. "Kaitlyn, are you okay?"

"Your wife … said you … were here," she exhales between breaths, bending over and putting her hands on her knees. She then takes one deep breath and straightens up, gushing out the words all in one breath. "I was in the park when I saw *this post!*" She bends over again, extending an outstretched arm over her head, offering her iPhone to the Professor. "I ran the whole way."

He stares at the screen in shock. "Is this real?" he asks.

Still bent with hands on her knees but breathing slower, she adds, "I really have to start working out."

"Kaitlyn, is *this* real?!" he demands.

"Yes, I think so," she says, straightening up again, catching her breath at last. "I have to check it out. I just saw it and thought you'd want to see it before I contact him."

"It appears to be in pristine condition!" Howard says, getting excited. "We must contact him immediately! Do you know what this means?" He stares at them both for a moment, taking in their faces. "It means you just made my life a living hell, Kaitlyn."

Anthony and Kaitlyn look at one another with bewilderment.

"I have to call my wife right away and tell her I can't make tonight's dinner plans."

PLACE: FLORENCE, ITALY
YEAR: PRESENT DAY

Dr. Elizabeth Davidson catches up to the Taylor family on the street. "I asked Dr. Macaluso if he recommended a place for dinner."
All three look at her strangely.
"I know?! Stupid question, but he suggested a terrific place, and it's right around the corner." She heads off in the direction of the restaurant.
"Great! I'm starving," Trevor says, turning to follow her.
"Me too," Cassandra adds, chasing after Trevor.
Jonathan shrugs to himself, then brings up the rear, like a good father duck watching after his ducklings.
They find the small, intimate restaurant, and, like most places in Florence, it's crowded and noisy but filled with an abundance of flavorful, mouthwatering food. The air is thick with garlic, basil, and oregano, together with a hundred other aromas that exude the very essence of Italy. Unlike their night in Paris, the party of four is now more comfortable with one another, laughing and joking in a way Cassandra wishes her father and mother could have done. The unspoken romance Cassandra suspected now manifests itself in subtle glances and tender

touches between patient and doctor, man and woman, eligible bachelor and desirable lioness.

On the walk back to the hotel, they stop at the Cathedral of Santa Maria del Fiore, just as the Italian sun sinks behind the cityscape. It's a smaller but still impressive cathedral that resembles the Notre Dame back in Paris. The elegant white marble glows brighter than Italy's famous rosé in the dying moments of the setting sun. The four gather with many others to watch as twilight sneaks across the sky, snuffing out the last moments of daylight. Illuminated by 21st century electric floodlights, majestic stone priests and bishops awaken from their slumber to keep watch over the slate blue heavens. In the distance, a flash of light streaks across the night sky. The crowd slowly disbands to seek shelter from the impending storm.

"We should get going," Jonathan urges, quickening their pace. Moments later as they pass Via degli Alfani, he adds, "One block over is the Galleria dell'Accademia. That's Italy's famed art museum which houses Michelangelo's 'David' statue."

"We have to go!" Cassandra shouts.

A bolt of lightning hurls from the heavens, cracking through the sky and making its way to Earth.

"I'm not sure if now is the best time," Trevor pleads.

"It closed three hours ago," Jonathan says, looking at his phone.

"Wait, how do you know these things?" Cassandra asks, peeking down a side avenue, not seeing her father's face is lit by the screen of the smartphone.

She looks up to see him waving the device at her.

"Touché," she says with a laugh.

"That would have been appropriate if we were still in France," Trevor says.

Another crack of thunder, this one much louder than its predecessor, and the entire group quickens their steps. They make it to the Piazza della Libertá just as the first raindrops begin to fall. Light but massive drops promise to make tonight's tempest one that poets and authors might write about. They run the last couple of blocks to the hotel as raindrops the size of heavy marbles strike the pavement.

The rain-soaked group cram into the lobby, hair dripping and clothes drenched. The kids rush to the elevator, but Jonathan hesitates, not wanting the night to end. Elizabeth joins the children though, so he follows behind. As they board the lift, all Jonathan can think to do is ask, "Alright, so, breakfast at 8?"

"I was hoping to sleep in tomorrow," Cassandra says. "Can we make it 10?"

"Sounds good to me," Trevor agrees with a nod.

The elevator stops on the second floor and Elizabeth steps out. "I usually go for a run in the morning," she says softly, "but text me where you'll be, and I'll meet up with everyone there."

Like a child denied a piece of candy, Jonathan feels scorned. "I thought—"

"Good night, kids." She cuts him off as the door begins to close. "I'll see you all tomorrow at breakfast."

As the doors slowly shut, the kids bid Elizabeth goodnight. Jonathan stands with his mouth agape, trying to think of any excuse to join her in her room. Two metal doors meet in the middle, obscuring Jonathan's view and filling the quiet elevator with a resounding clang.

The elevator ascends, slows, and then jerks to a stop. The doors open, and the Taylors clump down the hall like three wet zombies.

"Can we see the David tomorrow?" Cassandra asks.

"Sure, peanut. Let's just get out of these wet clothes and have ourselves a good night's rest. It's been a long trip."

Stopping at a doorway, Cassandra retrieves the room key, inserts it in the brass keyhole, and opens the door. "Okay. Good night, Dad."

Trevor opens his door, across from his sister's, and wishes his father goodnight too.

"I'll see you guys at breakfast tomorrow around 10," Jonathan calls as he continues down the hall to the last room on the right. "Goodnight!"

Removing his clothes, he lays them out on the steam radiator under the window, and makes his way to the bathroom, turning on the shower. Over the rush of water, Jonathan hears a low, barely audible tap on the door. Assuming one of his children forgot something, he throws on the hotel bathrobe and heads for the door. Another tap, this time a little louder, and a little longer.

"Hold on! Hold on, I'm coming!" he shouts. A flash of lightning illuminates the bedroom followed by a violent crackle of thunder.

Not bothering to check the peephole, Jonathan swings open the door. "Alright, what did you forget?"

Elizabeth stands before him in a matching white bathrobe. "I forgot to say goodnight," she whispers in her best sultry voice. "Is that the shower? I could use a nice hot something right about now." She moves past him, allowing the soft terrycloth robe to slide from her shoulders, revealing the subtle arch of the small of her back. Jasmin and lavender beckon him to follow as her strawberry blonde hair sways in the wake of her steps. She gathers a handful and twirls it into a bun, exposing the nape of her soft, slender neck. The bathrobe finds a comfortable place on the floor. The last thing Jonathan sees is her amazing ass as she disappears into a steam-filled bathroom.

The next morning, Elizabeth wakes to a loud knock on Jonathan's bedroom door. *Not again!* she thinks, opening her eyes.

Rinsing the toothpaste from his mouth and wiping his face with a hand towel, Jonathan emerges from the bathroom wearing his hotel bathrobe. "One second," he yells. "Er, un minuto!"

"Good morning," he says, crossing the room. "I hope you don't mind, but I ordered room service. I'm one of those people who needs their coffee in the morning."

Opening the door, Jonathan motions to the young bellhop to set the service at the small table in the corner. As he rests the tray there, the young man's eyes wander, trying to catch a glimpse of the bella donna— *beautiful woman*—lying in bed.

Jonathan ushers the young man to the door and thanks him with a tip, which he realizes is probably too much, judging by the way the boy keeps repeating, "Grazie Signore." He cranes his neck again on the way out, hoping for one last look at the Venus lying beneath the sheets.

"Make sure the door is locked," Elizabeth says, getting out of bed and slipping on her robe with one fluid motion. "Before we eat, I want to see something." Jonathan's face beams. "No, not that!" she says, dismissing his silliness. "Jeez, you men are all alike!"

He smirks.

"Come here," she orders, standing next to the bed.

He happily obeys, and she kisses him tenderly before pulling the bathrobe's belt tight and sliding her hands between the folds. She caresses his bare skin, then lets her hands travel up to his shoulders. Moving her arms apart, Elizabeth forces the robe open and off his shoulders. The sleeves fall, allowing the back of the robe to fold behind him. She runs her fingers over his exposed flesh and traces the lines of his body, stopping at a small imperfection here, a scar there, a birthmark on the right side, a long track of raised skin between his ribs, a slice across his abdomen. *Could be from an operation, or a self-inflicted wound as in the case of Seppuku,* she thinks. She kisses his neck. He remains motionless all throughout her sensual inspection. As her fingers move around his waist, she smiles, watching as the white terrycloth rises between his legs.

She turns him around slowly then, examining his broad back. The two scars, joined by a smaller dime-size impression, make a triangle of wounds. Her hands move up to his shoulders next, where she applies the slightest pressure. He responds to her touch as he did in bed, and kneels in place before her. She tenderly pushes his head forward away from her, exposing the nape of his neck as the tips of her fingers comb through his hair, gradually moving upwards. Fearing what she suspects might be there, her middle finger brushes against another dime-size entrance wound, ten centimeters above the base of his neck and similar to the scar on his back.

Elizabeth circles around and stands directly in front of him, then she raises his face to meet hers. His eyes catch the light briefly, causing his brow to furrow, and for the first time since they met, she notices a small, circular dimple directly in the center of his forehead.

Draping her body over his then, and cradling his head to her breast, she weeps silently for the many lives—and deaths—he's endured. *How many lives lost, how many heartbreaks, how many lovers has this one soul had to bury?* She kisses the top of his head before he looks up, straining to meet her lips with his. She falls to her knees, holding his head between her hands. With tender kisses, she moves from his lips down to his neck, shoulders, and chest, wishing she could love away his centuries of pain. She pulls at the tightly tied terrycloth belt, opening his robe to her. He undoes her robe too, feeling the soft flesh of her waist before his hands move up, feeling her ribs, then the smooth, perfect teardrop shape sides of her breasts. His fingers fan across her back as he tries to pull her close to him. She pushes him backward, forcing him to the ground.

"Last night was all about me," she murmurs, lowering her head to other parts of his body. "This morning is all about you. Tell me what you want me to do, Jonathan. Tell me … in Italian."

"Fai l'amore con me," he whispers.

She lifts her head. "Yesss. Now say it in French."

"Je veux faire l'amour avec vous."

She smiles. "Ooh, yes. I still like French better."

"Je souhaite que nous puissions faire l'amour pour toujours," he says.

"Mmmmmm, Jonathan. I don't know what you're saying, but keep talking," she pleads, as her lips travel down his body.

For the next half hour, Jonathan spoke, begged, and cried out like a native-born Parisian.

At 10 o'clock sharp, all four of their happy team were together, once again sitting down at a table to eat. Jonathan with black coffee and scrambled eggs, Trevor a muffin and coffee, Cassandra a scone and some tea, and Dr. Davidson, to everyone's surprise, sits in front of a large platter of French toast, eggs over easy, bacon, sausage, hash browns, rye *and* wheat toast, and a tall glass of orange juice. The three of them watch in polite shock as she devours the equivalent of a small Thanksgiving dinner.

Cassandra fakes a sip of tea and whispers sideways into her cup over to her brother, "She must have run to England and back to work up *that* kind of an appetite?"

"Where does she put it all?" Trevor leans in to whisper back.

Popping the last bite of French toast into her mouth, Elizabeth can't help but mumble, "She can hear you, you know?" then smiles as she washes it down with her orange juice.

"Right," Jonathan says. "So now that breakfast is taken care of, what shall we do?"

"The David! The David!" Cassandra pleads. "We can't come to Florence and not see The David!"

Trevor nods his head. "It's true!"

"Okay, I did promise we'd see David today," he concedes.

"I'm going back to the hotel to rest," Elizabeth announces.

"Oh, you must see The David!" Cassandra argues.

"I didn't get much sleep last night. That second floor is quite boisterous," she lies, stealing a look at Jonathan. "Anyway, I've seen David before. And besides, you three should spend some time together as a family without your father's therapist tagging along."

"But you're more than Dad's therapist," Cassandra says, making Elizabeth's eyes widen. "You're a part of our traveling adventure!"

"Right, and you may stumble upon the cure for Dad's illness," Trevor says.

"Yes," Jonathan adds. "You're the Scarecrow in our little trip to Oz."

"Oh?!" Elizabeth protests, tossing her napkin across the table and hitting Jonathan. "So I haven't got a brain?! Is *that* what you think of me?!"

He laughs. "On the contrary. The scarecrow was the smartest one of them all. We'll have to watch the movie together sometime. He solved every one of Dorothy's problems."

"I'd like that," Elizabeth says with a smile. "Well at least you didn't make me the Wicked Witch of the West in this little scenario."

Cassandra smiles to see the openly flirtatious exchange between them, then breaking the awkward silence, she stands and announces,

"Well, I'm going to see The David. You coming, Trevor?"

"Right after you two guys pay the check, I hope?" Jonathan asks, only half joking.

"I've got this," Elizabeth says, taking out her credit card. "And if you start in with that male ego bullshit, I'll double my rate from what I'm charging you!"

"Hold on!" Jonathan balks as they all rise to leave. "You're charging me for being here?"

"Just wait till you see my bill!" She waits for the kids to leave then before walking past Jonathan with a playful giggle. "Don't worry. I'm sure we can work something out in trade!"

"Hey, I'm pretty sure that's sexual harassment," he retorts with a smirk.

Out on the street, Elizabeth reminds them of Dr. Macaluso's 7:30 dinner party. "So we should leave the hotel by 7 o'clock."

They all agree. Instinctively, Elizabeth leans in to kiss Jonathan goodbye. She sees him starting to reciprocate, knowing he shares the same feelings. "I think it's this way," Trevor calls out, his face buried in his phone. They both awkwardly pull back quickly and nod to one another, fumbling with their hands, not knowing whether to shake, hug, or simply walk away.

Cassandra rolls her eyes. *Just kiss her already.*

Moments later, Cassandra can hardly contain her excitement, and she begins skipping down Via Giorgio la Pira with great anticipation. She's about to see one of Michelangelo's most celebrated works—in person!

In the convergence of four grand hallways, Michelangelo's David stands tall, forever ready to do battle with the colossus from Gath, whose name became synonymous with ginormous. While most sculptors of his day depicted David as victorious, having defeated Goliath in battle, Michelangelo chose to show David looking thoughtful, busy formulating his strategy moments before Goliath attacks.

Jonathan leans into his children, whispering, so as not to disturb the many admirers, "In 1501, Michelangelo began working on David when he was only 26 years old. He completed it in 1504 when he was around your age. Can you imagine creating something this perfect? Originally people thought the marble had too many imperfections. This enormous block lay abandoned for 25 years in the courtyard of the Opera del Duomo. But where others see imperfection, a true artist can create a work of immense beauty, one that will span countless lifetimes and touch the hearts of so many."

"Did you know Michelangelo, Dad?" Cassandra asks.

Jonathan laughs. "No, no, but I remember when he unveiled it in the entrance to Palazzo Vecchio. It replaced Donatello's bronze sculpture of Judith and Holofernes."

"Really?!" Trevor asks, turning around quickly with great enthusiasm.

Jonathan tousles his son's hair with a ridiculous smile. "No, I'm just teasing." He searches his memory, wishing he could say for sure. "Not sure where I was in 1504?"

For the next three hours, they walk around Florence, taking in all the charm and warmth the city has to offer. Narrow cobblestone vicolo— alley ways—barely wide enough for a motor scooter suddenly open to enormous piazzas filled with tables and chairs. People gather about, enjoying espresso and discussing the day's events. Modern storefronts, set into ancient stone facades, combine classical architecture with hi-tech fashion.

"I never knew a city could be so beautiful," Cassandra comments, filling her phone with picture after picture, each one more amazing than the last.

They stop at a small panifici—bakery—for freshly baked rolls and breads to snack on as they walk. Jonathan explains many of the structures, teaching them as much as he can about the architecture. Every so often, an old part of the town feels familiar to him. Shying away from such thoughts, however, he wants only to spend this time, this life, with his children, and not think too much of any other time but now.

By five o'clock, they enter the hotel lobby. In the elevator, Jonathan pushes the buttons for floors two and three. "I'm just going to stop in and tell Elizabeth, er, Dr. Davidson that we're back now."

The doors open and Jonathan exits the lift. Cassandra smiles and mouths, '*it's okay, Dad*', leaving Jonathan wondering as the door slides closed again.

When Elizabeth answers the door, Jonathan can tell she's been crying. "What's wrong? Are you okay?"

Before he can even enter, she throws her arms around him, squeezing so tightly, he thinks, *this tiny woman is going to break my neck.* "Hey, hey, what's wrong?"

Wiping her eyes, she turns away from him, "Nothing, nothing wrong."

"Something's wrong, now what is it? Did I *do* something?" He gently takes her by the arm and turns her around.

She shakes her head.

"Did I *not* do something?"

Again, she shakes her head.

"Is it because I went off with the kids? *You* told me to go."

She wipes her nose. "Don't be silly."

"I forget your birthday?" he tries making her laugh. "When *is* your birthday?" His eyes widen and his face freezes in mock horror. "Oh, crap! It's our anniversary and I was out drinking with the boys."

She giggles and slaps his chest. "No, you big lug!"

He raises his eyebrows as if to say, *then what is it?*

"It's just—"

"Yes?"

"It's just—" She starts to turn away, but he grabs her arm and holds her fast.

"I think I'm falling for you. You big, stupid oaf!"

PLACE: NEW YORK CITY
YEAR: PRESENT DAY

Howard winced as he held the receiver to his ear.

"Yes, I know we made plans over a month ago, and I didn't say I *won't* be there. I simply said I may be a little late." Professor Convery, apologizing to his wife, tries his very best to appease her. "I know. Yes, I know ... Yes, dear, but—Yes, I know, but something came up, and—Yes, of course it's extremely important—"

"I have him on the line, Professor," Kaitlyn interrupts.

"I know, darling, something *always* comes up. I'll try to be there ... I have to go. No, that wasn't some sick innuendo. I have to go. I love you." Howard fumbles the receiver into its cradle as Kaitlyn hands him another phone.

"Hello! Hello, is this the young man who posted the photos of the Aeternum tablets?"

"Trevor. His name is Trevor. Trevor Taylor," Kaitlyn whispers in the professor's other ear.

"Aeternum what?" Trevor asks on the other end of the line.

"Tablets—or markers, if you prefer?" Howard stammers into the receiver waving Kaitlyn away like an annoying gnat.

"Tablets? Markers? What are you talking about?" a confused young voice answers back.

"Let's start again, shall we? Hello, my name is Professor Howard Convery. My assistant, Kaitlyn, with whom you just spoke, showed me a photo you posted … Trevor." He makes an *'are you satisfied'* gesture with his eyes at Kaitlyn and then continues. "A photo of some tablets or, as *we* call them, markers. I believe you asked in your post if anyone knows what they are?"

Trevor finally understands the nature of the call. "Ohhh! Oh, yes, the little plaque. I was hoping someone could help me."

"Yes, well, I'm not sure if I can help, but I would very much like to know where you unearthed the items … from what dig site?" He waits in silent anticipation.

"Dig site, Professor?"

"Yes, where did you find them, Trevor? At what archaeological dig were they discovered? What country?"

"I'm a little confused, Professor." Trevor is bewildered, but intrigued. "I didn't dig them up from anywhere."

"How did they come in your possession?" Howard asks.

"People have been giving them to my father—"

"*Giving* them to your father?" Now Professor Convery is the one who's bewildered.

"Yeah, we've been traveling to other countries. He's been meeting with a bunch of people, and then they just give him these tablets, or markers, as you call them."

"Just *giving them* to him?" the professor responds, dumbfounded.

"Yes. Well, from what I understand, and believe me, I don't understand much of what's happened the past few days, but from what I can piece together, they're his."

"*His?!*" Howard emits an incredulous gasp.

"Yeah, they belong to my father. It seems my dad has been leaving these things all over the world," Trevor reveals with some skepticism. "Now he's trying to find them. Professor, do you know what the tablets mean?"

"He left them?! All around the world?! Is this some kind of a joke?" The professor's tone drastically changes from excitement to anger. "Young man, I have tablets like these dating back before the birth of Christ!"

"*You* have some?" Trevor's voice bellows through the receiver. "He was hoping to locate as many as he could."

"And your father actually believes these markers belong to him?!"

"Yeah. That's why wherever we go, people have been returning them to him."

"Returning them?!"

"Well, yeah."

"Trevor, I think your father and I should meet. Perhaps he can help me with something I've been working on, and maybe I can help him locate some of *his* missing tablets."

"Okay, sure," Trevor says. So how many do you have?"

Howard turns and gazes at the vast map upon the far wall. In almost every country on every continent, there's a marker accompanied by an approximate date.

"Oh, you might say, I have—" He smirks oddly to himself. "A few."

Jonathan presses the doorbell at number 2 Via Mazzetta and looks at his watch. *7:31, almost to the minute.*

Moments later, Dr. Macaluso pulls open a beautiful antique wooden door and welcomes them into his home, an exquisite home at that, much larger than most owned by those in his profession. Jonathan expresses his admiration and presents his host with a bottle of wine sheathed in burlap.

"Grazie, signore. La casa has been in my family for generations. I like to think I am merely its inhabiter," he says, winking at Cassandra. "Much like our bodies, until we move on to better things." He slides the expensive wine from its sleeve. "Oh! Very nice. Thank you, this is much too generous!"

"It is we who should be thanking you for welcoming us into your home. You are most gracious."

"Nonsense." He ushers them into the central part of the house. "Ladies and gentlemen, our guests of honor have arrived."

Several couples turn and greet the visitors, raising glasses and flashing smiles in acknowledgment. Dr. Macaluso's wife joins him and wraps her arm around his waist.

265

"You must be Jonathan Taylor," she says, extending her hand.

"Signore Taylor, may I present my wife, Jessica."

"Please, call me Jess." Jonathan takes her hand. "And you must be Dr. Davidson, and these are your children?"

"My children," Jonathan corrects her. "Dr. Davidson is my—"

"Physician," Elizabeth proclaims a bit too loudly, taking Jessica's hand.

Jonathan motions to his children. "Trevor and Cassandra—Cazz for short."

"It is a pleasure to meet you all," Jessica says with sincerity. Her husband presents her with the bottle Jonathan brought. "Oh. We must have you over more often, Signore Taylor," she adds, smiling at her husband.

"The pleasure is all ours, and please, call me Jonathan."

"Well, now that everyone is on a first-name basis, I would like to introduce you to some of my guests."

Jonathan nods and gestures for Dr. Macaluso to lead the way. "Let the games begin."

His wife takes the bottle and returns it to its burlap home. "I will put this someplace safe, maybe to partake in a more *intimate* setting, after the party." She flashes another smile and disappears into another part of the house.

"Jonathan Taylor, Dr. Elizabeth Davidson, Trevor, and Cassandra, may I present Dr. William Koch and his wife, Iris."

"Nice to meet you. Please call me Bill," Dr. Koch remarks, shaking Jonathan's hand, trying to mask his Italian accent with one from Tennessee.

"Very nice to meet you," Jonathan responds.

The introductions continued in much the same way: Richard & April Casciato, Michael & Debbie Spano, Denise & Fernando Vivero, Edward & Lori Colon, Jack & Carole MacKnight. All lovely people. All fascinating people. All very engaging, entertaining, and stimulating people. Unfortunately, none of them, Jonathan was sure, was his sister from a past life.

As Dr. Macaluso introduces Jonathan to the last couple in the room, Jaclyn and Zachary McMullin, a young couple who enjoy the pleasures of the Italian countryside as opposed to the urban setting, one of the servers catches Jonathan's eye as he moves about the room, refilling drinks.

Oblivious of other staff members working the party that night, Jonathan is positive he is seeing this particular individual for the first time. Jonathan watches with predatory instincts as the young man moves from person to person refreshing drinks. Zachary asks if Jonathan does much fishing in the States, but his words fall on deaf ears. Dr. Macaluso notices Jonathan's intent stare, as does Elizabeth. In a trance-like state, Jonathan leaves the conversation to pursue the unsuspecting server. Other guests, unaware of the nature of the dinner party, notice Jonathan cross the room.

Stopping 10 feet away from the man, Jonathan utters a single word. "Camille?"

Bent to refill a glass of chardonnay, the young man stops mid-pour and stands erect.

His eyes meets Jonathan's. He puts his hand to his mouth and begins to cry. "Clara!" he shouts.

Jonathan rushes over, throwing his arms around him. The two embrace and cry like the long-lost sisters they are.

Dr. Macaluso swiftly moves to the two, taking the bottle of chardonnay from his hand lest he spill some down Jonathan's back, and he asks the man he hired as a server, "Do you know this gentleman?"

Through tears of joy, he nods rapidly. "Yes. He is my sister, signore!" He looks at Jonathan. "I haven't seen you since … since—" He can't bring himself to say 'since the Germans shot and killed you'.

"Since that day in the nursery," Jonathan finishes his sentence. "When you were brushing Antoinette's hair, and I showed you my tablet."

"When the Germans—" the young man starts before he breaks down sobbing.

"I know, it's okay," Jonathan says, comforting his long lost sister. "It was a long time ago, and we're together now."

Dr. Macaluso's posture stiffens as if he has seen a ghost.

"What's wrong, Doctor?" Elizabeth asks.

"This young man, Matthew, is my patient. I have been treating him for anxiety for several months. I couldn't figure out the cause, so, some weeks back, I tried hypnotherapy. Under hypnosis, Matthew told me that when he was fourteen years of age, he lived in France where he witnessed a German soldier shoot his sister."

Elizabeth nods affirmatively. "Under hypnosis, Jonathan claimed that a German soldier shot him."

"Yes," agrees Dr. Macaluso, "but all that could have been researched, except Matthew also told me he had a doll named Antoinette. On the day her sister, Clara, was murdered, she had been brushing her doll's hair."

The room filled with an audible gasp. A phenomenon few people could ever comprehend, much less believe, was witnessed by every guest that night.

Both therapists suddenly remembered the dinner party taking place around them.

"Perhaps it would be best if we continue this in another room, Doctor?" Elizabeth suggests.

"I think you are right, signora," Dr. Macaluso agrees and then graciously announces, "Ladies and gentlemen, signore and signora, thank you all for coming. My esteemed colleague and I have some business which we must attend to. Please enjoy the rest of the evening. Eat, drink, and get home safe. Thank you all again for coming. Now, I am afraid we must take our leave."

The small party of six break from the larger party and move down the hall to Dr. Macaluso's study. Jonathan and Matthew enter the room together, fearful they will lose one another for a second time.

Once inside, everyone finds a place to sit—the children on a small sofa against the wall, Jonathan and Matthew in two chairs facing his desk, and Dr. Macaluso pulls up another chair for Elizabeth. He sits opposite the two gentlemen on the other side of his desk. The folder from his office lays before him, with the name Matthew Romano taped to the out-jutting tab.

Several seconds pass before Dr. Macaluso speaks. "Jonathan, why do you think Matthew is your sister?"

Jonathan looks at him, puzzled. "Because he is!"

"But he is a man. You see that? Can you not?"

"Of course, I can see him," Jonathan says, annoyed. "But, I also see him as Camille."

"So, Jonathan," Elizabeth asks, "you see a young girl sitting next to you?"

"No!" Jonathan answers, even more annoyed. "Do *you* see a young girl sitting next to me?"

"Jonathan, please don't get angry. We're just trying to understand all of this," she pleads.

"Matthew, you are sure this is your sister, the one who was shot in 1940?" Dr. Macaluso asks.

"Oh, I'm positive! I don't know how or why, but the man sitting next to me is my sister Clara."

"So you do not see Jonathan?" he asks.

"Of course I see Jonathan."

"It's not like we're two different people," Jonathan interjects. "I'm Jonathan Taylor from New York. I'm also Clara Dumont from Verrines." *Among other people.*

Dr. Macaluso opens the folder. "Jonathan, Matthew has told me some key elements of his past life. Would you mind answering a few questions?"

"Fire away, Doc," Jonathan replies, fanning his hand like a prizefighter taunting his opponent.

"What is your mother's name?" Dr. Macaluso begins.

"Jacqueline Dumont," Jonathan sighs. "Father's name was Charles Dumont, although mother had other names for him."

Matthew chuckles. "What was it she called him when she was mad at him?"

He looks at Jonathan and they both say it in unison, "Ma petite citrouille," and then they laugh. Around the room, faces show varying levels of shock and delight.

Jonathan translates for Elizabeth, "My little pumpkin."

"Listen, Doc. We can recite all kinds of things," Jonathan says. "We had an Aunt Marguerite—"

"Who lived in Orleans," added Matthew. "We stayed with her after you and Father were—" He stops, still unable to bring himself to say the word.

"Killed," Jonathan says softly, looking at his sister. "It's okay. You can say it."

"It was horrible!" Matthew blurts out. "I can't get the images out of my head! To this day, in this new life, when I close my eyes, I see Father lying there. And you! Oh, God! Your lifeless body just lying on the walk, rivulets of blood flowing between the cobblestones." He puts his hands to his face and weeps uncontrollably.

Clara hugs her little sister. Camille throws her arms around Clara's neck. "I was so mean to you. I was such a bitch because you made that stupid wooden tablet, and you carved that English word into it! I thought I was such an aristocrat. We were bourgeoisie at best. But I thought I was better than you. I'm so sorry! Please forgive me!"

"Là mon petit ange," Clara comforts her. "There is nothing to forgive. We were children. We couldn't help the terrible thing inflicted on our family."

"I waited so long for forgiveness," Camille cries, as tears run down his face.

Jonathan wipes Matthew's tears away. "Look what I have." He pulls a small wooden tablet from his coat pocket and hands it to her.

Camille smiles and begins to laugh. "You have it? How? Where did you get it from?"

"From our house. I went there and saw your daughter and granddaughter. I saw so much of you in her face. She must have looked exactly like you when she was 14."

Matthew studies the small piece of wood, turning it over and over again in his hand.

"Aeternum?" Matthew looks at Jonathan. "What does it mean?"

"It's Latin, *not* English, and I still have no idea why I carved it." He pulls two more tablets from his pocket. "One is from India, and this black one is from Australia. I have one of my own as well." He shows his sister the highly polished metal tablet made for him in Manhattan.

Dr. Macaluso closes the file slowly and places it in his desk drawer. "Well, I am now convinced." He looks at the two men sitting in front of him with a stern sort of smile. "The both of you planned an elaborate hoax, one not seen since the Loch Ness photo of 1934."

Elizabeth stands up right away to object, but he raises his hand. "Please, let me finish. I suspect Mr. Taylor and Mr. Romano here had heard about this poor family in France whose child died a horrible death and they decided to concoct a story." His tone hardens, building in intensity. "You sought out two experts in the field and gained their confidence by putting on one hell of a performance pretending to be hypnotized, even dragging your family into the scheme—unexpectedly, I suppose, unless they are in on it too?"

He throws a doubtful eye the way of the children, both of whom are sitting there now with their mouths wide open, and then he continues. "Only to play out your little charade here for us tonight. All for the sake of God knows what? It is either that, *or*—"

Emotions in the room are running from anger and frustration to bafflement and confusion, all hanging on his every word. Then his demeanor changes on a dime and he says in a much softer, understanding tone, "*Or* you two truly are the reincarnation of Clara and Camille Dumont." A smile crosses his face. "And that's exactly what my official report will indicate. I do not understand how or why this happened, but Clara Dumont, who died in 1940 at the age of 16, and her sister Camille Dumont, who died in 1998 at the age of 72, are in fact, right now sitting in my office."

"You lived to be 72?" Jonathan asks. "What happened to Mama after that day?"

The two men lapse into French, each asking questions of one another.

Dr. Macaluso gets up and motions to Elizabeth and the children, "Perhaps we should let them have the time that was stolen from them. This is an intimate moment, one we should not intrude upon. My apologies for the drama, but I could not help myself. I used to imagine myself on a stage when I was young. Perhaps in a previous life, I was an attore on stage like my papa." Dr. Macaluso leads them out of the room and turns to close the door with a big smile. He no longer sees a 58-year-old American architect talking to a 24-year-old patient. He sees two sisters laughing and crying and rekindling a love lost so many years ago.

In the weeks that follow, Dr. Michelangelo Macaluso will happily report to Dr. Elizabeth Davidson that Matthew Romano no longer suffers from anxiety, but also that he has no further memories of Camille Dumont or the life he once lived. *Forgiveness is a powerful thing.*

Jonathan and Elizabeth walk hand in hand back to the hotel in quiet reflection. Having told the children she would wait for their father, she sent them back to the hotel hours earlier, making the excuse she needed to discuss the case some more with Dr. Macaluso, yet secretly wanting one last night alone with Jonathan. She knows he must continue his journey to Scotland, to find Moira MacNaughton and the other markers. She's done the math, and there's an excellent possibility Moira is still alive. She also knows that watching the man she is falling in love with reconnect with his past love, especially the way he talked about Moira under hypnosis, would break her heart. Certainly, if the scene is anything close to what she just witnessed in Dr. Macaluso's study, she wants no part of it. *Better to build that wall up now, Beth. A moment of hurt vs a lifetime of pain.*

"Elizabeth." The sound of her name breaks the still Italian night. "I want you to know—"

"I know," she says softly, dipping her head as she continues to walk.

"I don't think you do." She stops and looks at him. "I'm going to—"

"Scotland, yes, I know," she says, quickly. "I hope you won't get angry, but I can't go with you."

Jonathan is both confused and annoyed. "I wasn't going to say that."

"You're not going to Scotland?" Now she's the one who is confused.

"No, I'm going. I mean, yes, I am. I mean, I have to—"

"No, you're going? Or no, you're not going?"

"Yes, I am going. I think I have to. I mean, I have to see this thing through. If Moira's alive, she may know something … something vital, possibly the key to this entire thing!"

"I know. You have to go," she says, growing melancholy.

"I don't want to hurt you."

"I'm a big girl, Jonathan. I can take care of myself. It's just, I don't want to be in the way. It may be difficult, you know, if you truly are Daniel MacNaughton and she's your wife? It may be awkward when you show up on her doorstep—" Her voice changes to a playfully teasing, coquettish girl. "And you're sleeping with a younger, hotter, sexier woman. A woman with a perfect body. A woman willing to do anything to keep her man." She laughs, despite her feelings.

"Anything?" he asks, witnessing now the same contemptuous expression he saw back in the hotel room when she asked to *see something.*

"What is it with you men? I just offered you my body, and you still want more!"

"I understand," he says. "I guess the thought of seeing me with another woman may be too much for you to bear." Now, Jonathan is the one laughing.

"Oh, yeah, that's it! Have fun wheeling her around the nursing home." She turns and starts walking back the way they came. "You think that cute guy at the party is still there? You know, the one checking me out all night. Maybe I can still catch him?"

Jonathan scoops her off her feet, taking her into his arms, and spins her around once before carrying her back toward the hotel. "Oh, no you don't, lady. You're coming home with me! You offered your body to me. You said you're willing to do anything, and I still have a few things I want to try!"

"Big, strong caveman wants woman!" she mimics in a deep, manly voice.

"Damn straight. I want woman! I want woman now!" he says in his best husky Neanderthal tone before kissing her gently and carrying her in his arms down the small, dimly lit Italian street.

"Ah, amore," an elderly Italian man remarks as they pass by.

"So that's three tickets from Florence to Edinburgh Airport, departing 1:30 p.m., arriving at 5:10 p.m. on Lufthansa Airline and one ticket departing 2:35 p.m. Florence to London, and that's on Air Dolomiti? Right, got it. Thank you, Margaret. Yes … Okay … Great, thank you. Orocco Pier Hotel. One night stay, yes … M9 to M90. I'm sure one of the kids will GPS it on their phone. Thank you, Margaret. No, no, I'll find someplace up north to stay, thank you."

Elizabeth motions to the clock that reads one in the morning, then mimes to thank Margaret for her. Jonathan nods and interrupts Margaret, "Yes, I got it all. Thank you, Margaret, and thank you for doing this at such a late hour. Really? Seven at night. What are you still doing at the office? Go home. Oh, you're making flight arrangements for your boss, very funny. Good night, Margaret. Thaaaaaaank yooooooou."

"Okay, we're all set," he says to Elizabeth after ending the call.

"You wouldn't keep poor Margaret working all night if your insatiable appetite for sex hadn't gotten in the way," she teases, snaking one leg out from under the covers and poking him in the ribs with her toe.

He grabs her leg and she spontaneously screams as he pulls her close, sliding her across the sheets. They roll in the covers and wind up entangled in an embrace.

"I see *someone* is ready for round two," she giggles.

"Hey listen," he says, pausing to kiss her. "Laughter is never something a man wants to hear when referring to his—" he motions down with his eyes.

"I'm sorry," she says, starting to kiss his neck.

"There's something I need to tell you."

"Yes?" she breathes, in a low, seductive voice, making her way up to his ear.

"I tried to tell you on our walk back to the hotel."

She nibbles his earlobe.

"Elizabeth, you do know—"

"*You* find me irresistible? Sexy? Adorable? Playful and cute?" she whispers in his ear as her hands tease other parts of his body.

"Yes, all those things, but I need you to know—"

"*You're* madly in love with me and can't live without me?" she giggles and moves to kiss his lips.

"I am." He returns her kisses. "But I'm also—"

She kisses him deeply.

"I'm going to—"

"*Quit* your job and move to London?" she optimistically asks.

"I'm going to *die!*" he blurts out. His voice grows somber. "Elizabeth, I'm going to die."

She stops, frozen by his words, unable to move or breathe, trying to process what he just said.

"I—" he starts. But with a single glance, her face tells him, *this is not the best time to speak.* He sits on the corner of the bed and contemplates his words.

Finally, she breaks the silence. "When you say you're going to die, do you mean—"

"Yes, Elizabeth," he answers definitively.

"Is it cancer?" She turns and looks at him.

"No."

"Brain disease?"

He shakes his head.

"Heart disease?"

Again he shakes his head.

"Blood, liver, kidneys?" All met with the same negative shake of his head.

"Then what? *How* can you say you're going to die?" she pleads.

"Elizabeth, believe me, I don't know how, I just know. The same way I knew I had to go to India and then Australia. It's some driving force within me. *It* called to me. *It* woke me from a dead sleep weeks ago. That was the morning I knew I was going to die."

She struggles to comprehend. "You said *it*. What's *IT?!*"

"I don't know? A voice inside my head … a dream buried deep in my subconscious … a warning from my past lives, maybe? I don't know. You tell me. You're the expert."

"Jonathan, your past lives don't *make* you do things. And they *certainly* don't inform you when you're going to die!"

Jonathan bends, placing his head in his hands. "It's like a whisper in the dark room crying out so loud, constantly reminding me my time is running out."

"Send your children home. Don't go to Scotland. Don't go see Moira. Come home with me. I'll stay with you, take care of you. We'll run tests … see specialists … you'll see, there's nothing wrong with you!" She wipes tears from her eyes. "And come next year, Cassandra and Trevor can come to London and spend holiday with us!"

"Believe me, there's nothing more I would want to do right now than sell my company, move to London, and be with you."

"You know, Jonathan, it's *really* easy to commit to something when you know there's no possibility of it EVER HAPPENING!" She gets up, throws on a T-shirt, and paces the room.

"I understand you're angry—"

"I wouldn't say angry. *And* don't try to *understand* what I'm feeling," she says. "I don't even know what I'm feeling. One minute we're about to make love, and the next minute you're telling me you're dying and my world is crashing down around me. How would *you* feel?"

"Well, there is kind of a downside for me too you know," Jonathan says, trying to lighten the mood, but this is met by yet another expression he has never seen before.

"Elizabeth, I didn't intend to hurt you. I didn't intend for any of this to happen."

"Oh! I'm pretty sure you intended to make love to me!"

"I didn't intend for *that* to happen, no guy does. We hope and pray it will *happen*, but we never *count* on it happening." He looks bewildered. "Hell, we can't even count on it *happening* even when it's just *about* to happen. It's only *after* it happens that we *know* it happened. And, even then, we're *amazed* it happened. Why do you think we're so happy afterwards?" he asks with a smile.

"Don't try to be cute."

"You think I'm cute?" he jokes. I'm cute! I'm cute!!!!" he yells, remembering a scene from *Rudolph the Red-Nosed Reindeer*.

She throws a pillow at him. "Keep your voice down. The kids will hear."

"Oh, so now you're worried the kids will hear? You didn't seem so worried 30 minutes ago." Jonathan rolls over onto his back laughing.

She jumps on the bed, attacking him, straddling his waist and punching his chest. "You're an idiot."

"Does this mean you're not mad at me?"

"I didn't say I was mad at you."

"Does this mean we're not going to make love?"

She leans down and kisses him. "What do *you* think?" she asks, once again in a deep, sultry voice.

He laughs. "Did you not hear what I just said? Guys *never* know *if* it's going to happen, until it's over."

She kisses him again, tenderly this time. "It's a good possibility."

But not a definite possibility, he thinks. Afraid to say anything that may change the outcome of his current situation, he simply smiles up at her.

"Promise me one thing," she says.

He laughs again. "In this position, a man would promise you *anything*!"

She smiles. "Okay, I'll give you that one." She kisses him sweetly. "I think that's why I love you. You make me laugh."

His face grows serious. "You love me?"

277

Her hand snakes between their legs and she grabs a sensitive part of his anatomy. "Shut up, you big dope. It's an expression."

He looks up at her and asks in a playfully high octave, "So what can I promise you?"

She releases her hold and collapses on his chest, staring into his eyes. "There's a strong possibility that this won't be your last time on earth."

He shakes his head. "Probably not."

"So when you do—come back, return, reappear, whatever you want to call it."

"Whatever *I* want to call it? *You're* the professional! It's your field of expertise. What do *you* call it?"

She scrunches up her face, which Jonathan finds adorable. "I don't know, we never had someone come back more than once, let alone multiple times." She smiles down at him. "As I said, you're an exceptional case, Mr. Taylor."

"Well, when you figure it out, let me know. I want to tell people I'm a multi-reoccurring reincarnation of myself."

Her brain goes into overdrive as she processes the phrase. "Hey, now that's actually not bad. Mind if I borrow it?"

"It's all yours. A gift from me to you."

"Ah, my first gift from you. I'll treasure it always." Although said in jest, Jonathan can see tears well up in her eyes. "Anyway, when you do your multi-reoccurring reincarnation thing next time around, I want you to contact me! Promise me you'll find me!"

"Elizabeth, I don't know when or where or even who I may come back as. I may be a woman next time."

She raises one eyebrow. "That may not be a bad thing," she says, smiling cryptically.

"Why couldn't we have met years ago?"

They begin to kiss. "What if I don't remember you in my next life?" he asks.

Her hands travel down his body. "Well. Let's see if I can do something for you that you'll never, ever forget." With a wicked laugh, she drapes the comforter over the top of them, disappearing into darkness.

The next morning, Jonathan texts Cassandra that he's having breakfast in his room, and he'll meet them, along with Elizabeth, in the lobby at 9:30 to head to the airport. Their flight is at 1:30 and he wants to straighten out some things before they leave. The sunrise washes over the ancient city of Florence as it had done even before the Romans settled it in 59 BCE, but on this morning, it feels different. Golden rays of heaven's light illuminate the room. Elizabeth stirs in bed, blurry-eyed and tired from the night before. Jonathan rests on one elbow, watching her.

"Good morning," he says softly, with just a hint of slumber still resting in his throat, making him sound a bit like Sam Elliott.

Her lips curl into a smile. A few strands of hair cover one eye. "Have you been watching me all night?"

"I didn't want to miss one moment," he says, leaning over to tenderly kiss the soft part of her neck. "I ordered breakfast. Should be here in 30 minutes."

She smiles another wicked grin.

Twenty-five minutes later, they rise, gather their things, and begin to pack for their respective flights. Occasionally, like honeymooners, they stop for a fleeting kiss or a gentle embrace. Over breakfast at the table, they talk and eat as though they've been dancing this waltz all of their lives.

Jonathan lets out a long moan. "Mmmmmm, even their room service is delicious."

"I just noticed," she says, waiting for him to take the bait so she can set the hook.

"Noticed what?" he asks, letting out another audible groan.

Hook, line, and sinker, she thinks. "You make more noise when you eat than when you—" Her head tilts backward toward the bed and she bursts out laughing.

Jonathan turns a bright shade of red. "In college, most of my earliest sexual experiences were in a dorm room with a roommate sleeping across the way."

"Oh? That explains the sock on the door knob." She chuckles again, enjoying the last sip of her espresso.

"We better get going. Don't want the kids banging on the door again," Jonathan says.

"I'm getting very good at hiding under sheets."

He kisses her. "That's just it," he says, gazing into her eyes, trying to make fleeting seconds last an eternity. "I don't want to keep you a secret."

Elizabeth and Jonathan walk down the hallway to the elevator, board the lift to the first floor, then stroll through the lobby, hand in hand to meet the kids.

"All set?" Cassandra asks without batting an eye.

"Taxi should be out front," Jonathan says as they exit the hotel, Elizabeth still by his side. A satisfied smile covers his face.

"Did you know about this?" Trevor asks Cassandra as they follow behind the couple.

She gives him a *don't be stupid* smirk. "Of course."

The ride to the airport is somber even though the city is alive and bustling.

Inside the terminal, they check the departure board. The gate for Elizabeth's flight, on Air Dolomiti, is in the opposite direction of the Taylors. She turns and sees the heartbreak on Jonathan's face as well as Cassandra's sorrowful expression.

She musters all her strength then and puts on her best British face. "I have to be going, and all of you have to catch a flight to Scotland."

Taking Elizabeth quite by surprise, Cassandra throws her arms around her surrogate mother and new friend. "We're going to miss you! Please say you'll come to visit us in New York! You have to! We have to tell you everything that happens in Scotland!"

Elizabeth hugs her tightly, wanting desperately to say yes, but in the back of her mind, she knows Jonathan's path will not lead to a 'happily-ever-after' ending. "Of course," she lies. "As soon as I can clear my schedule." She pronounces 'schedule' in a distinctly British way that turns Cassandra's tears into a giggle.

Trevor remains dumbstruck, still attempting to piece it all together when exactly his father and Elizabeth had become a couple.

She smiles at the young man before her, seeing so much of Jonathan in him. Trevor shakes her hand. "It was very nice to meet you, Dr. Davidson." He smiles, realizing too late he should accept her, in a more proper way, into the family. "Elizabeth."

She surprises him then by pulling him in close and whispering in his ear. "I'm going to need you to watch over Cassandra. She'll need your strength and support these next few months." Pulling away, their eyes lock. "When the time comes, I'm only a phone call away."

He gives her a puzzled look but agrees with a nod nevertheless.

"Would you kids give us a moment to say goodbye?" Jonathan asks.

Trevor and Cassandra smile and begin to walk away with waves but then Cassandra stops and runs back, rising onto her tippy-toes so as to whisper in her father's ear. "You better kiss her goodbye, Dad, and I don't just mean a peck on the cheek." She flashes Elizabeth a big smile before running off to join her brother.

"Smart girl," Elizabeth says.

"Yeah, she gets it from me," he mutters, slipping his hands around her waist.

"You know, as an English woman, I'm not accustomed to public displays of affection."

"Get used to it." He focuses only on her, and as every other person in Aeroporto di Firenze-Peretola fades from existence, Jonathan and Elizabeth embrace in a kiss that seems to go on for lifetimes, neither one of them ever wanting to let go.

When their lips finally part, he sighs and says, "Je t'aime mon amour."

"I understood that one," she squeaks out before she begins to cry, then repeats it back to him as best she can, butchering the French language as only a citizen from Britain could. He smiles and wants to laugh. She strongly disagrees with Dr. Macaluso's quote. *Not everyone can learn to speak Italian or French for that matter.*

"I'm giving you one month. One month. Then I'm coming to the States, and we're going to make this work!" she says firmly.

He kisses her again, whispering just soft enough for only her ears to hear. "I don't care how long I have. I want to spend every last minute with you."

She wipes her eyes and turns to walk away. "One month!" she yells, not looking back. Jonathan Taylor watches Dr. Elizabeth Davidson disappear into an ocean of people and out of his life … forever.

As Trevor heads off by himself to buy coffee, his cell phone rings. Cassandra, meanwhile, ambles up to her father.

"I want this to be the last one," he says as a tear finds its way down to his jawline before he wipes it away.

"The last one, Dad?"

"The last place. The last life. The last life I have to relive. I can't take it. I can't take any more of these memories. It's too painful. I can't take seeing people I loved, as much as I love you and your brother, knowing they're gone, and I'm still here, knowing they lived their life and I wasn't a part of it … knowing I can't be part of their lives *here* and *now*! None of this makes sense. I want to live this life. I want to be with—" he wants to say Elizabeth, but settles for, "someone who loves me."

Jonathan hangs his head and shakes it back and forth, wishing he could shake all these feelings off of him. For the first time in her life, Cassandra sees defeat on her father's face.

"I want it to end. I want to go home and forget I ever woke from that dream. I want to turn back the hands of time, go back to when you and your brother were young. I want to take the two of you to Central Park and play in the grass on hot summer days."

He then looks at his daughter with tears in her eyes. "But we can't do that. No one can catch a moment after it's gone. If only moments were fireflies, easily scooped up and kept in mason jars." *Moments of our lives always glowing bright, kept forever on a shelf.* He hugs his daughter and whispers, "Never grow up, peanut."

She responds as she's always done ever since the age of four. "I promise, Daddy."

"And I promise," he says. "We'll go to Oldshoremore, and see if we can find Moira MacNaughton, if she even exists. Then we'll head home to New York just in time to watch the fireflies dance in Grandpa's meadow, on our yearly pilgrimage up to the cabin."

Trevor walks over, ending a call and putting his phone in his pocket. "You'll never guess who that was."

"Mom?" Cassandra replies.

"Noooooo," he responds in a snarky kind of way, as though they were nine years old. "Some professor at the Museum of Natural History. He saw my post about the tablets. He called them markers. Anyway, he wants to meet you, Dad."

"Fine," Jonathan answers curtly. "Tell him we'll be back in New York before the first leaf hits the ground." Jonathan storms off toward their boarding gate.

"What did I say?" Trevor asks his sister.

She shakes her head and races off after her father, leaving Trevor alone with the luggage.

"Hello? A little help here?"

PLACE: HIGHLANDS, SCOTLAND
YEAR: PRESENT DAY

Jonathan steps off the plane at Edinburgh Airport.

The brisk Scottish air kisses his face, welcoming him home like an old friend. There is something familiar in the air. Maybe it's the faint sound of bagpipes playing in the distance, or the underlying pride of the Scottish people, or maybe it's simply a feeling that time has left this country back in the Middle Ages, that the threat of clan warfare could still break out at any moment. Either way, Jonathan loves this land, and for the first time in his worldwide journey, he feels more at home here than in any other place he's visited. It wouldn't take much for him to hang up his hat and call this place home once again.

He rents a car and they make the short 15-minute drive to the Orocco Pier Hotel. As they dine at the hotel's restaurant a little while later, Cassandra can see her father's mind is preoccupied, heavy with lifetimes of ruminations and reawakened truths, personalities, and people. Perhaps he's reliving moments from Paris and Italy, thinking of Elizabeth, of being in her arms and dreaming about a life together. Cassandra announces, in part to shake her father alert again, that she'd like to explore the quaint

Scottish town with its stone buildings and narrow cobblestone streets. Trevor says he's up for a night of exploring as well, and perhaps downing some pints at a local tavern.

Queensferry where they're staying, just 10 miles west of Edinburgh, is gorgeous at night. It's everything a Scottish village should be. On any other night, Jonathan would have offered his kids a guided tour, spouting historical facts and telling tall tails of Scottish lore, making his children wonder if he was making it all up or actually recalling some distant memory back when he walked these streets in another body, in a time when inlaid cobblestone streets and stone buildings first replaced dirt roads and wooden huts. But for now, all Jonathan wants to do is forget.

The following day proves no better than the previous night. As they make their way out of Queensferry and head north into the Scottish countryside, Jonathan is still brooding over Elizabeth. Cassandra remembers trips to her family's cabin in the Catskills when Jonathan often made the three-hour drive listening to an audiobook, not uttering a single word. She wishes for an audiobook now. Even Leo Tolstoy's *War and Peace* would make the six-hour drive up into the northernmost western tip of the Scottish Highlands, out to the small town of Oldshoremore, far more bearable.

If they drive to Loch Lomond and The Trossachs National Park and follow A82 up the crack, they'll drive along most of the coast of Lock Ness. Perhaps they'd even get a glimpse of old Nessie herself that way, but it would add three and a half hours to their journey. Instead, Jonathan chooses a much more direct route, taking them around Cairngorms National Park for the majestic mountains and long stretches of Highland Meadows. They stop at Costcutter in Lairg for some petrol and fresh-baked goods, and Jonathan jokes about buying some haggis, but Trevor suggests they stick with meat pies. All around them, the foreboding gray sky churns, warning of a constant storm that never seems to arrive.

The small, one-lane road seems to narrow as the trip progresses. Jonathan constantly reminds Trevor to 'stay left' every time a car approaches. Long wire fences line the roadway, supported every 14 feet by weathered wooden posts. Huge rocks jut up from the moors, breaking free of their eternal earthly slumber: frozen, unchanging, unmoving throughout the centuries—an isolated land protected from man's brutal industrialization. Here, the soil is virtually the same as when Robert the Bruce traveled upon it by horseback more than 700 years earlier.

Unlike himself, the Taylor family travel not by horseback but by hatchback, in a small rented car winding along narrow farm roads. The closer Jonathan gets to Oldshoremore, the more familiar the territory becomes.

"Ower there!" Jonathan cries out. "Ower there, I used to herd sheep as a wee boy."

Cassandra and Trevor stare at each other in the rear-view mirror. *Wee boy?* They both notice the sharp change in their father's speech all of a sudden. At first they suspect he is having fun, getting caught up in the whole spirit of the Scottish highlands, but soon it becomes clear his manner of speech and accent has changed, almost unrecognizable compared to his usual New York accent.

As they approach the town of Oldshoremore, Jonathan becomes increasingly more excited. The car rises and dips, turns and sways as they traverse the barren landscape. Long-haired cows graze alongside herds of puffy, white sheep scattered along the hillsides. The small car struggles up a long incline then, and as it crests over the hill, the long-awaited town finally comes into view.

"This is it! We're here!" Jonathan cries. "I know this place! I lived in this town!"

Town? Trevor thinks. It's barely five houses.

Among the green meadows and patches of pale-gold, overgrown grass, white plaster houses with dull, gray roofs sit planted like giant ivory teeth dropped onto the landscape from above. A cluster of pine trees stands on their right as they drive past.

"That must be their forest," Trevor jokes.

"Is this it, Dad? You lived here?" Cassandra asks, twisting her head from side to side, surveying the landscape. "Why?"

"Not here," Jonathan says. "Up ahead. Take a left to Oldshoremore."

"Where?" Trevor asks, before spying a road sign indicating a left turn for the town of Oldshoremore. "Never mind," he says, as both Jonathan and Cassandra stretch their arms forward, pointing to the sign. "Thanks, wise guys." He makes the left turn and drives up a small hill.

On the right side of the road, Cassandra stares at a small white house with a bright red cattle gate blocking the driveway. The car turns left and clucks up another slight incline. At the top of the hill, it appears another metal cattle gate blocks the road. But as Trevor gets closer, the narrow asphalt road bends again to the left. A small white house sits on the right side of the road, perfectly positioned in the middle of the rocky Scottish hillside, with a beautiful view of the Minch shoreline. The white sand beaches of the horizon seem out of place in this isolated mountain terrain.

"A beach?" Cassandra shouts. "What's a beach doing here?"

Jonathan laughs. "Aye lassie. The ocean's gawt ta meet the land somewhere."

The water is a stunning hue of turquoise, more suited for an island in the Bahamas than the northern tip of a cold and harsh country landscape. The car heads downhill, and continues along the narrow road.

"Stay left. Stay left," Jonathan warns.

"Dad, there is *no* left," Trevor says. "Or right for that matter. It's just one long lane. A small, narrow lane." He then maneuvers the car a little to the left, causing tiny pebbles to kick up from the shoulder of the road by the tires.

"Stay on the road!" Both Cassandra and Jonathan shout.

Trevor takes his foot off the accelerator, slowing the car and steering it away from the shoulder, but still favoring the left side of the quiet country lane. "Better?!"

Cassandra leans back in her seat. Jonathan remains alert, watching every bend and curve. They pass a one-room stone structure on their left, and Jonathan's face changes.

"Go slow now," he calls out to Trevor.

Having learned his lesson in France, and not wanting to zip by another one of his dad's many houses, Trevor slows the car even more.

"Right here, right here," Jonathan waves frantically. "Past this wee white house on the right. Be careful now, lad. It comes up mighty fast."

The car slows to a crawl. Jonathan points past a small fence on the right and screams out, "Right here! Right here! Take this clearing on the right."

Created by decades of wear, two small dirt paths with grass growing between them is the first inviting driveway they've seen on the entire road. The tire-track path gives way to white stone pebbles that crunch beneath the car's tires. A small, well-tended garden is held back by a weathered wooden fence. The car slows to a halt in front of two wooden posts with a wooden two-by-four nailed across them. A small but average size house for the area stands facing south. To the west, a beautiful view of the beach and the North Sea. Two chimneys stand on each end of the dwelling, and two windows are situated on either side of a small mudroom which sits dead center in the front of the house. The house is perfectly symmetrical. Across the lawn, Jonathan spots white sheets hanging on a clothesline.

I strung that line, Jonathan recalls, but for the first time on this entire journey, he is unexpectedly apprehensive. He sits in the car wringing his hands as beads of sweat gather at his temples.

"Dad, is this it?" Trevor asks. Nothing. He and Cassandra glance at one another and wait. "Dad?"

"This is it," is all Jonathan can muster. Cassandra can't help but wonder if his answer has another meaning, remembering their conversation at the airport.

A brown wooden door opens on the side of a mudroom affixed to the center of the house. Jonathan steps out of the car, holding on to the opened door for support, as he watches an older woman emerge from the shadows into the bright midday sun. He can hardly believe his eyes.

"May I help you?" she begins, before she can see Jonathan's face.

He closes the car door and drifts toward her. Suddenly, her hands fly to her face, covering her mouth. He starts towards her, slowly at first, but then faster. By the time he reaches her, he is almost sprinting.

The two embrace. Jonathan takes the woman's hands and kisses them deeply.

Trevor's gaze falls to his sister. "So is he her husband?" he asks.

They watch their father kiss the woman on her forehead, cheeks, and finally, he cradles her face within his hands, closes his eyes, and draws her into him for a long, deep kiss.

Cassandra answers her brother softly, but unequivocally. "Yep. He's her husband."

"She's alive!" Trevor grabs her arm. "Cazz, this is *that* woman, the redhead?"

Cassandra nods her head.

"Does that mean Dad's a fireman?"

Cassandra's face contorts. "How are you not following this?" She shakes her head. "I can't believe Mom thinks *you're* the smart one."

"Daniel? Is it really you?" The woman sobs as she holds him close, nuzzling her head under his chin, absorbing the warm protection only a wife can feel from her husband.

"Daniel?" Cassandra and Trevor repeat to one another.

Jonathan kisses her over and over again, getting lost in her embrace.

"Moira," he whispers her name ever so tenderly. "I've missed you so much."

She kisses him passionately then, just as a wife kisses her husband who has returned from war. The world fades away, and for that one, brief moment, there is no one else on earth but the two of them. They hold each other in a tight embrace as only two souls who have known true love can. Cassandra and Trevor stare on in shock as their father embraces a total stranger—a much older total stranger—as though she is his wife.

Trevor interrupts the reunited couple with a loud, throat-clearing, "Um, Daniel? Hello?"

"Oh, kids," Jonathan calls, turning around without releasing his embrace. "Moira, I want you to meet—" He stops then, at a complete loss for words, or maybe, they think, desperately searching for the right ones. When none come, he finally chokes out, "My children."

"Kids, this is Moira MacNau—um, is it still?"

With a shy smile, she nods. "Yes, it is still and has always been MacNaughton."

He pulls her closer to him. He can't believe she hasn't remarried after all these years.

"Mrs. Moira Greer MacNaughton, these are my children, Cassandra—"

"Hello," Cassandra offers with a peculiar smile.

"And Trevor, my oldest."

"Hi," he says curtly, with no trace of a smile.

"It's so nice to meet you both. Please, please come in."

Jonathan holds the door open and Cassandra enters first, cat-like and cautious. Trevor follows with a glance at his father. "Years of therapy, Dad. Years."

They enter the quaint dwelling and all look around.

"I'll be right back," Moira tells them, already on her way to the kitchen where she picks up the phone receiver. "Can I get ye anything?"

"No, we're good," Cassandra responds.

She dials the phone. "Make yersel at hame," she chuckles. "How odd does that sound, Daniel?" Her attention snaps to the receiver, "Hello, Shannon? Put Liam awn."

She smiles in their direction, then seconds later, "Liam!" She whisper-yells into the receiver. "Go fetch Angus and come straight over. Daniel's home! Sure, sure, bring them too. Yes, yes, of course, and tell Angus to do the same. Okay, see you in a bit. Cheers."

She comes back into the living room with a pint of Tennent's Lager, biscuits, and three teacups on a serving tray. "I put on the kettle. Tea will be ready in a minute." She places the tray on a coffee table in front of the couch where the kids are sitting.

"Still fancy a pint?" she asks Jonathan. He nods affirmatively. Moira hands him the tall, amber pint and touches his arm. "Here you go, my love. It's so good to have you back."

They smile at one another.

"What, no Guinness?" Trevor asks.

"Guinness." Jonathan snickers. "If we were in Ireland, maybe, but we're in the Highlands o' Scotland."

Moira smiles and shakes her head. "Oh, how the Irish love their Guinness! Now, whit do I call you?"

Jonathan and his children are momentarily puzzled.

"Come, come, you weren't born Daniel MacNaughton," she says. "Whit do folks cry you?" She notices the blank, dumbstruck stare on the children's faces.

"They call me—" Jonathan stops and takes a big swig of beer. The distinctive aroma of the frothy-headed ale releases years of memories, memories of growing up in Scotland. He closes his eyes, drinking the memories in before saying, "My name is Jonathan Taylor."

"Oh," she jumps up, hearing the kettle's whistle, and hurries to the kitchen. "That's a beautiful name."

"Dad!" Cassandra snaps. "Why is she acting like none of this is weird?"

"Yeah, Dad," Trevor agrees. "And why is she okay with a perfect stranger kissing her?"

"And why is she inviting people over?" Cassandra adds quickly.

Jonathan waves his hand, motioning for silence, as Moira re-enters the room carrying a steeping kettle.

"I'm sure the both of you have many questions for us." She sets the tea down next to the plate of cookies. "I'll try, with your father's help, to put all of them to rest."

She joins Jonathan, sitting on his knee and wrapping her arm around his neck. "You'll have to excuse us. We were very young when your father left me." Her aging eyes smile at his bright, relatively youthful ones. "My body may be old, but having you here with me now, I feel like a wee bairn again."

"Left you?" Cassandra asks softly.

"Yes, left me. Of course, it wasn't his choice. The fire took him." Something clicks inside Trevor's head. *The schoolhouse.*

"Should I tell them or do you want to?" she asks.

Jonathan smiles. "Kids, this is … my wife. We were married when we were, well, I was eighteen, and Moira was—"

"Seventeen, dear," she says. "We grew up here. Your father noticed me at the beach, and we knew." She looks at Jonathan sideways. "Well, I knew it was love at first sight. I think it was lust at first sight for you, Daniel. Oh, I'm sorry, Jonathan."

"You can call me Daniel," Jonathan says, a bit too eagerly for Cassandra and Trevor's tastes.

"Why do you think our father is Daniel?" Trevor asks.

"Because he is! Just as I know Daniel was Clara Dumont before that."

"What?!" Cassandra's body shakes. "You *know* about Clara Dumont?"

"How do *you* know about Clara Dumont?" Trevor asks, right after Cassandra.

"When I met Daniel," Moira begins, "we were both quite young. He would tell me the most outrageous stories. Tall tales of his life as a Viking killing people … and you had a funny name for hiking too—" She turns and looks at her long-lost husband. "I called it a walk-a-round. What did you call it, Daniel? That thing you did in Australia?"

"Walkabout," Jonathan gently corrects, taking her hand and holding it closed in his.

"Right, walkabout. Daniel would say he went walkabout as an ab-o-rig-i-ne." She sounds out the word with a peculiar pronunciation, complements of her Scottish brogue. "And he met a famous gunfighter in the old west. That was my favorite story," she adds, kissing his forehead. "Didn't end too well for ya, from what I recall."

They laugh together.

"I thought they were just stories, of course. I thought to myself, this lad certainly can spin a mighty yarn—"

"What does spinning yarn have to do with Dad's stories?" Cassandra interrupts.

"Spin yarn," Jonathan starts, "or spinning yarn, is an expression people used when someone told an especially long, sometimes embellished tale. It was a compliment."

"Like, *'Boy that guy can spread the bullshit',*" Trevor suggests.

"Well, no, not exactly," Jonathan clarifies. "*Spreading bullshit* is more like yer bum's oot the windae. That's like lying. *Spinning yarn* is simply telling a long, drawn-out, sometimes exaggerated story."

"Yeah, but didn't you think Dad—I mean, Daniel—was lying?" Trevor asks.

"Not so much lying, no, lad. I thought he was just telling me a story for my amusement. You have to understand, we didn't even own a telly back then."

"We were too poor," Jonathan adds.

"We could barely afford a radio."

"Oh, my God! I would kill myself. What did you guys do? Sit around and—" Cassandra blushes. "Um, never mind. I don't want to know."

"Aye, we did a lot of winchin too," Moira says, then shoots a devilish grin to the man sitting beside her. "But no, mostly he told me stories. Every night." She brings his hand to her lips and kisses it tenderly. "I think I grew more and more in love with him with every story he told."

"Ahh," Cassandra sighs, reacting as every girl does when hearing of true love, momentarily forgetting it's her father sitting with a woman who isn't her mother.

"And yes, Daniel also told me of how he was a little French girl playing with her sister in an upstairs nursery. He called himself Clara. Clara Dumont. Do you remember, Daniel?"

"I remember." He kisses her hand in return. "I remember everything."

"His stories had so much detail, all so vivid; I swear you'd think he was actually there. Then one day, shortly after we were married, I asked him, 'How do you come up with these stories?' I think if he'd told me the truth before we were married, he thought I'd say yer aff yer heid, and I wouldn't marry him, eh?"

"Aye. Ya right, ladybug." Jonathan lets his old nicknames for her slip from his lips as easily and comfortably as slipping into a warm bed on a cold highland night.

A tear falls from Moira's eye. Then another, followed by another.

"Are you alright?" Cassandra asks, immediately concerned, already developing sincere affection for the old woman.

"I'm fine, dearie. It's just, I haven't heard that name in almost 50 years. The last time I heard it, the love of my life ran into a burning building, promising he would be right back."

Jonathan hangs his head in shame. "I'm so very sorry, my love."

Moira lifts his head with her hand. "You have nothing to be ashamed of. If you came here today and saw the same building on fire, and heard those wee bairns crying out for help, you would do the same thing now as you did back then. It's who you are, and who you were, and who you always will be. It's why I fell in love with you."

"Dad … I mean, your husband, Daniel, ran into a burning building, to save *bairn?*" Trevor asks.

"Children," Jonathan translates.

"Not just any burning building," Moira continues, tears in her eyes. "The old schoolhouse, filled with wee bairn. The teacher got most of the students out, but there were several smaller ones still inside. Your father—Daniel—saved two. He carried them out in his arms. Then he run back for more." Her eyes close. "That was the last I saw of him. All but one of the children were saved before the roof collapsed. Poor Timmy MacNeil, and my Daniel, were both killed."

Jonathan pulls her in to him and holds her tightly in his arms. No one speaks, observing a minute of silence out of respect for the dead boy and Daniel, the man their father once was and somehow still is.

A soft, frail voice breaks the silence. "But I knew I would see him again." This petite Scottish woman had lived an entire life alone, yet unwaivering in her faith, never letting go of the absolute belief her husband *would* return one day. "I knew, and I waited. I knew you would find me, and I kept it safe."

"Kept what safe?" Cassandra asks, but before Moira can answer, they hear a car, maybe two, pull up in the driveway.

"Oh, speak o' the devil! They're here," Moira says. "Am a pure nick," she mutters to herself, her hands fanning across her cheeks. She gets up and grabs a tissue from a box on a small table in the hall, wiping away her tears before turning to Jonathan. "You're going to love this."

A brass door knocker clangs. "Come in, come in, please," Moira calls out, and the door opens. A colossal man enters with his wife and two children. Behind them, an even larger gentleman and his wife with three children join the group. The small room, suddenly full, seems to have rapidly shrunk even smaller, and the Taylors can't help but wonder what's going on.

Moira takes both of the huge gentlemen by the arms. "Boys," she calls them, even though they're grown men the size of lumberjacks, "I want ye to meet someone."

She presents them to Jonathan. "Liam, Angus, this is—"

Before she can finish, Liam grabs Jonathan's biceps in each hand as if to crush him. "Moira told us the stories when we were growin' up. She said you would return one day." He pulls Jonathan close and hugs him tightly. Angus wraps his arms around both men. The two men hold Jonathan in a death grip. The room falls silent as Angus and Liam tearfully embrace a man who is a total stranger to their wives and children.

Jonathan—like the others in the room—has no idea what is happening. Only Moira, Liam, and Angus are privy to this strange reunion.

Finally, Angus releases his hold, as does Liam. "I wanna thank ye with all me heart," says the towering giant.

"Me too!" adds the other.

"What did I do?" Jonathan asks, overwhelmed beyond words.

"Daniel, dear," Moira says, taking Jonathan's arm. Tilting her head back to take in the height of the Highlanders, she continues, "This is Liam McMurphy and his younger brother, Angus McMurphy."

Their names, however, hold no meaning for Jonathan.

"These are the wee lads you carried from the fire some 58 years ago," she announces, beaming from ear to ear, "though they're not so wee now!"

"You saved our lives, sir," the older brother says. "You gave two sons back to their dear mother when fate and fire had other plans for us."

"You gave me brother back to me!" Angus says.

"And him to me!" Liam says, wrapping his massive arm around his brother and hugging him.

Liam's wife walks up and kisses Jonathan on the cheek. "You gave me my husband."

"And mine as well," adds her sister-in-law, with a kiss on Jonathan's other cheek.

"You have given us our children," Angus says, "and our nieces and our nephews, and all the children they will one day bear as well. All that we have, we owe to you, sir."

Jonathan's eyes fill with water and he hugs the grown boys once again.

"We're so sorry you had to sacrifice your life to save ours," Liam whispers in his ear. "Thank you so much!"

Realizing the tremendous gift her father has given to this one family, Cassandra starts to cry. She sees Jonathan's loving gaze fixed on Moira, and she feels tremendous sorrow about the time he lost with this woman—his wife—who loved him so deeply that she sacrificed her whole life waiting alone for his return.

Trevor takes Cassandra by surprise and pulls her in for a hug, a single act of love he hasn't shown her in several years. She turns into him and cries against his chest.

Jonathan asks the brothers to introduce him to their wives and children. One by one, they make introductions. He shakes their hands, asking them their age. Recounting stories of when he was their age in response, making them laugh. Jonathan's brogue becomes more and more pronounced the more he speaks. "When I was a wee lad and lived down the lane, I had 12 sheep and two cows I had to look after up on the hill."

"Up by Old Man Sullivan's farm?" the youngest child asks. "He's Crabbit!"

"Haud yer wheesht! He's still alive?!" Jonathan exclaims, and lets out a hardy laugh. "Yon dafty eejit scared me as a wee one too."

Moira smiles and thinks, *it's been a long, long time since this house was filled with such laughter and good friends.*

Slowly the brothers and their families bid them farewell, and Jonathan accompanies them all to their cars.

"I don't know how, and I don't know why," Liam says, "but God has put you on this earth for a good reason, and if that sole reason was to save me brother and me, then we can never thank ye enough. We are here because of you."

"We are, because of you," Jonathan mumbles, "Ubuntu."

"I'm sorry?" Liam asks. "Did ye say something?"

"Nothing," Jonathan responds, then hugs the brothers one last time and waves goodbye as Moira joins him.

"What was that you said to him?" she asks. "Ubuntu?"

"Roughly translated, it means 'I am because of you'. It's South African."

"Another life?" she asks.

"Another life, another time," he answers.

"Zulu," she guesses correctly.

"Yes, part of the Nguni Bantu tribe," and then he smiles fondly as yet another distant memory sneaks into his head.

They walk arm and arm back toward the house: Daniel's house, their house, the house he was meant to live his life in with Moira, a life where he dreamed of raising a family, growing old, and ultimately dying in her arms.

"It's so unfair how this life cheated us—cheated *me* from a life with *you!* It's not fair, Moira, *not* fair at all!" He's shouting now as his anger rises. "Why do they get to live their lives with each other and have families, and we're denied all that!?"

She stops before the door. "If ye had it to do over again, Daniel, would you choose not to run into that burning schoolhouse? Could you stand outside, letting helpless children burn to death, just to have a life? A family with me?"

He hugs her tightly, "No, of course not."

"No, Daniel. You couldn't. That's not the man I fell in love with and married." She kisses her husband. "We can't change what happened to us or know why it happened. We just have to live our lives the best we can and make what little time we have left count."

She always did have a way of calming his Scottish temper.

"You have two bonnie children in there and a lassie right here who's going to love you till the day she dies. Let's not dwell on the past. I only invited the McMurphy clan here to show you that your sacrifice was not in vain, and has blessed so many other lives!"

He nods. "I suppose you're right."

She smiles. "Dae ye remember that movie we watched at Christmas, the one with that Stewart fella and Donna Reed, eh?"

"*It's a Wonderful Life,* by Frank Capra?"

"Aye, that's the one. Remember what the angel said … what was his name, eh?"

"Clarence."

"That's right, remember what he said to George Bailey. *Each man's life touches so many other lives.* I loved that line. That first Christmas after you—" She stops for a moment, fighting back the tears. "That was the hardest time, Christmas without you."

"I'm sorry," Jonathan begins, but she waves him off, wiping her tears.

"Every year they played that movie on the telly. I'd watched it alone, our favorite movie, and I knew, I absolutely knew you saved those boys for a reason."

Jonathan—Daniel—embraces his dear wife. *How can I ever make up for the lifetime of loneliness I caused her?*

Moira holds her husband, beyond happy to have him back in her arms.

As they walk back into the house, Cassandra hugs them both, and Jonathan looks at Moira for a moment and then at his daughter.

"I'm just so happy you two can finally be together," Cassandra says. "I see how much you care for one another, and if the fire hadn't happened, you two would be so happy."

Moira smiles. "Maybe, dearie, but then maybe you and your brother would not be here."

"Crap. I didn't think about that," Cassandra says, and the two of them start to laugh.

"I want to know," Trevor says, "how you knew my dad would return one day."

"Oh, that's easy," Moira answers as they settle back in the living room.

"Let's see … where did I leave off before Liam an Angus arrived?"

"Daniel told you about Clara Dumont," Trevor says.

"Aye, I remember. Right! Shortly after we were married, I asked Daniel, 'How do you make up all these stories?'. They were all so thick with details. Your father sat me down and explained he didn't make them up at all. They were memories. Things that happened to the people in his stories actually happened to him. I thought it was just another one of his tales, o'course, but then he told me specific names and places where he previously lived. He was earnest, and it started to scare me. Finally, I said, 'If you truly believe it, let's go to one of these places and meet one of these people.' So that's what we did. We saved our money and traveled to France, to a little village called—"

"Vérrines!" Trevor jumps in.

"Aye! Vérrines, that's the name. Daniel said he was a young, 16-year-old girl named Clara."

"Clara Dumont," Cassandra adds.

"Aye, Clara Dumont. Anyway, we made our way to the town, if you can call it that. I think we stayed in Néry that night.

"Remember the house where we stayed?!" Jonathan blurts out as though the memories had just jumped back into his head. "Oh! And the old couple? They were very nice! We stayed in their daughter's bedroom. There were crucifixes everywhere, and a paintin' of Jesus right there above the bed. Made it mighty difficult that night to—"

"Daniel!" a rosy hue fills Moira's cheeks. "I'm certain nothing of the sort happened that night." She offers Cassandra a confessing wink. "I do, however, remember the fresh baked croissants the next morning."

"Mmmmm, absolutely heavenly," Jonathan says, and Moira knows part, if not all, of his comment was directed to the overnight activities.

"Excuse me, Moira. I have to make a quick phone call," Jonathan interrupts, heading to the kitchen. "Please, keep telling the story."

Moira smiles then continues, "When we arrived in Vérrines, we asked if anyone knew of a Clara Dumont. We got the most mockit looks. You would probably say *nasty* looks."

"Remember that one guy? Talk about rude!" Jonathan shouts from the kitchen.

"Aye, but you weren't that nice to him either, if I remember correctly! Now, are you goin' to let me tell the story or keep interruptin'?!" she shouts back with a giggle.

Speaking into the phone's receiver, Jonathan gives a wave of his hand.

"Where was I? Oh, yes. Daniel walked around the whole town telling me where he went to school, who lived in which house, and for all I knew, he could have been making it up as he went. There was no way of proving any of it. But then he saw his house. Clara's house I mean. His entire demeanor changed. We knocked on the door and asked if a Clara Dumont had lived there. To both our surprise, well, to my surprise anyway, because Daniel was absolutely certain he lived in this house, the woman said yes, she used to live there, this Clara girl. When Daniel tried, however, to explain why we were there, they turned us away, and quite rudely too, I might say. Later we discovered that Clara Dumont, who lived in that house, had been killed by a German soldier."

"This time we were able to talk with them, Moira," Jonathan tells her on his way back into the living room.

"You did?! What happened? Did they believe you?"

"It definitely took some convincing, but aye, I would say they believed us." He removes a wooden tablet from his pocket and hands it to her. She carefully examines it, turning it over to check its authenticity, then looks back up at him. "Just like the others."

"Others?" Trevor and Cassandra ask in unison.

"Daniel made one before we left for France. In case anything happened to him. Anyway, I promised to keep it safe." Her eyes fixed on the word on the back of the tablet then. "He never did tell me what this word meant. After the fire, I put Daniel's tablet with the others."

"Do you still have them?" Jonathan asks.

"Of course. I kept them safe, just like I said I would. Don't ye remember? After France, we went to—"

"Denmark!" Trevor exclaims.

"Aye, your father told ye? Then he must have told ye about the box?" Her face lights up as she remembers.

"Wait, what box?" Jonathan asks.

Moira, now equally confused, asks, "How does Trevor know, and you don't?"

"We went to a therapist," Cassandra says. "She hypnotized Dad."

Moira laughs. "Did she turn you into a chicken, my love?" She gently rubs the side of Jonathan's face with her palm. "Oh, how I would have loved to see that! Do you have her number? Can she do it again?"

"I'm pretty sure Dad got her number," Cassandra says, a little too playfully. Moira nods her way, but Cassandra isn't sure she grasps the double entendre.

Moira leaves the room and returns with a well-worn 50-year-old backpack. "I haven't opened this since I placed yours amongst the others."

Jonathan opens the old canvas bag and looks inside. "It's all coming back to me." His hand pats the side of the backpack. "This is the reason we started this journey."

"How many are in there, Dad?" Trevor asks.

"It's getting late. I think you guys should be going."

"Huh? *You guys* should be going? Shouldn't the *three* of us be going?" Cassandra asks as she and Trevor just stare on with confused looks, awaiting his answer.

Jonathan moves to Moira's side. "We talked it over outside. I'm going to stay here tonight. I made arrangements for the both of you at the *Mountain View*. It's down the road, past the old schoolhouse." He shakes his head. The mere name brings back such bad memories.

"They converted the schoolhouse into a place of lodging too," Moira tells them, "but I can't imagine you would want to stay there."

"I'm sure you won't have any trouble finding the *Mountain View*," Jonathan continues. "Just drive slowly. The roads are narrow and winding. And stay to the left."

"Oh," Moira interrupts again. "Remember that nice young man from Liverpool and his wife? Yoko, I think it was? They were up here on holiday with their two children when he crashed his car and had to go to hospital."

Trevor looks at his father. "Wait. Is she talking about John Lennon?"

"Aye. That's him. I don't think he stayed left," Moira says, letting out a tiny giggle.

Jonathan nods and continues as if nothing fascinating had just been said. "I put your room on my card, so everything is taken care of."

"Dad, don't you think you should—?" Cassandra starts, but Trevor stops her.

"Cazz, they waited over 50 years to be together," he says, already walking his sister to the door. "I'm sure nothing you or I say could separate them tonight."

Jonathan and Moira just smile at this, and then accompany them back to the car. Standing together, they watch as Jonathan's kids drive away.

"You did a wonderful job raising those two," Moira says. "They're smart kids. She's beautiful, and I see a great deal of you in yer boy."

"Thank you, but I had help." They walk back inside the house, and Jonathan asks, "So what would you like to do now?"

"Oh, I think you know what I'd like to do," she says in a girlish, come hither voice.

"Really?"

"Aye! As your son said, I've waited more than 50 years for this!"

She heads toward the staircase with an old, familiar dance in her step. Briefly she pauses, removing a decorative dragonfly comb from her hair, allowing her ginger locks to break free. Turning her head back to him with one more fetching glance, she stops at a desk in the hall. Opening a drawer, she retrieves an old notebook and a deck of playing cards. They sit on opposite sides of a nearby table and Moira opens the notebook carefully. The date at the top of the page reads January 28th, 1964. Below that is their names, Moira and Daniel. Further down, a series of numbers add up to 525 for Moira and 340 for Daniel.

As she did so many years ago, she writes both their names on a fresh sheet of paper, followed by today's date. "You still think you can beat me?"

"Last I remember, it was three games to two, and I was winning."

She laughs. "The score is correct, but I believe I was winning. Would you like to check the book?" She shuffles the deck and hands the cards to Jonathan.

"I don't think so," he responds with a smile. Then he cuts the deck and deals the cards. Placing the remaining cards in the center of the table, he turns over an ace of hearts. "Oh, that's just grand! Here we go again, Ladybug!"

That night, they lay in bed holding each other. "Can I ask you, Daniel, does it hurt? I mean, did it hurt? Dying an' all? I'm so afraid."

He holds her tightly and kisses her forehead. "It's like slippin' into a dream. You have nothing to fear. But let's not talk about such things. I'm here now, my dear, and God willin', we have many more years together. I'm going to make up for all those years we were apart."

She kisses him deeply. "I love you, my handsome, young highland man."

"And I love you, my bonny Ladybug."

She closes her eyes. "Oh, don't look at me, Daniel. My hair has lost its fire, and my eyes have clouded over and lost their sparkle."

He cradles her head softly between his hands. "Open your eyes." She does. "You are more beautiful today than on the very first day I saw you on the beach. You had my heart then, and you have it now." He leans in and kisses her tenderly. "And you will have it tomorrow and all the days to follow. I have traveled to heaven and back to be by your side. I would give my life a hundred times over to make you happy!"

"I don't ever want to lose you again." A tear rolls down her cheek. "It tore me apart last time. I don't think I can go through that again."

"I'm not going anywhere, Ladybug."

The candlelight burned bright and long in their bedroom that night, but as morning approached, the light that filled the small Scottish cottage after so many years surrendered to the darkness.

The following morning, the kids came over the hill only to see flashing red and blue lights of an ambulance and police cars. Trevor stops the car and Cassandra runs to the front door. Several officers standing outside try to stop her, but before they can, she runs inside. Her father is speaking with an officer who is jotting down Jonathan's statement in a notepad. He speaks with such a heavy Scottish brogue, the officer mistakes him for a local, perhaps someone checking in on his elderly neighbor.

Cassandra throws her arms around her father. "We thought it was you!" she cries.

Trevor enters the house and explains to the officers that his father was staying with Mrs. MacNaughton.

Jonathan looks at his daughter with tears in his eyes, his nose red from crying all morning. "Moira's gone!" is all he can say as tears pool in his eyes again.

Leaving the three of them alone in the living room, the officer closes his notepad and joins his fellow constables outside. "Poor chap. He must have loved her so very much."

Moments later, the paramedics move down the stairs, removing Moira from her home, the home where she waited 55 years for her husband to return. As she's carried past them on a stretcher, Jonathan breaks down completely. Turning his back to everyone, he exclaims, "No! I can't see her like this!"

After watching Moira MacNaughton leave her house for the final time, Trevor places a gentle hand on his father's back. "She's gone, Dad," he says. "I'm so very sorry."

"I need to know where they're taking her," Jonathan says, almost frantically.

"I'll go find out," Cassandra says, tears running down her cheeks.

Trevor locks eyes with his father, and for the second time since they began this journey, his father hugs him. Once at the beginning, and now near its end. For the very first time in his life, Jonathan draws on the love of his son, allowing Trevor to help shoulder his emotional hurt in some small way. The young man embraces his father and feels all his pain and sorrow, together with the torment of love lost. His father shakes in uncontrollable agony for the loss of this woman he'd only met for the first time in this lifetime less than one day earlier. Trevor pulls him closer in an attempt to take away some of the hurt, but anyone who's suffered a loss so deeply knows the pain is theirs and theirs alone to bear.

"It's going to be alright, Dad," Trevor says, with not much conviction in his voice.

"It's not fair!" Jonathan cries, breaking free. "We just found each other again! Why? Why was I given a second chance only to have it ripped away like this? Why would someone play this horrible fucking joke on me?!" Jonathan paces the floor. "Why?! It's as if God said, 'Here, Jonathan, remember this person? The love of your life … the person who watched *you* die?'!" He was yelling now, with tears streaming down his face. "Well, we could let you two get back together and be happy, but no. Sorry, asshole! *You* don't get that! We're taking her away from you now!"

"IT'S NOT FAIR, TREVOR! IT'S NOT GODDAMN FAIR! AND I DON'T WANT IT ANYMORE!" He paces about the house like a caged animal. "AND THIS ISN'T THE FIRST TIME! YOU KNOW HOW MANY MOTHERS, FATHERS, WIVES, HUSBANDS—" He looks at Trevor, almost apologetically "—CHILDREN I HAD TO BURY?! Why?! Why would God do this to me?"

The room turns chillingly quiet. He sees Cassandra in the doorway. Beyond her, the officers stand outside on the lawn, all of them staring into the house.

"Sorry, Dad," Trevor says in a low, demure voice, "but I don't think God had anything to do with this."

"She's going—" Cassandra starts, whispering in a sad voice before clearing her throat. "She made all the arrangements ahead of time, and—"

"I want to be with her—"

"Dad," Cassandra searches for the right words. "She's going—"

"Where are they taking her, Cassandra?!" Her father's voice is stern, with a hint of anger.

"She's going … to be buried with *you*, Dad." Then she glances at her brother and corrects herself. "She's going to be buried with her husband, with Daniel."

Jonathan's face, like his entire body, turns stone cold, motionless, as he attempts to process the words he's just heard. With everything that has happened to him, Jonathan never even considered the possibility of coming face-to-face with his past self. Up until now, his former lives were generations removed. Daniel was only one lifetime ago. Too close to his present life, and the thought of confronting his own demise, seeing his own headstone, is too much for him to bear.

It will be here soon enough.

"I don't think I can. I don't want to see Moira go in the ground." Jonathan's hands tremble at his side. He looks around and surrenders this life to the past. "This isn't my house. It *was* once our house. It could have been *our* house again, but not now. This was their house, but not mine, not anymore." *All the love we had she took with her, and I will never get that back, not in a hundred lifetimes.*

"It's time," he says in a whisper, barely audible. His children wait for him to continue. "I want to go home."

He picks up the old backpack and walks to the door. They leave the house, but before they close the door, Jonathan turns back. "Wait. I'm going to take one last look inside."

As he moves throughout the house, Jonathan sees memories from a lifetime long ago play out before him. A young couple laughing and hugging. A youthful red-haired woman dancing with her newly married highlander man in the living room. In the kitchen, a new bride pulls a roast from the oven. A young man comes up behind her, slides his arms around her waist, and whispers something in her ear. She smiles with her emerald-green eyes. They run past Jonathan up the stairs, and he follows the phantom figures as they jump onto the bed. Jonathan see every room, every doorway, filled with loving memories of their life together.

He stands in the bedroom, where a recent memory intertwined with the ones from long ago echoes within his mind. He picks up a picture frame from the nightstand. An old photograph of a young couple. A girl with blazing red hair and emerald green eyes gazes lovingly into the eyes of a fledgling, handsome Scottish highlander.

Jonathan kisses the picture softly, looking at it one last time before placing it into his backpack. He leaves, vowing never to return, no matter how many more lifetimes he is forced to walk the earth.

Downstairs, he stops at the desk by the staircase and retrieves the notebook. He turns to the page dated the previous evening. Moira's name is circled twice. Daniel's only once. *Two games to one,* he thinks. *I don't know how she does it, but I know she cheats.* He places the notepad and playing cards into his backpack as well, then leaves the house. Slowly closing the door, he says goodbye to another life that might have been. Forever denied, a life of happiness lost, as lost to him as a life lost with Elizabeth. An officer unrolls the yellow police tape across the entrance to let him pass back out to the street.

A gentle wind blows easterly from the Atlantic. It touches the tops of the tall sea grass along the shore and floats across the rich, green grass of the meadow. It rests upon Jonathan's cheek with a soft kiss. Jonathan closes his eyes, lost in a time long ago. An image of Moira in a soft white T-shirt standing in a field of green, wind blowing through her long, wavy red hair, is forever frozen in time like the picture in the bedroom, only this one he vows to keep locked away in his memory forever.

"Let the breeze remind you of me. It is there, in your heart, where I wish to live," Jonathan recites to himself.

"Pardon me?" one of the officers asks.

"Just something she once told me," Jonathan answers. Walking to the car, he places the backpack on the seat. He turns to his children and says, "I'm ready. I'm ready to go home."

Jonathan sits quietly on the plane, mourning Moira in silence. *It's best we didn't attend her funeral. The endless chatter of small talk, answering countless questions from people who knew her best, 'How did you know Moira? Were you there the night she died? How long have you known each other?'* But what Jonathan fears the most of all is seeing her lifeless body lying on a bed of silk. Returning to New York spares him the grief of watching her lowered into the ground, seeing his own name already carved into the granite stone. Knowing she's lying next to a soulless corpse, the shell of his former self reduced to nothing more than decaying flesh and bones, all of these thoughts and more are too much for Jonathan to bear. He closes his eyes and sees Moira's face, a happy, young, red-haired goddess, strolling the moors of Scotland. It's strange how when you love someone, their outward appearance fades. Every flaw and tiny imperfection disappears, and we see them for who they truly are. From the moment Jonathan saw Moira again, he did not see the frail older woman his children saw. To him, her inner beauty shone through. The sweet, loving, nurturing woman, joyful and full of life, was still young and vibrant in his eyes.

Ask any person over the age of 50, and they'll say, 'I don't feel fifty-eight. In my mind, I'm still 23'. At the age of 60, you may feel like 30. At 70, you're just reaching 50. It's sad to think you only have one lifetime to live on this earth. You work your ass off throughout your entire life, maybe sitting in a small cubicle in an office building, maybe breaking your back at a dead-end job making minimum wage only to get a few years at the end of your life to really enjoy it. Time has stolen your youth away, and you find yourself fighting like hell for one more chance to feel young again.

Jonathan thinks of Moira, once the love of his life, a relationship ending. Then he thinks of Elizabeth, the potential love of his life, a relationship just beginning.

He wants Elizabeth. No! He *needs* Elizabeth. He needs her to share his pain. Isn't that what couples do? They lend support, shoulder the burden, lift the other up when they're at their lowest. They grieve together, laugh together, cry together, share their lives, their hopes, their dreams, their fears, and every ounce of their joy. *Wouldn't it be wonderful if all people did that for one another?*

None of this will Jonathan have. Was he denied it in this life because he was blessed with it already in so many previous lives? From what he can tell, most of his lives were filled with pain and torment though. And for what reason? Why was *he* cursed? What was his crime, what offense could he have done to justify such a harsh punishment? And what awaits him at the end of all this suffering? What is *his* reward? Where is *his* happily ever after?

Cassandra sits down in the empty seat next to him. "Hey, Dad. How are you doing?"

"I've been better," he responds quietly. "I won't lie to you, Cazz. That was really hard. Harder than when your mother and I decided to split up."

Yeah, but Mom didn't die. You both chose to walk away, she thinks. A faint smile crosses her face. She searches for the right words to ease his pain, but none come.

"Cassandra, right from the start, you've seemed much more accepting than your brother is of what's been happening with me."

"He's come a long way, but I'm still not sure if he truly believes it, Dad."

"Yeah, it's funny. After everything he's witnessed, he still asks me how I'm suddenly able to speak different languages." Cassandra smiles. "And yet your mother thinks *he's* the smart one?" This makes her burst out laughing.

"You're going to be fine, Dad. In a couple of weeks, Elizabeth will visit, and who knows?" She shrugs. "I like her, Dad. I think she's good for you."

"I like her too, Pumpkin. Elizabeth told me you were on to us from the very beginning."

"Didn't take a detective to figure that one out. Besides, men have no idea they're in a relationship until a woman tells them they are."

Jonathan laughs but his eyes convey a note of deep sadness. "Cazz, I have to tell you something, and I don't want you to be sad. The reason Elizabeth couldn't come with us, or why I couldn't stay in London was—"

"I know—"

"You do?"

Her smile fades and she nods before responding. "I knew you had to take this journey. I knew nothing would have stopped you from searching for those markers. Even with or without us, I knew it was something you were going to do. I saw the determination on your face right from the beginning. It was that *'take charge, must-do attitude'* look you get."

"You have that too." he says.

She smiles halfheartedly. "I'm glad Trevor came."

"Me too. I'm glad you both came."

She lowers her head. "I also know—" She hesitates, trying to say the words without breaking down.

Again without saying it, Jonathan knows what she's trying to say. "You know—"

"I think I always knew. Right from the start. That first morning, when you woke me and told me your dream. I mean, since you knew in all your other past lives that you were going to die, I figured, it only stands to reason you also know now." Her eyes well up. "And then you went and had Giorgio make that stupid tablet for you. I didn't think anything of it, but when I heard the story in India, and they gave you her marker. I didn't want to believe it. But then in Australia, when it happened again, I knew. I knew why you made it." Tears run down her face.

He wipes away a tear from one of her cheeks.

"You're smarter than you know."

A wide grin crosses her face as she's holding back tears.

"I don't want you to be sad, Cazz. Most people never know how much time they have left. I'm lucky in that way. I'm not sure how long I have, but let's make every moment count."

She nods in the affirmative, wiping her eyes and sniffling. Suddenly, the little girl who used to look up to him for comfort is sitting next to him.

"You know how your brother is always saying Arizona is nice, but he misses the winters in New York? Especially our place upstate?"

"It gets so cold there. I think the weather starts changing in mid-September."

Jonathan laughs. "Yeah, I love that time of year. The wind changes; it whispers through the trees, making them sway and rub together. I can see how easy it was for Washington Irving to write *The Headless Horseman.*"

"Yeah, up there, you really know when summer is over."

"Anyway, the reason Trevor misses winter is because winter *is* the season that makes summers so much better. The reason *why* life is so precious *is* because we all die. Every moment we live should be treasured. We've got to live every day as though it's our last. Never let a single day go by without telling someone that they are loved, because standing at a gravesite in tears, saying, 'I wish I could tell them how much I loved them', is a fucking joke! You had *your* entire life … no, you had *their* entire life to tell them."

Cassandra's lips quiver as she tries to keep her composure. "I love you, Daddy."

His eyes fill with tears. "I love you too, sweetheart. I wish I could dance with you at your wedding."

She smiles. "Maybe you will."

Jonathan leans over and hugs his daughter, then makes a promise. "I will never forget you. I will find you in my next life, and I *will* dance with you at your wedding." To anyone else, such a statement would sound absurd.

She hugs him tighter.

"Just wait to get married till I'm out of diapers," he says. "Better odds of me making it."

She laughs so hard at this she almost wakes up the entire plane. "You've got a deal."

"Now peanut, you have to make me a promise." He takes a marker from his pants pocket. "I'm going to entrust these to you. Keep them safe until I return." He stares at the small tablet and ponders, "I'm starting to feel the reason I'm coming back over and over again is because of these damn things."

"Dad, do you ever wonder if maybe you're returning just because you're *making* those markers? Like, maybe, just maybe, if you stop making them, you'll stop returning? Stop the markers, stop the cycle?"

He looks down at the tiny metal tablet. An overwhelming feeling of helplessness comes over him, knowing whatever has caused this is out of his control. "Yeah, I'll have to try that next time," he sighs and stands up. "I'm gonna go talk to your brother. I'm not sure if he'll be as accepting as you."

She smiles. "Yeah, but *he's* the smart one."

Jonathan sneaks past her, pausing long enough to tousle her hair. "Don't be a wiseass."

Jonathan sits in the empty seat next to his son. "Listen, Trevor, I want to thank you for coming with me on this journey. I know it went a lot longer than you expected."

"It's fine, Dad. The entire thing just kinda snowballed."

"Like writing a story."

"Writing a story?" Trevor gives his head a jerk. "How so?"

"A writer friend once told me it starts with an idea. The idea presents itself to the writer, so they compose an opening sentence, which leads to a paragraph that forms the first chapter. A coworker reads it and encourages the writer to continue. Next thing you know, the writer is up every night till four o'clock in the morning banging away on the keys of their laptop, and 100,000 words later, three months have gone by, all because the damn voices in their head won't shut the fuck up!"

Trevor just stares back at his father.

"Sorry, I went off the rails. Kind of like this trip. Anyway, I'm so glad you were by my side. I couldn't have done this without you."

"I just hope that, whatever you needed to get out of your system, is finally out."

"Trevor, you do know —" Jonathan starts, then stops himself, realizing with all Trevor experienced and saw, if he still can't bring himself to accept his father's situation, he probably never will. "Yeah, I think it's out of my system."

"Good. The sooner we get home, the sooner I can get back to work."

"Do me a favor, Trevor? I know it's a lot to ask, but please stick around for a couple more days, just until after the weekend is over."

Trevor is about to protest, but looks at his father's face and concedes. "Okay, Dad. Sure. What's two more days?"

"Thanks, son." He places his hand on Trevor's knee. "I'm also going to ask you to watch over your sister."

"Why does everyone keep telling me that?"

Jonathan laughs. "Because it's your job, man. Preordained from above."

"Now don't start that shit again."

"It's true. Before you were born, your mother and I knew we were going to have a girl, and we decided to name her Cassandra." Jonathan rolls his eyes. "You know how your mother loves Greek mythology."

"How did you know you'd have a girl? Did someone tell you? Like an old gypsy woman read Mom's palm or something?"

"No, nothing like that. In my heart, I always knew I would have a daughter, way before I met your mother. And if I ever had a son, I told your mother we have to name him Trevor."

"What? Why Trevor?"

"Trevor means 'destined for greatness'. We were surprised when you were born first, which was probably a good thing. Had your sister been born first, we might have stopped with her. Your mother interpreted your birth as a sign, that Cassandra was going to be, well let's just say a handful, and she was going to need someone to help her along the way. And watching your sister grow up, I'm now convinced the angels sent you first to always watch over her."

Trevor laughs at his father's wacky story. "She *is* a handful."

Jonathan smiles. "That's just because this is her first time on Earth, and everything is new and exciting for her, whereas you ... you're an old soul."

Trevor smirks. "Oh, come on, Dad. You don't believe that."

"It's true. Things come easier to you because deep down inside, you've done this all before. You're wiser beyond your years. You're her guardian angel. I truly believe you were sent here to watch over her."

"Alright, now you're just pulling my leg. Or as Moira said, spinning a yarn."

Trevor sees his father's face return to sadness.

"Oh, shit. I'm Sorry, Dad. I didn't mean to—"

"It's okay, Trev. We can talk about it if you want?"

Trevor searches for the right words to cause his father the least amount of pain. "You really think she was your wife?"

"A long time ago, in another life, yes. I believe this is why I had to make this journey. All these events were like breadcrumbs, and they all led me to her." Jonathan ponders it for a moment. "Maybe the same angels who brought you to us told me in a dream that Moira was close to death, and that's why I needed to find her, to have one more day with her, before saying goodbye."

Trevor—forever doubting his father's theories—just smiles. "You know what, Dad? That makes sense. So maybe it was Moira destined to die all along, not you."

Jonathan knows this to be false, but he nods in agreement with a fake smile. "Maybe you're right. Who am I to argue with my daughter's guardian angel?"

PLACE: NEW YORK CITY
YEAR: PRESENT DAY

Jonathan drops his luggage off in the foyer and heads

straight to his study, with an old canvas backpack slung over his shoulder. Cassandra heads for her room to unpack, while Trevor throws his bags in the spare bedroom before using the en suite. Jonathan drinks in the office, filled with so many small knickknacks, trinkets and souvenirs he's collected throughout his years of travels. *It all makes sense now.*

He places the backpack on the desk and removes the wooden box, the box Moira kept safe all these years. Retrieving the tablets he collected from their journey around the world, he lays them on the table next to the box and pauses. *It's hard to believe I was all these people. It's even harder to accept I'm everyone within this box too.* "Well, Akal, Kilara, Clara, you ready to join the rest of us?" He opens the box and gazes in at the many tablets inside. *Is it possible? Was I ... am I all these people?* Jonathan searches through the markers as historians search through archived records. Cautious fingers gingerly separate one life from another. He notices the dates, each one older than the last, and realizes they're in chronological order. He checks the date on Akal's stone: February 29th, 1876. He finds her slot and slips it in place. He then looks at Kilara's stone. No date, but Jonathan remembers Minjarra telling him Kilara lived sometime in the 1600s. He finds the appropriate placement and slides the black stone in front of a wooden tablet from 1593. A memory of a young Shakespearean actor dying from the plague flashes before him. He picks up Clara's marker and thumbs through the small tablets.

Finally, the last tablets of his past lives is safely filed away. Jonathan then checks the dates of the other markers before removing his own tablet from his pocket. *It's time, old man.* He lays his marker in front of Daniel MacNaughton's. He says goodnight to Daniel and to all his other lives as he closes the lid and fastens the clasp. Then he summons his children to join him in his study.

He slides the box across the desk as the two of them walk in.

"Trevor, I asked Cassandra to take care of this for me. Please, and I can't stress this enough, please keep the contents safe! I've traveled around the world to find them, and spent, I suspect, many lifetimes to collect them all." Jonathan places his hand on the top of the box. "Moira guarded them her entire life. Before her, my family in Dragor, and now … now it's your turn to keep them safe."

He focuses his gaze on Trevor. "The contents are priceless. Do *not* get rid of this box."

Trevor's face turns stern as he pledges a solemn oath. "I promise, Dad."

Jonathan sighs in relief. "When the time comes, you can sell any of my possessions, or throw them away, I don't care. But one day, someone will come. I can't tell you who they will be, whether a man or a woman, young or old, but they will come. They'll come for this box. For the markers within."

"But Dad, how will we—" Cassandra starts, but her father cuts her off.

"You'll know," he says with a smile. "The same way all those people we met knew it was me."

He looks at Trevor again. "I realize you don't want to think about this, but if your sister passes before you, swear to me you'll carry on, always protecting the markers." Jonathan looks down, gently placing his fingertips on the lid of the box. "And when the time comes, God willing, when you have children of your own, tell them my story. Make them understand. Impress upon them the importance of these tablets, and make them swear, as I am asking you to do now, to keep them safe." He looks up again, holding each child's gaze for more than a few seconds, before he continues. "It may be longer than one lifetime before I return, but I will return. I promise you." Trevor opens his mouth, but Jonathan stops him. "I know you don't believe in any of this, Trevor, but *please*, for the memory of your father, please swear to me."

Trevor sees the sincerity and fear in his father's eyes. "Okay, Dad. I swear," quickly adding, "*but* you're not going to die any time soon. We discussed this and agreed, it was a premonition of Moira's passing, not yours."

"You *had* a premonition of Moira's death?" Cassandra asks.

Trevor turns to his sister. "Yeah, we talked about it on the plane."

She can see her father standing behind Trevor, eyes closed and shaking his head. She nods in agreement, and Trevor mistakes this as an acknowledgment to him, not to their father. *He's the smart one, yeah right,* she thinks.

"Now if you don't mind," Jonathan says, "I'm feeling a little tired from our journey. I'm going to lie down for a while."

"Okay," Trevor agrees. "But don't forget, we're meeting with that curator guy from the museum tomorrow."

"I won't forget," Jonathan says.

"I'm just going to grab a bottle of water. You want one, Cazz?"

Jonathan and Trevor leave the study together, but Cassandra remains alone with the box.

In his bed, Jonathan reflects on the long journey he's just made with his children. Memories of the past weeks fill his head. Not only those memories, but all the memories from previous generations swim through his mind as well. He recalls brothers, sisters, mothers, fathers, children, and grandchildren from all parts of the globe. He sees the faces of men and women he has loved. He sees parents through the eyes of a child and great-grandchildren through the eyes of a very old person. He smiles and laughs out loud to himself, recalling the happiest moments in his life, but soon begins sobbing uncontrollably for all the sorrow and tragic times too. He feels both joy and sadness, pain, and happiness. Millenniums of emotions spanning lifetimes flood through him.

Why? Why did I make this journey? Why couldn't I just live my life, running my company, going about my days like every other person on this planet? Content in ignorance? Why did I wake from that damn dream and act upon those feelings?

It was a voice, he realizes. A voice that called to him like an invisible stranger whispering in his ear.

Find a mark.

What mark? His mark? Are those damn tablets the mark? Are those the marks he's been tasked to find? Why the obsession with finding those markers? The desperate need, the yearning, the cravings a hundred times stronger than any desire Jonathan has ever experienced in his lifetimes. A junkie crying out, his body shaking from withdrawals, knows no hunger compared to the craving that woke Jonathan that morning. And nothing could beat the overwhelming satisfaction he experienced after creating a marker of his own.

Leave a mark.

Why is it so important to leave his marker with the others? A fellowship of forgotten lives all huddled together like tiny gravestones in a small wooden box. What's the point? Aren't we all just future headstones waiting for the last of our lineage to eventually forget about us?

But as Jonathan lays there, it occurs to him: it's not about leaving behind a metal, wood, stone, or clay tablet. Those kinds of markers are insignificant. They're not the marks meant to be left at all. The only true marks, the ones most important in this world, are the ones we leave on one another. For every life Jonathan has lived, he has touched so many other people's lives. For every child he's raised, every brother or sister he shared his life with, every couple he was born to, he affected, changed, and enriched their lives. Every friend, lover, colleague, neighbor, or passing stranger somehow, in some way, had their life forever altered, simply by interacting with him.

Moira's voice jumps into his head reciting the words from *It's a Wonderful Life*: *each man's life touches so many other lives*. Jonathan closes his eyes and agrees. No words were ever truer. In some strange way, we are all connected on this planet. He thinks back to what Terry had told him in Australia. *Remove the water, and each island becomes a connected piece of land*. Be kind to one another. Love one another! It is the single most consequential message every religion tries to impress upon its believers. So why is it so difficult to follow? *How many people of faith actually live by that rule?* The stranger you help today may never repay your kindness in this life, but in a life to come, destiny could make them your savior.

It is time.

Jonathan hopes to get some much-needed rest. A smile grows across his face as he slowly drifts off to what he hopes will be a long, restful sleep, only to be awakened by a flood of bright, white lights. Unable to form words, he wails. The soft, warm blankets of his bed are gone, and he is naked and cold. But not for long. Someone wraps him in a cloth, and he soon feels the comforting, steady heartbeat of his mother's chest.

Back in Jonathan's office, moments after Jonathan and Trevor walked out, Cassandra approaches the wooden box with all the curiosity of Pandora. She undoes the small metal clasp and gingerly raises the lid, anxious yet eager to inspect the contents. As the cover flips backward, her gaze falls on two rows of small tablets, much like the ones recently given to her father. Carefully, she removes several small tablets and inspects them. She turns over the first, then the second, and then the others, noticing the same word inscribed on each and every one.

$$A\epsilon T\acute{\epsilon}r\!\!\sim\!\!N \mathsf{u} M$$

On the other side of each one, a name identifies the person her father used to be in a previous life. Most markers bear a date under the name, but some have two dates. She stares down at them puzzled at first, before realizing it's their birth date and date of death. One by one, Cassandra removes each small tablet, examines it, and then returns it to its original position in the box. The dates on each tablet move a generation or two back in time, sometimes skipping entire centuries. Missing markers, Cassandra surmises.

Some tablets are inscribed in what looks to be Chinese characters, some have the Cyrillic alphabet, some are in languages she has never even seen before. Nevertheless, all have the word 'Aeternum' on one side. The oldest marker is wrapped in cloth, and ever so gently, she unwraps the delicate clay tablet. It too, like the others, has the word 'Aeternum' scratched into it on one side. On its reverse side, however, the cuneiform characters for KU and ŠIM, for the name Kushim.

Cassandra thinks back to her history classes. The name Kushim had appeared on a Sumerian clay tablet used to record transactions, circa 3400 BCE. She looks all around her Dad's study—at African wood carvings, Native American pottery, Australian tribal art, a framed Japanese kimono—and she starts to piece it all together. All around her are paintings and sculptures collected by her father over the years,

collected not because he admired them, but because they reminded him of who he once was. He spent a lifetime surrounding himself with things from his own past.

She then picks up the newest tablet added to the box, a beautiful, highly polished piece of steel, and her hands shake as she reads the name and dates.

Jonathan Adam Taylor

02-29-1964

2022

Crying now, she turns it over.

AETERNUM

Pulling an oversized dictionary from the bookshelf, she flips through the first few pages. Her finger scans down the columns of words: Ad-verb, ad-vice, aer-o-bic. She continues until her index finger comes to rest.

Aeternum (adverb). Eternal; forever. Everlasting.

Cassandra hears her brother's voice from the other room. Her brain doesn't fully comprehend the words he is saying until he starts to shout.

"Dad, I'm heading out," Trevor announces. "Dad? DAD?! OH, GOD! DAD?!!!!! CAZZ, CALL 911!"

Cassandra places her father's metal tablet—along with the others—carefully back into the box and closes the lid. She understands all too well now. Her eyes close. Tears run down her cheeks.

PLACE: NEW YORK CITY
YEAR: PRESENT DAY

The funeral was beautiful, as funerals go. It seemed like

half of Manhattan turned out to pay their respects to the city's favorite architect. An endless line of mostly strangers passed Trevor and Cassandra, shaking their hands and offering them their sincerest condolences. Even their mother was there. If not for the fact he would soon be covered by dirt, Jonathan would have remarked, *'she's only here to make sure I'm really dead'*.

One face blurred into another, and slowly the stream of people dwindled to just a few good friends. Margaret and Bruce were among the last to leave.

Trevor looked out at the city of headstones—*a small metropolis dedicated to the dead*—He then squinted out toward the Manhattan skyline in the distance, his vision melting as the cityscape blends together in the sea of headstones before him. A tiny city behind iron gates, each occupant a skyscraper in their own right.

Markers, Trevor muses. *We're all just markers, names on slabs of marble, if we're lucky.*

323

"You okay?" Cassandra asks, noticing Trevor staring off into the graveyard.

"Remember when Dad would take us up to Grandpa's cabin in the Catskills?"

"You mean his 'fortress of solitude'?"

"He only called it that when he wanted to get away from Mom, but yeah."

"What made you think of that?" she asks.

"I remember driving through those small towns and passing all those graveyards. I couldn't help but think that everyone buried in there—" Trevor motions to the landscape around them. "Everyone buried here, they all had lives, they all had hopes and dreams." He looks around. "And then I wonder, did they worry about paying their mortgage? Did *this* one have an affair, or did *that* one cheat on her husband?"

"I don't know," Cassandra answers.

"That's the point. When all is said and done, nothing matters. All our hopes and dreams, our worries, and transgressions—none of it means a thing. All we really leave behind is a name on a marker in a field." He shakes his head. "And when the very last person who ever knew us dies, that's when we're truly gone from this earth, for good, because there's no one left to remember us."

"Unless we do something memorable," she says.

"Like write a book, maybe?" He nurtures a seed within Cassandra that was planted weeks ago in Australia.

One person remains at the gravesite. Someone unknown to Trevor, a stranger paying his final respects. Either this man had an attachment to his father or he wants to talk privately with the family after the service. Trevor suspects the latter and excuses himself. His shadow crosses Jonathan's headstone, joining the stranger's, and the man offers his condolences.

"I'm very sorry about your father. Much too young to be taken."

"Did you know my father?"

He shook his head. "We never met, but I was scheduled to meet with him on his return to the States." The stranger extends his hand. "I'm Professor Howard Convery. I believe we spoke on the phone."

Trevor takes the man's hand. The name Convery registers. "Oh yes, from the—"

"Museum," the man concurs, as Trevor continues.

"I'm sorry I didn't get back to you."

"Quite understandable. Was your father ill? You made no mention when we spoke."

"He was as healthy as a horse, but I think he knew."

"Why do you say that?"

"He told me he was dying. That's how he convinced me to go along with him on that trip overseas." Trevor plays back the last couple of weeks in his head. "It wasn't supposed to last as long as it did, but looking back now, I wish it had lasted a lot longer. Another 30 years or so."

Cassandra joins her brother, and Trevor introduces her to Professor Convery, who once again conveys his condolences.

"Trevor, Cassandra, I know this isn't the appropriate time, but I must ask about these markers in your father's possession, the ones we spoke about on the phone."

"Markers?" Cassandra asks. "Oh, you mean the tablets with his names on them?"

"You mean people's names? You said *his* names," the professor asks, now bewildered.

"Yes, he had a tablet made with his name inscribed on it before we left for India. But I think you misunderstood. I did say *his names*, because from what we learned, every name on those tablets … they were all his names."

Howard Convery stands at the grave of a man he never met, yet had been searching for his entire adult life, confused and puzzled. "But from the photos Trevor posted on the Internet, only one of the tablets said Jonathan Taylor."

"Mister Convery—sorry, Professor—this may be impossibly hard for you to comprehend, and I have no intention of standing over the body of my dead father and debating what I already know to be true. But I'm telling you in all earnestness, my father *was* the people whose names are engraved on those tablets, or markers or whatever you want to call them."

Howard can see Cassandra getting flustered. "Please, I assure you, I have no intention of upsetting you, especially here, on this day. I'm merely trying to wrap my head around a larger picture." He pauses for a moment, reflecting on the exhibit he's worked on for more than 40 years. "A much, much larger picture, I assure you. You mentioned your father made one of these tablets before he embarked on his trip?"

"Yeah. Apparently, he always made a marker when he felt he was—" Cassandra breaks down and sobs, before she can bring herself to utter the words, *close to death.*

"Mister Convery," Trevor interjects, rubbing his sister's back, "it seems my father lived several lives before this one. I don't know how, and I don't know why. All we can surmise is that the people whose names are on those tablets … they were all my father, in former lives."

"There were more in the box," Cassandra says quietly.

"You have more?" Howard asks in amazement.

"Yes," she repeats. "I believe there are more out there too, many more from what Dad alluded to. I just wish he could have found them."

Howard Convery smiles as if a life-long quest is finally coming to fruition. "Well then, Cassandra, Trevor, have I got something to show you!"

A few days later, Trevor makes arrangements to meet with Professor Convery at the museum before he heads back to Arizona.

It's early autumn now, and the leaves in upstate New York have all turned brilliant hues of red and gold. The city landscape remains a never-changing shade of gray, but despite the slight chill in the air, it's a beautiful day in Manhattan, so Cassandra and Trevor decide to walk to the museum.

"I'm catching a flight out tomorrow," Trevor says. "I spoke with the office. They're gonna let me work remotely. So now I just have to pack up my apartment, rent a truck, and drive back to New York. Are you sure it's okay if I stay with you for a while, until I can find a place of my own?"

"I told you, Trevor, you can stay as long as you like. There's plenty of space."

Jonathan left all of his assets in a trust to be divided equally between the children. Still, Trevor insisted Cassandra keep full ownership of the New York apartment, especially since he can live quite comfortably on his half of the inheritance.

In turn, Cassandra signs her half of the cabin over to Trevor. "I think Dad would want you to have it. He found a lot of peace up there, and he was hoping you would too. Maybe meet a girl, get married, and conceive a child up there." She giggles. "You know, that way you can tell them how you were both conceived up there."

"I was not!" He sways, bumping into her shoulder with a smile. "Dad just made that up … I hope. I can't believe Grandpa purchased the land way back in 1976, almost 20 years before we were born. I remember Dad saying that before Grandpa built the cabin, they would sleep in a small trailer with no heat. Can you imagine?"

"Dad loved to remind us," she starts, clearing her throat so as to best impersonate her father. 'When I was your age, we didn't have indoor plumbing. We had to use the outhouse in the woods.'"

Then they both recite the phrase they'd heard so many times: "Many cold nights I laid in bed trying to decide whether to use the outhouse or hold it till morning." A burst of hardy laughter follows, looking like a couple of lunatics to their fellow New Yorker passing by.

Cassandra remarks that this was their father's favorite time of year.

Trevor agrees. "Dad loved to go to the cabin this time of year."

"His *fortress of solitude*," Cassandra says, still smiling.

"He always said, 'It's a magical time of the year, when the leaves change colors and the north wind blows through the trees.'"

"Yes, Trev! And he'd always say, 'I can easily see how Washington Irving could have written *The Legend of Sleepy Hollow* up here, especially when the trees creaked and rubbed up against one another.' He would come into the cabin and say, 'I swear, this time of year, those woods *are* haunted,' and I'd laugh, thinking, how could a grown man like Dad be afraid of ghosts?"

Trevor chuckles. "I can't imagine Dad being afraid of anything, especially of ghosts. He'd probably light a bonfire in the fire pit and invite them in for a cup of coffee to discuss the afterlife."

"A glass of scotch is more like it," Cassandra says.

"Yes, scotch," Trevor agrees. "He loved his scotch."

"Although he didn't drink much at home," Cassandra adds. "Only when he was upstate sitting around the fire. He said it just felt natural."

The two walk on for a while in silence, both contemplating why that was. Before they knew it, they were walking up the steps of the Museum of Natural History. Inside at the information desk, they announce their appointment with Professor Convery. Moments later, an attractive woman, maybe a year younger than Trevor, introduces herself as Kaitlyn, Professor Convery's assistant. They follow her past the admission desks, where Kaitlyn makes a small motion with her hand as if to say, 'they're with me', and the ticket takers and security guards all give her slight nods of approval with their heads. She leads them to a side door that opens with a swipe of her badge, and they continue down a long corridor, making several turns, passing offices and labs where researchers seem to be hard at work on future exhibits.

"We're all very excited. I think Professor Convery was here at 5:00 a.m. this morning. He's had us working on the presentation ever since he spoke with you on the phone, Mr. Taylor."

"Please call me Trevor," and, even though he tries hard not to sound like the cartoon character Crush from *Finding Nemo,* a sea turtle surfer dude pops into his head when he adds, "Mr. Taylor is my father."

Kaitlyn lets out a small giggle, detecting an ever so slight 'sea turtle' accent from one of her favorite movies. Trevor's cheeks flush red.

They stop at a door with Professor Convery's name painted on the glass. "Here we are." Kaitlyn holds the door open. Her gaze focuses on Trevor as he walks past. "I love that movie," she whispers, making him feel less embarrassed. He notices her entrancing, brilliant blue eyes, and for the next couple of moments, all previous thoughts escape him and he blushes once again.

More people than they expected to be there file into the room.

"Seems like the entire department is here for this," Trevor says.

Howard shakes their hands hello. "We're all very excited, and I have to tell you, I'm also a little nervous." He motions for them to sit as he tries to compose himself. "I give lectures three or four times a year, all over the world, but this is something very close to my heart. You see, I've been working on this project for over 40 years."

He waits until they're both seated and everyone else has taken their seats or found a place to stand in the back of the room. "Let me begin by extending our sincere condolences on the loss of your father. And thank you for being here so soon after his passing. As you all know, I've been working on this project for many years. For the longest time, these small tablets were nicknamed the 'Mystery Markers'. I think a few too many of us grew up watching Scooby-Doo on Saturday morning." He smiles and waits for the low chuckles from the audience to die down. "Well hopefully today we are one step closer to solving this mystery." He points to the back of the room. "A couple weeks back, Kaitlyn brought something quite interesting to my attention, a post she'd seen online."

Trevor cranes his neck, searching the back of the room till he catches her gaze. Once again his cheeks glow red and his stomach fills with fluttering butterflies.

"The post was from Mr. Trevor Taylor, and the photo attached showed three markers in his father's possession. Even more astonishing is what they told me after their father died. You see it's their belief that their father, Jonathan Taylor, has been responsible for leaving these markers behind every time he passes from this life, only to be reincarnated when he starts the process all over again. Trevor's sister Cassandra told me her father recently made one of the markers. Is that correct?"

Cassandra nods her head. "Well, that's not actually correct. Dad didn't make it. He had a jeweler make it for him. We stopped on our way to the airport and Dad picked it up."

Professor Convery smiles, admiring Cassandra's honesty and literalism, tenets he values highly in his field. "Please tell us, why do you believe your father had the marker made?"

Cassandra clears her throat. "Well, at first, I don't think even my father knew why he had it made. Later, when I asked him about it, he just said it was something he had to do, but couldn't tell me why. I think he was more surprised than Trevor and me when he received the first marker in India."

"The first marker? Someone gave it to him? In India. Interesting, very interesting!"

"Yeah, we thought it was strange. But I think Dad was surprised, yet also hoping or expecting to find one there."

"You have to understand, Professor Convery," Trevor interjects, "a lot of strange things happened in India."

"Like what?" Professor Convery asks. "And please, call me Howard."

Mr. Convery is my father, Kaitlyn thinks, giggling again quietly to herself, and picturing her professor as a giant pot-smoking sea turtle.

"Like for starters," Trevor answers, "Dad spoke Urdu, a not so popular language in India. And he didn't just pick up a word or two. He started speaking it fluently."

"Xenolalia," the professor says, looking around the room, noting how many of his colleagues' faces register varying levels of shock and amazement. Some are even taking notes. "The ability to speak a language one never spoke before. Very rare. And very intriguing. Please go on."

"Well, Dad took us to a little village, and although he had never been there before, he was able and point out several landmarks, including the house where he claimed to have lived as a woman. Apparently, our father, Jonathan, was a mother of two children in a former life. He died more than 96 years ago—well, she died, as a result of a train accident. Coincidentally, Dad was also struck by a train at the exact spot, only there was no train."

Howard looked confused, as did most of the people in the room.

"Yeah, that's exactly how I felt. Now you know how weird this all was to us."

"To you!" Cassandra objects. "Even after Australia, you still doubted it. It was only after Elizabeth and France when you started to accept it, although I don't think you fully believe it."

"Elizabeth? France? Accept what?" Howard asked.

"Professor Convery," Cassandra says, then corrects herself. "Howard. As I tried to tell you in the cemetery the other day, all these … these markers, as you call them, they all belong to my father. They're all that's left of him."

Professor Convery still looks puzzled.

"With everything my brother experienced with our father on this trip, he still struggles with this concept. And I don't expect you to take our word for it either without any proof, but I'm telling you, these markers all represent the people my father once was."

"So, you're saying the people whose names are on these tablets are—"

"Yes. They're him! They're *all* him!" Cassandra shouts this loudly enough for everyone in the room to hear. Her voice returns to a quieter, softer tone. "They are—or what I mean is, they *were* him, or he was *them*, however you want to phrase it. These markers represent our father's past lives."

The room falls silent. Cassandra waits for the room to erupt into laughter, but nothing of the sort occurs. Instead, there's just a long, eerie silence.

"That *would* explain a great many things," Howard finally says.

Both Trevor and Cassandra's eyes widen. Trevor more than his sister's.

"As hard as it is to believe or even accept, and I don't mean any disrespect, but let's say reincarnation is possible. That alone opens up a whole number of new questions, but let's stay on topic. Cassandra, you said you have more of these markers, not just the two that Trevor posted."

"Which two did you post?" she asks her brother.

"The ones from India and Australia."

"Dad received another one in France," Cassandra tells Howard.

"And Moira gave Dad a whole box of them in Scotland," Trevor tells him.

"Moira?"

"Dad's wife," Cassandra answers. "She passed away when we were there."

"Your father's *wife?*"

"In his previous life," Cassandra clarifies, speaking slowly and looking not just at Howard but at every person present to make sure they understand. "Right before this present one. He was married to a woman named Moira MacNaughton. She was still alive when we traveled to Scotland. She was waiting for Dad to return. Waiting for her late husband Daniel to return. Dad *was* her late husband Daniel in his last life." Her eyes water, still thinking of Moira. "I guess, once she knew Dad had returned, she was able to move on."

"And she gave your father a box? With some markers in it?"

"About two dozen markers. Each and every one of them a past life he collected over the years. From what we can gather, Dad has been walking the earth for a few centuries. And the proof is all in the box."

"Amazing," was all Howard could say. He puts his head down and brings his hand up to his chin, cupping it as if pondering how best to approach the next subject. "Did you examine them all? Look at them? Turn them over?"

Cassandra nods, already anticipating his next question.

"And? The word? Did they all have the word? Was it there?" he asked with all the enthusiasm of a schoolboy.

She nods again. "Yes. On every one of them."

"Do you know the meaning of that word?" Howard asks her.

"I looked it up."

It was as if they were now linked, the two sharing a secret about to be revealed to the entire room. They said it together. "Eternal."

"Professor, do you really think it's possible that my father could have been reincarnated 24 times?"

Howard smiles. "Cassandra, I think you may have just solved a riddle I've been working on for the past 40 years. And your father, well, he may be the key to all of it. Wait till you see this. You'll be amazed." He motions to Kaitlyn and Anthony at the back of the room. "I must apologize to my assistants. They've worked weeks on this presentation, but I think we should skip right to the main event."

Both nod understandably. "But first, Anthony, I've told you the story enough times. Could you please share with Cassandra and Trevor what started me on this endeavor?" He bids Anthony to come forward.

Anthony, surprised and a bit nervous, makes his way to the front of the room. Howard introduces him and urges Anthony not to be shy. He knows public speaking will play a significant role in his career one day. Howard smiles at Kaitlyn too. "This goes for you as well, Kaitlyn. I may call on you next."

Anthony clears his throat. "Well, as the professor constantly points out, it all started some 40 years ago, in Deadwood, South Dakota. It was there in that small town where Professor Howard Convery was introduced to Mr. Joseph Kehm, and when I say introduced, I mean dug up from the ground."

The ensuing laughter is quickly silenced by a correction from the professor, "Exhumed, Anthony. The proper term is exhumed. For the sake of our guests, let's try to sound a little professional! Perhaps you can tell our guests what is so special about Joseph Kehm?"

"Mr. Kehm was the first person Wild Bill Hickok killed in Deadwood," Anthony recites proudly.

"That is correct, but what was it about Mr. Kehm that was *even* more paramount?" Howard urges.

"Oh! It was the first time you found an Aeternum Marker."

Trevor moves to the edge of his seat. Cassandra raises one eyebrow.

Professor Convery then motions for Kaitlyn to come forward, "And what is an Aeternum Marker, Kaitlyn?"

She joins Anthony, and in a more professional manner tells them, "An Aeternum Marker, or as we call them around the museum, the *Mystery Marker,* is a small tablet typically measuring 3 inches long by 2 inches wide. The marker can be made of stone, wood, clay, or, in Mister Kehm's case, metal. It bears the name of a person on one side, sometimes with the date of the person's birth and sometimes with the year of the person's death. In cases where the tablet was created BCE, Before Common Era, only a name is present."

She cocks her head and talks out of the side of her mouth, "In the professor's youth, they used to refer to it as BC."

Trevor looks at Cassandra and mouths the words, *'before Christ?'*

Kaitlyn smiles at Trevor. "Before the introduction of the Julian Calendar, established in 45 BCE by Julius Caesar, the year began on the 31st of March, and—"

"I'm sure our guests haven't come here to get a lecture about ancient Roman timekeeping, Kaitlyn," Howard interjects. "Let's bring it back to the markers, please."

Trevor nods an encouraging grin her way, mouthing the words, *'you're doing great!'*

A red-faced Kaitlyn continues. "They're named the Aeternum Markers because the one constant on every tablet from every period in time is the word *Aeternum*. It's engraved, scratched, or carved into each and every tablet."

Professor Convery gives Kaitlyn an approving nod, and she returns his gesture with a smile.

"I don't understand," Cassandra says. "You have a couple of my father's markers? I thought he had found almost all of them."

"As I said at the cemetery, I've got something to show you. Now if you would be so kind as to follow me, I think I can answer all your questions by showing you what I've been working on."

Trevor and Cassandra file down the hall behind Professor Convery, followed by Kaitlyn, Anthony, and several other colleagues, professors, and interns. Howard stops at a door with the words *Aeternum Exhibit* stenciled on it. Cassandra and Trevor follow him into a dark room lit only by the light filtering in through the doorway, and wonder what awaits them inside.

Howard flicks on the light switches. One by one, each section of the massive wall map illuminates, presenting itself to the two unsuspecting visitors. Standing in front of Cassandra and Trevor is a detailed representation of every continent, country, state, province, and territory around the globe. Oversized pins, together with identifying plaques, have been placed on the map to indicate the locations where each marker was found.

The two of them can't believe their eyes. There must be hundreds. In comparison to the markers Cassandra has in her possession, this seems like her couple of dozen markers were like Greece's King Leonidas with his band of 300 about to face off against the entire Persian Army.

"As you see, Cassandra, Trevor, we've been diligently working for a very long time on this project, which my colleagues have named *Mystery Markers*. Tablets like the ones in your possession have been discovered all around the world, in every country, from just about every century. The oldest arrived several days ago, in fact." Professor Convery approaches a section of the wall standing in front of Africa. "An archaeologist unearthed this tablet next to the remains of a woman in Ethiopia." Howard stops, catching his mistake, and corrects himself. "Well, I'm sure they didn't call it Ethiopia back then. Historically, it was called Abyssinia, but back then it wouldn't have been called anything. I'm sorry. I'm getting off track. Nevertheless, this particular tablet is the oldest tablet we now have in our collection. Through carbon dating, we've ascertained it dates back to more than 8,000 years BC. Sorry, old habit. BCE, Before Common Era." He smiles at Kaitlyn who grins back. "And this is the only marker we have with just the word Aeternum inscribed on it. No dates, no name. We believe it may very well be the very first marker." He sees the eyes of his guests widen.

His last statement hits the children with all the force the invisible train must have hit their father with in India. *The very first one!* Both know that this one tablet could hold the key to freeing their father from his eternal cycle.

"Professor," Trevor says softly, "you said this first tablet is more than 10,000 years old?"

"That's right," the professor answers with a nod.

"Well I guess there's evidence that people were alive 10,000 years ago, but did they even communicate with a written language back then? Just how old is the human race?"

"Those are excellent questions. As to how old the human race is, there's a great deal of evidence that people lived millions of years ago. For the longest time, Lucy held the title of the oldest woman. She lived 3.2 million years ago, but I seriously doubt she had the mental capacity to create a marker. Almost 17 years after they discovered Lucy, another female skeleton, nicknamed Ardi, was discovered, and she dated back 4.4 million years, 1.2 million years older than Lucy. So as a species, we've been here a pretty long time. Your first question, however, brings up a greater mystery, one I hoped your father would clarify. Now, unfortunately, I'm afraid we'll never know the answer."

"What is that, Professor?" Cassandra asks.

Well, as Kaitlyn explained, the one constant on every marker is the word Aeternum. Now that *can* be explained somewhat on the tablets created after the 6th Century BCE. But tablets preceding that century? Those are the ones that have us puzzled." He points to the most recent addition to the exhibit, the one from Ethiopia. "Especially this one. This one is a real paradox."

"How so, Professor?" Trevor asks.

"The earliest known Latin inscription was found on a golden brooch in Rome called the Praeneste fibula, loosely translated as the "brooch of Palestrina," which reads, *Manios Med Fhefhaked Numasioi,* translated from ancient Latin meaning, *Manius made me for Numerius.* The piece dates back to the 6th Century. So that's our starting point."

"Starting point?" Cassandra shakes her head, not understanding.

"The first evidence of when Latin was used."

"Ohh," they both say.

"Many of these tablets date back 700, 800, even 1,000 years BCE. That one," he says, pointing to Africa on the map, "is from 8,000 BCE."

Trevor then asks the same question Howard asked some 40 years earlier. "So how could a Latin word be inscribed on a tablet some 7,000 years before Latin was invented?"

"You see our enigma?"

Trevor nods, as does Cassandra.

"That's precisely why I was so anxious to meet with your father. Unfortunately, I'm afraid that secret may be lost forever."

"Or," Cassandra says shyly, "we may just have to wait a while before he, or she, surfaces again."

Howard smirks, then contemplates the possibility. *It may be at least 20 more years. I'll be 82. With the right diet and exercise, God willing I just may live long enough to ask him.*

They step back from the map to take it all in.

"Why do you suppose he does it?" Howard asks them. "Why do you think he leaves these markers?"

Trevor and Cassandra stand frozen, unsure what to say or how to answer. Having never addressed the question to his colleague, Kaitlyn timidly raises her hand like she's back in high school. Trevor sees her, and despite everything going on, thinks *that's so adorable.*

Howard furrows his brow. "Yes, Kaitlyn?"

"That's an easy one," she says, lowering her hand. "Don't you see? It's simple."

With an encouraging nod, Professor Convery urges her to continue.

Kaitlyn clears her throat. "From the dawn of time, man has been leaving pieces of himself behind, as if to say, 'Hey, look at me! I was here!' Consider the cave paintings in Lascaux, France. Some of the oldest Paleolithic paintings date back 20,000 years." She glances around at the esteemed men and women gathered there, and beams. "None of you figured this out?"

Her question is met with a sea of shaking heads.

"It's what makes the artist paint … or the author write … or the actor perform. We're all looking for something to leave behind, something so great we'll be remembered by future generations. Shakespeare will live forever. Whenever someone quotes 'To be or not to be', he'll be remembered. Whenever someone reads Melville, or Yeats, Edger Allen Poe, Pat Conroy, or even J.K. Rowling, these authors live on. Whenever a person gazes upon the work of Michelangelo, looking up at the Sistine Chapel, marveling at the fresco upon that ceiling, or a small child looking upon the statue of David for the first time, Michelangelo is reborn and lives on. Botticelli, Rembrandt, Monet, Edvard Munch, all these artists continue to live through their work. No man or woman will ever be forgotten if a single person remembers them. *No one* will truly die if they live within the heart of another."

She stares at their faces, contemplating her words. Then continues. "Think of the great movie stars, Bogart, Gable, Monroe, DeNiro, Pacino—hell, even Kevin Smith will live on for all eternity on the silver screen. 'I'm not even supposed to be here'," she says, quoting a line from *Clerks,* Kevin Smith's first indie film, then pauses, looking for recognition. Only Trevor laughs. She smiles and continues. "In a manor of speaking, they've all achieved immortality."

Trevor recalls something his father once shared with him. "A great Roman poet named Quintus Ennius once wrote, 'Let no one weep for me, or celebrate my funeral with mourning; for I still live, as I pass to and fro through the mouths of men.'"

Howard freezes, as do Kaitlyn and Anthony. "Who did you just quote?" Howard asks him.

"Quintus Ennius. I think he lived like 150 years before Christ."

Howard corrects Trevor, "169 years to be exact."

"Oh, you've heard of him? Yeah, Dad made us study ancient Roman civilization. I always loved that quote, so I memorized it."

"I'm guessing you never came across *The Douglas Aeternum Stone* in your studies?" Howard asks, walking over to the wall and pointing to Italy on the map.

Trevor's jaw drops. Cassandra murmurs a barely audible, "Shut up!"

"I'm afraid it's true. If this theory is correct, your *father* wrote those words almost 22 centuries ago."

Tears start running down Trevor's cheeks as he suddenly starts weeping openly.

Kaitlyn flattens her hand to her heart and turns away. Anthony opens his mouth, but before he gets the first word out, Kaitlyn shoots him a look through watery eyes. "Not a word, Tony! Not. A. *Word*!"

Professor Convery rests his hand on Trevor's shoulder. "Perhaps some part of him wanted you to discover who he was long ago. He may not have even been conscious of it. But he wanted you to find him, and that's why he urged you to study Roman culture."

Cassandra puts her arms around her brother and comforts him.

"Thank you, Kaitlyn," Howard says, turning to address the group. "Ladies and gentlemen, let's give the Taylor family some privacy now, so they can get acquainted with their father's many lives and his long journey on this earth."

One by one, the gathering leaves until only Kaitlyn, Trevor, Cassandra, and Howard are left. Kaitlyn takes Cassandra's hand and forces a smile as tears well up, unable to express her emotions. Quite unexpectedly then, she throws her arms around Trevor's neck and hugs him before running from the room.

Cassandra stares at her brother. *What was that for?*

Professor Convery tries to make an apology. "She's a very—"

"Odd person?" Cassandra fires off.

"Sensitive, caring, captivating," Trevor says, still staring at the empty doorway where she ran through seconds earlier.

"Emotional," Howard says. "I was going to say emotional, but odd works too." Howard shakes the incident from his head, then says, "Take as much time as you need. I'll be in my office. Please see me before you leave. And thank you. You've given my life's work so much meaning."

Cassandra embraces the humble professor. "Thank you for finding our father for us!"

He hugs her back. "I only wish I had the chance to know him personally."

She turns, glancing at the map. "I think you may have known a lot more of him than we did."

"I'll be right down the hall. I suggest you start here," he says, pointing to South Dakota, "and work your way to the right. It's what I did." He smiles and leaves the room.

Cassandra joins her brother, and for the next couple of hours, they read every plaque, tablet, location, and name their father used to be, starting with Joseph Kehm in Deadwood, South Dakota. In one place he was a Viking killed when attacking an English monastery, and in another he was a Samurai, killed during Japan's Sengoku period. He was a Roman poet, a Zulu warrior, a Russian Cossack, a Chinese merchant, an Egyptian slave, and a Persian warrior in the Sassanid Empire. In one life, he was a soldier in the Napoleonic Wars. In another, he fought with Hannibal. He fought in both the Revolutionary and the Civil Wars. It turns out, in fact, their father fought in almost every major war in history.

Before leaving, they find Professor Convery in his office. Cassandra makes arrangements to have her tablets delivered to the museum. Howard assures her that he'll treat them with the utmost of good care, and that they will remain their family's property. The museum still has much research to do, and with the addition of her father's markers, names have to be searched, verified, and added to the exhibit in chronological order. Howard is optimistic the exhibit will open in a year or two. He then tells them he would love to dedicate the AETERNUM exhibit in honor of their father, and sincerely hopes they will attend the official opening.

Trevor shakes his hand and Cassandra hugs him one last time. Both agree, stating they would be honored to be there.

Kaitlyn accompanies them as they leave the museum, and stops Trevor before reaching the revolving doors. "I wanted to apologize for my reaction in there."

Trevor motions for Cassandra to wait for him outside. "There's nothing to apologize for—"

"It was very … unprofessional." She raises her head, and her eyes capture his gaze once again. Trevor is at a loss for words and can feel heat returning to his face. "I'm going to do one more thing that's not professional," she says, handing him her business card. "My cell number is on the back. Call me. You know, for a cup of coffee … or something?"

It's the way she said, *'or something?'* that will haunt Trevor.

With a quick peck on his cheek, she disappears into the crowded lobby.

Trevor pushes the heavy rotating door, exiting into the bright sunlight overlooking Central Park West. Cassandra waits by the Equestrian Statue of Theodore Roosevelt. "What did she want?"

Trevor flashes the business card. "I think a date?"

Cassandra walks away shaking her head. "A date with you? Like I said, *odd* girl."

Professor Convery sits back in his chair and ponders what he will do with himself now that his life-long project is coming to a close. He also wonders what life has in store for the Taylor children. *Will they ever meet their father again? And if so, who will Jonathan Taylor be in his next life?*

Trevor remains in New York, watching over his sister as he promised his father he would. Every year, they celebrate Jonathan's passing by visiting a different country and going to a specific location where their father lived in a former life. For the first few years after Jonathan died, Elizabeth came to New York to visit on the day she and Jonathan met, a symbolic anniversary of sorts. As the years pass, Cassandra grows closer to Elizabeth, and she looks on Cassandra as the daughter she never had.

The leaves upstate have long since made their metamorphosis, changing color before falling to earth. Autumn has come and gone. Trevor stuffs a small journal and a pair of rolled-up socks into a backpack more suitable for climbing Everest than anything they'll do up in the Catskills. He prefers traveling as if going on an expedition, whereas Cassandra's carry-on, overnight, and travel suitcases sit in an even row, waiting by the front door, for their end of the season weekend trip up to the family's cabin. One last visit before closing it up for the winter, something Jonathan did every year, so the kids faithfully honor the tradition.

Kaitlyn sits cradling a small bump in her belly and casually turning her wedding band. Trevor joins her, kissing her forehead and placing his hand gently on her tummy. "Are you sure you're up to going? We can cancel. I'm sure Cazz and James will be okay with it."

"Nonsense, we go every year. Besides, I want this little one to see where they were conceived." She giggles and adds, "the same place where their father was conceived," happy to keep the family joke alive.

Down the hall, Trevor can hear his sister on speaker phone with their mother.

"Honey, I'm so proud of you," Hannah's voice resonates through the receiver. Cassandra removes a hardcover book from a small brown box.

"Thanks, Mom." She studies the cover, where her father's face smiles back at her. In bold type, the title reads,

My Father's Many Lives

"I can't believe it's been five years already," Cassandra says, opening the book to read the dedication as her mother continues talking.

For my father, Jonathan Adam Taylor,
and for all his many lives.
May your journey be swift, your obstacles be few,
and may you soon find the rest you so richly deserve.

"Cassandra? Cassandra, are you listening to me? Did you hang up?" Hannah's voice struggles to pull Cassandra from the swampy quicksand of her thoughts. "God, I swear, sometimes you're just like him."

Trevor hurries into the room, holding the house phone. "Cazz! You have to take this. Wait till you hear—"

"I didn't hang up on you, Mom. How could I answer you if I hung up?" She flashes a glare at her brother. *You know not to disturb me when I'm on the phone with Mom.*

"You need to take this call!" His outstretched arm extends the phone to his sister.

"Here, talk to Mom," she says, trading phones.

"Mom? We'll call you back." Trevor hangs up the phone before his mother's response even makes it through the receiver.

"Hello?" Cassandra's puzzled eyes squint at Trevor's excited face.

"Hello, Ms. Taylor? I can't believe I reached you. I mean, I didn't think this was a real number. My son Connor saw the Aeternum exhibit at the Museum of Natural History, and, well, this is going to sound crazy, but he wrote down this phone number and … I'm sorry Ms. Taylor, please don't think I'm crazy. He's only five, but he can be very persistent. He demanded I call this number. I thought he made up your name, and I was honestly shocked when your brother answered and said you lived there. Ms. Taylor, this really is crazy, but my son said, 'Mommy, call this number. My *daughter* is expecting me. We made a deal that I would dance with her at her wedding'."

The End

Time goes by so quickly.

What will you be remembered for?

What mark will you leave upon the earth?

A Note from the Author

Facebook posts, Instagram photos, or tweets are a great way to stay connected with people, especially all around the world. But I have found my greatest friendships are the ones that were forged face to face: sharing a bottle of wine with friends, laughing over a pint in a pub, getting to know someone you care about by playing a game of chess or backgammon with them, or maybe as Daniel and Moira did, developing a lifelong—and lives-long—obsession with gin rummy.

Our lives go by so quickly, and as far as we can tell, contrary to Jonathan's experience, we may only get one chance to experience it. So put down the latest iPhone, or hell, hide your phone if you have to. Experience actual reality instead. It's going on all around you every second of the day!

Every character in this book represents someone who has touched my life in so many ways and has definitely left a mark on my heart.

We're all going to die. From the moment we're born, we have one guarantee, and that's death. Some people don't want to face that, but the ones who do, the people who truly accept death as a reality, seem to live a much happier, more productive, more rewarding life.

When I went through my divorce, I would go to work every day smiling, happy, listening to people's problems, giving advice, always projecting a positive, carefree attitude.

A co-worker asked me, "With all that you're going through, how can you stay so happy?"

I looked at her and said, "I live my life by four words: I AM CANCER FREE!" She looked at me like she had no idea I was also battling cancer. I reassured her I wasn't, but from the moment the doctor utters those words, *"I'm sorry, it's cancer,"* your mind changes, nothing else matters, you're in a battle for your life, and you are literally fighting every day to hold on to that life. So let me ask you, why wouldn't you fight for every day of your life now as if you had cancer? Why wouldn't you enjoy every moment? We only have a limited number of days on this earth, and no one knows when their time will come, so why not be happy? Why not tell everyone around you how much they mean to you while they're alive, instead of mourning them at their funeral, saying, *"I wish I could have told them how much they meant to me."*

Bill Murray said it best in the movie *Scrooged*. *"For a couple of hours out of the whole year, we are the people that we always hoped we would be."*

Why not be the person you always hoped you would be
every day of the year?

– Gary MacKnight

ACKNOWLEDGMENTS

I am truly blessed to be surrounded by so many wonderful friends and family members who supported me through every step of the creative process. Everyone has been tremendously helpful and encouraging. If you are among those who ever asked me, "How's the book coming?" consider yourself among those I thank here. It's been a long journey, but one I'm certain was worth every second. This is truly a story that wanted to be told; I merely typed out what the story was telling me.

First let me thank Laura Williams. If not for her, this book probably would not have even been written. She was the one who, when I told her about my dream, said, "That would make for a good book." And so I wrote the first and last chapter that very same day. After reading it, she encouraged me to write more. So I did. And after that, with more encouragement, I wrote more. And more. And more, until I finally typed, 'The End.' I also want to thank Laura's husband Rande, who in the early developmental stages of this book's first draft deciphered my chicken scratch and helped me form basic sentences. Time, after time, after time. Thank you again!

I'd also like to thank Amar and Manini, the owners of Armán The Green in New Delhi, India. When I asked them if I could write about their Bed and Breakfast, Manini was delighted and congratulated me, saying both she and Amar have a special love of writers. If you're ever in India, I highly recommend staying with them!

And to Russell and Lindsay Smith, owners of an adorable cottage I fell in love with in the town of Oldshoremore, Scotland. When I asked if I could write about their ancestral home, Russell immediately sent me pictures and emails, telling me of the amazing history surrounding his home that has been in their family for over 500 years! I sent him the chapter in the book that took place in Scotland, and he helped me with the language, making it truly authentic. I also have to give him full credit for the story about John Lennon. When he told me that, I knew I just *had* to add it to the book. He even offered me and my son a sporty convertible to use when I come to visit. The world could use more friendly strangers like him! One day, God willing, we will toast in person with a couple of pints of Tennent's Lager!

And to two people who have left a huge mark in my life, my friend Iris Koch and her husband Bill. Iris was among the first to read an initial draft of the book and undertook the immense task of editing and elevating the language through countless hours and thousands of corrections. I can never thank her enough.

To James Murphy, Vilma Velazquez, and Marty Charters who read advanced copies of *Leave a Mark* and critiqued key issues essential to the story.

Last but never least, I'd like to thank Sean Patrick Brennan, who cleaned up every inconsistency, comma, and grammatical mistake I made when writing this thing. If you think you can write well, just give your manuscript to an editor and wait till it comes back covered in little red marks. Sean did an amazing job, not only with punctuation and the like, but also by adding just enough of his own voice to make mine sound better. I thank you from the bottom of my heart.

One last note. Even though the characters in this book are fictional, many have the names of family and friends in my life who have left a mark on my heart. Hopefully I have left my mark on them as well!

All my love. —Gary

Thank you all for reading my book. I hope you enjoyed it! I'd love to hear from you, so please email me at LeaveaMark4me@gmail.com and let me know what you thought.

If you liked this book, please go to Amazon and add a review (but please, no spoilers).

If you enjoyed this book, you may like *An Englishman in Prattsville.*

IT'S A LITTLE DIFFERENT.

PLEASE ENJOY THE FIRST CHAPTER...

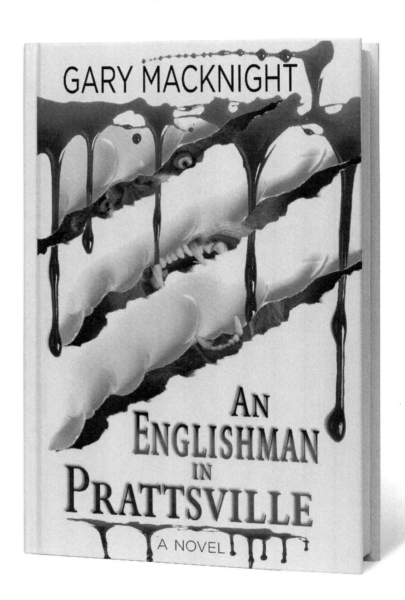

Chapter 1
A Quaint Little Town

Prattsville. *It's a quaint little town.* That's what Louis Kessler likes about it, he thinks as he pulls off the interstate. It would be another forty-five minutes driving through the towering green, picturesque mountains of the Catskills before he reaches his destination. Far from the city where he would often remark, *"There are more people on one city block than all five of the surrounding towns,"* Louis feels his stress shed from him like the winter snowfall on a rusty tin roof melting away in early springtime sun. Town after town speeds by, never changing, never growing old. Louis scarcely notices the wooden buildings and dust-paved gasoline stations as he slows to the required limit of thirty miles per hour in the little towns, before applying a slight bit of pressure upon the accelerator, coaxing the Land Rover back to a cruising speed of sixty. Whether for enjoyment or out of necessity, acquiring the 120-acre property was the best thing he has ever done. Between the sale of the estate in England — a not-so-small sheep farm — and Louis's uncanny ability to make money in the stock market, the price had been a minor setback he's never regretted.

He takes his foot off the pedal a hundred yards before entering the small town of Prattsville quietly cruising in just under twenty miles per hour. By the time he reaches the center of town, he's barely creeping, never having to once tap his brakes as he makes the turn into Jim's Great American's parking lot. You can't quite call it a supermarket, even though it has everything this town could ask for. All six aisles would fit nicely in the checkout line of his big box store back home. But that's what Louis loves about it.

Louis has an air about him. If you've never heard him talk, you might think he comes from Park Avenue royalty. But with the delivery of one syllable, his English upbringing cannot be masked. He is British through and through. Truly proper in the way he dresses, in the way he speaks, even the way he walks. But there is something off about his demeanor. Like a convict who's spent too many years in a cell. Longing for companionship, but standoffish.

Everyone knows *of* him, but maybe not *about* him, which he is quite content with. To the locals, he is the Brit who rides into town once, maybe twice a month, picks up just enough provisions to last three or four days, before heading across the parking lot for one last essential element to help him make it through the weekend.

The Catskill Mountain Liquor store was a recent addition, added shortly after Hurricane Irene swept away most of the town. It is a much-needed refuge in Louis's mind.

The crisp mountain air fills his lungs as he exits the truck. The long, hot days of summer have passed, and now the icy, cold fingers of winter are eager to return. It is noticeably cooler, at least twenty degrees below the place he left four hours ago. *May need to light the fire tonight.* He makes his way through the store, gathering milk, eggs, butter, and orange juice. A pound of cold cuts, or "deli meat," as the locals correct him every time, reminding him he's a flatlander no matter how many years he's been coming up to this haven.

Definitely will be needing a fire tonight. He pulls his coat collar up around his neck.

"Winter's coming early," an old man passing by remarks.

"I should say so," Louis responds.

Reason 342 why he loves upstate. People are just friendlier.

It's a town where mud-covered pickup trucks and rusted cars fill the parking lot as the locals stop to cash their paychecks and fill their shopping carts with the weekend supply of Coors Light. A group of men, clad in camouflage vests and bright red baseball caps, hover outside the hardware store. The barbershop of rural America. Louis feels their eyes upon him as he walks to the truck. No doubt the next subject on the agenda of the *"What's his fucking story"* club.

Reason 27 why he hates upstate. If you weren't born here, it's tremendously hard to fit in.

With the groceries comfortably nestled in the truck, he makes his way to his second stop. High-pitch tinny chimes announce his arrival as he steps through the door, breathing deep the musky, oak-aged barrel aroma of the shop.

"Morning, Mr. Kessler," the salesgirl says, flashing him a smile as her only other customer concludes his business and heads to the door.

"Morning, Jenny, how's your mum?" He holds the door open for the weekend tippler before starting down the aisle.

Jenny breathes deeply, drinking in the words pouring from Louis's lips like fine brandy her customers seldom purchased.

"Oh! I got your bottle all wrapped up for you, and Mom is fine, thanks. A little touch of arthritis. Happens like clockwork around this time of year." Jenny has a wholesome, Donna Reed, *It's a Wonderful Life* kind of look. That's not to say she's plain; she's a natural beauty in the way a summer sunset captures one's attention, makes them stop to drink in the moment before it's lost and gives way to twilight.

"How did you know I was coming today, Jenny?"

"It's been almost 30 days since your last visit. You were due."

"Twenty-six," corrects Louis, and changes the subject quickly. "Yeah, I'm always surprised how people seem shocked that winter comes around every year right after fall."

"When are you going to take the leap and move up here for good?"

"Couple more years, Jenny, a couple more. Just have a few more things to straighten out." He places a hundred-dollar bill on the counter. "As usual, keep the change."

"Mr. Kessler, how many times have I told you, it's way too much—"

He cuts her off. "And how many times have I told you to call me Louis?"

His Fab Four tonality makes her smile girlishly and she buries her chin against her chest. "Thank you, Louis."

He waves the bottle overhead behind him as he makes his way toward the door. "No, thank you. Cheers, Jenny."

Through the store's window, nearly covered with town fliers and illuminated with a red neon OPEN sign, her gaze follows him as he saunters through the parking lot. Like some ancient predator stalking an unaware prey, she remains motionless, eyes fixed. As he slips into the driver's seat, she blinks and is released from her trance. She licks her lips and clears her throat.

Made in the USA
Middletown, DE
05 December 2022

15977365R00217